Penny Lace

My thanks to John Granger of New Tythe Mills, Long Eaton, and to David Chambers, historian of Nottinghamshire

Penny Lace

Hilda Lewis

Bromley House Editions

Nottingham

Penny Lace
by Hilda Lewis
was first published in 1942 by Jarrolds

This edition was published in 2011 by Bromley House Editions, an imprint of Five Leaves Publications,
PO Box 8786, Nottingham NG1 9AW
www.fiveleaves.co.uk

ISBN: 978-1-905512-96-6

Five Leaves acknowledges financial support
from Arts Council England

Cover image courtesy of R Iliffe,
Nottingham City Council and www.picturethepast.org.uk

Typeset by Four Sheets Design and Print
Printed in Great Britain by the MPG Books Group,
Bodmin and King's Lynn

Book One

Chapter 1

Nicholas was angry. He stood on the platform of his silent machine, chafing at lost time.

He hadn't got half his bobbins yet! Those bitches were taking it easy again! All very fine for them! But a chap couldn't afford to be held up, not on piece work! Trouble in the lace-trade! No wonder! How did they think to get along when a chap had to stand about idle because the Union told him to! Here he was, capable of winding bobbins, ay and threading them into the carriages and all, and here he had to stand idle because the Union said it was none of his job!

Last year — the worst year ever known in the trade — so they said! He'd remember it all his life — 'eighty-nine — remember the lock-out. And the lack of work. And the hunger! And the masters sitting snug in their fine houses. And then, to crown all, the big slice cut out of the men's wages! No wonder a chap couldn't always pay his way punctual! The wonder was that a chap managed to live at all!

Drat those girls!

He cast an impatient eye down the great bare room, lit, though it was barely ten in the morning, by fish-tail flames; driven by draught, they jerked like live creatures imprisoned in their wire cages. As far as he could see, all the other machines were at work — every one. Clatter, clatter, shrieked the machines. Pistons rose and fell. His feet pricked with the vibrations. The whole place was full of deafening, rhythmical sound.

Only in the frantic, lunatic noise, his machine was silent.

He jumped impatiently from his platform. He'd go and see what had happened to the blasted things himself! Frowning he strode past the long table where a dozen girls were threading bobbins, thin and flat as autumn leaves, into the carriages. Head bowed over the delicate, finnicky work, they had no time to look up at Nicholas, not even at handsome Nicholas! Flick went the clever fingers, so fast, he couldn't catch the movements. No fault there! And no wonder! Fourpence a thousand didn't leave time for day-dreaming!

He turned on his heel, and still frowning, strode through the arched opening into the next room.

Bluebeard's chamber! Yellow hair, white hair, grey hair, dangled helplessly from hooks — raw silk yellow as buttercups, silk, white as curd, ash-grey cotton, waiting to take their turn upon the swifts that whirled madly, feeding the wooden bobbins. The bobbins themselves rotated rapidly, almost imperceptibly filling with cobwebby filaments of silk, or with coarser threads of cotton.

At the other end of the long room, at small high tables, the girls were filling the disc-like brass bobbins from wooden ones. Their hands moved with mechanical precision upon the bobbin winding machines.

"What's oop?" Nicholas asked truculently.

"Fault i'th'twisting. Five 'stead of seven to th'thread. Us had ter wait!"

"I can't afford ter wait!" Nicholas growled. . . Mrs Preen was turning nasty about her money. Said he'd coaxed her long enough with those brown eyes of his! Said if he didn't pay up good and soon, she'd put him out, bag and baggage!

Still scowling, he retraced his steps through the great room, back again into the shop. Casting a look of fury upon his own useless machine, he strolled round to his neighbour.

He stood watching. The iron rods thrust upwards against the jacquard band whose pierced holes directed the pattern. The threads jerked obediently sideways and then back again, filled with pattern; the lace moved slowly upwards, wound itself upon the roller.

And all the time, the thundering, insane clatter.

Standing there, annoyed and aimless, he sensed a slight disturbance at the end of the room, a momentary break in the rhythmic movement of the workers. He cast an irritable glance in that direction.

A girl, a rather tall but quite ordinary girl stood in the doorway nodding and smiling. And smiling, he thought more irritable than ever, as though she expected folk to stop work and smile back! Who on earth was she, marching into the din of work as if the whole damn place belonged to her? He turned to his neighbour.

"Miss Ware!" The man on the machine shouted the information above the clattering din.

Nicholas flicked another glance to the end of the room, and since he was not attracted by the appearance of Miss Ware, moved towards his own machine.

"Ay, Miss Ware. Heriot Ware!" The man called after him, standing on tip-toe so that his voice might carry above the forbidding barrier of the machine. "John Ware's dowter. On'y child. Th'whole works —" he jerked his head to include the immense shop and the massive thundering machines, "'ll be hern, one day!"

Nicholas took another look.

No! She didn't interest him — not as a lass! But — his irritation increased, because she, a mere female, would one day possess Heriots, this great factory. Mebbe in the future, as owner of Heriots, she'd be interesting enough! Meanwhile, he wouldn't want to look at her twice! Not his sort! And it made him sick, all this bowing and scraping!

But all the same, his eye, practiced in a woman's points, slid sideways, missing no detail of Miss Ware's appearance.

Not much to look at, in spite of the airs she gave herself! He was glad he didn't care for her appearance, it robbed her of her superiority!

He saw a tall thin girl, the smartness of her tight-fitting jacket wasted upon her undeveloped figure, her sophisticated hat tilted oddly upon her immature face — a young face, thin and eager; a pale clear skin with a powdering of faint freckles on the short straight nose. A strand of light hair had fallen beneath the polka dot veil and she lifted a gloved hand to tuck it away. He was struck by the contrast between the elegance of the glove and the childish gesture of impatience with which she thrust the hair beneath her hat.

Because he resented her appearance here, he missed no detail of her unhurried progress down the room. From beneath lowered lids he saw and detested the way in which not only men, but women, too, rose and stood for Miss Ware. It was not the fact of their rising, nor even the hasty bob, that Nicholas resented. It was something else, something submissive, as these workworn women in their decent shabby black — old enough to be her mother, some of them — stood humbly before the young girl. It left a nasty taste in his mouth!

The girl herself, he could see, felt nothing of this. She seemed to think the humble attitude her due. Or, mebbe, she didn't think at all! There she stood, mouth smiling, eyes smiling, holding up the work and grinning away as though every minute wasn't so much brass!

Nice sort of smile she had, though — friendly. He stood scowling at his own silent machine. What did he care about her smile? She was Miss Ware. She was as impersonal to him as the machine he worked on. A machine — it wasn't really impersonal at all. A man could alter it, adjust it, rule it. You could set it to work for you, scrap it if it were no good. . .

"Pity she's nowt but a lass!" shouted Nicholas's neighbour. "Nobbut she i'n't a right good lass. Teks int'rest in all on us, I'm tellin' yer!"

"Let her keep her int'rest to hersen!" growled Nicholas. "Silly madam!" Let her come this road, he'd not look at her! He didn't hold with bowing and scraping to any woman — be she the Queen herself!

He lounged there, smarting under an unaccustomed sense of inferiority, he Nicholas Penny, as good as the next man and better than most! Who did she think she was, anyhow? Dressed up maypole! She'd be an old maid for all her father's brass! A chap liked something plump and cuddlesome, something with a bit of colour, something a chap could. . .

Deep in the pleasant thought of what a chap could do, he was lost. A poke in the ribs from his informative neighbour, brought him indignantly back.

Heriot Ware was standing and looking down at him with a hint of amusement in her face. She held herself erect, making the most of her height. It seemed to him, smarting under a sense of inferiority, that she deliberately looked down on him, that she intended to make him feel small. He straightened himself to his own good height, furious with himself for caring about her attitude, or even noticing it.

She said, "I don't think I've seen you before!" He detested her voice, though it was pleasant enough — detested the crisp voice of authority, speaking a tongue different from his own.

He said, with faint, but quite unmistakable impertinence, "yo' wouldn't!"

Her eyebrows went up, dark brows, clearly marked in her pale face.

"I suppose not!" she agreed, And then, with sudden sharpness in the pleasant voice, "well, now that we have met, I'd like to know your name!"

"Nicholas Penny." And damn her for a sarcastic bitch!

"Nicholas Penny!" He liked the sound of his name on her tongue. Her clear voice lent it authority.

"You have not been with us long?"

"No!" *Us indeed! Yo' mind yer own business!* He hoped the resentment he must not show would somehow communicate itself to her.

"I hope you will be happy here," said Heriot Ware.

Damn her swank! He would not thank her for her pious hope! A girl came hurrying down the aisle of machines. She said, dropping a bob, "Yer feyther's gone to th'office, Miss Ware. He says will yer please goo right oop."

"Thank you, Lizzie," Heriot said. "How's your mother?"

"Comin' on nicely, thank yer. The shawl yer sent were right comfortubble."

"I'm so glad!" Heriot lifted the heavy folds of her braided skirt, and all smiles and nodding head, made her way back along the machines.

"Saucy madam!" Nicholas said.

The man stopped to wag a tiresome finger. "Boot's on t'other foot ter my way o'thinkin'. Clever yer may be, young Penny, but yo're damn lucky ter get into Heriots — best mill i'th'Midlands, best conditions o' work, best everything —"

"Is that so?" drawled Nicholas, exasperated by the exhibition of patronage just witnessed.

"Forgot last year, hev yer? Heriots pressed for th'cut in wages same as all th'rest — di'n'it? Heriots locked th'men out, same as all on 'em — di'n'it? Heriots were closed along wi' all t'other mills — weren't it?"

"Ay, those are facts I'll not deny! An' I'll not deny, neither, th' cut came cruel hard. But wi'out that cut th'mills would mebbe have closed down for iver. Times are hard — an' when times are hard, lace is first ter know! Luxury trades — they're like a thermometer! John Ware had ter toe th'line along wi' all t'other mesters. But all th'same he were out ter mek things easy for us men. He were on that there Board o' Conciliation. Twenty-five per cent cut th'mesters wanted, blast 'em, for us Levers hands, but he made 'em accept twelve-an'-a-hafe. Ay, he were right good! An' what's more, all th'time Heriots were closed, he paid ivery hand five shillen a week, men an' wimmen alike. He wouldn't have it known, though!"

"No wonder! Runnin' wi' th'hare an' huntin' wi' th'hounds!" Nicholas said slightingly.

"Nay, lad! He had ter stand in wi' th' mesters, but he *felt* wi' th'men! What us'd have done wi'out him, I dunno!"

"Us di'n't ought ter live on'y by th'goodwill of any mester!"

"If yer were a mester yersen, yer'd think diff'rent."

"Mebbe! But I'll tell yer what!" Nicholas was suddenly fierce. "Females di'n't ought ter be in mills, not wi'out they come ter work. Females like yon stuck-oop maypole ought ter stay in their own parlours. She'll be an owd maid fer sure — an' serve her darn well right! Some fowks thinks as they ought to have iverything wi'out so much as liftin' a finger — ay, iverything set before them in one big pile so as they can pick and choose!"

His brow dark he sauntered back to his own silent machine.

Nicholas wandered discontentedly about the castle grounds. Nottingham Castle, foursquare, squat and respectable, not unlike the Queen herself in shape, frowned from its rock southwards over the slums, frowned northwards over the bright grass of its lawns set about with formal patterns of daffodils and hyacinths.

He leaned over the high parapet and looked down to the city spread below.

What ailed him now? For the last week he hadn't been satisfied — not since that day he'd hung round his empty machine and asked himself why the masters should have it all their own way. Just a week ago, it was. He remembered it was the day that stuck-up Ware girl had come marching in... *If yer were a mester yersen yer'd think different...* old Britwell had said. *If yer were a mester...* That had stuck! He hadn't thought that way before. He'd always been a satisfied sort of chap — worked when there was work, tightened his belt a bit when things were slack; eaten heartily when there was food and cadged from Mrs Preen when there wasn't; went to the music-hall when he'd brass to spare and walked the streets with a pretty lass when there wasn't. Now, he wasn't satisfied any longer. He wanted something better than being another chap's beast of burden. Turn and turn about — it was only fair! Why not? *Why not?* He had the brain. And he had the will. Ay, that was it — *the will*! Why shouldn't other chaps sweat for him? Why shouldn't he be able to talk free-and-equal with high-up folks? Why shouldn't he speak in a well-off voice and look down his nose at people. . .?

Straight down beneath him, he could see little slummy houses — the sort of house he had known and been content to know, ever since he could remember. The white-washed walls of The Trip to Jerusalem stood out clear against the grimy houses. He went there of a Saturday night for his pint. Well, he wasn't satisfied to do that any longer. He wouldn't be satisfied till he went along to The George Hotel, a carnation in his button-hole, to drink his champagne along with the rest of the masters.

He walked round to the front entrance of the castle and came into the dark quiet hall. Now what? He looked about him. He had the place to himself. Pictures and statues and things? Not in his line. He'd go down and have a look at the lace.

Alone in the empty gallery, he wandered slowly, peering at lace flounces yellowed with age from a great lady's gown, at ruffles from a fine gentleman's shirt. Incredibly fine. . . every thread twisted by hand, every knot made by patient long-dead fingers.

The thought of those laborious fingers vexed him. He strode over to look at the machine-made lace. Early attempts, the net coarse and heavy, but less durable than the cobwebs human fingers had spun. First attempts at decoration — the designer in him stirred in sympathy with these first attempts. Clumsy patterns worked upon plain net — the first embroidered lace. And then the first real lace — as he counted lace — made by twisting the threads themselves. Twist lace, clumsy, coarse, ugly. . .

No wonder the lace was coarse and clumsy, look at the machines that had made it! He wandered through the narrow alley flanked by obsolete machines. Huge and cumbersome, they too had clattered and chattered; had been fed and tended by their slaves. Now they stood grim and silent in this quiet place, fit only to be stared at by the curious.

Heavy. Motionless. Silent. They had taken their toll of strength, of life, even. Not only men and women, but children even, little children, had been broken by the machines. When he himself was a little chap, his own dad had told him. . .

He looked. And looked again. Annoyance rose within him, swift annoyance, quite unwarrantable annoyance. Someone was at his end of the room.

The pleasant feeling of being king of this particular castle, fell from him. A woman, ay, a woman! Standing as still as one of them statues and staring for all she was worth! Could you beat that? Of all the damn nonsense! A woman's place was to stare in shop-windows. Or at pictures — if the pictures were respectable. But not at machines!

The woman at the other end of the room, unconscious of his criticisms, went on staring at the machines. When she moved from one exhibit to another, she lifted a careful skirt, as though she were not yet used to its length.

Surely there was something familiar about that movement! Something familiar about her altogether! He'd seen that young woman before... taller than most girls she was, childish, though, for all her height... smart, in a way, and yet with a sort of carelessness, the rather fetching carelessness of the young girl.

She swung round on her heel with a clean graceful movement, in spite of the hampering skirts.

"Good afternoon, Nicholas Penny," said Heriot Ware.

He felt again that quick resentment, because she had not granted him a handle to his name. He looked her up and down with a clear suggestion of insolence.

"Good arternoon, Harriet Ware."

Up went her startled brows. There was temper in the set of the mouth. Suddenly she smiled her wide, rather sweet smile.

"It isn't Harriet," she said and tossed her head under the stiff be-ribboned sailor-hat.

"Oh?" said Nicholas inadequately, and — he hoped, indifferently.

"After my grandfather Heriot. Andrew Heriot. Though perhaps," the acid sweetness of her tone reduced him, fuming, to a two-year-old, "you haven't heard of Andrew Heriot."

"Mebbe not!" Treating him as though he were daft! As though you could live in Nottingham and not know the name of Andrew Heriot! His voice took on a note of aggressiveness. "Anyroad, 'tis a daft thing ter do — naming a young lass fer an owd codger!"

"Not at all!" Heriot replied with a flash of temper. "It's a fine name. And I love it. I wouldn't be anything but Heriot Ware for anything in the world!"

Nicholas raked her with an impertinent eye. Just as well! his eye said.

She stood flushing at his impertinence, for all her height and elegance, childishly helpless. She felt surprisingly different from the Miss Ware who talked easily and kindly with papa's work-people. Here was one of them — a mere hand — and it was not at all easy to talk to him.

She fidgeted at the button on her glove. And yet — he was just a twist-hand, like all the others!

But he wasn't. He was *not*! She was surprised at her own swift denial. You had only to look at him standing there, with a dark lock of hair flung across his forehead — a very good forehead: and those golden eyes with reddish angry lights dancing in them. And the long hands, fine against the coarse corduroy. Yes, and even the workman's handkerchief, bright and careless about his throat lent him an air — almost as if he were playing a part. But all the same, in spite of that air of his, she knew he was a twist-hand — a twist-hand, neither more nor less. Why, she had seen him at work!

She felt the silence, ridiculous, embarrassing. She tried once more.

"What are you doing here on such a lovely afternoon?"

"I med ask the same o' yo'!" None of her business if he were on short time. "A lass among th'owd machines — that's a bit of aw right!"

Heriot laughed — a laugh as clear and unaffected as a boy's. "It's the machines!" she said. "I cannot keep away from them! It's odd — so I'm told. And you think so, too, I can see! But I don't think it odd at all! It's a bit of old Andrew coming out in me. I'm like him, too. To look at I mean. I'm glad. It makes me proud — rather."

He was liking her better now, warmed in spite of himself by the unstudied friendliness of her voice. Here, among the old machines, she had forgotten she was Miss Ware. She was talking, he thought, with the eagerness of a rather lonely person. Though why Miss Ware, young and friendly, should be lonely, was more than he could figure out!

"*Do* you think I'm like him?" she demanded, as if everyone, as a matter of course, must know the face of Andrew Heriot.

Nicholas shrugged.

"Come and see, then! There's a picture up in the Long Gallery."

He followed her, half-resentful that she should command and he follow. And yet, he told himself, it was not Ware's daughter that he obeyed, but some urgency she possessed within herself.

They mounted the wide shallow stairs, Heriot's hands careful about her trailing skirts.

"You don't know," she said, "how I bless those machines. Even if I didn't really care about them, still I'd bless them! You see, it's the only way I can be free, really free to be by myself!"

Nicholas was bewildered and showed it.

"You don't know what it is to be a young lady!" she sighed. "I wish I didn't, either! I'm always tacked on to mamma, or to papa, or to a female friend, or to one of the maids. But the machines — I can't pretend to follow the reasoning — somehow or other they supply the place of a chaperone. For instance, at this moment, I am supposed to be shopping with mamma. I find shopping tedious. I shall never be a proper young lady!"

She sighed again. "So when mamma had hung about an hour over the silk counter at Jessops, I told her I was off to look at my machines. And here I am! And here —"

They halted beneath a large dark canvas, "here's grandpapa. Good-day, grandpapa." And Heriot dropped a mock curtsey.

"Well?" she demanded.

Nicholas was embarrassed. The old boy was no beauty! But then, neither was the girl!

He studied the painted face.

Blue eyes with a brownish sort of fleck to them — hazel, didn't they call it? But more blue than hazel. She had those eyes, too. Quick-changing eyes, proud one minute, and friendly the next. The old boy's nose was long and hers was short. But the mouths were alike — wide and full, with a good shape to them. He'd bet when the old fellow grinned, it'd had been a nice sort of a grin. As for the chin — tempers both!

Heriot said "I'd rather be like him than a raving beauty!"

"Yo've got yer wish!" Nicholas said bluntly. And they both laughed.

The laugh cleared the air. They stood chatting away in the friendliest fashion. She forgot that this odd and attractive young man was, after all, one of her father's twist-hands. And he, easily accepted by this elegant young lady, forgave — and even enjoyed — her social superiority.

He thought as he sat down beside her on one of the inadequate cane chairs, that he had never talked to a real young lady before. It occurred to him, as an interesting point, that the charm which had never failed with girls who were not young ladies, had not failed him this time, either.

Chapter 2

It was quiet in the Long Gallery and dim. Evidently the authorities saw no point in pampering the public when it came to looking at pictures. And evidently they were right. For after that first very personal inspection of Grandpapa Heriot, neither Heriot nor Nicholas cast a single further glance in his direction. There they sat under the knowledgeable eyes of Andrew Heriot and talked.

Heriot said, "whenever I look at Grandpapa Heriot, I'm glad I've got his name. He was a great man, my grandpapa. I never knew him. I wish I had. I *do* wish I had! He died before I was born. He made Heriots, you know. In fact, he *was* Heriots."

"Ay?" His tone challenged the importance of Heriots.

She was not one to let a challenge go by. "Heriots is the biggest factory in the Midlands, in England, perhaps. And my grandfather started without a penny — no friends, no influence, no money. Nothing. His father, Simon, came to Nottingham — tramped all the way from Glasgow to find a job — his wife and children trailing behind him, begging as they went. I'm not ashamed of it!" she tossed her head. "I'm proud of it! That's *living*. . . even if it's a bitter sort of living. At least they weren't suffocated with cotton wool! They found work in a lace factory, all of them! Plenty of work then. Golden days — for the masters. Andrew — that's grandpapa, wasn't seven when he started. It was awful in factories then, papa says."

"Us down't need yer feyther's word fer that! Th'air were filthy. Poison to body an' soul. And fowk had ter breathe it in all day long. And then th'machines! Yer've on'y ter goo downstairs ter picture the weight on 'em."

"I know. I think of that sometimes. I go down and look at them, and I try to imagine Andrew lifting his hands to them — little boy hands. They died of course, the children! All of them — except Andrew."

He nodded. Children dying at the machines — it was old history. No good getting worked up about it this hour of day!

Heriot said, pitifully, "Just think of it! Little children dying off like flies! Every day it happened. No-one thought much about it. It wasn't anyone's business. Children were cheap. The owners got rich. I'd like to have *killed* them — the brutes!

Nicholas said with lazy good humour, "it's ovver late ter mind now!"

"Not when it's your own family! It comes close, then — you wouldn't believe how close! You feel it in your own blood! Andrew's mother and father died, too. But then they were quite old — thirty-five or so. Still, it was a horrible way to die. T.B. both!"

Nicholas nodded. "Lace-mekker's disease. My own feyther died that way. Came from breathin' blacklead all day. Shoved it on the combs like they do now ter mek 'em run easy — on'y it were real lead they used."

Heriot said gravely, "I know. Papa tells me things — often. But not mamma. Mamma won't talk about it, ever. I think she doesn't like to remember the way her grandparents died."

They were silent. Slowly a smile widened on Heriot's mouth. "But nothing could kill off Andrew. He went on and on, working and learning and thinking — saving a penny here and a penny there, where another man wouldn't have found enough to live on."

"Penny saved is penny earned — but yer don't mek fortunes that way!"

"It was grandpapa's way — his way of beginning, anyhow! When he'd saved enough, he hired a machine and set it up in a room of his cottage. Two rooms the cottage had — the whole family lived in one — Andrew was married then. They slept and ate and lived there. But the machine had a room to itself. It was lighter and warmer and bigger, the room where the machine was, But it was going to make their fortune — and nothing was too good!

"So there was grandpapa with his hired machine working by day and by night — and all the family helping! And all the time be was working, he was thinking. That was the difference between grandpapa and most other hands. He thought while he worked. He thought and thought — and at last he got his great idea. He'd been wondering a long time about the bobbins. He'd been thinking they were too thick, too clumsy. And really, when you look at them downstairs, you wonder why nobody had thought of it before! Why shouldn't bobbins be thinner and larger, grandpapa wondered. They'd take the same amount of thread — more even. They'd be easier to work. You could stack more of them in one machine —"

"Is that so? I'm a twist-hand mysen!" Suddenly he dropped his sarcastic drawl. "I'm dead keen on designin' and them flat bobbins made it possible ter get freer patterns, finer patterns. Yer've on'y got ter look' at th'owd lace ter see that! So it was yer grandfeyther! I'll tek off me cap to him!"

"You may well do that! Having the idea wasn't enough. He had to have money, too. And of course be hadn't got any! So he had to persuade someone who had. That wasn't easy, he didn't know anyone with money. And then he thought of Ware. Ware was a friend of his — afterwards he became my other grandfather. Ware had a few pounds left to him, but he didn't mean to risk them — naturally. But Andrew made him. Andrew got his own way — always!

"They had bobbins made the new thin shape. But of course they weren't any good without the right sort of machine. So they bought an old machine — so old, they bought it as old iron. But it cost them all they had — and a bit over. And there was many a night sleepless through cold and hunger for all of them! Andrew and Ware took the machine to pieces and they had new parts made to take the new bobbins. They were head over heels in debt when they started. But they'd started — that was the thing. They'd started!

"And that was the beginning. Andrew had been right — as he always was right. The new machine worked more easily, more quickly; and as for the patterns — but I mustn't say anything about patterns."

Nicholas grinned.

"Andrew moved his family out and took the other room for his machines. Then he took the cottage next door. Ware got his money back — and a partnership. Before he was thirty-five, Andrew had the biggest mill in the Midlands — Andrew Heriot who had tramped England barefoot!

"And that's not the end of the story. The story goes on and on! Because Heriots goes on and on. Think of it, Heriots touching all sorts of lives, moulding all sorts of lives — yours and mine and hundreds and thousands of people we don't know and shan't ever see. Heriot lace going all over the world, into all sorts and conditions of houses. Rich women wearing it. Working-women wearing it — and that's better. Poor women who'd always worked hard and never had anything, like my great-grandmother! Heriot's lace is cheap and it's good. Penny a yard, some of it. Lovely patterns, too!"

"Is that so?"

She was beginning to recognise that drawl. She sent him an angry glance.

"I work on Heriot lace," he reminded her with a twinkle.

Her brow cleared. She laughed outright. He thought she had a good sort of laugh. It came out clear and honest as a bell.

"It isn't only that though — more people having pretty things," she said thoughtfully. "It's the fact that there's work for hundreds where there wasn't any work before."

"None so much ter showt abowt," Nicholas said a little stiffly. What did she know of work, soft-living little madam? "Conditions weren't niver too good i'th'lace-mills, yer said so yersen. And they're not all that better now!"

"They are! And they were at Heriots. Always. That's why I'm proud of Heriots, I'm prouder of Heriots than of anything in the whole world. You see when grandpapa started Heriots there wasn't anything to stop the owners from doing what they chose, no factory acts —"

"Us knows all abowt that!"

"No you don't. Or you wouldn't talk the way you did!" Her blood was up. She didn't allow anyone to slight Heriots. "And when the first factory act did come at last — the lace-trade got left out!"

"Ay, us knows abowt that an' all! No rhyme nor reason. Used ter puzzle my feyther. Mek him rare wild, it did!"

"Oh, it was reasonable — in its way. But reasonable things aren't always wise things!" She stopped to let this pearl of philosophy sink deep. "You see the act only applied to mills that used power. Well in those days, most of the lace-machines were worked by hand. There was so little steam used — a machine here, a machine there — that nobody bothered."

"Ay!" Nicholas said drily. "A few dozen done to death here, and few dozen there, down't signify!"

"It did to Andrew!" she said very quickly. "Grandpapa didn't have to be told that children oughtn't to be kept hanging about for twenty-two hours out of twenty-four — he remembered too well! And he didn't have to be told, either, that they oughtn't to be dragged out of bed at midnight, or later, just because the piece was finished and had to come off the machine. He knew an extra set of bobbins would settle that problem. And he knew that children oughtn't to be allowed to fall asleep where they stood. He used to say if they got caught in the machines, it wasn't only bad for the machines!

"And more than anything, he knew it wasn't enough to give children just food and clothes and sleep. So he started a little school in the Heriot works, and he paid a teacher, even when he didn't know where to turn for money.

"Nobody would lend him any. They hated his ideas. They said he was pampering the workers and ruining the trade. Even Ware got frightened. He broke off the partnership. But not their old friendship. Andrew never held it against Ware, not even when Ware's son wanted to marry mamma — there wasn't anything mean about Andrew!"

Nicholas said, "so that was the way of it! Less handpower and more steam. Th'more steam, th'more kids done to death. Kids were cheap, like yer said, so who cared!"

"Andrew cared. Andrew cared so much he just couldn't let things go on and do nothing! He was a rich man by then and he'd got a lot of influence. One of his friends was a Mr Charlton. Mr Charlton wasn't in the trade at all, he was a country gentleman — he lived at Chilwell Hall. He hated things as much as grandpapa did. So the two of them went about trying to wake people up. All sorts of people — parsons who ought to have been awake before, and teachers, and country gentlemen, and shopkeepers. Then they drew up a petition begging Parliament to bring the lace-trade in under the act. Lots and lots of people signed — but more didn't. Not the owners. Of course not the owners! They thought treating human beings like human beings would ruin the trade! So that petition failed. And the next. And the next. But they went on, trying and failing and trying again, hammering on in spite of all failures, till in the end they didn't fail!

"When grandpapa was an old man, he used to say — papa has often told me — *I built Heriots out of my own blood and sweat, not the blood and sweat of the children.* Grandpapa — oh!" she stopped very suddenly, "I'm doing it again. When I begin on Heriots I don't know when to stop. I'm afraid I've been boring you. I'm afraid I often bore people. I've got the bore's habit of thinking that everyone must like the things I like. And I'm a little mad about Heriots. I wish I were a boy! My parents were sorry I wasn't — I'm the only child, you see — and I'm sorry, too!"

He sent her a deliberate glance. "I'm glad yo're not a lad!"

She tapped an impatient foot — a slender foot, well-arched. He had the connoisseur's appreciation of that foot! A frown gathered on her dark brows. She said sharply, "I don't like that sort of thing! Keep it for other girls. I'm different!"

He drew in his breath with surprise. She had put herself on a level with other girls he might know, she, John Ware's daughter! She had forgotten the distance between them. Well — he wouldn't be the one to remind her! And she *had* a temper. He'd guessed right about that chin!

Suddenly she laughed. If she had a temper it was soon over! He couldn't abide a Sulky Sue!

"I should say I *am* different! What other girl in the world would talk by the hour about her grandfather?"

"Not one! But then fowk did ought ter be diff'rent. I mean, people didn't ought ter be like a row of houses — each one th'spit o' t'other. I'm diff'rent mysen!"

She sent him a swift glance. Why was he so certain about that? It couldn't be just be because he was so good-looking — that would be foolish. And he looked anything but a fool!

She said, "Why are you different?"

He was silent, his face turned away. He was so long silent that she thought he hadn't heard.

"Why are you different?" she asked again.

He turned his head and gave her a long look. The bright colour stained her cheeks.

"I'll tell *yo'* why I'm different, though I don't b'lieve in a chap gassin' abowt hissen. But yo'll unnerstand. Yo're diff'rent an' all! I'm like th'owd chap theer" he jerked a thumb in the direction of Andrew Heriot Esq. "I wain't stay put! I've got ter do things. Mek sommat out o' my life. I want ter know things, ter learn, ter find out. I've *got* ter find out! An' find out quickest way an' all — life i'n't all that long! Th' School of Art, fer instance. I could learn quite a bit, theer. Some o' th'hands laugh at it. They say a little experience is worth a lot o' gab. I down't think so. I think a word in season med be a short cut to a lot of experience. I want ter learn about designin'. I want ter be able to put my hand on books that tell abowt it. I down't believe in mekkin patterns out o' yer own head an' nothing more to it! I mean theer's boun' ter be laws that govern the job o' designin'. And when yer've learnt 'em, yer'll mek a good design — if yer have it in yer. I have it in me!

"But it i'n't on'y designin'. It's lace. I want ter know abowt th'diff'rent kinds o' lace. An' how and why we got just those sort o' patterns. I want ter know how they're mekkin' lace in other countries, an' the sort o' machines they use, an' how they market th' stuff. Ay, an' even what colour card they mount th'lace on, an' why they chose that special colour. There i'n't anything I wouldn't want ter know."

Heriot said, "I'm mad about lace, too. But they won't let me learn, they won't let me learn a thing about it — it's not ladylike!" she said bitterly. "But you — there's nothing to hold you back, nothing at all!"

"I'n't theer?" Nicholas echoed her own bitterness. "*I'n't* theer? Nothin' — on'y lack of opportunity!"

" I could speak to my father —"

"I down't sponge on my friends!" he said fiercely. Damn it all, he wasn't going to be beholden to a lass! Suddenly — a little cooled — he realised what his remark might imply. Well, let it stand! He said softly, "That were a bit cheeky, weren't it? But — us cares abowt th'same things, so in a sort o' way us med be friends, medn't us?"

She felt her own withdrawal, "I don't know. Being friends — that doesn't happen in a minute, does it?"

"All th'best things happen in a minute, like bein' friends, and" he held her with a dark and meaning eye, "fallin' in love!"

She turned away, angry with herself for so stupidly blushing. "I don't agree," she said coldly.

"Yer will!" he assured her.

Nicholas watched her closely. He knew enough about girls to read this one aright. Romantical. For all she was Miss Ware and husband-high, for all her fine education, she was as full of soppy-sawny notions as an egg is full of meat! Well, he'd brought himself bang into the middle of the romantical picture. What could be more romantical than the poor lad, the clever lad, ay, and add to that the handsome lad — starting out on his great struggle? That ought to fetch her, grand-daughter of Andrew Heriot!

But fetching though the picture might be, his pride was in revolt. He could not resist the desire to boast, to produce for her some respectable family background.

He said, "I med be right down comfortubble, if I pleased. I've an uncle wi' pots o' brass. Got a big business an' all. Done more'n aw right for hissen. I'd be well away if I went in wi' him. I wain't, though. I'll not be no-b'dy's tame cat. Dead men's shoes down't attract me. Not these partic'lar shoes, any road! Buyin' an' sellin'. Lapdog work — if yer look at it th'way I do. Mekkin' — creating' wi' yer own blood an' yer own sweat th'way yer grandad said — that's work fer a man!"

Her flushed cheek, her bright eye encouraged him.

"Buyin' an' sellin' an' nothin' more to it — it's livin' on th' life of others, th'way some plants do, like —"

"Parasites." She supplied the missing word.

"I were gooin' ter say that mysen!" he rebuked her. "What I think is, ne'er mind how grand th' buyin' an' th'selling, ne'er mind how much brass a man may handle, it's still lap-dog's work. That's why I wan't goo in fer it!"

Heriot said softly, "that's wonderful!"

"Nay! It's just th'way I am."

"No, but it *is* wonderful. I envy you your freedom to choose — and the chances you'll have. And the chances you'll make for yourself."

She sighed a little, turning the watch upon her breast. "Heavens! I'll be late for dinner. I must fly!"

She was going. Soon she would be gone. And he wouldn't be able to talk to her any more. It was fine talking to her! All sorts of grand ideas came into his head when he talked to her — ideas he didn't know he had. And they were all true — except mebbe he'd made her believe that the old man's piddling little shop was something right-down grand. Everything else, though, was true. He *was* going to do things, to be someone. . .

"Good-bye, Nicholas Penny!"

He must see her again. Must talk to her — that was all he wanted to do, talk. She wasn't the sort of girl a chap would want to kiss and cuddle. She was the sort a chap would want to talk to — not because she had any ideas in her rabbit's head, women never did — but because she brought out ideas that were in your own head. . . the sort of girl a man wanted to be with just to talk to! He hadn't known such girls existed!

She said again, "Good-bye, Nicholas Penny. And — good luck!"

"No luck wi'out a friend! Heriot Ware —" Be damned to it, he would not call her *Miss*. "I'd give all I've got i'th'world — on'y I'm afraid it i'n't much — if yer would let me talk to yer — sometimes!"

She was troubled. She didn't want to refuse. She had enjoyed talking to him. He was so different from anyone she'd ever met. He had brought her right into a new world, Andrew Heriot's world, the world of the worker. . . *Heriot Ware. . . Heriot Ware. . .* No one had ever addressed her like that before! Heriot, Or Miss Ware. But never the two names. . . Heriot Ware, the two names together, each as important as the other. She was no longer Heriot, nor Miss Ware — she was quite a new person, Heriot Ware.

But for all that, she could not say *Yes*. How could she say *Yes?*

"That wouldn't be easy for me," she said at last.

He swallowed his pill. And it was not so very bitter.

He looked at her steadily. "But yo're still crazy abowt th' machines!"

Her candid eyes dropped. Now why all this difficulty, she wondered, in answering so simple a question. But perhaps after all, the question was not so simple. Then, eyes still lowered, she said softly, "I'm still crazy about the machines."

And gathering the folds of her long skirts, half-ran from him down the Long Gallery.

Chapter 3

He thought of Heriot Ware as he walked up the cobbled High Street of Thrapstone village. She stirred his mind so that he must think of her incessantly. But she stirred neither his emotion nor his heart. For all his thinking, his pulses moved not one whit faster, his blood remained cold.

. . .A grand lass. . . He was anxious to give her full due. Ay, something right down fine about her. Quality. Not his sort, though. Not the sort of lass a chap would want to cuddle — nor yet to wed wi'.

He kicked at a stone with a shabby boot; he watched it spinning and bumping its way along the cobbles.

Just as well! Nicholas Penny with just abowt a bob in his pocket deciding that he didn't want to wed with the Ware heiress! Crazy!

He sent another stone spinning after the first.

Not half so crazy as it looked on first sight — not when you took into account the girl herself. Romantical she was, for all she fancied herself hard-headed. She was the sort to hop into your hand easy as winking — ne'er mind what her folk might have to say. And they'd say plenty! Gentle she might be, but she didn't have that chin for nothing! Romantical — you'd only to bear that in mind and the salt was as good as on the dickybird's tail! All that silly gab about the nobleness of work! Work was what gave you food and drink — and as much more as you were clever enough to grab! He'd played up to her quick as lightning, spouting about the dignity of creating! The funny thing was, while he was spouting, he'd actually meant it. Looked like being romantical might be catching!

Silly kid! She'd lived all her life wrapped round in cotton wool — like she said. And so she thought she was in love with the working-class. She thought that, just because her grandfather had come from it. But he hadn't stayed in it! She'd forgotten that! If he had, mebbe she'd be singing a different song. Let her come down and live in the middle of the stink and the meanness and the belly-aching hunger and the cold of the workers, the way he did. Quick enough she'd change her tune!

But meanwhile she was soppy-sawny with her notions. And meeting a chap like himself wasn't likely to alter her mind! Just because he was a working-chap that gave him a pull. Yes, it gave him a pull over the dressed-to-the-nines fat-arses she met every day! Queer, the very thing that would down him with any other girl in her position, was like a gift in his hands. She was his for the asking — if he asked right!

But — a third stone went bouncing after the others — he wouldn't want her that way. To get her because she was at a silly age wasn't any good!

She was romantical and she was silly — but there was something right down fine about her. He was certain that if he'd asked her for a bit of brass to help some poor chap, she'd have emptied her purse then and there and no questions asked. Silly and trusting — but fine. No, he didn't want to get her because she didn't know any better. He wanted her to respect him, to admire him. . .

Walking there, kicking at the stones, it occurred to him that if he could not win Heriot Ware's respect, then maybe he wouldn't be able to do those wonderful things he'd planned. Without yeast the bread won't rise!

Dignity of the worker be damned! Ear cocked, eye skinned, elbow up, boot ready — that was what worked the trick!

Queer. Twenty-three he was, and all the time satisfied to take life as it came — doing his bit of work and not caring overmuch how he did it; wanting nothing but a bit of cheap food and a bit of cheap fun. And then — suddenly meeting this girl and finding everything changed.

And this was queerer still! She was penny plain and he liked them twopence coloured. She was tall and thin — and he liked them shoulder-high and cuddlesome. She talked a great deal — and a lass's mouth wasn't meant for talking. But all the same, since that day up in the Long Gallery, everything was changed.

Perhaps, though, things weren't as simple as that. Mebbe without knowing it, the idea had been growing, growing steady, growing slow, the idea that Nicholas Penny had got to do something, be someone! A very good idea too — but how did a chap start to go about it?

He could answer that one all right. The only answer in spite of bad times! Lace. The way old Heriot had made his fortune. The way fortunes were still being made — ay, and being lost! But he wouldn't be a loser, not he! Like old Andrew he was cut out for a winner!

He knew more than a bit about lace already — been working in twist-lace ever since he was twelve! He knew blindfold whether the thread was right, knew by merely tossing it in his hand, whether the unwound hank of cotton would make good thread — fine but not too fine, smooth and even and unravelled. Just as he knew whether the thread was five or seven ply, or even whether through some accident a strand was missing — though it seemed the eye could not detect the difference because of the incredible fineness of the filaments. Still he knew. Aye, he knew! And as for the machines — not much he didn't know about them! Not a thread nor a screw but he knew its purpose.

Ay, he knew a bit. But not enough. Not nearly enough! Plenty to learn! He wanted to know it all — every bit of the process — gassing and bleaching and starching — even though he never need to put hand to it.

And then the lace itself. He'd learned more than a bit about different kinds already from looking at specimens in the castle — Point de Venise and Honiton and Alençon and Mechlin and ever so many others. He'd met Heriot Ware wandering round, more than once, this last fortnight, and he'd got her to talk about the specimens so as he'd know how to say the names. And then he'd practiced them to himself at nights so that the names came easy off his tongue. Yes, he'd practiced the foreign-sounding words just as he was practising to speak well-off. Saying the words the way she said them, made them seem as queer almost as foreign ones. It came hard, learning your own language all over again; but if a chap kept his ears open in trams and in shops and in the street, he'd soon be speaking like the best of the nobs!

His step slackened, halted by habit at his uncle's shop. His mind registered something new about the window, something unexpected. It looked different, somehow. Sort of gay. Jolly. Someone had given the old wax figure a brush-up. Saucy! And all those ribbons bunched up in gay rosettes to look like flowers! Yards and yards of ribbons crumpled up — the old man would have to sell it off cheap! Careful old soul he was as a rule, whatever had come over him?

At the tinny tinkle of the bell, Miss Bird, his uncle's assistant, turned her yellow face towards him. It seemed to swim disembodied in the gloom of the little shop. Her grey untidy head, always inclined to shake a little upon her thin neck, trembled quite violently. She opened her lips.

"Yes, sir, what can I do for you?"

Nicholas jumped. Not the old bird's voice at all! A young voice, a young voice speaking in that dark and ancient shop.

He stared. A girl, a young girl. . . pretty as paint. Prettiest piece he'd ever set eyes on! This lass, standing there in the dusty shaft of sunlight that struggled through the dirty skylight, beat all the others at their own game!

He went on staring. Pretty figure she had — and the black tight-fitting gown she wore didn't leave you to guess much, neither! And that narrow white band she wore at the high neck — well, it wouldn't be whiter than the neck it hid, he'd swear. Artful that dress! Set you thinking of the white throat. . . blue veins there'd be, branching under the white skin and little hollows at the base of the throat where it went curving down. . .

He wrenched his thoughts from the tantalising picture.

Her hair now. . . a chap couldn't keep his eyes away. . . no more than when the landlord lifts a glass of good ale up to the gaslight. Same kind of leaping fire drawing the eye! Those curls. A chap would want to twist his fingers in those curls. Springy to the touch they'd be, flying back again as it might be elastic. And that mouth — bright and soft, the underlip pouting a little — a promising sort of mouth, the way a girl's mouth should be!

A chap couldn't think clearly, standing there and star-ing. . . a chap still had to go on thinking about that red mouth and the white neck and the round breasts under the tight black dress.

"What can I do for you, sir?" There it was again, the young voice, while he stood and gawped.

Miss Bird, her head shaking more than ever, said sourly, "He don't want serving. That's the boss's nephew!"

"I'll go and see if Mr Penny can see you," the girl said. And swinging on her heel, went back the way she had come.

He had not taken in the curious import of her words. His thoughts were on that waist, on the roundness of those slim hips. A peach. . . where on earth had the old chap picked her up?

"My niece. My sister's gal!" Miss Bird's grudging voice informed him. "Never cared for her, no, nor for her mother, neither. Bold as brass, both!"

In the blank made by the girl's absence, he turned an ear to Miss Bird's grievances.

"Never had much to do with either of them. . . never cared for their goings-on! And now her mother's dead, she comes to me — bold as brass — like I said. And never so much as *by your leave!* Walked straight into this shop she did, because of mislaying my address the shiftless way she would! And when the old man set eyes to her, nothing would serve but she must come here. Wanted a housekeeper! A fine excuse! As if I haven't done for him all these years. Looked after him proper, I can tell you. And never an extra penny piece! Cooked and mended and dusted, and cleaned — and never so much as a *thank-you! And* the shop an' all. Took it all for granted, because I'm mebbe not so young as some! And now it's Miss Wade this (that's her name, Wade, Stella Wade), Miss Wade that, Miss Wade upstairs and down, inside and out, till I'm fair sick of the sound. Pushed out of my rightful place, I am! Treated like dirt! All my years of experience — nothing! Did you notice the window? Ever see such a sight? Not a pair of stockings, nor a flannel petticoat, nor a roll of calico, even — nothing to show what the shop sells, the way a shop-window ought. A decent family draper's — and all decked out like the kind of shop those women go to who aren't any better than they ought to be! But nothing I say makes any difference. The old man's crazy about her. *Everyone knows what I sell,* he tells me. *Got to tickle up their fancy, like Miss Wade here, says!* Miss Wade, oh, she's tickled his fancy all right! Whatever she says is right, whatever she does is right, whatever she wants —"

The girl was back again, sauntering down the narrow aisle between the two high counters. He could have sworn she waggled her hips at him as she came.

"Mr Penny's resting. He says please to come back in an hour!"

"What's that?"

"I said Mr Penny was resting. He says —"

Resting! The old boy! And him as tough as a horse! And making appointments! And sending people away, sending his own nephew away! The girl might be pretty — but damn it, this was going too far! This was plain daft!

His sympathies began to stir in Miss Bird's direction.

"Look here," he said, "yo' look here!"

He wanted to explain that it was all damn silly nonsense about the old man resting — the old man never rested; that it was all bloody eyewash about going away and coming back in an hour; that he was the old man's only living relation and he would come and go as he pleased. . .

But he was lost, he, Nicholas Penny, who believed in his own star, his own fortune, his own self.

"Well, what's th'matter wi' him, any road?" he asked lamely.

"Heart. So doctor says. Doctor ordered him to rest after every meal, so rest he must, and that's all there is to it!"

Her voice was quiet enough. But she stood there, shoulders squared, with the suggestion of carrying out those orders by the strength of her own body — if need be!

She roused his temper, standing there, flaunting herself, giving her orders. He wanted to shout. Out of th'way yer goddam silly bitch! But she looked grand standing there, with her little chin thrown back, and her fiery head. He didn't want to quarrel with her! If the old man were that set on her, it wouldn't be too clever to start off with quarrelling. Not that sort of a quarrel, any road! A love quarrel, mebbe. And then, kiss and be friends! Ay — he wouldn't mind that sort of quarrel!

"Aw right!" he was pleasant. "I'll be back. When?"

"To tea. Come back to tea." And then, with a sudden betrayal of adult dignity, "There's a Bakewell tart. I made it myself!"

And by God, as if she weren't pretty enough already, there was a dimple in the cleft of her round chin!

Miss Bird sniffed with a toss of her trembling head, a sniff that expressed her opinion of men both young and old.

"Aw right!" he was annoyed that he could think of nothing smarter to say, no wise-crack.

In the doorway he turned and saw her bright head in the gloom bent above a box of ribbons. Her white fingers flicked above the glossy ribbons.

He sauntered down the narrow street, temper struggling against this new-found pleasure... Something new this was! Being ordered out of the old man's shop! Being ordered to come back at such and such a time! And all as soft as butter!

He crossed the stream by the scabby stone bridge and stared down into the sour water.

A peach! Good enough to eat!

Another face, eager beneath its fair hair, challenged him. He remembered Heriot Ware, her quality, her air of breeding, her clear voice... Nice enough, but she wasn't his sort! He forced himself to remember her quick friendliness, her young eagerness to make him understand... ay, to make him understand... But she wasn't his sort!

The challenge grew faint, died upon the air. His interest was stone-cold.

He wandered over the bridge. His feet trod the scant grass that stubbled the mean road. He kicked at the poor and shabby grass.

... That girl back in the shop... sort of girl to enjoy yourself with. Everything would be fun with her, everything a sort of adventure. Even an ordinary thing like a walk... ay, certainly a walk. You never knew where a walk might lead you...

He grinned, looking about him.

Grim little houses, poor little shops... General shop with its wretched show of cheap tinned goods, cheap biscuits, stale slab of currant cake... hard to tell which was currant and which fly! Dreary little fish-shop displaying tired-looking kippers and bilious-looking dried haddock, and a yellowing piece of cod.

The grin died.

If he married that bright girl he knew where his walks would lead to — he knew well enough!

Not for him! Not for Nicholas Penny! For him the broad streets of Nottingham, the grand shops. When he had to pass through streets like this, he'd lean back in his carriage and never notice them. Why, he'd rather be dead and put away decent in his coffin than drag out a living death in a hole like this!

But he didn't mean to die, not he! He would live in a fine house in Nottingham. The Park, maybe. Or else in that new district, Mapperley they called it. Open and high it was, and they were building fine houses there!

His mind played with the house he would have.

Towers and turrets and a stone staircase going down to the flagged area. A fine kitchen, bigger than two of these hovels knocked into one. An enormous fire roaring up the chimney, yes, even in the hottest weather... and a cook, fat the way cooks ought to be, and red from the fire, preparing his fish, his joints, his puddings.

His mind leaped two storeys.

The drawing-room. It would run from back to front of his house. Curtains of velvet it would have. Or stiff silk maybe, in changing colours. Gold mirrors decorated with angels sitting on fat behinds; twinkling, tinkling chandeliers of cut glass — prisms, like the one his mam had picked up long ago, one day when she'd gone out cleaning. He'd been a little lad, then, but he had never forgotten holding it up to his eye and seeing it break into a wonder of orange and blue and green light.

Yes, that was the sort of house to have — the house he meant to have — one day!

But a man couldn't live in a house like that all alone. It would need a mistress to keep it bright and splendid. Well, why not the lovely girl, the saucy smiling girl? Because — he ground his heel upon a springing coltsfoot, because she wouldn't fit any more than this coltsfoot would fit into the fine greenhouse he meant to have. Take her away from her right setting and pretty though she was, she'd look common — the way this coltsfoot would. She wouldn't fit — not the way some girls would — not the way that Ware girl would. . .

But she was sweet, standing there in the dark shop, lighting it up — like when you put a match to a fire in a cold, dark room. . .

The shop-bell tinkled as he brushed through the door. He strode through the shop, empty except for Miss Bird tidying away, trembling head nodding darkly over trembling fingers. He passed through the little lace-curtained back door and up the dark stairs.

Her gay head, her gay smile, flamed at him above the jug of wallflowers on the checked tablecloth; the flowers, deeply warm, caught up the colour of her hair. She and the flowers flamed crazily together. He thought, dazzled, It's like when you light a fire. . . And came, unthinking, towards its warmth.

Chapter 4

Life was coming real to Heriot. It was coming real and living, full of salt and savour as she had always known it should be!

And time, too! No-one would ever know how she had gone about sickened by the comfort, the eternal everlasting sameness, the tabulated good manners of the life she led! No one would ever know how she had gone about stiff with rebellion beneath her quiet face. What was the good of rebelling when there was no definite thing to rebel about? No, she must stand firm inwardly. She must save herself for the crucial moment — because that moment would certainly come. Then she need be afraid of nothing, no, not even of being smothered beneath the paraphernalia of tedious respectability. *Paraphernalia of tedious respectability*. . . a good phrase that, and all her own! She would tell it to Nicholas. . .

The right moment! But till it came she had to go on playing the part of Miss Ware; to go on accompanying mamma to endless tea-parties; to hover about mamma, twittering prettily on At Home days; to follow mamma obediently to the hateful, ever-growing round of dances.

Dances! She wished she could make mamma understand that she disliked them intensely, that each invitation brought with it a sinking of the heart. She was always anticipating horrid things! She would, she was certain, tread upon the tail of her gown and land shamefully upon the floor. Or she would contrive to lose a slipper, neither so unobtrusively, or so usefully as Cinderella. Or, she would allow herself to become flushed and untidy, with — horror above ladylike horrors — her nose pearled with moisture. She had never done any of these things, so far. But she was always terribly afraid she was going to. Yes, she had escaped so far, but next time, next time, it must certainly happen!

And another thing was certain, too. She hadn't got the right kind of conversation for parties. Mamma accused her, sometimes, of not trying! Much mamma, with her assurance, knew about the agony with which one pursued the ever-vanishing thought. Hunting the weather through every shade of vicissitude, capturing it, pinning it down the captive of one's bow, only to find it running free, escaped, gone from one for ever!

It was so difficult to get on with young men. . . ordinary young men. It was hateful when her partner left her quite quickly after a dance; hateful — and hurtful — to look round and see other girls a-sparkle behind their fans, while their partners stood above them, nodding with smiling ease. They all thought her stuck-up and conceited — and all the time she was crying inside because of being such a stupid failure.

Yes, she bored the young men — all except Edward Jebb, who bored her. When he talked, she found she wasn't listening — after a while. She did try, honestly she did, but she just couldn't be interested in his eternal hunting and farming. Her mind would go wandering off on its own — wandering to Heriots and the machines; and to the men and women who worked on the machines.

Even when he had taken her to the Theatre Royal — mamma smiling and nodding and speeding them off — and she had sat entranced by the sorrows of Iolanthe, and had laughed more than a young lady should, over the vagaries of the Lord Chancellor, even then she had caught herself thinking once again of real things and real people — how she was here in her best gown enjoying herself; and how, though it was quite late and night dark in the streets, the lights would be flaring at Heriots, and the machines clanging — the twist-hands of the night-shift earnest about their work.

Heriots — it was an obsession with her, mamma always said. Well, what else had they expected when they christened her? Even a boy with an uncommon name like that, would be conscious of it, but a girl! Of course the name was branded into her consciousness, of course it was part of her very self... Heriot, Heriot, in every condition, in every place... *Good Heriot. Naughty Heriot. How do you do, Heriot? Good-bye, Heriot, Good morning, Heriot. Good night, Heriot...* Of course she could never escape from Heriot, Heriot, Heriot...

Not that she ever wanted to escape. She wouldn't have things different, not for the world! Only — it would have been easier for her if she had been born a boy. She had longed to be a boy, agonised to be a boy — once. Nobody had understood that, ever. And now she was not at all sure that she, understood it herself. But she had understood it well, then. And it had set her apart from all the people who had not understood — from mamma and papa — who had wished it themselves, once. It had set her apart at school, too. Other girls hadn't understood, they just hadn't understood. When she had tried to make them understand, *Oh Heriot!* they had said or looked or implied, *However could you want to be a boy? How could you even imagine it?*

And that, of course, had made it difficult for her ever to have a real friend. Not only had she imagined it — but she couldn't imagine not imagining it! Because she had longed with all her might to take her part at Heriots, as her father's son would have done — to belong to Heriots.

To belong to Heriots! It had been her heart's wish ever since that first time papa had taken her down to the factory. Five years old she had been, and she remembered it as if it had happened today. She would remember it if she lived to be a hundred; she would remember it, she was sure, on her death-bed, hearing above the rushing of great waters they talked about, the clash and clatter of the Heriot machines.

She could see herself, now, a minute figure, staring up at the immense machines, feeling herself no bigger, no more important than a fly, as they towered above her. And the men and women, she remembered them, too, standing respectfully for papa, yet showing by their very courtesy how much they respected themselves. And papa — papa moving with kindness, moving with authority. Papa's hand stretched out, a clever hand that knew its business, touching this, touching that, while he spoke with his people, asking about their children, or their husbands, or their wives... whether the new baby was a boy or a girl, whether Bob was home from sea, or whether Nancy was happy in her new job. Papa knew them all, knew their sorrows and their joys. It had seemed to her then that papa and the hands worked for Heriots together; that it was papa's job to look after everyone, think for everyone, as a papa should. Or God.

After that, Heriots would never leave her in peace. It was like a live thing, always at her. When she was sick, the voice of the machines was in her ears and she could only be comforted by the promise to be taken to Heriots as soon as she was well. If ever a special treat was offered, she was prompt in her preference for Heriots. It was irritating to her parents — she knew that, but she could not help it. The matter was beyond her. She was always talking of Heriots, asking innumerable questions about Heriots, demanding insistently to be taken again to Heriots. And again. And again...

She might, given patience, have got over her childish enthusiasm, but when she heard, for the first time, the story of Simon Ware, the thing was finished then, and for ever. The story of that pitiful trek into England, and across England, touched her heart like a ballad. But when she heard, eyes dark with pain, how the Heriot children had been put to the machines, and how they had died, one after another, pitiful victims of the machines, then her grief left the realms of legend and became her own personal, unbearable grief.

She began to understand, for the first time, that quite young people, children even, could die. Then it followed that papa, who was not quite young, could die, too — die at any moment. There was no reason, of course, why this should happen — but then so many things happened without reason. And this might happen, too! What would become of Heriots, then? Who would care for the machines, and the workers?

The thought tormented her, keeping her awake at nights. Lying in the darkness, she would ask herself, weeping, who would look after Heriots, if papa should die? And then, later, with the realisation that not only might people die, but die they must, yes even the Queen at

Buckingham Palace, the question, who will look after Heriots *when* papa dies?

It came between Heriot and her play; between Heriot and her eating; between Heriot and her sleeping. *Who will look after Heriots?*

She grew thin and peaked, until mamma packed her off with Nanny to Skegness, for the benefit of the air; and there, among the golden sand and the blue sea and the long line of scarlet-saddled donkeys, the question became less urgent. But even there, as she lay warm beneath the patchwork quilt, watching the moonlight travel across her bed, watching a dim patch spring to sudden colour, there would come, with the breaking of the sea, a faint echo of the question to trouble her dreams.

As she grew older, the idea lost some of its urgency. After all, papa had not died — nor did he show any intention of so doing! And then, away at school, with Nottingham sights and sounds grown dim, she was satisfied to leave the matter at the back of her mind. She knew it was there, and that was enough. After all, she was not yet strong enough or clever enough to help Heriots. Besides — Heriots didn't need her — yet.

But when she left school behind her, when she set foot again in her native town, Heriots was at her again. And for good. She was no longer a child swept by childish enthusiasms, she was almost a young woman, with the clear consciousness of her ability to serve Heriots.

But neither mamma nor papa had grown with time. She begged papa to take her into the factory; She wasn't a boy — well, what of it? She would work harder than any boy to make up for it. Papa should see, let him only try her, and he should see!

Papa had pinched her ear and said he would think about it. But she had known by his voice, by that light and careless tone, that his mind was already made up — if you could call a mind made up when it hadn't registered the thought at all!

Mamma had referred to the matter later. Quiet and firm, and in the tone that expected no argument, mamma had said that it would not do.

But in spite of the non-arguing tone, Heriot had argued.

"A factory," mamma said flatly, "is no place for a lady!"

"But there are women in Heriots, lots and lots of women. . ."

"I said *ladies* —" And so, unwitting, mamma showered glamour about those women who were free, free to work. "A lady's place is in her home!"

"Nonsense, old-fashioned nonsense!" Heriot cried passionately, knowing the battle already lost, for mamma's lips were drawn as if in pain, mamma's eyes remembered. . . And then, quite briskly, she had gone on to discuss the new gown Jessops were making for Heriot to wear at Lady Jebb's garden party.

Clear. Clear as daylight, what mamma had intended. She had intended to bring you back to what she considered realities. Edward as going "to offer". And obviously the garden-party would provide a suitable occasion.

Well, let him offer! She would not accept him. She had decided that swiftly, suddenly. It was not that she disliked Edward, she had even a mild affection for him, but if they would not give her Heriots, she would not give them Edward! Nothing but sheer blind rebellion. Afterwards, though, she had been able to rationalise her unreason. Edward, with his devotion to the Jebb estate, his passion for crop and beast, would be useless, utterly useless, to Heriots.

And putting Edward out of her mind, she had put marriage. After all, she was barely eighteen and heart-free. Save for Heriots.

And now Nicholas Penny.

Yes, there was Nicholas. Nicholas who was her friend! How could it be otherwise? Together they shared a devotion to the old machines. Together they learned about lace. They could discourse quite learnedly to each other on the romantic history of lace. In the quiet of the Long Gallery they talked — and it was not always about lace.

Nicholas was a worker. She shied from the fact that he was a working-man, with all the habits, pleasant and unpleasant, of his class. To her, he was that abstract thing, a worker — as Simon had been, as Andrew had been, as all her forebears had been. She never stopped to consider that she had not known her forebears, that time had gilded them with romance, or with success. It was enough that Nicholas was one of their company, he spoke the rich strange tongue of the worker — except when he remembered and spoke his careful foreigner's English.

She had gone her way, lonely and rebellious and dissatisfied. And then — click! It was like the kaleidoscope that lay neglected in the nursery cupboard. Something had clicked in her mind and the whole pattern had changed. And in the new pattern, she and Nicholas and Heriots were bound together.

Did Nicholas care for her? She thought he did. Surely, he did! But he had never said so. Not in so many words, perhaps, but surely, in other words... *I'd give all I have in the world if you would be my friend...* Surely, surely, he must care!

If Nicholas cared! If only he cared! How they would work for Heriots, she and he, together! Already his hand served the machines, he had the designer's joy in fine and delicate patterns. With Nicholas she could do more, incomparably more, than she could ever have done alone. Women choose husbands to help them bear their responsibilities, mamma had said, pushing the claims of

Edward. Mamma in her foolishness had let fall a pearl!

But suppose it had not been Nicholas whose heart was set upon lace, not Nicholas, but some other, without his eyes, his smile — would she have been so certain, then, that only in marriage could she best serve Heriots?

She never asked herself that question. She only knew that her heart leaped at the thought of Nicholas.

She had stood by the machines, but her eyes were not for the machines. She had wandered the lace gallery, but her eyes were not for lace. Her heart might leap at the thought of Nicholas, but her eye had not lit up at the sight of him. Three weeks since she had seen him! One day and another day, adding up to three whole weeks.

She went about her daily duties. She smiled, she poured tea for mamma, she sat beside mamma in the carriage... Three weeks, three whole weeks. He was ill. He was lying sick and uncared for in that dismal room of which he had told her... He was not ill! She could not imagine Nicholas ill, splendid Nicholas! Besides had he been ill, she must have known it, in her heart she must have known it! But why had he not come, for three weeks not come? In the true spirit of the romantic she came upon the reason. He had suddenly realised that this was more than friendship. Nicholas so poor, so proud and so simple! Nicholas would never come running after Miss Ware. Miss Ware, if she wanted him, must make the first advance.

And Miss Ware did want him, oh she wanted him!

But for all that it was not easy for her to make the first movement — even if she could be sure what that movement should be. She must, she supposed, throw away the silly notions she had been brought up with, the fantastic notions of what constituted proper behaviour in a young lady. It was right to be retiring when one was dealing with Edward Jebb, but this was Nicholas!

I'm glad you're not a lad... you're different... I'd give all I have in the world... all I have... Searching in her memory for a word she might have forgotten, endowing the word remembered with significance even Nicholas had not dreamed of, she strengthened her failing purpose. Mahommed and the mountain; the dear and gracious Queen and her long-ago example — all in one glorious muddle to stiffen her faint courage.

That Nicholas might be running after another girl, did not occur, even remotely, to Heriot. Nicholas was her friend! He was simple and kind and honest. Also he was poor and proud... Certainly, if she wanted him, she must do the seeking!

Not so easy to find Nicholas, however firmly she stiffened her courage. A humble young man, even if he were as handsome as Apollo, may be rather like a needle in a haystack when it comes to looking for him! Of course there was Heriots — she could find him at Heriots. But — her cheeks flamed at the thought — to put him at such a disadvantage, to seek him where he must bow respectfully to her position! Unpardonable! And foolish. He would never want to speak to her again!

Walking along the streets of Nottingham, sitting upright in the carriage, trotting on her mare, her eyes darted this way and that. She even played with the notion of an insertion in the personal column of the *Nottingham Express*. But — suppose someone saw it? Suppose Nicholas himself saw it — Miss Ware advertising for her lost young man. . .?

Fortunate Nicholas! Simple liking driven to the point of anguish! And no effort on his part! Had he sat down to consider the matter, he could have done no better.

Blessed, blessed accident, thought Heriot, meeting Nicholas one afternoon where the hollow Lenton Road runs down by the castle, to Friar Lane and the Market Place. And Nicholas did not enlighten her. The high Castle Rock was ablow with daffodils. It was a Saturday afternoon and the quiet road was alive with people — women hurrying down into the town for last minute shopping, families in their best clothes hurrying into the Castle garden to listen to the band; men, women, children, perambulators, all hurrying, hurrying, to miss none of the fun.

Heriot stood, her eyes on Nicholas, not even hearing the music that came delicate upon the air. . . This was Nicholas, standing with her here, this spring afternoon, Nicholas. . .

Nicholas said, “That’s my favourite tune!”

Was there music playing? Was there?

He said carefully, “Can’t hear it properly, not from here! Come in and listen?”

It was more than a casual invitation and they both knew it. Saturday afternoon and the band playing! All Nottingham’s working-folk released from the factories would be there, lads with clean gay handkerchiefs about their throats, girls in bright cotton frocks, pretty as the posies that stood stiffly in the borders. Saturday afternoon and all Nottingham taking the air.

She thought, in sudden panic, I can’t. . . I can’t. She thought in greater panic, This is my chance. He’s waiting to hear, Yes, or No.

Take a pair of sparkling eyes, hummed Nicholas.

Had she thought to play Victoria to his Albert? Then play it now, now!

Mamma... papa... She shrank a little from the thought of them. It wouldn't take long for such news to travel, and then... then... What? The more public the performance the better!

And a pair of rosy lips, sang Nicholas softly. "I wish you would!" Even in his eagerness he held fast to his new manner of speech.

Now or never... now or never... She shrank a little from *now*; she shrank woefully from never. She traced with her toe a pattern in the dust. Now or never.

Heriot looked up at Nicholas; she smiled her wide sweet smile.

Miss Ware passed through the gateway before Nicholas Penny.

Chapter 5

Ellen Bird was not pleased.

Fools men were, the whole lot of them! Fools to be taken in by the nearest pretty face!

A bad day for her — and for old Nicholas and for young Nicholas, though they didn't know it yet — when Stella came swinging, the audacious way she had, into the shop. Tinkle of the bell, swinging inwards of the door — and Stella beaming and gleaming in the dark shop, well-pleased with herself and all the world — just like her mother before her!

And since that day everything changed, spoiled; she herself, put upon, flouted; her experience flicked away with a snap of the old man's fingers. Forty years of experience! And Stella, flushed and smiling and full of new ideas, trying this, trying that, going on her triumphant way — leaving all the mess to be cleaned up by someone else — and who that someone but Ellen Bird?

Well, it was nothing new — though none the less bitter for all that! Stella's mother had played that trick all her life, drawing the lads after her with the toss of her head and the smile of her lips. Even when she hadn't wanted to, still it had happened. All the lads had followed, even when she hadn't piped. Even Mr Nicholas. Older than the lads he'd been, a man and steady, and master of his own shop.

Nicholas hadn't thought much to Margaret — so he'd said. At first. Nicholas hadn't cared much about women at all. Shy he'd been with them, and short. He'd been like that with herself once. And then he'd come to rely on the things she could do for him, so he'd got into the way of speaking pleasant, not sort of to the air, the way he had used! Yes, he'd been well on the way to caring — though he hadn't known it himself.

And then, Margaret.

Margaret hadn't thought twice about Mr Nicholas — except to laugh out loud at the very notion of him. No, she wouldn't so much as look at him, though he'd been just about on bended knees to her.

That had been the worst of it! That had tore your pride to little tiny bits! Even Margaret's leavings you couldn't have! Because after Margaret had gone, Nicholas went back to his old ways, short and cold and all shut up inside of himself — and he disliked women more than ever. . . Nicholas, the only one who'd ever come near caring for you. Margaret had hurt him and gone away. . . and even her leavings you couldn't have!

It had taken her a long time to accept that fact, long minutes in front of the glass, facing herself, facing the thin untidy hair, the thin sallow face, the thin long nose. No, it couldn't have been otherwise... but it was bitter.

And then, when Margaret had gone awhile, not so bitter. She had thought, she's gone and I'm free. Free to be my own self. I'm not a beauty, but I'm not a fool. I'll show them, *show* them... But what had all her *showing them* amounted to, but doing things for Nicholas? She had bought and sold, dusted and swept and cooked, washed and mended — and never a penny piece better than her fifteen bob a week! Fifteen bob rising by miserable sixpences to thirty-five! After forty years' slaving, thirty-five bob! And he, he'd grown from young Nicholas into old Nicholas. And she herself — she wasn't as young as she had been! Well, what did you expect? All these years and no service too great or too small she hadn't done for the old man. Why, last winter, only, when he'd gone about spitting and coughing so bad, she'd even put up the shutters for him, she, Ellen Bird, slipping and sliding on the frosty pavement, the heavy wood dangerously swinging. And he could have got butcher's Bob to do it and willing, only he'd been too mean to spare a few pence!

Yes, she'd worn out her strength and thrown away her woman's dignity to save his miser's pocket. Well, she was being paid for it! Not a word of consideration, not a word of gratitude! And now came Stella, young and strong as a horse, and there was the old man fussing about and bleating, Miss Stella mustn't lift this, mustn't lift that... Give Miss Stella a hand... Miss Stella this and Miss Stella that, till she could scream!

Do Stella justice, she never asked to be fussed over — not in so many words. It was the way she had of looking sort of helpless out of those brown eyes of hers. Just her way! But you didn't like her way — her harum-scarum flibberty-gibberty way! No, nor the sound of her voice neither as she sang about the house... too much like her mother's.

Maybe there wasn't any real badness to Stella — except she was her mother's daughter, high-coloured and noisy. Only it wasn't fair of her to drag you back again to those unhappy days, the way she did with sound of her strong sweet singing.

All your life you'd worked and worked. After it was all finished with Nicholas, you'd asked for nothing but a bit of peace. It had been a long, long time in coming, that peace. And now, seemingly, that was to be taken away, too!

Why did you come? Who asked you? You were doing all right down in Torquay, you were serving at the ribbons in a good establishment, you were being paid a sight better than what you are here. Why didn't you stay! She'd thrown those questions at Stella, Stella standing there, with her hands outstretched, and sure of her welcome.

"Because blood's thicker than water," she'd said, smiling the sort of smile that would have sent old Nicholas off his nut. "Because I couldn't bear Torquay after Mother died." She'd said that with the sort of look that would have melted young Nicholas. But neither smile nor look had cut any ice with you. It was hard not to hate Stella for her own sake as well as her mother's.

Ellen's head began to tremble on her neck. She knew it was trembling and she hated the knowledge... Made her feel like one of those old women sat out in the sun by almshouse doors, their hands shaking and shaking. She noticed them every time she went into Nottingham. Down by The Fountain, the almshouses were. And, when it was warm enough, the old creatures were sat out like dead plants rotting in the sun. She never wanted to look at them. But her eyes got drawn in that direction. Every time she went into Nottingham she swore she wouldn't look at them...

...But she had to. Always she had to! And more than that, if she had a few minutes to spare after the round of buying, she would go down Friar Lane to have a look at the old women there. She didn't want to look at them, any more than she wanted to look at those down by The Fountain. But it was a sort of fascination they had. Frightened her too — a bit. Not that she had need to be frightened. She had her job. Knew it from A to Z. Had a bit put by an' all. Not much but there was still time to save, still time. After all she wasn't old — hardly middle-aged, even. It was Stella, bright and shining and taking the eye like new paint, made her feel old.

And now things had come to a pretty pass. Old Nicholas skipping like an old ram to the piping of red lips. And young Nicholas, he was always coming over nowadays — he followed Stella about with his eyes as if he'd like to eat her!

She'd tried to warn them both. But she might just as well have saved her breath to cool her porridge. Young Nicholas had looked at her — and never a word. But she'd known what he meant all right, she was nobody's fool! It was young Nicholas was the fool, thinking she could be jealous of a chit like that! She had her own gifts — she had her experience, and the sort of dignity that comes from experience. She wouldn't demean herself by being jealous of Stella. Just didn't like her, didn't trust her, that was all!

As for the old man, when she'd tried to warn him, to remind him that Stella was her mother's daughter, he'd turned on her, and his eyes were snapping like an angry old dog.

"Ah'll thank yer not t'interfere wi' my concerns, Ellen Bird!" he'd said, not even giving her the benefit of a handle to her name, the way he wouldn't when he was wild. And then, forgetting himself, he'd bawled out, "Yo' damn interferin' owd bitch!"

Such language! From him! And to her! Speaking to her like that, after forty years' devoted service. That's what you got for putting everyone in front of yourself — everyone put you down like dirt!

There was the old man, still following the girl about, wagging his tail whenever she so much as glanced in his direction. Couldn't he see how unproper it was? Didn't he know that an old man like him didn't ought to look at a young girl that way? Old enough to be her grandfather he was. Disgusting. . .

A shuffling springless footstep sounded from the back of the shop. She drew out a drawer and busied herself with a pile of tapes. Let him see that he had, at least, one faithful worker! She tutted with vexation over the tumbled heap — wide tape, narrow tape, black tape, and white, all jumbled together. Messer, that's what the girl was — a messer!

Old Nicholas came shuffling forward. Ellen Bird made great play with the disordered drawer. The old man stood peering downward, drawing a knotted hand through his sparse grey beard.

"Why, Mr Penny, you gave me quite a start! I was that busy I never heard you! Ever see such a drawer in your life? I ask you!"

Hands on hips, Ellen Bird surveyed the drawer in triumph.

Did you ever! The old man, instead of flying off the handle, was standing there and grinning, yes actually grinning, as if he was looking at a nice tidy drawer instead of a tumbled, tangled mess.

"Mustn't be too hard on th'young, must us?" And he was chuckling, actually chuckling. "She'll learn in time, ay, she'll learn!"

More than anything Miss Bird resented his suggestion that they were of an age, the old man and she! Why, she was in her early fifties — still. And him, sixty-five, if he was a day! Let him remember that! She was only middle-aged, while he was well on the shady path that led to the churchyard!

He played with the heavy chain looped upon his woollen waistcoat. He said, "yer down't like th'lass, now do yer?"

"What lass?" *Lass indeed! Slut, that's what, slut!*

"Yer niece o'course! Little Miss Stella, yer down't like her!" She couldn't control her burst of temper. "I'd like her a deal better if she was a bit tidier round the place!"

"I like her th'way she is! A sight fer sore eyes!"

"My eyes aren't sore!" She was tarter than green apples.

"A'n't they now?" His tone held doubt. He turned his back in its shabby broadcloth and shuffled to the back door. Suddenly he turned and pointed a commanding finger. "I expect yer ter help her — see? She's yer niece an' it's yer duty. She's young, but she's got a good head on her. That winder, now, down't it draw th'eye?"

"That it does!" Miss Bird's sniff removed the faintest hint of compliment from the words.

"Ay, she've got th'brain, and yo've got th'experience — and between yer y'ought ter do summat!"

"Open up in Nott'nam. Jessops'd just about lose their sleep, I shouldn't wonder!"

"Well, yer niver know! Even Jessops had ter mek a start sometime! Anyroad, that's neither here nor there!"

His temper changed suddenly. "Yo' do what I tell yer, see? An' I'm telling yer to look after her, unnerstand?"

"I'd need more'n one pair of eyes ter do that!"

"Meaning ter say?" He was suddenly back again at the counter, moving as he sometimes did, with speed surprising in his corpulent old age. His face, dark with anger, was thrust into her own.

"Don't ask me, I'm sure!" Ellen Bird tossed the thin waves of her piled hair. "And —" with the sudden courage of anger, "I'll thank you not to bully me, neither! If I don't suit, I can always go, I s'pose!"

"Ay, that yer can!"

Her heart sank. She felt a little sick with fear, even though she knew well enough that he would not, because he could not, replace her. It would take years before another assistant could discover how to clear up his muddles — even suppose one were willing. He was old — so much older than his years; since his last year's illness he forgot so easily. He would forget what he'd ordered, and what he'd sold, and what he'd paid, and what he'd been paid for! He had set customers by the ears more than once by demanding payment a second time — even while he held the change in his hand! It was she who did everything now-a-days, she who was responsible; she who bought, sold, dealt with travellers, checked and paid invoices, went into Nottingham to buy, and until lately, had dressed the window.

The window. . .

At the thought of that, her anger against Stella flamed anew.

Here he stood the old man, chin thrust out, showing you clear enough that his monkey was up. He was so near she could almost count the grey stubble on his chin. He was a beast! All men were beasts, that's what they were, beasts!

"Running a shop and running it right, isn't to be learned in a day, nor in a week, nor yet in a year, neither!" she reminded him, her head trembling slightly in spite of her defiance.

"I've learned all I want!" he said blandly, "an' I'm mester here, and I'll thank yer ter remember it! See?"

He turned his back and shuffled heavily away. She looked after him, noting with savage pleasure the creases ridged clumsily between bent neck and shoulder. She thought, "turn me off and see where you'll land! The workhouse, I shouldn't wonder!"

Her thoughts, dismissing the old man as useless, turned to young Nicholas... He ought to be learning the job — everything'll come to him, one day! And there isn't anyone could learn him better than what I can. We could make a right good job of it, him and me!

But he wouldn't, not young Nicholas. Crazy about lace he was, and didn't care two pins about the shop. She'd put it to him, pointing out that once a twist-hand, always a twist-hand, at the beck and call of a master, he who could be his own master... she'd talked to him like a mother, but she might just as well have talked to the wall! He'd laughed, with just that bit of temper in his eyes that warned you to go easy. "Summat better ter do than sell flannel drawers t'owd ladies, ay, *an'* young 'uns, come to that!"

Not a very gentlemanly thing to say! One didn't expect much in the way of manners from the old man, but Nicholas, he was different. He lived over to Nottingham, he could speak well-off, same as she could herself, when he wanted!

Old Nicholas and young Nicholas. They both needed the steady sort of help a good woman could give. But what did they care about that! Beauty's only skin-deep — so they say! But it draws the eye. It draws the eye! Old and young alike, men don't care about beauty under the skin — not when there's a pair of red lips about!

Miss Bird's head shook slightly as she stacked the tapes into neat bundles and put each in its appointed place.

Old Nicholas went slowly up the steep uncarpeted stairs...

Stiddy, now stiddy! His hands were shaking. His legs were shaking! Ay, he was shaking all ovver. But he'd be damned if he'd let that old bitch see it!

He stopped, catching at the handrail. Coloured spots jigged before his eyes. Bent over the handrail he considered the flying spots.

Yellow... red... green. Like the colours Stella put in ter brighten th'window.

His hand crept upwards to his breast.

...Couldn't catch his breath. Hateful when yer can't catch yer breath...

He stumbled through the kitchen door.

...Stiddy now... stiddy does it! Not so far to th' chair. Tek it easy... easy...

He lay back, eyes closed, lips blue in his blue face.

...Damn th'owd hag fer upsetting him this road! She knew he had ter go easy! Then why didn't she think a bit before she let that tongue wag! By God, he needed someone to look after him, to see that bitches like that di'n't aggravate him and mek him ill. . .

Through his heaviness came the sound of singing — Stella at her bed-making.

. . .A kind voice. A kind lass. She'd be along soon — time to put th'joint in th'oven. Stella mustn't find him this way. Upset her it would. Tender little heart she had — not like that black scarecrow downstairs. No, Stella mustn't find him this way! She'd niver thowt of him as an owd man — she'd said so! Fine figure of a man — that's what she'd said. Di'n't like young chaps. Selfish, the lot of 'em. Ignorant an' all. She liked a man wi' a bit of experience. . . Ay, a fine figure of a man.

Gradually his pulse calmed. His heart took on a slower beat. His head fell back upon the red-and-white flowered cushion. . . an old man asleep.

Chapter 6

Stella lay with young Nicholas in the grass under the alder tree. It was chilly this spring evening and she shivered in spite of the warmth of his body pressed close to hers.

Suddenly she sat upright. "I don't know what to *do*, Nick!" she burst out nervously twisting and untwisting her fingers.

Nicholas looked at her lazily. Silly lass to go jerking about when they were laying so cosy next to each other!

"I don't know what to *do*!" she said again.

"Come an' lay down an' I'll show yer!"

"Don't be so daft!" Still her fingers wove their frightened pattern. "You don't think, Nick, you don't think of anything except kissing and cuddling and making love!"

"Yer own fault fer bein' so cuddlesome! I mean — yo' an' me laying close together in th'dark. Yer wouldn't want me t'act diff'rent, now would yer?"

"Nick!" She was beating at him with frantic hands. "Don't talk yourself away from me. I need you. I need you bad. But you don't listen. You don't listen. You didn't hear what I said just now, did you, Nick, *did* you?"

His only answer was to take her wild hands and mumble kisses over them.

She was frantic to pull her hands free, to bring them crashing full into his selfish, greedy face. Her young body went rigid. She felt herself stiffen with purpose.

"All right, then!" She was quiet. "If I can't get help from you, I'll do what he says — he's asked me often enough, goodness knows!"

"Whativer are yer talkin' abowt?" He was still lazily amused.

"If you'd been listening, you'd have heard! But you weren't listening, you never do!" She wrenched her hands from his mumbling mouth. "Stop that! I don't belong to you! I don't belong to you, never no more!"

"What's come to yer, my lass? Whativer are yer talkin' abowt?"

"I told you. But you didn't care enough to listen — even to pretend to listen. All right, I'll say it again. I belong, from now on, to the chap I'm going to marry!"

He stared stupidly, bending forward a little to read her face in the half-light.

"Are yer daft, Stella? What th'hell are yer talkin' abowt?"

She said drearily, "I *told* you... only you were too busy kissing to listen. Well, now you've *got* to listen! I'm marrying the old man!"

He sat up suddenly. “What th’devil — what owd man?”

“You know very well, what old man. Your uncle!” Stella said and smiled in his face.

“Then yer *must* be daft!” He still wore his air of banter, but behind the lazy smile, the brain worked.

“I’d be daft if I didn’t!”

“Do yer like him?” Nicholas was curious.

“*Like* him! I hate old men — all old men. They’re dirty!” She shivered a little. “Though,” she added more quietly, “Mr Penny’s kind — ever so kind!”

“An’ what will yer do wi’ his kindness when yo’re in bed wi’ him!” cried Nicholas, brutal at the thought.

She flinched. But she answered calmly enough, “Same as I did with yours!”

“Oh no you wain’t!” He pretended to fair consideration, but all the time he felt the pricking of jealousy goading him on to hurt, to humiliate — chiefly to humiliate. “An owd man in bed, an’ a young ’n — that’s a diff’rent pair o’ shoon!”

“I’ll say it is!” she flashed wild with anger. “When the old one’s as kind as kind, and the young one’s as selfish as hell! You never even paid me the compliment of a bed, did you, Nick! You couldn’t wait, could you? Out in the fields, like —”

Quite suddenly her anger went. “Nick,” she said piteously, “help me, *you* help me. An old man in bed — like you say — I can’t face it! Help me, you’ve *got* to help me!”

“Help yer? That’s a good ’un, when I can’t hardly help mysen! Help yer! What do yer want me ter do?”

She beat her two hands softly together. “You know well enough! But you make me keep on asking. You *like* me to keep on asking — almost as if you want to punish me. Well, if I’ve got to ask again — marry me, Nick. Marry me like you said you would that first time you had your way with me — remember? Save me, Nick, save me from the old man!”

“Marry yer? On what — i’ God’s name? I’m out of a job an’ yer know it!” He was lying to gain time. “Know what I’ve got in my pocket? Just abowt two bob to last th’ week out. An’ my room not paid for, neither. We planned out I should learn a bit, study, gi’ mysen a chance — that’s what we promised each other an’ yer know it!”

“I know it. I do know it! But I never thought things would turn this way! Nature won’t wait for anybody! And I can’t wait, neither! Get a job, Nick, any job! Never mind about the chance. You’ll make your own chances. You’re clever, Nick, and you’re young. And you’re strong, too! You can’t keep a good man down — like you always say. I’d work, too. I could work quite a bit, yet! Afterwards, too. It isn’t work I'm afraid of. Work never killed anyone. It's being ashamed, gets me down. Thinking what folk'll say of me, thinking and thinking. ". . .All the little folk in their little houses laughing behind their hands. And then, not behind their hands! Aunt Ellen — she'd throw me out. I wouldn't have nowhere to go — nowhere. But if I was married, I wouldn't mind. I'd be proud! And when it was all over, I'd get work again, I'd get someone to look after the kid —"

"Whose kid?" he asked just too quickly.

"Whose kid?" she repeated slowly, as if the question didn't make sense. "Whatever do you mean, Nick? Whose kid? The one that's coming, — ours. Mine and yours, of course!"

"Why o' course? Th'owd man's bin kind, iver so kind!" His mimicry was cruel. "Ha'n't he? Well, *ha'n't* he?"

Stella said in tones of wonder, "You beast! You dirty beast! You know well enough whose child it is! You know I never went with a man till I went with you. You know I've never been with a man in my life — but you. Don't you?" Her voice rose, "*Don't* you?"

Nicholas shrugged.

She took a long breath, steadying herself. "If that's the way of it, I'd best be going. I don't need to be beholden to you, thank God! I've got my remedy."

"Meanin'?"

"You know my meaning. I've got to have a husband, haven't I? Well, *haven't* I? And what better can I do than take the one that offers? It isn't every girl in my position," she added bitterly, "finds one ready and waiting and —" she flung the taunt at him, "able to keep her, too!"

He said, very quietly, "Yer can put that right out of yer head!"

"And why?" She took quietness from him, but there was danger in her quietness.

"Because he wain't marry *yo'*. Not when he knows."

"But he won't know. Why should he? He doesn't suspect a thing — he wouldn't. Not about me. He thinks I'm the sort of girl — I was. I'd be married long before — before anything began to show!"

He made no answer. She waited in the silence. Fear began to stir. She thrust forward her face, trying to read his, to translate this fearful silence. Her face was candle-white in the dusk.

"You — you wouldn't *tell*?"

"Me? O' course not!" He was smooth. "But — what abowt th'owd bird?"

"Aunt Ellen?" Stella laughed, a little hysterical from sheer relief. "She doesn't know a thing! She wouldn't know the way a girl gets together with a man when it's dark and quiet, and they're young. She's old, so old she's forgotten everything— forgotten, if she ever did know, the way a baby comes. She lives in a world of her own, gone back to childhood inside that shaking old head of hers."

"Yo' listen ter me, Stella, an' listen hard! Ter begin wi', she's none so owd — not above fifty, as I guess. And she's none such a fool, neither! She knows more'n what you think! Not iverything, but still enough! An' what she down't know, she'll guess! She down't love yer, even if she is yer aunt! She's got all th'owd maid's jealousy agenst yer, because yo're young and yo're pretty! Wild wi' jealousy she is! It wain't let her rest. She's got a sort of horror, and yet she's got a sort o' satisfaction an' all, because of what she calls yer *gooin's on*! She trailed us once. . . yer di'n't know that, did yer! I knew it, though, an' I were careful, you bet! 'Member once us was walkin' down by th'river and I shut yer up. I di'n't speak, nor yet I di'n't let yo' speak neither! An' afterwards I said I were list'nin' to a bird. . . an' so I were — on'y us didn't mean the same sort o' bird!"

He chuckled.

"Oh yes, I were careful! She knows yer've got a man. She towd me that much, hersen. But she down't know who — I were one too clever! Asked me to keep an eye on yer, she did! I near laughed in her face. Warned me, iver so solemn, she did, yer'd find yersen in Queer Street one o' these days!"

"Good prophet!" Stella said hopelessly.

For a while neither spoke. They sat remote, strange to each other.

"Listen, Nick!" Stella's voice came from the darkness brittle with nervousness. "You've *got* to listen to me, you've got to understand. I'm in dead earnest. I'm not knuckling down. I've got my life to live — even — even if I've got to live it without you! You can break my heart, Nick, but not my spirit. I won't let you break my spirit! I can't afford to be romantic and all that! Because there's my child's life, too. I've got to think for the child. And I'm taking the old man!"

"An' if he alters his mind? If he wain't take yo'?"

"He won't alter. He's mad for me!"

"If he alters his mind?" Nicholas asked again, gently.

"You mean," she could hardly bring herself to the words. "You mean — you'll tell?"

The nodding of his head was only to be guessed at in the darkness.

"Then —" her voice was shrill with fear, "I'd tell him something, too! I'd tell him outright who it was brought me to it!"

"An' if I deny it?" Nicholas asked softly.

"You wouldn't! You couldn't!"

"Wouldn't I? Couldn't I? Mebbe I wouldn't want to — but us can't all do what us wants! See here, Stella, we've just abowt got t'unnerstand each other!"

"It's over-late for that!" she said bitterly.

"Stop play-actin'. Yer not th'first lass, and yer wain't be th'last! I'm fond o' yer, Stella, I am that! An' I'm downright sorry yo're in this mess. I'd marry yer if I could. A chap could be happy wi' yo', Stella! But a chap's got ter look out fer hissen before he can tek on th'job o' looking out for anyb'dy else! My job — as I see it — is ter look fer mysen first! If yer tell th'owd man, I'll deny everythin', ivery single word yer say, an' so. I warn yer! And what's more I'll put yer in court for slander! Can yer prove it? Who's iver seen us tergither? Who's iver heard me so much as mention yer name? Ay, or yo' mine! We've bin too clever. Prove it! Go on, prove it! Yer'd have a job!"

She tried to speak, to utter his name. The sound came voiceless, without meaning.

He looked at her, and his face was wry. "My lass," he said, "it down't sound pretty, an' it i'n't pretty. An' it's not th'way I *want* ter do! But every man has got ter to do what he must — an' there's no other man can judge fer him. Gi' me a chance, Stella. Lay off th'owd man an' trust me. Trust me, Stella. Yer wain't be sorry — that's a promise!"

Her laugh cracked out. "Trust you! You and your promises!"

She rose stiffly to her feet, brushing blindly at the twigs that clung about her skirt. Her hands trembled violently about their work. She said slowly, "I wouldn't marry you now, not if you were on your knees to me, with the whole world in your hands. You don't believe that, do you, Nick? But it's true — it's true! Because you're no good to anyone! A woman couldn't trust you when she had need to trust. You're like a grand piece of china that's cracked — no use except to look at. So, goodbye, Nicholas Penny — I'm taking the old man!"

"Not in this life, yo're not!"

"You can't stop me!" Defiance fell suddenly from her. "Oh, Nick," she said pitifully, "why do you want to stop me?"

"Because I need th'brass! There it is, gloves off! Because I can do more wi' it than yo' iver will, ay, do more for both on us, yo' as well as me!"

"Stop that fine talk!" she commanded harshly. "Gloves off, like you said! For a bit of money you'd sell me — sacrifice us both, me and the child, together!"

"Plain speaking. I'd sacrifice yo' an' th'kid, ay, an' anyb'dy, anyb'dy at all that gets in my way! Mysen, even. Mysen most! On'y yer wouldn't unnerstand that, yer wouldn't *want* t'unnerstand! Yer think I'm hateful, down't yer, hateful an' wicked an' mean! Yer think it's easy what I'm goin' ter do, down't yer? Yer wouldn't even want t'unnerstand — it i'n't easy. . . Stella, this minute, by my own act, my own will, I'm losin' yer — mebbe for iver! There'll niver be anyone like yo' in my life, niver any more. Whativer comes ter me, I've lost yo'. Yo're sweet an' yo're lovely — yer wouldn't know how lovely! But a woman i'n't enough by hersen, not even when it's yo', Stella. Yo've got ter live — yer said so just now! So've I, Stella, so've I. I've got ter do things — big things. That's the on'y way I *can* live!

"Listen, Stella. I niver had a chance! Niver will have — except I get this. Th'owd man's brass. It's all I iver had ter look to! All I iver will have! An' it i'n't much when all's said! Let me have it, Stella. I'll do big things wi' it — big fer yo' as well as fer me. Down't come between me an' th'brass, Stella, an' yer'll live soft fer th'rest o' yer life. I swear it!"

She said, "What sort of a man are you, Nicholas? Twisting round dirty shabby thoughts to make them look grand? It's dead man's shoes with you, neither more nor less! And if they're not so large as you'd like, you'll put up with the pinching! As for your swearings and your promises —" She shrugged. "I know the worth of them — and much good they've done me! No, Nicholas, I've learned the lesson you've taught me! Each person's got to look out for theirselves! and that's what I'm going to do! And when I've married the old man, don't think there'll be a bite out of the cherry for you! Because there won't. Because I play fair, always! So good night, Mister Nicholas Penny — and when I'm your auntie, I'll slam the door in your face, your handsome hateful face, so help me God!"

She was half-running, half-stumbling over her skirts, and crying as she ran.

Chapter 7

Nicholas was helping Miss Bird in the dusty gloom of the shop. Every now and then she sent him a look, her eyes surprisingly sharp beneath the crumpled lids. Nicholas whistled cheerfully, swinging the heavy black boxes from their shelves on to the counter. Now that the old man seemed ailing, Nicholas had taken to coming over several evenings a week; and every Sunday morning, behind closed shutters, he and Miss Bird checked up stock.

To Miss Bird it was tremendously exciting, working alone with Mr Nicholas. All the week she looked forward to Mr Nicholas asking her this, asking her that — information which she, alone, could supply. It gave her back her rightful place, that place Stella had stolen. And it was exciting, too, being shut in with Mr Nicholas, the yellow gaslight illumining just the two of them — and all the sunny outside world shut out.

Nicholas found these Sunday mornings tiresome, but it was time well spent. He was getting a fair idea of what the business was worth, and how much he could get for it when the old man went. And more than that, it gave him an excuse to be near Stella. He was restless away from Stella, not because he had any need of her — in the press of more important matters, that was thrust aside. But he had to find out what she meant to do! He had to prevent her from carrying out her threat.

His constant presence, he was certain, would frighten her from speaking.

Ellen patted and folded and tidied.

. . . Mr Nicholas must have taken those words of hers to heart, after all! Keeping an eye on his own, and very right and proper! Didn't so much as look in that girl's direction, for all she followed him about with those big eyes of hers! Preferred to learn his job, learn it from a woman with twice as much sense in her little finger, as that slut in the whole of her mischief-making body! Sensible young chap, Mr Nicholas. . .

She sent him another look beneath her crumpled lids.

. . . Sensible — maybe! But she hadn't been so sure about him, once. That night, not so long ago, when she'd followed Stella in the dark, Stella and a man whose face she couldn't see. No need to see Stella's face — you'd know her anywhere by the way she flaunted her body! She'd followed those two — and she'd come home sickened, the way a decent woman would, from the sight of Stella laid out in the dark grass next to a man! Watching Stella — and then walking home all alone in the darkness, tripping and stumbling in the darkness, and all the time tormenting herself. . . Was it Nicholas laying there with Stella? The man was tall — like Nicholas. But though she'd waited ever so quiet, ever so still in the darkness, waited and waited, she hadn't seen the face nor heard the voice.

Was it Nicholas? She'd hoped and prayed it wasn't Nicholas. She didn't want Nicholas to get tangled up with Stella. The same shop wouldn't hold them both, her and Stella — not with Stella set above her, the mistress! After all these years to have to clear out for Stella!

That night, waiting for Stella to come in, and praying, praying real prayers that it mightn't be Nicholas. . . and all the time clear anger burning in her heart. . . It was a shame for a decent young chap to get mixed up with a dirty slut like that!

Was it Nicholas? Was it? *Was* it? Twisting and turning in her bed, and no answer at all from the silent house.

And then, at long last — and later than a decent woman had a right to be, Stella's foot upon the stair; and then, Stella's soft breathing from the room across the narrow passage, Stella's breathing mocking, *wouldn't you like to know, to know, to know!* Stella breaking up your poor peace, casting it like dust on the wind. . . bringing back other nights when one other's breathing had mocked your wakefulness!

Who had been with Stella hidden in the dark grass, acting wicked in the dark grass? She *had* to know! If it had been Nicholas. . . She'd had to drive away the thought of those old women set out in the sunshine, rotting in the sunshine. . .

Had it been Nicholas? No good asking Stella — she was artful. But Nicholas himself — that was another matter — he was simple!

She'd caught him soon after, pinning him into a corner of the shop. She'd nothing against Stella she'd explained. Why should she? But the girl was young and heedless the way young things are, and it was only a mother's part she was trying to play to a motherless girl. . .

And all the time she'd watched him, and he hadn't turned a hair! Even when she'd owned to following the pair, even then he hadn't fluttered an eyelid — he'd just gone on nodding and smiling and agreeing, agreeing with every word she'd said.

It was then she'd been sure it hadn't been Nicholas. She'd been so glad it was like a stone rolled itself away from her heart. She could have sung because of the happy, happy future, with the old man gone to the rest he well deserved, and Stella sent away, and she and young Mr Nicholas running the shop together. She'd gone down after that to take another look at the old women. There they sat peacefully out in the sunshine; she hadn't minded looking at them at all!

Yes, the more she thought about it, the more she knew she was right! Nowadays he never so much as glanced at the place where that girl stood! Stand there, she would, and fix her eyes on him, sort of trying to make him look her way — *willing* him to look her way... You could almost feel the power coming out of her. Yet he ignored her as she might be a stock or a stone!

Nicholas balanced a great drawer of ladies' chemises on his right hand. The box swayed and dipped. She watched. Would they fall? He sent her a smile. Not they! Ellen was sure. His hand was too steady. Handsome he looked, standing there and balancing the heavy box as if it were a feather, and smiling so pleasant. He had a way with him you couldn't but say!

Suddenly she had the feeling they were no longer alone... something had broken in on their pleasant intimacy... something, or someone... Wasn't that a deeper shadow, there, in the dark doorway at the back of the shop? Ellen lifted unwilling, unsmiling eyes. She knew by the rising tide of anger within, who stood there.

Stella Wade, pressed against the unyielding door, looked at them. Her glance ignored Ellen, fixed itself upon Nicholas. She stood there, speechless, imploring him with her wild eyes.

Nicholas felt the urgency of her need coming out towards him, commanding, demanding, drawing him against his will.

Ellen's glance flicked from one to another. "Shameless!" she said clearly. The pale face quivered as though drowned beneath flowing water.

"Shameless!" Miss Bird said again. It was as though she spat at the girl. Stella's face slid further into the shadow, disappeared. They heard her footsteps dragging upon the stair.

"Never saw such a thing!" Ellen spoke with satisfaction. "Eyes all over anything in trousers!" She fixed Nicholas with a calculating glance. "Better keep those eyes of hers on the old man she's going to marry, that's what I say!"

Nicholas dropped the black box. The chemises fell in a white flutter.

"What's that?"

She smiled secretly. Hark at the edge to his voice! Might be a knife! Sharp enough to kill you! He didn't mean Stella queening it here, neither!

"Didn't you know? Surely *you* knew, Mr Nicholas! I mean to say — a secret it may be, but they didn't ought to keep it dark from *you*, now did they?"

"I down't know what yo're bletherin' abowt! What are yer tryin' ter say? C'mon, out wi' it!"

"Don't look at me like that, Mr Nicholas! It's not my doing, I'm sure! Don't tell me you never knew! I thought you did, or I wouldn't have breathed a sound, not a sound! I don't want to get into trouble letting out secrets! Not with milady queening it here! Pleasant she may be — when it suits her. But those that gets on the wrong side of her — they aren't to be envied! I wouldn't want to stay on — not if she's to be Mrs Penny Senior — and you couldn't blame me, neither, could you? Got to keep an eye open for another job, I have. Shouldn't have all that difficulty getting one, should I? I mean to say experience, it's always valuable, shouldn't you think!"

He wanted to shout in his anger that the muddled miserable experience she had picked up in this mean shop was not likely to get her anywhere — except, maybe, to the workhouse. But he couldn't afford to give way to anger. He had to think, to think calmly and quietly, he had to work things out.

Stella, the bitch! She meant to be as good as her word! Well, so would he! And this nidding-nodding hag, poisonous with spite against Stella, she'd work the trick for him!

"Of course it is," he agreed softly. "Yer can't get far, not wi'out yer have experience. But — yer wouldn't leave Penny's would yer? Yer couldn't do that! I mean — Penny's wi'out Miss Bird, well, it's like mustard wi'out meat!"

She flushed all along her stringy neck with pleasure. He knew her worth! He knew! Oh the lovely future, the safe future!

He saw the ropy veins take on the hot flush. He leaned to her across the black box.

"I down't know what've got into yer head, but yo're wrong about th'owd man. He likes young things th'way he med like a puppy. It's his way an' it down't mean a thing! Now *yo'*, that's diff'rent — he thinks th'world o' yo', Miss Bird. Yer can tek my word fer it! He sees a lot, th'owd man, an' he thinks a lot, but he down't say much! It were on'y t'other day, though, he said to me, *Wi'out that little lady* — meanin' yo', Miss Bird, *I could not run this shop*! An' no more than yer due!"

She flushed again, drinking in his words, thirsty for words of praise, come at last. Again he saw the hard and ropy veins take on the red.

. . .*That little lady*. . . Didn't sound like the old man! Still, if Mr Nicholas said so, so it must be! Maybe she'd been wrong about the old man and that girl! Maybe it *was* like being fond of a puppy — the way Mr Nicholas said! Maybe. . . and maybe not! She wasn't born yesterday, not Ellen Bird! Why, the way the old man looked at the girl! Like he wanted to eat her! *That little lady*. . . and only the other day he'd offered that little lady the sack — and none too polite, neither. . .

"Thinks the world of me, does he?" She tossed her grey untidy head. "Funny way of showing it!"

"It's *his* way! He wasn't brought up la-di-dah! It i'n't a pretty way, but it's *his* way! And his heart's i'th'right place! Look here —" Nicholas was almost lying across the black box, "I down't know what maggot's workin' in that head o' yourn, but th'idea's daft. Yer can see that fer yersen. I mean ter say! How'd I look wi' an auntie like that! Th'idea's ridic'lous — an' th'owd man's th'last person i' th'world to mek hissen ridic'lous!"

"December has mated with May before now!" declared Miss Bird on the strength of a piece she'd read once in the *Penny Magazine*.

"Not this May, an' not this December! Yer can count on that! I mean," Nicholas was pious, "*It* wouldn't be *right*! I'm not talking abowt, abowt — th'conventions." He flung the magnificent word at Ellen's trembling head, "I mean what fowk'd say an' all that! That's none o' my business! But I've got ter think fer th'owd man — that's where my duty lies! He's owd and he's more'n a bit childish, and there's nob'dy ter look out fer him, barrin' me. He's a right ter wed, I'm not denyin' that! Ivery man's got th'right ter ple'ase hissen — in reason! Mind yo', *in reason!* Now if he was to set his mind on someb'dy as'd mek him happy, someb'dy as he'd known an' trusted all his life," Nicholas paused and fixed significant eyes upon her flushed face, "I wouldn't want ter say a word, not a single word! He've got th'right ter be happy. But that gel — I wain't say naught agenst her, she's good enough — so far as I know. But she's not th'one to mek an owd man happy, now is she?"

"Not the one to make anyone happy!" she agreed with sour fervour.

"I wouldn't want ter go as fer as that! I wouldn't want ter call anyone! So correct me if I'm wrong. That niece o' yourn, she's a bit — well, a bit fly, i'n't she?"

Ellen's head thrust forward on her skinny neck. "Meanin', Mr Nicholas —?"

"Nothin'. Not really! Nothin' but —" Candour broke through his unwillingness. "Yer saw her yersen, more'n once, out wi' a chap. An' yer asked me ter keep my eyes skinned, di'n't yer? Well, I weren't goin' ter spy on a lass, not likely! But yer can't allus shut yer eyes quick enough!"

"Mr Nicholas!" Ellen's head began to tremble slightly.

Nicholas said slowly, "I'm not one ter tell tales, but I've seen her abowt — an' I wouldn't swear 'twere allus same chap, neither! Kissin' an' cuddlin' they was, an' pressin' so close, yer wouldn't know rightly, was it one person or two! I remember askin' mysen, more'n once, whativer time she'd get home. Must have kep' you up iver so late!"

Miss Bird nodded. "You may well say that! When she first come, I'd wait up for her. There I'd be, nidding, nodding in my chair, like a fool! Then I up and told her straight she'd got to be in to time! But tell her nice, or tell her nasty, it's all one. She does what she pleases. She'd say the air indoors stifled her; she'd say as she had to get a bit of exercise

— though if she worked the way I do, all day long on my feet, she wouldn't want no more exercise. So after a bit I gave over. Stubborn she is, like her mother before her. And sly with it, too! I don't wait up any more. I go to bed. Sleep with half-an-eye open till milady comes in. And late enough, too — like you said! Hours no decent girl would keep! But she's a deep one and it's no use arguing . . . . Kissin' an' cuddlin' did you say?"

Nicholas nodded. "Ay, an' she down't look too well on it, neither!" He was feeling his way carefully. "Keepin' late hours down't agree! Down't look half th'lass she were! Lost that good colour! Gone scraggy an' all! An' those eyes! Looks like she dipped her fingers in soot and give 'em a good rub round!"

"You've done a power of noticing!" she said sharply.

"I'm gen'rally reckoned a noticin' sort! But yer'd have ter be downright blind if yer di'n't mark th'change! That niece o' yourn looks downright poorly!" He fixed Ellen with a look charged with meaning, "th'way she drags hersen abowt! Poorly in body, ay, poorly in mind, an' all!"

"Mebbe there's a reason!" She leapt all excitement to the suspicion.

"What way do yer mean?"

"Never you mind what I mean!" She was filled with sour triumph.

Nicholas lifted the black box and with an easy movement swung it into place on the high shelf. He whistled under his breath and slid down a box of overalls. . . But he hasn't picked up what he dropped, she thought, and stooped obediently to the dirty floor.

Chapter 8

Stella measuring three yards of Oxford shirting felt the material slip from her loosened hand.

. . .Aunt Ellen at it again! Standing there and staring. Eyes stabbing at you as though they might be needles, pinning you down just wherever she wanted you pinned, so that while she looked at you that way you didn't dare to move! What was it this time? Had she seen you cut an extra inch or two of shirting? *Cut accurate, my girl, cut accurate!* You'd scream if you heard that bit of advice once more! And then that other gem of wisdom! *If you can't cut accurate, then don't give any advantage!* And when, nervous under that grim eye, you had once more offended — *We'd all like to be generous with other folks' property, oh yes, we'd all like to be generous!*

Hateful, Aunt Ellen's mincing way of repeating a phrase as though it were something precious! Hateful, the way her head thrust forward, quivering on her skinny neck! Look at her now, all trembling and shaking! And a funny bit of colour to her cheeks as if she'd put it on out of a box and hadn't looked in the glass while she did it! Didn't look right in the head, the old woman!

She folded the material with careful trembling fingers.

. . .Why ever had you left Torquay? Why ever had you left Bliss and Garland? Something like a shop that was, full of light and colour. . . Box upon box of ribbon, rich and glossy ribbons, and all the colours of the rainbow! Not like the cheap tape that passed for ribbon here, red and white, sky-blue and pink and navy and black! And one shade of each! And facing the ribbon counter, instead of these calicoes and red flannels and black sateens, there'd be silks and satins thrown across — careless you'd think, unless you stopped to look how careful the colours were blended — yes, careless and gorgeous! And lots of customers with plenty in their purses and smiles on their faces. And something going on all the while! Not like this dead-and-alive hole, with its one or two customers a day, and the dust settling everywhere no matter how many times you flicked it away with a duster. But most of all you missed the company — the young ladies and gentlemen all pleasant together. Jokes and fun and a little bit of flirting. No harm meant and none taken!

She tore a piece of flimsy brown paper from the roll behind her, and placed the folded shirting in the exact middle.

. . .Jokes and fun and all pleasant together. So long since you'd heard a joke now! You wouldn't know whether to laugh or cry now, supposing you heard a pleasant word! Aunt Ellen was hateful! She hadn't wanted you and she never let you forget it. Her tongue was always wagging about you — and what was worse — about mother. Seems like she couldn't let mother's memory rest in peace!

She rolled the corner of the paper over the shirting and snipped off a piece of string.

Funny! Aunt Ellen must always have hated mother! And mother hadn't known! Mother wouldn't have understood, she never had understood that people wanted, really wanted, to be hateful to each other. She'd talked sometimes about her little sister Ellen. She'd got it fixed in her dear simple head that Ellen was lonely. And then, towards the end, when she'd known she was going to die, she'd begun to worry about you, too. So what more natural than that you and Aunt Ellen should comfort each other!

Comfort! There was about as much comfort in Aunt Ellen as in a cup of cold poison!

She leaned over the counter, making up the bill.

That was why you'd gone with Nick at the beginning. Just for the comfort of hearing a kind word, for the comfort of feeling a hand warm on your hand. But after that — after that you'd gone with Nick because you couldn't help yourself. You'd come to love him with all the strength of your body — the way mother said a woman should love her man — the right man. . .

But Nick hadn't been the right man. There was all your sorrow in a nutshell! No help in Nicholas! And soon enough, if you didn't help yourself, people would begin to talk. . .

"Bobbin o' thread, number forty!" Mrs Biddle was saying it sharply, as if she'd said it more than once already. Stella searched blindly in the drawer.

. . .Yes, they would begin to talk and you'd lose your job, and even if you got another one — which wasn't likely — you wouldn't be able to work for long. . . and those that don't work must starve. . .

She put the cotton beside the parcel and added the cost to the bill.

. . .And so you were going to marry an old man, you, with your strong young body and your heart that was set on another, going to marry an old man, old Nicholas, with his fat paunch and his thin goat's beard. . .

You couldn't do that, couldn't. . .

She walked slowly over to the dark corner where the cashdesk stood.

. . .And if you couldn't bring yourself to it, where would you turn for a helping hand when you couldn't help yourself any longer? Aunt Ellen? She'd enjoy turning you out! Nothing for it but the old man, nothing. . .

At the cash-desk she handed in four shillings and received three-farthings change — and a sly squeeze of the hand into the bargain. It was as much as she could do not to rub her hand against her black alpaca apron. She thought wildly, I can't stand the touch of his hand even, not even his *hand*. . .

She passed the three-farthings and the bill to Mrs Biddle, and remembered to wish her good morning, before she lifted the heavy bolt of cloth back to its place. Ellen, with her long inimical stare, missed nothing of the effort, missed nothing of the slight backward thrust from the hips.

Pushing back the roll of cloth with ineffectual fingers, Stella was afraid to look round.

. . .Aunt Ellen would be staring again, staring and staring. Something queer about her, the way she kept following you with those eyes. Had she seen the old man squeeze your hand? And was she jealous? Oh God, God, jealous of a feeble, snuffling old man! Made you feel queer, the way her eyes went sliding over you, raking every inch of your body. Made you feel queer, too, the way she never spoke to you nowadays, unless she absolutely had to! And then sort of hissing out the words — toads and snakes, the way it was in the old tale!

The hours you spent with Aunt Ellen in the cottage, the long, long hours, the long silent hours. All time banging between one tick of the clock and the next. And the silence between you thick with distrustfulness and hate. . . Had you really flinched from the thought of the old man, the kind old man? You'd take him and thankful! Give him back kindness for kindness, gentleness for gentleness. . .

Miss Bird withdrew her eyes from their long staring, dusted one hand upon the other, and strode by Stella as though she were not standing there, trembling flesh and blood. She stopped in the dark corner to whisper to the old man. There was a slight shuffling as he got onto his feet, as he followed her.

They passed through the back door together.

Stella's heart began to jump about in her breast.

. . .Funny the two of them leaving the shop like that! The old man never left *cash* once he'd come down for the morning! Whatever did Aunt Ellen want with him? What *could* she want with him! Nothing. Nothing at all. Just worrying yourself sick with fancies! But all the same it *was* queer, Aunt Ellen going off with the old man like that, both of them together, in shop hours!

Well, what did it matter? What did it *matter*? Soon she'd be married and Aunt Ellen could look out! She wouldn't have Aunt Ellen running upstairs and down, as if the place belonged to her! She'd had enough of Aunt Ellen to last a life-time!

But — Stella caught the back of her hand against her mouth. What *was* the old woman doing upstairs in shop hours? And why hadn't the old man sent her down again? He didn't hold with Aunt Ellen being anywhere *but* in the shop. He'd said that scores of times!

She heard the movement of their feet above, the scraping of chairs drawn close.

. . .Looked like they were going to sit down to it! She began to feel a little sick, as she did nowadays, when she was upset — or frightened.

Frightened? Whatever had she got to be frightened over? The old man didn't guess a thing. He was too straight. And too innocent. As for Aunt Ellen, she was spiteful enough, but in her queer way, she was innocent too. She was shut up in her own queerness, so that she didn't see what was going on outside. Not that — Stella pressed her hands over the sickness in her belly — not that there was anything to *see*. . . yet. She was getting a bit queer herself, letting worry run away with her! Better find a job of work to do, that'd put the silly notions out of her head!

She looked about the empty shop.

Wanted dusting. Wanted it ever so bad! Soon as you got the slightest bit of sunshine, the dust showed up something terrible.

She looked under the counter for her duster.

It wasn't there. Of course it wasn't there. She'd washed it. Only yesterday she'd washed it. And she'd put it to dry on the rack upstairs in the kitchen. That's where it was now, drying on the rack in the kitchen. She'd go upstairs and get it and give the shop a bit of a dusting. Yes, she'd do that!

She remained rooted in her place.

Well, why didn't she *go*? Why on earth was she standing about here?

Afraid of going upstairs? Afraid?

Yes. . . afraid. . .

Afraid of that low-pitched buzz that went on and on and on. . . What could they be talking about? One thing. . . one only thing.

There she was again, imagining all sorts of horrors just because two old people were talking together in an upstairs room. . . just because she didn't like Aunt Ellen. And yet she'd come here ready to share Aunt Ellen's life, ready to take Aunt Ellen into her own life — the way mother had wanted.

But mother hadn't ever known Aunt Ellen. Mother hadn't seen her. . . shaking head cocked to one side like a mangy old bird, eyes spiteful, eyes stabbing. . .

Well, what did all that matter now? Soon you'd be married to the old man and Aunt Ellen would have to go. And she'd be made to keep away, right, right away. . .

It had stopped, that buzzing! When had it stopped? Had it really stopped?

She stood, ears straining into the silence.

Wouldn't it start again in a second — buzz, buzz, buzz?

Someone was coming downstairs. That would be Aunt Ellen, heavy on the wooden stairs. Queer so small a woman should make so much noise! More footsteps following... shuffle of slippers, flipping and flapping the way slippers will... the old man himself...

There they were, standing in the middle of the shop and looking downright queer, the both of them! Aunt Ellen, yellow with spite, and a red spot of fire on each side of her nose. And her two thin lips pressed so tight together it was like she was buttoning up her anger, keeping it back so as she could spit it out in one go! And the old man, looking ever so funny, facing you across the counter, one ropy claw on the counter, trembling on the counter. Looking away from you he was, face turned a bit to one side, and a queer shamed sort of look on it. Why, couldn't he look you in the face? What had he done, the kind old man, to make him ashamed?

He was saying something. But his voice was so low she had to lean to him across the counter. And even then she couldn't catch every word he said.

...Don't need your services... free to go... at once... What ever did he mean? What was he saying? She knew. She knew well enough what he was saying! She'd known, really, ever since he and Aunt Ellen had gone upstairs together! Look, he was pushing something across at her... an envelope. She could just catch, murmured ever so low, *in loo of notice*.

"What's it all about? I don't know what it's all about!" That was her own voice, ever so high, ever so thin! She hadn't meant to say that. She'd meant to take her time before she said a word. But her voice, it seemed, had acted independent. And she'd have to stick by her words now!

He wasn't answering, not a word, the old man. Only standing there, sorrowful, his mind shut up against her.

Her voice came out again. She could hear it, still thin, with a sort of crying to it. "You can't do this to me," it was saying, "I mean — what have I done?"

And still he stood silent and sorrowful, hating the way he had to act, but knowing he'd got to do it all the same. You couldn't help but be sorry for him, poor old man, poor troubled old man...

Maybe — she caught wildly at a gleam of hope, maybe she'd been scaring herself over nothing. Maybe Aunt Ellen had made mischief about that bit of shirting...

Maybe. And maybe not.

She'd got to know... simply got to know...

There was her voice again, her own voice acting without her permission. You wouldn't know it for her voice at all!

"Tell me what I'm supposed to have done. You ought to tell me. I've got the right!"

The old man's mouth was opening and shutting, opening and shutting like the goldfish in the round bowl in the parlour at home. Funny! Your mind was full of troubles, and yet you could think about the bowl on the table by the window, and the way the light would run along the ceiling. When the water wanted changing the fishes would come up for air, and their mouths would be opening and shutting... opening and shutting...

Aunt Ellen's mouth split open suddenly, the words came through it, whistling and spitting.

"Rights! You're the one to talk about rights! You've been about with men, haven't you? You've got yourself into a mess, haven't you? You've got a bastard in your belly, haven't you?"

...*And when she opened her mouth, toads came forth, and snakes*... Aunt Ellen glittering and shaking and frothing a little round the black O of her mouth. Aunt Ellen enjoying her madness, enjoying it ever so much... *Toads came forth and snakes*... So this was what Aunt Ellen was like when she forgot about being ladylike!

Listen, listen, the old man was speaking at last, speaking ever so quiet, ever so gentle!

"It's true, i'n't it? If it's true, y'ought ter tell me. I ought ter know!"

...Deny ...deny. He'd believe me. I could *make* him believe me. Deny, quick, deny...

She heard the thought go screaming through her head. She heard another thought, a tired voice inside her brain, "What's the use?"

...Standing there... standing there, blue lips, red-rimmed eyes, gummy eyes... used up and old...

Her whole body shuddered away from him.

What have I to do with him? Withered skin, withered face ...grey skin, black gaps between the brown and broken teeth...

Grey, black, brown. She saw him disgustingly daubed as in some obscene painting. Her gaze dropped to his hands, his trembling claw-like hands... Hands to hold, to touch, to take what belongs to him...

Her two hands gripped at the counter, slid away from the counter. There were marks on the wood where her wet fingers had been. There was no strength left in her body. Her body was relaxed with relief, relief of being free of him.

She said, panting a little against the counter, "Yes, it's true!"

The old man said, "Then there's nothin' more ter say!"

"There's a deal more, a great deal!" Aunt Ellen's voice, glittering with triumph. "A lie she is, a living lie, like her mother before her! She'd have cheated you, fathered her bastard on you! She... she..."

"Quiet!" He turned with that strange swiftness of his. "Yo've said enough! *Ha'n't* yer said enough? Is there no end to th' cruelness o' wimmin?"

He looked at Stella. "I thowt ter get my bit o' happiness, th'way other men do. Comin' late, I thowt, but comin' sure. Well, that's ovver!"

For a moment she forgot her own sorrow in his sorrow — the poor old man whom she had cheated.

He said, "Yer were abowt my house, an' up an' down my house. But I respected yer. I wanted ter marry yer. I was willin' ter face th' laughter that comes to an owd man when he weds wi' a young lass, because I respected yer. But yo' — yer held yersen cheap! Anyb'dy could have had yer."

Cheap! To this shambling, doddering old man. That was funny! It was ever so funny! She wanted to laugh away the sickness that rose in her. But she must do nothing, nothing that would hurt him further. Let him think what he would, it was his right!

"Cheap!" repeated Aunt Ellen and laughed a loud neighing laugh.

Stella said, her back to Aunt Ellen, ignoring Aunt Ellen, "I'm going to have a child. And I've lost my job. I need the work, I need it terribly. Mr Penny, you thought kindly of me once — only this morning you thought kindly of me. . . Don't make me lose my job! Let me work here a little longer, just a little longer."

"You be off to your fancy man! He's fixed you up with a job already!" Aunt Ellen's face twitched about the suggestion.

Stella only said, "Mr Penny. . . *please*!"

He was turning away. . . he was going. . . he wouldn't listen. She said desperately, "There's something I've got to tell you — alone!"

He said, "There i'n't nowt to be said between yo' an' me that all th'world can't hear!"

"You hate and despise me," Stella said, "but what about your nephew, what about Nicholas? Nicholas comes into this, too!"

Ellen thrust herself forward. His old bewildered glance shifted from one woman to the other.

Ellen's laughter spat out into the air.

"What did I tell you? What did I warn you?" She turned swiftly upon Stella. "You slut! You dirty, lying slut! You threw yourself at his head the first minute you set eyes on him! But he never so much as cast you a glance, never! You weren't never more'n the dirt under his feet! Dirt! I've seen. . . I've seen. . ." she choked a little over the words. "I've seen you late at night with a man, kissing and cuddling and hugging so close you wouldn't know was it one person or two. . . I've seen you laying in the dark with a man — and it wasn't always the same man, neither. You're a slut, a dirty slut, like your mother before you!"

Stella's hands began to tremble. She went close up to Ellen. She said, very slowly, "You keep your tongue off my mother! You've had your way about me — you and Nicholas together! He's been clever — the way he said he would! But say that again about my mother, you just *say* it!"

Ellen backed a step. Her eyelids blinked rapidly. "You take your money and clear!" she screamed. "Pack your things and go! Do you want telling again?" She flung a sudden arm towards the old man, catching him by a dusty shoulder. "Here, give me a hand with him and clear out! Looks like you're going to have murder on your conscience as well!"

Their cold fingers touched, recoiled from the touch, catching him, lifting him, as he fell.

Chapter 9

Nicholas thought, staring into Penny's shop-window, that even without the letter he would have known that things were wrong. Articles withdrawn and never replaced! Show-cards knocked awry and never straightened! The waxen lady, old Ellen's pride, grinning there, a toque perched upon her flaxen waves, and no rag at all to cover her nakedness!

He knew that when he pushed open the door and stepped inside, he would not find Stella. . .

Stella. . . the pen had been poison about her name! It was in his pocket now, the old woman's letter, with its spidery, quavery writing. Almost impossible to read, it was, with words written in, and words scratched out; words underlined, and words running into the line above! His first thought had been to pitch it into the empty grate. But second thoughts had reminded him that the old woman had never written to him before, never once in all these years. He'd known for certain then that something must be wrong.

Something wrong! Had Stella told her tale? Had they believed Stella? Bent over the disgusting sheet, he had thought that the damn woman's damn handwriting was bad enough to make out, without your heart leaping fit to choke you!

At last, from the incredible confusion of the writing, from the filthy epithets and the mad accusations against Stella, two things had become clear. Stella's secret was out — though not his own part in it; and the old man had had a heart-attack.

The old bird, he thought grimly, staring into the disordered window, had let herself go! Language free, very free! Who would have thought it from such a ladylike old bird? And in attacking Stella, she'd attacked, though she hadn't known it, Nicholas himself! Not so very clever of the old girl to attack the next owner of Penny's — even if she hadn't known what she was doing! She'd pay for it — in good time! It wasn't the kind of thing he was likely to forget!

There was no tinkle as he pushed open the door. Bell muffled. The old man must be bad!

An odd creature, like a startled jack-in-a-box, popped up from behind the counter and asked him what he wanted. He had not expected Stella — but he had a moment's nostalgia for Stella's bright beauty. The old bird, he thought, wasn't running any more risks! No-one was likely to fall victim to these female attractions!

"Where's Miss Bird?" The spectacled gnome, whose head barely reached above the counter, blinked and jerked an upward thumb. She must have been on the watch, the old crow! He could just picture her, ear flattened against the door! For there she was, standing in the doorway at the back of the shop. She, too, wore a dusty neglected air. Her grey hair was tousled so that the false pad showed through.

"Oh Mr Nicholas!" she said, and her head shook upon her stringy neck. "He's ill. Ever so ill!" And surprisingly the tears jerked out of her little sharp eyes, and bounced upon her sallow cheeks.

He thought, in spite of his anxiety, that ugly women shouldn't cry — especially ugly women that were old. Tears were for the young and pretty, tears for a chap to kiss away. . .

She said mournfully, "Come upstairs and I'll tell you all about it!"

Nicholas said a little stiffly, "You've told me quite a bit already!"

"Oh Mr Nicholas, you haven't heard the half, not the half of it! Such goings-on, you never saw the like! Near killed him it did! He's getting a bit o' sleep now — come along before he wakes up."

She laid a hand upon his arm. He resisted the impulse to shake it off. Best not offend the old thing till he'd heard what she had to say!

The glass-paned door swung behind him. Even in her eagerness to tell him of the important part she had played and how cleverly she had played it, she remembered her duty. She drew the yellowing lace curtains to one side and tapped smartly upon the pane. The jack-in-a-box jumped violently, and galvanised into duty, flung herself over a drawer.

Miss Bird followed Nicholas upstairs.

He was glad, as he stirred his strong sweet tea, that he had not shaken off the old woman's hand. From her chatter, confused though it was with self-praise and cunning insinuation, one thing at least was clear. She was his ally — and a powerful one! Alone with the stricken man, a man dependent upon her for his slightest need, there was no limit to her influence.

And she had already put herself about on his behalf — so she said! And there were promises for the future. . . *Nothing I wouldn't do for you, Mr Nicholas, nothing at all. . .*

Well, and why not? She knew which side her bread was buttered, the old crow! Her only hope for the future lay in him. She could hardly hope to get anything out of his uncle. The old man might be led by a pretty face — but not by generosity. He'd said more than once that he considered he owed Ellen Bird nothing. He didn't have to pension the woman for taking good wages, did he? No, nothing to be gained for Ellen Bird except by the goodwill of the future owner — and she was clever enough to know it. But, she'd been a damn sight too clever, this time, and that goodwill was already forfeited.

It was clear as daylight, as she sat there buttering him up, that she expected him to keep on the shop with herself in command.

A good little business! A gold-mine, really, if properly handled. And who could handle it better than Ellen Bird? Ever so many ideas she'd thought of, he wouldn't credit! The old man had let the stock run down a bit — only natural at his age. But, let Mr Nicholas wait a little, only let him wait, and then he'd see!

And now, sensing his lack of interest, she was changing her tone.

It was not to be expected, of course it was not, that a fine young man, a clever young man with ideas of his own, should be satisfied to bury himself in a quiet little place like this! She would carry on for him faithfully. She knew the ropes. She asked nothing more than her ordinary wages... with perhaps, if he were really, really pleased with her, a teeny-weeny rise...

The air of pretty coaxing sat oddly upon her. He let her maunder on.

...She with her snake's eyes and her crocodile's grin had got Stella turned off! She, with that actual hand that lay peaceful on her lap, had written those dirty things about Stella — about himself — though she hadn't known that! Well, know it or not, she'd pay!

On and on that harsh chitter-chatter... How she had watched Stella, and all the time the girl had gone about sure, so sure, that nobody knew her secret. And how she, herself, had sat night after night, planning this way and that, to tell the old man, and still save him from the shock. How when the thing was becoming evident, she'd told him ever so gently, and they had gone downstairs to tax the girl; how seeing the game was up, she'd owned to it...

"...So then when she said, *What about Nicholas, he comes into this as well*, I couldn't hold myself in any longer. I upped and I spoke. I said... I said..."

So, Stella had spoken. But they had not believed her — as he'd planned for them not to believe her — the old man because he was too sick, the old woman because she hated Stella. Oh, he'd been clever, clever, as he'd warned Stella he would be!

But the thought of his own cleverness did not bring him the pleasure a man might expect. He was downright upset when he thought of Stella alone and at her wit's ends, Stella at the mercy of a jealous old man and a sour hag.

"...So then I just stood over her till she'd picked up her few things, you know, hat and coat and that! And I never let her see Mr Penny no more — not after I'd got her to help me get him upstairs. He'd had quite enough, and so I told her, more'n enough, what with being so old and his bad heart and all..."

Where had she gone? Where could she have gone? Had she any money? Had she even a place to lay her head? She'd brought it on herself, of course! He'd warned her — and she hadn't listened! But that didn't seem to make it any better! Where was Stella? Did the old hag know? And if she knew, would she tell? By God, he'd like to take the old scarecrow and tear the answer out of her skinny throat!

Easy now, easy! Even if she did know, this wasn't the time! He'd thrown dust in her eyes — let it stay there till it didn't matter what she saw!

Just as well — in a way — that Stella had taken herself off. Give them both a bit of time! Possible, wasn't it, that she'd been wrong about a kid. Women often got bothered when they went off the rails the first time. And it was the first time with Stella, he knew that well enough — though he'd pretended to doubt it. He'd been aggravated the way she'd carried on! He would make it right with Stella, though — when he got his hands on the old man's brass. Got to have the brass before you can start being free with it! A chap had to help himself before he could think to help others. . . Lord, the old girl was still gabbing!

". . .So when I went upstairs again, you could have knocked me down with a feather! Laying on the floor he was, where he must have fell out of his chair. And his face! His poor face! Such a colour you never saw! Death in his face. I tried to lift him. He was too heavy, though! You'd never credit his weight! But then —" she simpered a little, "I'm only a woman. . ."

On and on, clacking and simpering and twittering. . . So she'd sent for the doctor. . . So she and Mrs Black next door got him into bed. "So Mrs Black had said. . ."

Nicholas nodding from time to time, offered her tribute in his charming smile.

". . .So then, when he come to a bit, and was more himself, I said, 'Mr Penny, why not send for Mr Nicholas? I don't want to alarm anyone,' I said, 'but Mr Nicholas, he's got the *right* to be here. . .'"

On and on, the silly tongue, the false tongue! Well, let it clack! With all its falseness, it appeared to have done him some good!

A slight movement from the next room, and the stream of gossip dried suddenly. There came the slow tapping of a stick as though the effort were much. Miss Bird went fluttering from the room. In a moment she reappeared. "Just a minute," she said and simpered. "I'm making him respectable!"

The archness of her manner disgusted him. Even the decency of the old man's room was mocked by her archness. It was, Nicholas thought, almost as though its spare cleanliness concealed indecency.

Nicholas stood by the bedside, looking down at the old man.

Pitiful he looked, downright pitiful, with his blue face and his bluer lips, and his old hands trembling on the red cotton bedspread.

Suddenly he remembered that this dying old creature, this pitiful caricature of a man, had coveted Stella. For one hateful moment he was glad that the old chap was dying, glad he wouldn't covet any woman any more.

He tried to push away the hateful thought, to make himself know that this was the last of his kin dying here.

. . .The only one in the whole world left. . . that knew me when I was a little chap. . . that knew my mother and my father before me. The only one in the world that remembers them as a grown-up remembers. When he dies, all memory of them dies too. . . then they are really dead, dead as they have never been. . . Our blood, his and mine, the same blood. And now dying. . .

He felt his throat work, he felt the tears prick in his eyes, they were wet upon his cheek. The old man gave a ghost of a chuckle. "Good lad," he said, "good lad!"

If he had planned his behaviour to the last degree, be could have achieved nothing as useful as these tears. He knew it. But the knowledge brought him no pleasure. He was genuinely moved by the thought that the old man was dying. . . but all the same the knowledge remained, sitting tight, sitting snug in a corner of his brain.

"Sit yer down, lad!"

He sat awkwardly. The basket-chair creaked beneath his weight.

"Come nearer — Nick!"

Years since he'd heard that boyish name upon his uncle's lips. Took him right back to the time when he was a tiny nipper playing about in the gutter, and rich Uncle Nicholas came a-visiting with all the world in his pocket.

Nicholas worked the protesting chair to the bed's side. The old man looked beyond him, peering with dim eyes at the doorway.

"That'll be all, thank yer, Miss Bird!" He stopped to draw reluctant breath. "The shop'll be needin' yer attention." He chuckled again in his ghostly way as the door shut sharply. The old chap, Nicholas thought, seemed to be finding death a bit of a joke — more of a joke than living!

"Yo're a good lad, Nick," the old man said again. "A bit of a flibberty-gibbet, maybe! But yo're young. Yer'll have time ter learn. . ."

He dropped into silence. Good to have time. . . how good the young never knew. . . nobody knew, really, until the hour struck and there was no more time. . . no time any more. . .

The cheap clock on the mantelpiece ticked away the minutes no more time. . . no more. . .

"Listen lad," the old man said at last. "All I've got — it's fer yo'. Mebbe it wain't seem so very much ter yo', but it seems a lot ter me. A rare lot.

Mebbe because I worked fer it — worked day in, day out. Niver spent a penny more'n I could help. Put it all back agen into th'shop… ay, th'shop."

He fell silent again, leaning back against the high pillows, painfully commanding his strength.

"Th'shop. I niver said much abowt it, not to nob'dy. I down't suppose yo'd think much to th'shop, Nick…"

He stopped. He wanted so terribly to hear Nicholas praise his shop.

He went on wistfully, "yo're used to th'grand shops in Nott'nham — Jessops an' Griffins an' th'like. All very fine in their way, on'y they're not friendly shops, an' they don't *count* — not the way Penny's does…"

He stopped, his face was waxen upon the high pillow; his hands plucked a little upon the red bedspread.

Nicholas said gently, "Down't yer talk no more, yer di'n't ought ter talk! O'course it's a fine shop. An' yer'll have lots o' years yet to tek care on it yersen!"

The old man said, "There'll be no more years fer me. An' it i'n't a fine shop. On'y it matters the way a town shop can't. In Nottin'ham a grand shop goes smash — well, then fowk can go to another one. But here, it's diff'rent. If there's no Penny's, there's nothin'. Penny's belongs — it belongs here. It's, it's as yer med say living — livin' th'life o' th'place th'way a person does. Not a christ'nin' nor a funeral, but Penny's knows. Not a baby's gown nor a weddin' veil, but Penny's teks its part. It counts. It *do* count! Down't sell my shop, Nick. I want it ter go on bein' needed…"

He stopped, panting. Beads of sweat stood out upon the grey skin.

"A little more, Nick, on'y a little an' I'm done — for iver. Ellen Bird. Often I've give her the rough edge o' my tongue. Couldn't help it. She's tiresome. But she's true. Ay, she's true. I've said in th'past I down't owe her but what I've paid her. Layin' here and thinkin' I see that i'n't true. There's things as yer can't pay for. An' bein' loyal's one. She've been loyal ter me. An' ter my shop. Look after her, Nick, an' yer wain't lose nothin'. She'll look after yo'. Keep her on, her an' th'shop tergither."

The head fell back upon the pillows; the creased old eyelids shut down upon the tired eyes.

Nicholas thought, He don't need an answer. He's not *asking*, he's *telling*. Taking it for granted I'll do what he says! Daft about the shop. Daft about the old Bird an' all! Got the two of them mixed up together in his head… wouldn't put it past him to leave everything to the old woman at the last minute…

He pushed the unpleasant thought away. "Don't yer worry," he said softly, "I'll tek care of everythin'!"

The eyelids drifted open. The mouth moved soundlessly. Bending over the old man, Nicholas fancied that the lips shaped the sound *Stella*, before they fell again into silence.

It was only when he stood on the dark landing outside the dying man's room, that he remembered, with relief, that he hadn't really promised anything.

Chapter 10

Nicholas looked smart. His new top-hat glistened. The crease in his new striped trousers was pronounced. He would have liked to sport a yellow carnation in the lapel of his new broadcloth coat, but, with the old man just buried, it was not quite "The thing".

"The thing", Nicholas knew, guided the lives of people like Heriot Ware, people into whose class he meant to push his way. But they, so happily born, so shaped from childhood by the demands of "the thing", had no need to trouble themselves. Further; he, the outsider, must ponder "the thing", must puzzle out its curious nature, must make himself free of its thousand thousand intricate laws.

Meanwhile one started by looking "the thing". Turning to catch a glimpse of his tall figure reflected in a plate-glass window, he was satisfied. And reason enough too, when you came to think what these clothes had cost. He'd never dreamed clothes could cost all that! Made a bit of a hole in the old man's two hundred! Still, you can't make cake without you break eggs — that's what Ma Preen always said. And true enough, too!

He turned to catch his reflection from the side. . .

. . .Looked like he might have worn togs like this all his life! Looked just like one of the nobs! And so he would be a nob, too — one day. And by God, not the least of them, neither!

The Exchange clock struck three. On the last stroke Heriot Ware rounded the corner of King Street. Catching sight of her he thought, good plain quality, warranted to wear. And sighed a little.

For Nicholas there were only two kinds of women, plain ones, and pretty ones — and only one kind that counted. Then where, he would ask himself, did he place Heriot Ware, whom not even her best friend could call pretty, and who very much counted! Heriot Ware, he would tell himself quickly, was the exception. She was in a class by herself and he was proud to be seen with her. Yes, she's different! he thought again, watching as she came swiftly towards him. A lady. . . a perfect lady!

She swung along, face glowing beneath the smart toque, young bosom rising and falling beneath the smart braided jacket, sending the spring sunshine twinkling in arrows of light from its innumerable silver buttons.

She's nice and she's smart. . . Nicholas sought in his mind for the right words. But. . . he sighed again, she isn't pretty. She isn't *pretty*.

Heriot looked at him as if not quite certain that this was indeed Nicholas. She looked again, and then came forward holding out her hand. He noted with satisfaction that the glove upon her slender hand was fine and supple. Her hands, he thought, marked her. She — Stella — had pretty hands, too. But she'd never had a pair of gloves like this — never. Come to think of it, he'd never seen her wear gloves at all. Stella's hands, they were small and white and pretty. . . the touch of Stella's hands, they made a chap. . . Oh, to hell with Stella's hands!

Heriot said in the high young voice he admired as hallmark of superiority, "I almost didn't know you, Nicholas!"

He flushed. Self-centred, and all too new to his fine feathers, he took this as a slight upon his usual appearance.

"I recognised *you*!" he said stiffly, and comforted his irritable pride by adding to himself, No wonder! A lamp-post like you!

But he could not keep his resentment long, for her mouth, though admittedly large, was beautifully shaped; and now it was smiling very sweetly.

"Like me?" He was boyishly naive, turning on his heel that she might see and admire.

"Very much!" Heriot said promptly.

"The same tailor as your father's."

His speech, she thought, was a little painfully matching his clothes. He felt her faint criticism.

"What's wrong with me?"

"Nothing!" she assured him quickly, "nothing at all!"

"But there is. What is it? Come on, out with it!"

Heriot said slowly, "Nothing *wrong*. Only — now you're everybody else — to look at I mean!"

"I want to be like everybody else. I've got to be like them. Got to talk like them an' all!" His thoughts came bursting through the unsure restraint of his careful speech. "Ay, talkin' — an' that's a sight harder than lookin'. But I'm learnin'. Lookin' like 'em, talkin' like 'em, but all th'time, inside o'me, bein' diff'rent. Because I *am* diff'rent. Yo' know that, don't yer?"

Heriot nodded. But — she liked him better with the bright handkerchief round his young brown throat, and the naive speech tumbling fresh from his lips. Yes, he was different then, so truly different. So altogether real! But Nicholas was right — though it was a pity! Even Grandpapa Heriot, strongest of individualists, though he had cherished his native Scots to the end, even he had bowed to the conventional in dress — witness his portraits in broadcloth and fine linen. So if Nicholas felt it right to adopt conventional speech and manners, though she preferred him natural, she'd help him — if he'd let her!

But she had not answered his question.

"Yer do know I'm diff'rent, don't yer?" he persisted.

Heriot said frankly, "You know perfectly well what I think — or I shouldn't be here. But," she faltered a little, "I don't know what you must be thinking of *me*! Meeting you — like this — on the sly, really — it's not the kind of thing I usually do. I've never done it before, really!"

"I don't think nothin'!" He was annoyed at her admission of secrecy. Time, wasn't it, to come out into the open!

"It was your letter!" Heriot said blundering on, and deepening his annoyance. "I simply had to know what the news was!"

". . .And the time before that, when there wasn't a letter? And the time before that? I suppose it was the machines — though we'd hung over them time and time enough and knew every nut and bolt by heart! And the time before that, when there wasn't any letter and there wasn't any machines, and you walked along of me in the castle gardens and listened to the band?

Heriot flushed. She knew his thoughts — how could she help but know? "What do we do now?" she asked.

"What's wrong with The Victoria?" He offered it lightly, as though there were no splendour at all in the invitation — The Victoria, where the nobs went!

"The Victoria!" Clearly she did not like the idea.

"Why not!" He was truculent. Did she think The Victoria too fine for the likes of him?

"We might meet papa there, and —" there was mischief in her eyes, "you haven't been introduced!"

"Not yet," Nicholas agreed. He meant to follow up that remark of hers, but not now; they must settle first where they were going. And if not The Victoria, then where? He knew of no other place where he might entertain a real young lady. In his own city he was as foreign as any foreigner.

"There's the museum." The brightness of her tone gilded the suggestion with newness.

They crossed the wide Market Place, threading their way through the bright alleys of stalls. They sauntered up along the narrow Friar Lane past Dorothy Vernon's house all weathered wood and golden stone, past the little curio shops where Chinese Buddhas contemplated their navels amidst a distracting medley of beads, plates, Chippendale chairs and Jacobean tables, past the little bakery where small cakes were set out in bright rows of pink and green and orange and white.

"Such a tiny street!" Heriot laughed. "Every time I come down it, I feel myself growing taller and taller — like Alice. I shouldn't be a bit surprised, really, if I suddenly found my head up among the chimney-pots!"

He didn't know who Alice might be! And he thought she talked a deal of nonsense. He looked at the tall girl by his side and wished her some inches smaller. She dimmed his male superiority. He enjoyed the sensation of a small woman tripping along by his side. She didn't trip, this girl, she walked with the long step of a boy.

The great wrought gate of the castle stood before them; they passed through the turnstile.

The gardens were deserted except for themselves. The formal lawns spread green and empty; the absurd pill-box of a bandstand looked forlorn. Tulips grew in neat pattern; exact tulips and wallflowers marked the turf's edge. Only the air was untamed, sharp and winy with the perfume of wallflowers.

He could hear the rustle of her skirts as she walked beside him.

. . .She was a lady. And she was nice. But she was queer all the same with her sudden way of changing. One minute she'd be just a bit of a lass, quick and eager and silly and romantic. There she'd be gabbing away, and letting out her *O's* and her *Ah's* just like a kid, till he'd forget himself and act like a kid an' all — like telling her where he'd bought his suit. And then he'd look up, and she wasn't a kid at all, but a young lady with her eyebrows up! You couldn't fathom her! Stella wasn't like that. Stella was simple. She was always the same person and always the same kind of age — the right age. . . at least till lately. . . lately. . .

Oh damn Stella. . .

They stood looking down from the castle parapet. The hill which bore the castle dropped steep and rocky into the road below; the grey and dingy street was alive with carts and horses and little dark figures. Heriot leaned her elbows on the parapet, careless of her smart jacket. Nicholas admired her carelessness — it was yet another hall-mark. On the other side of the mean street flowed the Leen Canal, its shabbiness thrown into sharp relief by the triumphant riot of willow-herb.

"My nurse used to bring me here for picnics," Heriot said, "It was so pretty and so quiet. . . a few years have made a lot of difference!" She sighed a little. "You could walk miles along the canal then — or perhaps you couldn't. I was so small, I expect anything would have seemed miles to me!"

He knew a moment's envy of the carefully-tended child she had been. Himself, even as a tiny fellow, he had played about the gutters till darkness fell; till his mother, returning from her long day in other folks' houses, came and gathered him in her arms and brought him into the poor room he called home.

Well, that was past now and they had come together, he and she, on equal footing — yes, for all the differences of childhood, on equal footing! All those advantages she had had, he could turn to his own advantage — if he married her!

If he married her! In God's name, why not? She was willing enough, he'd swear! His children would be her children, they would reap all her benefits, all the protected peace of her childhood, all the advantages of her class. . .

But what of that other child that was his child, too, his child and — Stella's?

The thought thrust at him.

Good Lord, was he always to be tormented by Stella? Always? He was too poor to help anyone! He had to help himself first! Afterwards he would help Stella. . . when he could!

Heriot, looking down over the city, said, "It's raw and it's ugly. But it's real! I wouldn't want to live anywhere else, ever. I belong — as grandfather belonged. I'm part of it. It makes me feel little and unimportant. And yet — in a way — terribly important, too! There's work to be done, no end of work. Making Heriots bigger still, buying new machines, more and more machines — finding work for the workless. . ."

She stood there, savouring her kinship with the dead man.

Staring downwards, he heard her words a murmur only, accompanying his own thoughts.

. . .Hateful streets, hateful houses — like the house I live in, have always lived in. Shabby men. Shabby women. Even in good times a little bit cold, a little bit hungry. . . Factory chimneys driving against the sky like they're the only thing that matters. And so they are! So they are! Serve the machines or starve! Machines banging and clanging and grinding out gold. From every factory door and window a stream of gold. Golden sovereigns, jumping and jingling to the feet of the chap that's smart enough to pick them up. And so it goes on. And so it will go. . . flesh and blood thrust into the machines for the clever ones to pick up — gold. . .

Heriot said softly, "Grandfather Heriot stood here, often — where we're standing. He must have looked down as we do, at the houses and the people and the river and the railway, and he felt he belonged. And maybe when things didn't always go right, he lifted his eyes and saw the trees of Clifton go marching up the sky and it comforted him."

She had broken the pattern of his thoughts, his deep and satisfying thoughts, with her chatter! It wasn't old Heriot he cared about, it was Nicholas. Nicholas. How much longer did she mean to stand mooning about her grandfather? He hadn't met her today just to muck about! He'd come to tell her that his uncle was dead and that he hadn't got the fortune he'd been talking about. A bit of a legacy, he'd say! He wasn't going to let her know that the measly two hundred was his uncle's life-savings, he wasn't going to belittle himself that way!

Suddenly the bright sky clouded. Darkness swept across the dappled blue. A scatter of rain, sharp and stinging, pattered. Tiny dark spots sprang out upon the front of the gay tartan. Heriot gathered up her skirt in her two hands, and with a swirl of white petticoat, ran across the wet grass. Her smart toque, her fair hair, the tip of her nose, glistened with raindrops. She stopped, breathless, beneath the covered portico of the castle entrance; Nicholas joined her a moment later, anxious that his silk hat had taken no serious hurt.

Inside the castle it was gloomy — like being beneath the sea, Heriot thought. White marble faces peered at them from the staircase; painted faces stared at the intruders from life. They walked up the wide stone staircase under the glazed eyes of pseudo Titians. Up in the gallery, the attendant sleeping over catalogues that no one ever bought, had a saurian aspect. Heriot led the way. Beneath the indifferent eye of Andrew Heriot, Esquire, they sat down.

Heriot said, "Quiet if not cosy! Now! I've been dying to ask you about that letter, Nicholas — only I've been practising self-control — hard! What is it all about? What do you want to tell me?"

He said simply and gravely — just as he had planned to say, "My uncle is dead!"

"Oh Nicholas, I'm sorry!"

"So am I!" Yes, he'd got just a hint of grimness in his tone. She was looking at him a little surprised, a little startled.

"You see I counted on him — really, though I kept on telling myself I didn't. Couldn't help it, I suppose — the only relation I had in the world. That's why it hurts. Now he's gone. And the brass as well — except for a bit of a tip — legacy they call it — sounds better! No uncle, no money — like I might have guessed."

"You mustn't mind — about the money I mean." She was stammering in her eagerness to comfort. "It doesn't matter. not really, not so very much!"

Daft little fool! All idealistic and romantic! He was irritated, even though he had known she would take it this way, had counted on it! But it was galling to see her throwing away money with both hands, his money. Always had too much of the stuff, didn't know the value of it — that was her trouble!

He could have shaken her. But at the same time he was impressed by her indifference. Class, he thought, class through and through!

He said, fortitude becomingly dashed with wistfulness, "I didn't ought to be disappointed. I've known it was coming. He was wild for me to carry on the business, but I didn't care about it. And I didn't make a secret of it, neither!"

He bent forward. "I want to make something of myself" Emotion caught at him, played havoc with his rehearsed speech, "I've *got* ter mek somethin' o' mysen —! I've got be somebody as counts. I've got ter —" he caught at the word that had won her at their first meeting, "*create*!"

"Grandfather was like that!" She nodded toward the picture. "You can see it in his face. Not this portrait, though. The artist was bent on making a gentleman out of Andrew. The impertinence! A "gentleman" out of Andrew Heriot! There's a picture we've got at home — it's in the dining-room, and it makes everything else look foolish — especially people. A great broad forehead and a chin like a rock. Eyes of a dreamer — and a chin to make the dream come true! You ought to see it!"

"I'd like to!" Nicholas sighed. His sigh said clearly, What's a poor devil with just abowt naught in his pocket to do with the Wares?

Heriot tapped smartly with an elegant foot. Tap. . . tap. . . tap. It went sounding away through the empty gallery, so that the saurian attendant raised a nictitating eyelid to stare.

"I want you to come!" she said imperiously, but her heart beat furiously beneath the silken plaid. "When will you come? Come on Sunday. Come to supper — it's always supper on Sundays!"

Nicholas smiled, a gentle smile reminding her of worldly wisdom.

"You think my people wouldn't welcome you? You don't know papa!" She avoided the question of mamma. "He's the kindest man in the world!"

"And what," Nicholas asked still gently, "will you tell papa about me?"

She looked a little uncertain. "What should I tell him? That you're my friend of course! My friends are always welcome!"

Nicholas played a faint incredulity. "Will you tell him, for instance, I once worked at Heriots?"

"That would be a recommendation," she faltered.

"Would it, I wonder?" He held her with a lightly-mocking gaze. "When that invitation comes, Heriot Ware, then I'll accept it!"

She rose, a tall tempest. "You don't trust people, Nicholas Penny, you don't trust them enough. You're ashamed, really, of belonging to the working-class, when you ought to be proud. You're a terrible snob, really, much, much worse than anyone else I know —"

She stopped suddenly. "Isn't my temper awful! Pop! Out it comes when I'm not expecting it. My nurse used to say that ladies never show temper. . . I'm afraid," her voice was half-rueful, half-laughing, "I'll never be a lady!"

There it was! From the self-possessed young lady she had turned suddenly into a little girl. What on earth was a chap to do?

Nicholas knew.

He said softly, "there's no lady, anywhere, can compare with you!"

He'd said the right thing — he could tell that by the look in her eyes — but all the same he felt a daft fool, sitting there and playing up to her romantical ideas.

He made the most of his moment.

"One of these days," he said, "I'm going to tell you — something. But I'll wait for that invitation first!"

"Mamma will write," she said again and her eyes were shining. "I must must go now, Nicholas. Don't worry too much about things — you're the kind of person that nothing and nobody could keep down!"

Those words... hadn't he heard them before? He shrugged away the burden of Stella. He took Heriot's hand. "I've been waiting for that invitation." He was grave, he was manly. "And hoping as well as waiting. I've got to think of the difference in our positions. If a chap has naught else, he has his pride!"

She nodded. Pride, a proper pride, she understood that perfectly.

"And —" he hesitated, fearing anti-climax, "I should take it very kind if you'd say naught about me — my circumstances and all that! Everything's so muddled up, I just abowt don't know where I am. Let your folk take me as they find me!"

She nodded. She did not know how admiring her glance at the handsome young man. He missed nothing of her admiration, though he was deep in the thought of just how they would find him... Handsome and modest — he must watch the way he spoke. Clever and ambitious — better not overdo the ambitious part till he got to know them better. Pleasant and respectful... respectful, there was a word stuck in a chap's throat...

They came slowly down the grey stairway together and out of the dim hall. The evening sunshine was clear about them. At the great gates she stopped. "Goodbye, Nicholas Penny," she said. She gathered her long skirts, not very deftly, in one gloved hand. "Goodbye," she said again. "And good luck!"

"Good luck," he repeated and there was a half-question in his tone. He gave her a long and steady look out of his handsome eyes. Beneath her fine skin the bright colour spread, burst into bloom upon her young cheek.

"Oh!" she cried. And again, "Oh!" She clutched desperately at her smart skirt as though clutching at dignity itself. But it didn't help. She was wholly a child, a confused and routed child, as she half-ran towards the safety of home.

Nicholas looked after her, rubbing a thoughtful chin... Women were easy — if you knew how to handle them!

Chapter 11

Mamma will write... She had said the words calmly enough, but the way her heart jumped when she'd said them, told her clearly it was not as simple as all that!

Since when had mamma taken to inviting friends without enquiring who? and how? and when? and where? And there was no reason to suppose that mamma would alter her habit in favour of any young man at all — especially an unknown and penniless young man.

Thinking it over, she was relieved that Nicholas had been sensible about clothes. She had been sorry at first, shocked even, to see him brought down to the level of all the other young men she knew. But — suppose Nicholas had been obstinate to show mamma and papa exactly what he was! Imagine Bell's face when he opened the door! Bell might even have tried to send Nicholas down to the servants' entrance. Imagine Bell! Imagine papa! And above all, imagine mamma!

Yes, Nicholas was wise! Fight for what you want, but don't wear out your strength on needless trifles!

How to proceed in this matter of the invitation — the invitation that must be sent? Suppose she mentioned it to papa? Papa was always to be counted upon for courtesy and kindness — he had a reputation for both. And one had only to look at him — whether he was with the hands, or with his friends, or with the merest acquaintance to know it was true. So kind a man, so genial, so easy!

Mamma was different. It was as though, remembering perhaps not with her thinking mind, but with something older and stronger, she was determined to put a barrier between herself and those not so securely placed — a high, strong, completely impregnable barrier.

But at the very best, supposing the inconceivable, supposing that there was no how, when and where, there would always be that last question, unasked maybe, but none the less urgent for an answer. Why did she wish to see the young man again?

And to that last question, no answer, no answer at all — except maybe the look one couldn't control, the colour flooding dreadfully in the cheeks.

And of course, the truth was she had nothing to say! There was the heart of her difficulty. If Nicholas had said right out, *I love you*, then she wouldn't have been afraid of anything; for what could they do but say *No*? And while her heart went on saying *Yes*, that wouldn't matter. Much.

But Nicholas had never said *I love you*. Not in so many words. . . .*Tell you something — one of these days...* What might that mean? It had only such meaning as she herself cared to give it. And suppose she cared to give it too much? And that look — that look! Even now, remembering, she felt the heat of blood in her cheeks. But what, after all, had it been but a look — a mere look? One couldn't fight mamma and papa on the strength of a word or a look!

A word. A look. But how spoken, how regarded! If only Nicholas had spoken! But perhaps once again he had been wise. To declare himself without first asking permission! It would have finished Nicholas for ever with them. They had such rooted notions of correct conduct, her parents, and they would tolerate no deviation from it, none at all.

But, she thought, restlessly pacing, this gets me nowhere! The invitation has been promised and the invitation must be sent. Nicholas was right to demand it — I ought not to have waited for him to ask. He owes it to his own dignity — and to mine. And after all — a grim little smile lifted the corner of her mouth — it will be nothing to the awkwardness when Nicholas tells them — as I rather fancy he will — that he means to marry their daughter!

She tackled papa after dinner as he sat in to his port. It was a good time; he was rested and well-fed, with the cares of the day behind him. There could not be any difficulty, she encouraged her fainting heart, papa so easy, so kind...

But there was difficulty.

Instead of papa signifying that any friend of Heriot's was welcome, he asked at once who was this gentleman and where had she met him? And though she had steeled herself to meet the question, the moment found her unprepared. Stammering, blushing, she informed papa that she had met Mr Penny — somewhere — just where she could not at the moment recall. But Mr Penny was — was interesting. She was sure papa would like him.

Papa, very pleasant, said, "No doubt! But you must see for yourself, my dear, that it is hardly the thing! One must know something about people before admitting them into the intimacy of one's home! Besides, why do you suppose that I should find this unknown young man interesting? I assume," papa was bland, "that he *is* young!"

Stammering more wildly than ever, she murmured the word *Lace*.

"Lace?" papa pricked up his ears. "But I know everyone in the trade, everyone. Penny — I cannot recall the name — *Penny*!"

Then, seeing something of her distress, he added kindly that if she had really set her heart upon this invitation, he would try to find out something about the young man, though the name carried no recollection, no recollection at all!

Kneeling later in the darkness of her bedroom, elbows propped upon the wide window-seat, she considered that neither she nor papa had behaved as one would have wished. She herself — suppose instead of hedging and lying, she had said, *Nicholas Penny was one of Heriots' hands. That's where I met him — at Heriots*. That would have, been the right thing to do! It would have safeguarded Nicholas's dignity and her own, against future attack. . . But Nicholas had forbidden it!

Let them take me as they find me! But how would papa find Nicholas, Nicholas who had been one of Heriots' hands? She had never really known papa. She had accepted him, without question, as the kind and genial person everybody said he was. But it was wrong. Papa was not really friendly. That charming manner of his — it might well mislead you — till you came up against him! His pleasant way with his work-people, that was genuine enough. He liked them — as you might like a horse or a dog that belonged to you. They belonged to Heriots. They belonged to him. And so he wished them well. If there was some kindness, wasn't there even more pride? Yes, certainly, there was pride! Heriots' hands must be the best-treated of all hands — because they were Heriots'. They must have good working conditions — because they were Heriots'. They must be allowed to stand face-to-face with the master and state a grievance, not because that was common justice — but because they were Heriots'.

They were Heriots' hands and he was the master. The master! There it was. It explained papa. He would put himself to endless trouble to help this man or that. When Betts, the foreman, had found himself innocently, or perhaps not so innocently, in trouble, papa had not spared himself; he had interviewed officials, written countless letters, had come in late to meals or missed them altogether; no, he had spared neither time nor energy to help Betts. There was nothing he wouldn't do to help one of his men, nothing at all. But — it came to her in a flash of understanding — he would rather be found dead, in dignified circumstances, than be found drinking a glass of beer with one of them!

No. . . She came to the surprising conclusion that papa was not at all what he appeared to be. She had thought him strong — and he was not strong. Neither kindness, nor yet a knowledge of what was right, would carry him one inch beyond the boundaries of conventional behaviour. He was not strong — but, like all weak people, he was obstinate. He would be awkward to deal with, but he would give way in the end to the stronger will. Well, if Nicholas loved her, when the time came, no-one should be as strong as she!

Her knees hurt from pressure of long kneeling. She stood up and pressed her cheek to the window. Down the dusky tree-lined road came the lamp-lighter. The gas-lamps flowered into light. . . blossoms of light among the dark mysterious trees; shadow and light moving in the dark mysterious room.

But — Heriot's eyes followed the magic-working progress of the lamp-lighter — mamma is different. She's strong, She's grandfather's daughter. She built up her wall because she knows what's on the other side. She was on the other side — once. But if I want to get over the wall? If I want to see for myself, what's on the other side? Well — I belong to grandfather, too!

But when she opened the subject with her mother, she was not at all sustained by grandfather's strength. And once again, she was met by a surprise. For mamma was indifferent. She said, calmly, that if Heriot wanted the young man to come, why then he'd better come! And that was all!

A curious world.

Heriot, hurrying away before mamma could change her mind, her heart singing in her breast, was not to guess that mamma knew a good deal about those meetings with Nicholas; that under that quiet face mamma was excessively angry — but this was not the time to show it.

When Mrs Pearks, the housekeeper, had returned one Saturday night, a few weeks ago, and told her mistress, with much excitement, that she had seen, with her own two eyes, Miss Heriot walking the castle garden with a young man, and him wearing no collar, neither, Ada Ware had felt the cold and bitter anger rise. She had not for one moment doubted the story, odd though it might seem — she knew her Heriot. She was aware, too, that Edward Jebb came no longer to the house.

She was thankful that it had been Mrs Pearks and not one of the younger maids who had witnessed this strange and distasteful exhibition — there would have been no stopping their tongues. But Mrs Pearks was sensible and she was trustworthy — and she was too fond of that fool Heriot to set her tongue wagging. But for all that Ada Ware had given Mrs Pearks a new silk blouse — and it was neither Christmas nor a birthday!

And there had been further confirmation... A tall young man, Mrs Broughton had said, passing her cup for a second time. A good-looking young man and very well dressed... Good-looking? Then certainly not Edward, whom Mrs Broughton, when one came to consider it, knew perfectly well!

She had said nothing to John. John was not the man to tackle difficulties with wisdom. He was charming — when things went well. But the unexpected, if it were unpleasant, threw him out of his stride. She knew it — and she kept the knowledge to herself. For the legend of his charm was her own creation; with her own vigilance she had cherished it. She knew, and she alone, how fragile that graciousness, how brittle. The perfection of his home had been her life's work — the casket for his charm. The factory which he loved, ran smoothly enough, though even there, in those early days, she had seen him, at rare intervals, helpless with indecision, or with rage. She had made him promise then, that when anger threatened, and she not by, he would lock his door on everyone until the anger passed. And chafing, furious, he had respected his promise, as he respected his lightest word to her. No one but she had ever seen John Ware helpless in the grip of fury.

She loved him. Beneath her cold manner her love was nothing short of idolatry, that he, debonair and handsome, had stooped to plain Ada Ware. She could not endure that her idol should expose his weakness to the servants, to his friends — least of all to his child. So through the years she had continued quiet and watchful, sheltering him in each rare spasm of fury, building for him his reputation for charm and goodness of heart.

And now, thought Ada grimly, this! Heriot rushing wildly to make a fool of herself! She would hurt John in his weakest spot — Ware pride. He would be frightened. And because he was frightened he would be furious. Heriot would see that fear. Quite possibly, in his anger, he would insult Heriot's pride — she had her own pride, Ware and Heriot mixed, though she had the good sense to keep it hidden! John would stiffen that obstinacy of his till there was no stopping her! She knew them both, husband and daughter. She had learned to read them both as she sat quiet, watching, always watching. . .

She had meant to break the news to John, to break it gently, making nothing of it. . . Heriot is behaving badly, she had meant to say. . . Heriot is in a difficult phase. . . growing up, you know. . . one must be careful. . . only a child after all. . .

But John had come to her instead. Restless of hand and eye, he had come to tell her of Heriot's peculiar request. An unknown young man, unknown in this city where anyone who mattered at all was known by everybody else! But of this young man, not a person, not a single person, knew a thing. . . not a single thing!

She had taken the matter calmly, smiling above her anger against Heriot. And quite soon she had brought John to see that, really, he was getting excited over nothing! Let the young man come, by all means! Whatever was in Heriot's mind, they would be in a better position to deal with it, once they had seen him!

And afterwards, still cold and furious with Heriot, she had thought over her advice and found it good. If the young man was the one Mrs Pearks had seen with Heriot, then by all means let Heriot bring him into her home. Let her see how his speech and manners accorded with the way in which she had been brought up! Let her listen to ignorance couched in uncouth speech! Let her watch him at his food — that alone should be enough! In any case, they could not afford to throw away any advantage — and what greater advantage than having seen him? In any case, to forbid was asking for trouble.

Mamma will write... And mamma had written! Nicholas sat on the bed in his shabby room, carefully avoiding the place where his best trousers lay folded beneath the mattress. Yes, mamma had written! He had never believed she would write. And yet she had written! But — wasn't the invitation a bit stand-offish? Heriot's precious mamma wasn't exactly tumbling over herself to secure his company! Looked almost as if the old girl had been forced to give way and was doing it as grudgingly as possible... Was mamma Ware arranging things so that a self-respecting chap would be forced to say *No?*

And why the devil should anyone expect him to say *No!* He was Nicholas Penny — and as good as the next man! If mamma Ware thought he would dance to her piping she had another guess coming!

He dipped his pen into the penny inkwell. He thanked Mrs Ware — in his best handwriting — for her kind invitation, which, he truthfully declared, he had much pleasure in accepting.

He examined his reply. Good bit of notepaper. Cost a damn sight more than he'd ever thought a bit of paper could cost. Silly to spend good money on what you could only use once — still you lived and learned. Good handwriting! He'd always been partial to a decent bit of writing same as he was partial to a decent bit of design...

He read and re-read his note. Every word, he knew, would be scrutinised, used for his undoing, by the stuck-up snobs that were Heriot Ware's parents. He knew it was correct, because he'd copied it straight out of *The Epistolarian's Companion*. Well, if they got a better-written, better-composed, better-looking letter than this one, he'd like to see it!

Rare clever chap he was, Nicholas Penny! He'd set his mind on this invitation — and the invitation was here. He'd set his mind on Heriot Ware — and Heriot Ware he would have. And if in future he set his mind on anything, anything at all — even if it were Heriots' great factory itself — that, too, would come tumbling into his hands. Yes, whatever he wanted he would get — because he was that sort of chap. And the stuck-up-look-at-you-down-their-noses Wares would be eating out of his hand when he said the word *Go*. And he hoped they'd enjoy their feed!

Chapter 12

Sunday afternoon and Nicholas Penny dressed in his fine suit, off to take supper with the Wares. The sun was bright and Nicholas knew that it shone on the fine figure of a man... The sun was grand, life was grand, and grandest of all was having money in the bank — even if it were only a little — and a cheque-book in your pocket!

A cheque-book. That seemed to pull a man out of the working class and lift him right up among the business men. He thought, If I want to write a cheque for fifty pounds, or for a hundred pounds, or for a hundred-and-fifty even, I could do it — and it isn't everyone can do that! But — a man should be able to write more than one cheque for a hundred-and-fifty — he should be able to write two cheques, three cheques, as many cheques as he wants! A proper man should have plenty of brass — either comes to him from his father, or made by his own brain. His own brass. Not his wife's... not Heriot Ware's...

Heriot Ware. If he had all the brass in the world, and she not a penny piece, he would still set his mind on her, because marrying her, he honoured himself; because she had all those things that, though he sweated blood, he could never reach without her.

Queer the way things turned out! If, a month ago, anyone had told him that he, Nicholas Penny, twist-hand at Heriots, was going to visit John Ware, free-and-equal, he would have said the chap was daft! Suppose he were to meet John Betts, now, this very minute, suppose he were to say, "I'm going to marry Heriot Ware." Betts would say, "You're daft. And she's daft — if she agrees. You're both daft to reckon without John Ware. In spite of those pleasant ways of his, he's hard as nails and obstinate as the devil!"

That's what Betts would say — and he was no fool, neither! Betts had got Ware taped up — and so he ought. Foreman at Heriots this last fifteen years! The things Betts said about John Ware were all of them gospel true — how in spite of his friendly way of speaking, he was obstinate and foolish and had let chance after chance slip through his fingers!

That evening at The Salutation he'd gone in for his pint, and there was Betts, that quiet man, tongue loosened by a couple, waving his mug about and talking... talking. He'd taken Betts over to a quiet spot, given him another couple — and listened.

"Heriots goos on because it's bin set ter goo! Owd Andrew set it, an' on it'll goo, till it goos — smash! Ter do well in lace yer need a sort o' sixth sense — an' Ware ha'n't got it. He's afeard — afeard of anythin' new. He'd turn down an offer made by th'good Lord hissen rather'n tek a risk!"

And he himself, crazy to hear more, had urged Betts on with expressions of disbelief — and more beer.

"Ay, 'tis so! Ware was th'first to get th'offer o' that there Barmen machine — matter o' seven-eight year agoo. An' he turned it down because o' not likin' th'look o' th'stuff it turned out. I begged an' I prayed him. I said, th'stuff is clumsy an' it's coarse, an' nob'dy wain't look at it — *now. Not now*, I said. But you wait! The thing's got possibilities. Buy it, I said. Get hold e' th'patent. Look, I said, if th'bobbins were shifted *so* — yer could mek a quick change-ovver from coarse ter fine. Buy it, I said. If yer down't use it right away, yer will some day. But he wouldn't lissen. What were good enough for owd Andrew were good enough fer him. Nay, he wouldn't lissen!"

"An' yer were right!"

"I'll say I were! Barmen is very diff'rent from what it were then, I'll own. It's bin altered, as yer med say, out of all knowledge. But not ter them as unnerstands. Th'principle's th'same. I saw then what that machine could do — and I were right!"

Nicholas nodded, stepping smart and fine down the Sunday-quiet road... Old history now. But Betts had been right! There wasn't any kind of lace couldn't be made on a Barmen from heaviest guipure down to finest cobweb. Couple of hours for the change-over, instead of the weeks required by the Levers. One line in lace didn't go, you just switched over. 'Stead of lagging weeks behind, catch the fashion as it flies!

Turning into The Ropewalk, he thought, John Ware turned down the Barmen. John Ware, leading the trade by the nose, turned his back on all the new trade — new trade for Nottingham. Nottingham's trade almost dead — and every lass in England wearing a lace stock — made on a Barmen. Switzerland grabbed that trade! Wonder what Ware feels like when he thinks those self-same stocks come back in their thousands of thousands to be finished here — here in Nottingham where they ought to have been made!

Shortage of work in the lace-trade. When you asked why, fluctuation in trade, they'd say — as if that meant anything! Fluctuation in trade! Weakness in the head, he'd say!

Standing upon Ware's gleaming white steps, hand to the brilliant door-bell, Nicholas thought it didn't look as though fluctuation in trade had caused much trouble for the Wares.

...Everything a house ought to be! The kind of house he'd have himself one of these days! A great big front door all massive wood with great nails like you'd see on an old castle. Ay, and a pointy arch over it like you'd find in church. And when he craned his neck a bit, he could see a round tower with a sort of balcony. And very nice too! A house didn't need to have a pattern like lace — it only needed to look grand. A house ought to have a little bit of everything and no expense spared!

But the magnificence outside had not prepared him for the splendour into which he stepped. The thick bright-patterned carpet that caressed his feet; the great walnut table carved in intricate patterns of griffins and cherubim; the enormous dark paintings whose subjects he couldn't make out, but whose gilt frames he was sure must have cost a fortune; the massive silver urns filled with roses although it was early spring and bitterly cold; and above all the neat man-servant, hovering there, hands outstretched for hat and coat.

The Ware standard of beauty became, then and there, his own standard for life. Though, later, he came to accept simplicity of line and purity of colour as criteria of beauty, his acceptance was outward only because these things were fashionable and a wise man moves with the times. But his soul never ceased hankering for the thick floral carpets, the hangings, the marble statues, the picture-crowded walls, the thousand-and-one knick-knacks that made the Ware house his first revelation of beauty.

He was nervous and embarrassed as the man announced him.

But hang it all — he sought to steady his nerves — I may be just about dithering inside, but I'm damned if I let them know it! I'm dressed as good as what Ware is and I've practiced what I'm going to talk about. I've just got to go easy, that's all!

His manner was perfect, easy, with the pleasant deference of a young man to his elders. He bowed over Mrs Ware's hand.

Is this the young man? He could hear the question as plainly as though she had spoken aloud.

Is this the young man? He could hear the clear echo in John Ware's mind.

He chuckled inwardly. He sensed their bewilderment because he was presentable, because he looked as if he might be of their own class. He'd turned the tables on them! They'd thought with their grand house and their high-and-mighty ways to make him look like dirt. But it hadn't worked. It just hadn't worked!

He sat down, all polite attention to the pleasant nothings of his hostess. He thought, trying to size me up and lost her way! Don't just know what to make of me! New experience for her — judging by that chin!

He was responding charmingly to Mrs Ware on the weather when the door opened and Heriot came in.

He rose, the merest fraction of a second after John Ware. Standing for

Heriot, he wondered whether this was just eye-wash or whether Ware always rose for his womenfolk.

He looked at Heriot. Funny to see her without a hat. He'd seen her lots of times, but never without a hat. Looked better this way. Pretty — almost. Mebbe because there didn't seem quite so much of her in this high room. And her face was all rosy with pleasure, and her teeth shining and white and even, between her smiling lips. Done something to her hair. . . he'd said once he liked a woman's hair to look sort of natural. He'd been thinking at the time how stiff her hair looked, all ridges — and how Stella's hair curled soft all over her head. She must have taken that to heart, because now it was brushed straight and shining and she'd plaited it round her ears. Looked like a head on one of those coins in the Castle Museum. Pretty she was not, but she had style. Ay, she had style!

He was not inattentive to Heriot, but she must wait. His mind was on her parents. Behind their commonplaces, he had to guess at character; behind their conventional politeness, friendship or dislike. He had to learn where he must give way, where to snatch his advantage.

His first attention was for Mrs Ware — later he would make his opportunity with Heriot's father. He thought, half the things she says don't matter. It's the way she says them! Sort of voice that makes things sound important even though it's naught but a nosy question. Been cock o' the walk too long! Would Heriot be like that at fifty? Not if she married him, she wouldn't! He knew who was going to be master in his own house!

And he said. . . Voice of Mrs Ware, imperative for attention. He called home his wandering thoughts and presented them a willing sacrifice to Mrs Ware.

He rose from the best meal of his life. If this was their idea of making do of a Sunday, he'd like to know what they ate other nights of the week! Fresh salmon — he'd seen it in Burton's often enough and he'd wondered what it tasted like. Well, now he knew! Tinned salmon was more tasty, specially with a spot of vinegar, still it was something to have eaten the real thing! Pity about the pineapple. He'd had to refuse it, because though the smell of it had drawn his mouth with water, he hadn't known how to tackle it. Well — next time he wouldn't refuse!

And now here he was, sitting in John Ware's study, just the two of them together, smoking cigars and gassing away like old pals. At least, Ware was gassing away while you led him on, heading him off very clever from the questions the old girl must have told him to ask! One tricky moment there'd been, when the old chap, looking up from the careful cutting of his cigar, remarked that he'd seen you before!

You'd turned that off very easy, though. *My double!* you'd said. And changed the conversation.

Ware watched the ash lengthen on his cigar. It was rare that he had so appreciative an audience as this young man — a young man who knew how to ask an intelligent question and then had the sense to wait for his answer!

"Ten years ago, we lace manufacturers had the ball at our feet — a golden ball. But we kicked it away! We had our chance and we lost it!"

Nicholas, all courteous attention, thought contemptuously, ay, you did your share, you and your Barmen!

"Seventy-nine. The most marvellous year. Simply enormous increase in our export trade. Couldn't get enough hands on the job. We didn't care what we paid — we had the work but not the men. A twist-hand could earn six, eight, ten pounds a week — more some of them! Didn't know what to do with the money. Easy come, easy go! Why some of them — you'll hardly believe it — would come to work in a hansom cab! Day in, day out, they'd come driving up, leaning back and taking their ease and smoking... I used to think of the way Andrew Heriot would come in, day in, day out, walking on his own feet, even to the day he died. It used to make me see red, thinking of the old man humbly walking and these beggars on horseback! And then I'd say to myself, that's just it! Beggars on horseback! Andrew left Heriots behind. These men — they'll leave debts and their children to the workhouse. So I learned to laugh. Just to laugh! But I didn't go on laughing when it came true. 'Eighty-three brought in one of those odd drops in the trade..."

Not so odd, Nicholas thought, if you knew how to add two and two together! Yes, Mister John Ware, you was like them men. You didn't think for tomorrow, neither. You thought everything would go on as usual, so you allowed yourself to get overstocked — Betts said. Overstocked and glad to drop the stuff at any price!

"Exports dropped that year. Wages dropped. The Union paid out-of-work benefits till there was no money left. Men, women and children starved in the streets."

Nicholas nodded. He remembered. Ay, he remembered. Half of the factories closed and those that managed to remain open, working on half-shift. Sixteen he'd been, and wandering from pillar to post in search of a bit of work... Feet shuffling through broken boots, belt drawn in until it hurt — and even then not shutting out the hunger pains... ay, he remembered!

"And then last year — the strike!"

Nicholas remembered that, too, would remember it as long as he remembered anything! Twenty-five hundred men on strike and marching the streets. Hot words on the tongue and cold hunger in the belly! And a deadlock because the masters couldn't keep the factories going at union rates, and the men couldn't live at less than the rate. And in the end — the cut. . .

"But for Heriots, it was as broad as it was long!" John Ware drew upon his good cigar. "We had to come into line with the other factories, naturally. We cut the price per rack — but if it hadn't been for Heriots, the cut would have been a great deal bigger than it was! I stood out for twelve-and-a-half when all the others were clamouring for twenty-five! And I had my way — in the end. I made it up to my hands — as far as I could — in other ways. Heriots looks after its hands first and last and always. When things are bad we go on hoping; and in the end they pull up. Fluctuation. That's the way it's been ever since there was a lace-trade at all. Up and down, down and up! It levels itself — if you don't go broke first!"

"Of course," John Ware waved a comfortable hand, "the small houses feel it first. Trade drops and they're finished. But the big concerns like Heriots, with all their resources, they stand steady. . . and as I said, it levels up!"

Nicholas felt his first pinch of disappointment. If things were bad, how could he hope to make even a humble beginning, let alone a fortune? If already established mills came croppers with the first fluctuation, how could he with his two hundred pounds and no credit, hope to make a way? But Ware was wrong — wrong somewhere, although, maybe, a chap couldn't put his finger on the place. Bad, trade might be, but yet, every day new names were coming to the front, unknown mills stood steady and grew to fortune. It was still being done. . . every day it was being done. But how? How? There was a clue, he was certain. If he let the old chap go on talking, maybe he'd find the clue for himself!

"Why does the trade go up and down! What *makes* it? There must be a cause?" It was not with deference, but with real anxiety that Nicholas leaned forward for his answer.

"Good times and bad times, as I said. And it isn't always easy to know why, Of course, every luxury trade feels the pinch first. Everybody knows that! There always have been fluctuations and there always will be. We know that the only thing to do is to sit tight and wait!"

"But there's bound to be some way of reck-on-ing!" There, even in his anxiety he had avoided the pitfall of *reck'nin'*. "I don't mean to the last inch, of course!"

"Seven lean kine and seven fat!" John Ware smiled. He enjoyed playing Nestor to this respectful young man.

"Ay, Joseph knew a thing or two," Nicholas said. "And it wasn't prophecy, neither. Just plain horse-sense!"

"It always has happened and it always will happen," Ware assured him comfortably. "But *why* it happens, who can say? Take the year before last. A damn bad year for lace — I can't remember a worse! Why? Some blamed the weather. Filthy spring if you remember, cold and wet. Others say we let our opportunities slip. *I* say trade was bad everywhere and, of course, lace was bound to feel it more than most! I say, the law of averages. There's your answer. Good times and bad times. Sit tight and wait for the good times!"

. . . But abroad they had the same bad spring. . . and yet they made brass hand over fist — and still are by all accounts. You can see it in the papers! Fool yourself, John Ware, if you please — you'll not fool me. . .

Aloud he said, watching his careful speech, "There's more to it than that! There must be! There are chaps out at Long Eaton, ay and Derby and Southwell and all, making money faster than eye can see — and have been doing this past few years! It's the same for them as for you, same bad weather, same bad trade everywhere, same everything!"

"Long Eaton! Southwell!" Ware's face was dark with anger, his voice shaking with passion. "There's your answer! You've put your own finger on the poison-spot. It's blacklegs like them that steal our trade. They thrive because they bleed Nottingham trade white!"

. . .Now, now we're learning! They thrive, do they, out at Long Eaton and Southwell when they can't even manage a living wage in Nottingham? Let them bleed Nottingham — if Nottingham masters are fools enough to stand for it!

Nicholas sat forward eagerly.

"It's taking the machines out of Nottingham that does the damage," Ware said. "No union rate outside Nottingham, you see! Inside, the masters have to pay strict union rate. Good year, bad year, the rate doesn't vary. Fixed by fools with no foresight and there it stands. But outside, you can pay a man as little as he'll work for! There's your profit straight away. It's damned unfair!"

"Of all the dirty tricks!" Nicholas was hot for the men working at cut rates.

"I'm with you, there! It works out like this. I must pay union rate at Heriots. But I can take a machine out, and pay the same man for the same work on the same machine from a third to half as much. For instance, at Heriots, I pay eleven pence per rack. At Long Eaton, I'd pay on the average fivepence ha'penny!"

"A chap'd have to starve on that!"

"Oh no he wouldn't. He can live — and live well, too! A twist-hand at Long Eaton gets less per rack but he earns more — a good deal more in the end. Why they average two pounds-ten to two-fifteen per week. Think of that! Compare it with Nottingham's twenty-five shillings a week. Some of those twist-hands out at Long Eaton earn as much as four or five pounds a week — steady wages!"

Then why is it wrong to take the machines outside? Hands benefit. Masters benefit. Trade benefits. Are you too damn lazy to see it?

"Five pounds?" Nicholas was politely incredulous.

"You may well be surprised. Of course there's another thing. It's a different kind of trade out at Long Eaton. They don't touch fine work or novelty lines. We have to. It's a vicious circle. We know we've lost the common trade, so we try to make up for it by tickling the public fancy. But you can lose on novelties more quickly and more heavily than on anything else — naturally! And when trade's slack everywhere — as it is at the moment — why then people don't want novelties. Of course, women will still go on sewing lace on their petticoats, and clothing factories will go on using cheap lace for garments. Let me tell you, there are mills at Long Eaton where all the machines are working all day, day in, day out, week in, week out. Never a lost minute!"

"How do you make that out?" Behind his casual question, Nicholas's heart was beating. Surely, surely, his clue was here!

"All these machines making the same pattern — day after day, the same pattern. It makes for cheapness, of course — a common, nasty cheapness. Plenty for your money. You'd know a Long Eaton pattern anywhere! If you want to make your fortune, young man, and you're not particular how you do it, if you can shut your eyes and your ears to the distress here in Nottingham and you don't mind adding to it — go out to Long Eaton!"

Nicholas's heart leaped in his body, as it had never leaped, even for Stella. Old Ware with his grumblings and his grousings and his woolly-headed maunderings, had pointed the way.

But John Ware, guileless of any pointing finger, glad only of this understanding listener, went on.

"No wonder there's trade at Long Eaton. Not only every mill, but every house, every room, almost, has got its machines. Machine-makers don't wait for us in Nottingham to buy — they know they'd wait till kingdom come! We're too busy keeping our heads above water paying at union rates to think of new machines — though God knows we want them badly! But you go and put down a hundred, fifty even, on account, and you'll get one, hire-purchase — the finest, newest machine to take the widest lace. No risk — for them! If you pay, you pay. If not, back goes your machine. . . you lose your money and your machine, but that's your risk! Not much risk the way those blacklegs work, though! You put down your few pounds, hire a room and round up the family. If it's the wife and children, why then you've no wage bill! And there you are! Today you're a twist-hand, tomorrow — a master!"

Tomorrow a master! It was as much as Nicholas could do to keep his seat. He was wild to leap from his chair, to rush through the dark streets and hammer upon the door of Jardines, machine-makers, until they opened and promised him a machine.

He forced himself down to sensible behaviour.

Sunday. It was Sunday. It was late at night! Jardines were closed. Of course they were closed. They'd be glad enough to let him have a machine tomorrow — ay, or even two machines! Tomorrow... tomorrow... *tomorrow a master!*

From somewhere in the house a clock struck delicately. One, two, three... Nicholas counted eleven silvery chimes.

"Eleven!" He was charmingly contrite. "I'm afraid I lost count of time! I could sit list-en-ing to you all night. Should have, I reck-on, if the clock had not given me a reminder. I am ever so sorry, I..."

John Ware waved away apologies. He, too, had lost sight of the time. The lad was a fine lad, sensible, quick to catch at an idea!

Nicholas knew when they went into the drawing-room that Mrs Ware was displeased because he and John Ware had sat so long together. It was no part of her plan, he guessed, that her husband should like Heriot's unknown, unsuitable young man!

"You must forgive us both, Heriot, my dear," John Ware said, a friendly hand upon the young man's arm. And Heriot nodded happily.

He went striding down the dark streets. Nottingham on Sunday night and all decent citizens abed and asleep. The silent streets were empty, except where a cat slunk shadowy among shadows.

Tomorrow a master... All the time the words were in his ear. *Tomorrow a master... a master...* They wove themselves in and out of his dreams; they were in his waking ears.

Chapter 13

Tomorrow a master... tomorrow a master...

The clanking of the tram, the rise and fall of the horses' glossy rumps beat out a rhythm to the magic words. Nicholas watching the countryside slip smoothly past, thought, I'll not be making this journey many times more! He was glad, gladder than he could say that he hadn't promised to keep on the shop. Man of his word, that's what he was, and if he'd really promised, then wild horses wouldn't have made him break his word. But he hadn't promised! There hadn't been time to promise. The old man had done all the talking and he, himself, had just sat by the bed and listened.

A man had to do what he thought best. No man could do more! Even if he didn't want money for his machines, even then he wouldn't keep on the shop. What use a shop without customers? Someone would crawl into the shop now and again for a card of buttons or a paper of pins, or at the most a yard or two of flannel. You couldn't live on that — couldn't even cover expenses. And you couldn't expect any improvement in trade, neither! When a woman wanted a dress or a mantle or a hat, she went into Nottingham. Of course she did! Smarter styles, better variety, better value! Went to the Co-op most of them. But even the grand shops like Jessops and Griffins could give better value than Penny's with its small turnover and its dependence upon old Ellen's taste. Taste! What she called smart had been dowdy this last ten year! Good tram service into town an' all! What could be pleasanter than sitting here behind the smooth backsides of the horses, and watching field and hedge slip by? Nothing. Except to sit in your own carriage and watch the smooth backsides of your own horses!

And so he would. One day! Old Ware had shown him how! In the middle of all that stick-in-the-mud nonsense, your way clear and shining! Of course, you hadn't taken anything for granted — not from a woolly old dunderhead like him! You'd made it your business to find out for yourself... been backwards and forwards to Long Eaton, you wouldn't care to count the times! Been asking questions of this one and that — questions in Nottingham, in Derby, in Heanor, in Long Eaton — wherever there were lace machines, in fact! And best of all you'd talked to Betts...

Knew a power of things did Betts! Would he come in with you? Wobbling a bit he was. Didn't want to leave Heriots in the lurch. *And suppose Heriots has to leave you in the lurch — one of these days?* That's what you'd said to Betts. And Betts had seen the force of it!

Because what old Ware said was true. There was work and to spare at Long Eaton! Out there, in big mills and small, in houses and in single rooms, there was the ceaseless hum and clatter of the machines. And what sweeter sound for twist-hand and master alike, than the voice of the machines, machines steadily, unceasingly, at work?

That was why the shop had to go! Money. Money for the machines! And it wasn't any good being soft. The old chap was dead and you were downright sorry. Wouldn't have wished him an inch nearer the grave for all his brass. But he was dead and buried and there was nothing you could do about it. A chap couldn't think to hold the world back with his two hands! If you didn't sell Penny's now, while you had the offer, then Penny's would creep downhill to its grave. And who would be the better then?

Nicholas jumped off the tram and strode down the cobbled street. He had stepped out briskly enough, but his step slackened. The old bird! He had to break the news to her! Poor old wretch — it would be a blow, an unexpected blow! He'd been down so often lately, watching how things went before definitely making up his mind, listening to all she had to tell, that she'd been dead sure he was going to run the shop himself. . . Things were rum! For a long time now he'd promised himself the pleasure of telling her that there wasn't a place for her at Penny's any longer, because soon there wouldn't be a Penny's at all! Yes, he'd been meaning to tell that ever since she'd been such a swine over Stella. Now he was going to do it, he was sorry! It would be a blow. Straight over the heart! He almost wished he hadn't got to give it!

Well, sorry or glad, here was the shop and the job had to be done!

He pushed open the shop door.

At the tinny tinkle, Ellen Bird looked up eagerly in the empty shop. Her yellow teeth showed between her smiling lips.

"Mr Nicholas!"

"Morning Miss Bird. How's things?"

"Mustn't grumble, must we?" Her tone was bright. "It's early in the day, yet."

He picked up her bill-book and stood flicking over its empty pages. She stood looking at him, ready to cry, convicted of a fault of which she was in no way guilty.

Nicholas said quite kindly, "Don't take it to heart. No good flogging a dead horse!"

She couldn't, or wouldn't understand. She just stood there, ready to cry, her head trembling slightly.

Because she rubbed his nerves raw with pity, he said suddenly, brutally, "It's finished. Penny's is finished. I'm going to sell out!"

She goggled at him as if English had suddenly become an unknown tongue.

Lord, she was damned ugly! He was sorry for her, but she was getting on his nerves so that he wanted to hit out and be damned to it! After all it was none of her business what he did with his own property! There she stood, peering at him in her shiny black dress like a moulted raven; and her bird's-nest head thrust forward and shaking.

"Mr Nicholas —" Her voice,came out with the breathless gasp of the drowning. "Mr Nicholas —" She was fighting for her breath. Well, thank the Lord she wasn't able to speak! He'd thanked the Lord, too soon! She'd found her breath again! Her words were coming out, spitting and spluttering and hopping and bouncing like a kettle boiling on a hob. And each word a single, scalding drop!

He stood silent. The kettle couldn't boil for ever!

Her words petered out in a thin stream. Only she repeated the word *promised* over and over again. *You promised*. . . as though the word was a talisman. *You promised*. . . as if upon the word her whole salvation hung.

"I *beg* your pardon?" It was his new manner, distant, frigid, reminding her of the distance that lay between them — employer and employed.

"You did promise! I heard you promise!" she insisted, one claw at her jerking breast.

"A pity to listen at doors!" He was savagely smooth. "I mean — you are liable to hear all wrong, aren't you?"

"I didn't listen. There isn't time to listen, ever! I'm at it, morning, noon and night!"

"Glad of a change, won't you be?" Nicholas was pleasant.

"Don't twist my meaning, Mr Nicholas. I never complained of work, did I? Well, did I? I love it. It's — it's as you might say my life! All the life I've got — all the life I ever had — is in this shop. You can understand that, can't you, Mr Nicholas? *Can't* you? You couldn't mean to get shut of it, not a lovely little shop like this!"

"I'm afraid I could." Good Lord, why in the name of goodness must she waste his time with her nonsense?

She looked at him. And went on looking. Then she turned away, her old head a-wag, her old grotesque hands a-tremble. She was huddled again over her work — work, the only thing she understood in this bewildering, terrifying new world. She bent over the ribbon-box, fingers jerking and shaking as she sorted out widths and shades. Rolling, smoothing, patting, placing them in shining gleaming order. . . as long as she could go on doing this, her well-known beloved work, then nothing could happen to her, nothing at all! Everything was safe! Safe!

Nicholas began to feel more comfortable. . . Managed that a treat! She understood good and proper. The matter was finished! Closed!

"Mr Nicholas!" Her voice came trembling in the silence; her strange eyes stared over the ribbon-box. "I was thinking — just thinking — wondering you know — how much do you — would you — want for the shop?"

He stared at her, wondering whether she had gone crazy at last. She faced him, staring back boldly.

"Well, that's hardly your business, now is it, Miss Bird?" He made his voice deliberately unpleasant. He was not going through all this again.

"I was thinking. . . maybe. . . you see I've got a little put by. I was thinking, maybe I could put fifty pounds down, fifty pounds, Mr Nicholas."

Odd that fifty pounds, fruit of forty years, painful thrift, should seem so little now, so very little. . .

". . .And then I was thinking I could put down so much a week —"

He burst into laughter, jolly friendly laughter, just to show the poor fool that he had taken no offence.

"I should want a good deal more than that," he assured her. "Two hundred, three even. More if I can get it. And I'd want it on the nail!"

He could not face her stricken look. Fool she might be! A pushing and irritating fool — but she looked dying.

He put a hand on her bony arm. He felt old and wise beside this doddering fool.

"It wouldn't do," he said kindly. "Even if I could afford to sell to you, I wouldn't. I wouldn't take your money — because you'd lose it. Every penny. The shop's finished. Done! You couldn't keep it going. Conditions are changing. There's no room for this kind of shop any longer — no room for this muddled sort of shop-keeping — living from hand to mouth. It's got to go!"

"I don't believe it," she cried pitifully. "Why *should* I believe it? All these years it's gone on and on. . . besides. . ." she peered at him sharply, "if it's all that rotten why should you expect to sell it so easy? Two hundred's a lot of money. You answer me that!"

"Because —" Nicholas was irritable with restraint put upon himself, "I'm not selling Penny's as a going concern. The Co-op's nibbling. That's why I'll get my money. And that's the truth! When the Co-op comes, goodbye to tuppenny ha'penny shops that make you pay through the nose for stale goods. And Penny's won't be the only one, neither! Listen, Miss Bird, neither you, nor me, nor anyone else could make a go of Penny's. I've known you too long to want to see you try. Penny's is a sinking ship. . ."

"And you're the rat!" Her voice rose thin and shrill. "You're the rat!

You — you — you're capable of anything, anything at all — if it's only mean enough and dirty enough and low enough! It was you got Stella into trouble. I know — I always knew — in my heart. Only I wouldn't *let* myself know! And I kept my mouth shut, I thought, *Penny's has got to go on!* I thought, *First old Nicholas Penny and then young Nicholas Penny, and them after him another Nicholas, and then another, keeping on the shop I helped to make.* So when I saw you slinking round after Stella like a tomcat, I shut my eyes. I pretended I didn't see. Because nothing mattered, really, except Penny's should go on. That's why I kept my eyes shut and my tongue quiet, that was why I told the old man it wasn't you acted dirty with her. . ."

Ellen Bird, driven beyond herself, losing her careful gentility, her shop assistant's airs and graces, driven back to the prurient language of her ugly childhood.

He lifted a hand as if to command her, strike her almost, into silence. Before the mad look in her eyes, his hand dropped.

"When I think of the fool I've been! When I *think*. . ." She hit her two claws together. He found himself wondering that the bones didn't crack. "Telling the old man how good you was. . . I could die of laughing I could! He was that poorly towards the end, that weak! He believed every word I said — gospel. I could 'a got round him to leave me everything. . . everything! He trusted me. If he'd 'a known about you — and her, you wouldn't have got a penny piece. He'd set his silly heart on that girl the way he hadn't wanted anything his whole life long — the light of his old age she was, just about! You broke his heart between you, you and her. And all the time I knew. I knew and I never said a word. Fool that I was, I never said a word!"

"You didn't know," Nicholas said. "You didn't know anything. And you know nothing now! And — let me remind you — there is such a thing as being had up for libel!"

"*Don't* you speak ladidah! And don't you play the gentleman with me, neither! I've known you from the days you wet your trousers, and it won't work! And don't you fool yourself, neither! I do know — I've known all along! And don't you think Stella wouldn't up and speak if she got half a chance? Don't you think she'd be glad to get some of her own back? Libel? *That* for your law of libel!" She snapped her fingers in his face. "Of course I knew. But I didn't care. Why should I? As long as that little bitch didn't get her claws into Penny's to make ducks and drakes of it, I was satisfied. I didn't want Penny's for myself. I only wanted it to go on. I thought you'd let me work for you, that's all I wanted, to be let to work for you!"

"My dear Miss Bird —" And damn her with her insulting reminders! He'd play the gentleman till she burst! "On your own showing you lied and lied. In fact you did nothing *but* lie! And you thought about nothing but feathering your own nest; from beginning to end it was yourself and yourself only! And if your plans didn't work out the way you thought they would, well, you've only yourself to blame!"

Excitement slowly fizzled out. She began to realise something of the enormity of her behaviour, to him, owner of Penny's. She said humbly, lips spread in an ingratiating smile, "It wasn't for myself, really it wasn't, Mr Nicholas. It was the shop. It was always the shop... Wanting it to go on... Seemed like it *had* to go on, because of us two starting it, him and me. The shop — it was something I'd helped to make... the only thing worth doing I ever had a hand in! And I could have got it for myself, before God that's true! But I'm old and you're young. Young blood. That's what the shop needs. That's why I played fair. You play fair, too, Mr Nicholas, let Penny's go on!"

It was intolerable, the implication that he, Nicholas Penny, could play other than fair. And he was sick to death of the whole damn fool chitter-chatter! "The discussion is finished." His manner was almost grandiose, "When my plans are settled you shall receive fair notice."

"Fair notice?" She repeated the words as though they made no real sense. And then again, "Fair notice?"

She went off suddenly into peals of laughter, peal upon peal. She stood there, old head shaking, while the tears slid down her withered cheeks into her laughing mouth.

"Stop that!" he ordered. "You stop that!" And because it seemed she had not heard, added, "You'd better stop that — you'll want a character when you go, won't you?"

The noise stopped abruptly. She stared at him, tears still in her unwinking eyes. Then without a word, she shuffled over to "cash," took her old black hat from its peg, and still holding it in her hand, shuffled out through the door.

He stood watching her shuffle down the sunlight street, rusty hat in hand, the keen wind playing havoc with the piled monument of her scant hair.

Looked like she didn't know what she was doing! Pity she'd seen fit to take herself off like that! Fair notice he'd said, and fair notice he'd meant, with maybe something in the way of a bit of a present. He was a fair man — in spite of the old woman's daft remarks, a fair man! Those insults of hers — he took them from whence they came! They wouldn't have stood in the way of him acting right by her... Pity she'd gone ramping off like a lunatic! Why did she want to go making things harder for herself? When it came to giving her a character a scene like that couldn't be forgotten. He wasn't angry — but a man had got to be reasonably truthful, he owed that to her next boss. ... Well, he needn't lose his sleep over that, she wasn't likely to get another job, hysterical old scarecrow, not unless the Lord sent down a miracle!

Still it was a pity!

Chapter 14

In the castle garden, tulips were over and done with; snapdragons flamed in formal beds. On the rose trees, tight-folded buds gave promise of summer's abundance. Heriot in an embroidered muslin, frilling beneath the chin, the slightness of her waist emphasised by a blue ribbon sash, long white gloves dangling from careless hands, waited for Nicholas.

Down in the town, the clock on The Exchange began to strike. Heriot, surprised, turned the little watch upon her bosom.

Nicholas was late! Again! If it were anybody else — Edward for instance — she would simply get up and go away. But Nicholas was different. To raise the question of keeping her waiting was a little like questioning his whole upbringing... and she knew how sensitive he was! That sudden way — almost defiant — of flinging out some fact about his childhood, his poverty, his lack of education; and then, just as sudden, careful of speech, overplaying the gentleman! It was enough to warn her. Not that she was afraid of Nicholas — though his temper was hasty, at times. But she — she was his friend, and she couldn't bear to hurt his feelings.

Still — she pulled his letter from her reticule. Half-past two, he'd said. And now it was past three! What would mamma say if she could see her daughter sitting on a public seat waiting about for a young man — a young man to whom she was not even engaged?

Mamma would have a good deal to say! But then, whatever Nicholas did wouldn't please mamma, no, not even if he turned out to be the Archangel Gabriel himself! Whatever he did was wrong, the way he sat and the way he stood; what he said and the way he said it — particularly the way he said it! Mamma was cruel about Nicholas, raising ostentatious eyebrows at every slight mistake, laughing at him, after he had gone, for the way he spoke. She couldn't see, didn't want to see, how plucky he was — and how successful! Why, every day, except when he was excited, he came nearer to the speech of the gentleman!

Nicholas came quite often to the house because papa asked him — and mamma could hardly turn him out. But she sat there politely and made it clear that he was not wanted. Nicholas understood, but he didn't care. He just did not care! He came to see Heriot, he said, and as long as she wanted him to come, come he should! So there he would sit, also perfectly polite, and ignore mamma's little game.

Papa liked Nicholas. Or had done — until lately... yes, just lately papa's opinion appeared to be changing...

The clock struck the quarter and Heriot frowned.

She really ought to get up and go away! Nicholas ought to know that a gentleman does not keep a lady waiting! Was he late because he was so frantically busy just now? Or was it that he simply didn't care! What did Nicholas really think about her? Was he waiting to see how this great venture of his turned out? Or was he simply satisfied to go on being friends and nothing more?

Well — she sighed — if he were satisfied, so was she!

But the hammering of the pulse in her throat told a different tale!

There he came, swinging straight across the smooth turf, in spite of the sign that requested him, please, to keep off the grass. So like Nicholas! If he wanted a thing he'd take the shortest way to it, and who cared about the rules?

Nicholas dropped lightly into the seat beside her. She thought, it doesn't even occur to him to apologise! She was a little resentful. After all she was Miss Ware and she was not accustomed to be kept waiting. She looked up at him and her resentment vanished. After all, this was Nicholas! That made everything right!

He said, "Congratulate me, Heriot Ware. It's my birthday!"

"Many happy returns!" She smiled, delighting as ever, in his use of her name. *Heriot Ware*. To the gentlemen of her acquaintance she was Miss Ware — even Edward in his most inspired moment had never got beyond *Miss Heriot*. To her own friends she was Heriot. But for Nicholas and Nicholas alone, she took on a new identity. She was Heriot Ware.

Suddenly she remembered the birthday gift sent less than a month ago — she was not likely to forget it considering the care she had spent in choosing it. "How many birthdays in a year?"

He laughed outright. "Sometimes lots. Sometimes not even one. It depends upon my luck. Today is a very special birthday, though. Today I make my entry — a master!"

Smile! She ought to be smiling, to be glad for the important thing that had come to Nicholas. . . Blackleg. . . that's what papa had said. . . that's why papa had stopped liking Nicholas. . . And the way he explained things, father was right. Blackleg. . . She could not spoil his pleasure with the ugly word; she could not express pleasure, since she felt none. She said nothing.

He said, "I've got my factory!"

"Nicholas!" Impossible to tell what was in her mind.

"Two machines! Heriots'll have to look out!"

She laughed with him at the absurdity. But in spite of her laughter, worry persisted.

"Tell me all about it, Nicholas. To begin with, where is it?"

"Where is it? What do you mean, *where is it*! Where I said it would be o' course!"

His tone was sufficient warning. But love Nicholas as she might, she was not afraid of him.

"Not — not Long Eaton?"

"Ay!"

"Oh Nicholas!" This time trouble was clear in her voice.

"And why not?" His own voice was hard with truculence.

"Long Eaton!" she said again.

"And what's wrong wi' Long Eaton?"

"You know perfectly well! You know it's taking the trade away from Nottingham!"

He shrugged. "Nottingham had th'trade and it was up to Nottingham to keep it. She couldn't. Well — you can't keep back trade from other towns just because Nottingham's played out! Listen to me, Heriot Ware. Every man's got to do what he thinks best. Th'trade's left Nottingham and all the fine talking in th'world won't bring it back again. It's gone, gone for good, to Long Eaton and to Beeston and to Derby and to Heanor! Why does your dad think that is, eh?"

"It's clear, isn't it?" Heriot was a little bitter. "If you don't employ union men, you can pay them as little as you like!"

"Sweat 'em you mean — as much as they'll let you! And why should they let you when they can get union rates? Answer me that! You can't, but I can. Because it's worth their while, that's why! Listen! In Long Eaton a twist-hand can earn three, four, five pounds a week. In Nottingham, biding by union rates he's lucky to scrape up thirty shilling. Lucky if he can get work at all! How d'you make that out?"

Heriot said nothing. She wanted Nicholas to go on talking, to go on justifying himself, so that she could go back and make papa understand that he was quite wrong.

"I'll tell you. It isn't only union rates — there's more to it than that! It's the whole spirit is wrong. Nottingham masters and Nottingham men, they're blind and stupid and greedy as hell! Neither wants to give way in case it might help t'other chap. If we've got to go to th'devil, let's all go together — that's the motto! And believe me, to the devil they'll go!

"The trade's rotten with old custom, rotten with old ideas, rotten with old age! Your father didn't tell you that, did he? No — because he ha'n't woke up to it himself. He's fast asleep and dreaming of the good old times. The good old times that wain't ever come back! Look, here's an example of what I mean. You've seen your father's machines. Grand they look — to anyb'dy who don't understand. There they go, the fine machines, clattering away in the fine factory.

"Well, never mind about fine factories. You go to Long Eaton and there you'll see something! The mill mebbe i'n't up to much. One single room, mebbe, wi' the floor strengthened to stand the weight. But the machines. The machines. In that one room you'll see the latest, the finest machines in the world!

"The latest machines. That brings us back again to the question of union rates. Because the newest machines are naturally the widest machines. Long Eaton machines are one third the width again of Nottingham machines! I don't need to tell *you*, Heriot Ware, that whatever the width, once you set out the machine, the labour you put into it is the same — ay, wide or narrow, it's all one. So in Long Eaton, whatever the width o' lace, a man gets same price per rack. What do you do in Nottingham? Abide by union rates. The wider the lace, the higher the pay, ay, every inch paid for! So up goes the price! In Long Eaton the twist-hand works no harder and th'master can afford to sell cheap — a darn sight cheaper nor Nottingham. That means more business; more business means more work; more work means more money — not only for th'masters, but for th'hands. And so it goes!"

Heriot said, "New machines! Papa's dream for years. But he couldn't afford them, he just couldn't afford them!"

"If he'd paid less than union rates he could have afforded them! But it's too late now. Trade's gone. No good locking the stable door when the mare is stole!" His hand went out in a gesture of impatience. "But it i'n't only the machines. It's more'n that — a whole lot more! Ay, it's more'n the cheap rent and the low rates I pay out at Long Eaton, more even than th'low rate of insurance. . .

"That's not the whole story, not by any manner o' means. It's the spirit between th'masters and th'hands that counts — it counts more'n anything. At Long Eaton there's fair give and take. It's that oils th'wheels and keeps th'machines going. In Nottingham —" he shrugged his distaste.

"But —" she was bewildered. He might be right about everything else, but not this, not this! "The spirit at Heriots — it's fine! You won't find a more generous, kinder owner than papa."

Again that fierce, impatient gesture. "Being generous i'n't enough. Being kind i'n't enough. Look alive and alter your step to fit the new tune — that's what counts! You go to your father's factory, but you don't unnerstand half what you see there! You go along at dinner-time and what do you see? All th'hands knocked off, and very proper it looks! But whether a chap's got a decent meal, or whether he's got naught but a crust o' dry bread, he's got to knock off th'same length o' time because th' union tells him to. Some o' those chaps have got to hang about and watch t'others eating. And th'machines have got to stand idle when they might be earning to put food into empty bellies.

"Now go to Long Eaton and what do you see? Not so pretty, mebbe! But a man's free to please himself — knock off, or snatch a bite while th'machine runs. And the last is what most of 'em do. Work and eat. That's the law. And working-men know it!"

"But —" this at least was all wrong, "men need food and they must have time to eat it!"

"Ay — if they've got it t'eat! If not they've got t'earn it, But it i'n't only that! That's only one o' the damn silly ways th'union interferes with th'best int'rests of the workers. You go round any factory when it i'n't snap-time, and like as not you'll find here an' there a twist-hand mucking about an' naught to do — same as I was mucking about myself that day I first saw you. Why? I'll tell you why! Some little thing wants adjusting and he's not allowed to touch. Bobbins mebbe need liftin' out. But th'union says *no*! He knows as well as th'next man how to lift bobbins out of th'carriages, but th'union says, *twist-hand, twist. Do aught else and we'll kick you out o' th'union!* So there he stands and twiddles his thumbs. An' even if your father was willing to pay extra, there i'n't a twist hand in Nottingham durst do aught but twist. No, there he must stand, wasting his own time, and your father's time, wasting his own power to earn and his master's profits.

"But you go outside the city where the union laws don't run. You'll find the twister puts his hand to anything that comes. He'll lift out bobbins, put 'em in again, tighten a screw, give a hand to himself — or his butty. Helps himself and his neighbour, ay, an' th'master an' all! He speeds up th'work and everyb'dy gains!

"I tell you, Heriot Ware, I wouldn't work in Nottingham not if you gave me your father's mill to put i' my pocket. Nottingham's lost the lace trade — all but, an' if she don't stop to see where she's bound for, she'll lose th' finishing an' all!"

Heriot said slowly, "You're clever, Nicholas, even papa says so! But you're young. Papa says that, too! You've plenty of ideas, papa says, but you haven't any experience. If what you say is really true, how do you suppose Heriots has gone on all these years?"

"I'm young. Got no experience — like your dad says. But what about Betts? Been your father's foreman these fifteen year — and what he don't know about Heriots i'n't worth knowing. When Andrew Heriot started, things were good in the lace trade — but we don't need Betts to tell us that! Nottingham hadn't any competition to face — there weren't any trade, not to mention, except in Nottingham. And there weren't so many skilled workers, neither! They multiplied along wi'th' trade — and they multiplied too fast. Any road, whatever th' conditions, your grandfather was one in a million. He'd a made his mark be the conditions what they might! If he'd 'a been alive now, Heriots would 'a been a very different pair of shoes. Ay, an' th'whole lace-trade with it! He would 'a led — t'others would 'a followed!

"But he's dead an' your father stands in his place. I'm going to speak plain and if I hurt you, Heriot Ware, I'm sorry. But I'll not apologise — this is th'time for plain speaking. You've got t'unnerstand once an' for all why I don't see eye to eye wi' your father. Your father i'n't a special person th'way old Heriot was. He's nice enough, but he's a gentleman — brought up soft! *From th'soil to th'soil three generatioms* — so they say! An' I reckon that's true. If you were a lad, Heriot Ware, you'd find yourself a common twist-hand one o' these days, I shouldn't wonder! No, to make your mark you have to go short, to starve even. You have to plan and fight and push and struggle every inch — th'way your grandfather did, the way I mean to do!

"Your father never knew what it meant to go short, no, nor what it means to stretch out your hand and find nothing there. He put out his hand and took, always. He did his best for Heriots, I'll not deny. He gave what was in him to give — such as it was! He played fair — according to his notions of the rules. Ay, he did his best — but his best weren't good enough — it just weren't good enough. He didn't *add* to Heriots. Not because he didn't put in new machines when they was wanted — though your grandfather would 'a found the brass! A great factory — it's a grand thing, not because of its machines nor its men, nor yet th'work it can turn out nor the money it can make. But because o' the life within itself, th'power and th'influence. Your father didn't add to that — that grandness. I can't put it diff'rent, but you unnerstand. You do unnerstand, don't you?"

Heriot nodded, turning away her head. For what Nicholas said about papa was true. She recognised truth when she saw it — but it hurt, it hurt abominably.

Nicholas said more gently, "he i'n't made on a grand scale. He let chance after chance go by. You ask him about th'Barmen — or rather, don't! He's sore still. No, the truth is this — and if you don't believe me, ask Betts — Heriots has carried on by its own momentum. It had a grand start and it's gone on. And so it will go — by its own momentum — wi'out power, wi'out direction, on and on down th'hill, going quicker and quicker, and then — crash!"

Heriot looked straight before her, her face stiff with self-control. Nicholas watching her, thought, time she learned to see straight with those steady eyes of hers!

He went on, sparing her nothing. "Heriots looks good and fine. From th'outside. You look at th'accounts — if they'll let you anywhere near th'books! I bet you wouldn't be so pleased! I've said it before and I'll say it again — I wouldn't take that factory of your father's, no, not as a gift!"

Still she sat wooden. Suppose the tears she could feel pricking under her lashes overflowed? Suppose they rolled down her cheeks and she had to put up a handkerchief to wipe them away. She, Miss Ware, weeping in a public place!

She thought, passionate behind her stiff mask, Heriots mightn't be what it was, and father isn't grandfather, but it's all right! It's all *right*!

She turned to Nicholas desperate to assure herself. "Heriots crash! *Heriots!* Why, it's as safe as the Bank of England! Everyone knows Heriots. And papa — he mayn't be a genius like grandpapa, but grandpapa thought enough of him to trust him with Heriots. Everyone trusted papa. And there isn't anyone in the country that knows more about lace than he does — he's president of the Lace Makers' Association, he's on every society and every council. Everyone respects his knowledge. . . they consult him, listen to him. . ."

"That doesn't make him worth listening to!"

She thought, terrified beneath the stiff mask of her face, I won't let him frighten me, I won't! Nicholas and papa, they're at cross-purposes, that's all! Nicholas is angry because papa disapproves of Long Eaton. As for papa, he takes Nicholas and his two machines too seriously. . .

Nicholas said softly, "Let's be done arguing! Don't turn away your face. Look at me, Heriot Ware!"

She looked at him then. He saw, for the first time, that her eyes were bright with tears.

Nicholas said, "Looks like I've made you unhappy. I di'n't mean to do that. I'd like you to be happy, always. It's my birthday, like I said. A special birthday. Want to know why?"

She nodded blindly.

"Because today I'm a master. Like your father said — Today a twisthand, tomorrow a master. An' tomorrow's come!"

He was silent, tasting his triumph.

At last he spoke again, "The day I became a master, I meant to ask you something — I always meant to. Will you marry me, Heriot Ware?"

. . .But he doesn't say he loves me. . . He ought to say he loves me.

"Will you marry me, Heriot Ware?"

. . .I love him whatever he says, whatever he thinks, whatever he does. . . But he doesn't say he loves me. . .

He stood there, his steady gaze bent upon her.

. . .He asks me to marry him. Doesn't that say everything?

Flame kindled in the swift colour of her cheek. She wanted to speak, tried to speak — and failed. Only her hands, her long fine hands moved towards him.

Nicholas thought, She's fine — in her way. . . but it isn't my way! And then, unbidden, unwanted, the thought — but Stella was lovely!

Chapter 15

A small mill can do as well as a big one, better in fact, Nicholas told himself. You could give the closest attention to every detail — not a single moment lost, not an inch of thread wasted. Just half-a-dozen folk giving themselves up to the job. He'd seen mills like that over at Long Eaton, scores of them. Family affairs — wife and husband and children all working, all saving, all giving themselves body and soul to the job...

Ay, but why should anyone work for him, body and soul? What claim had he on anyone, anyone at all?

Stella. If he'd kept in with Stella she'd have worked for him like that! Brain she had, and strength, ay and the will to work. Heriot Ware — what could she do for him? Her head was stuffed full of romantic notions about the working-classes, notions that would never suffer her to get down to the actual work itself — to work, nose to the grindstone day in, day out, through noise and heat and the close foul air... No, she couldn't do that. But she could do what Stella couldn't do. While he toiled towards success, Heriot Ware simply by being herself, could guarantee that success, could make it secure... Pity he couldn't marry them both!

Nicholas stood looking at the partly demolished shop that had been Penny's. The bedroom where the old man had died stood grotesquely, two walls with its dingy wallpaper shabbily exposed. Incredibly mean, incredibly dirty it looked against the clean spread of the sky. And yet, that last day he had seen the sick old man, it had not lacked a certain dignity. As if, Nicholas thought, a little ashamed of his fancy, as if the shadow of death had lent it a little grace... Over there, against the stained and faded wall, the bed had stood with its fly-blown knobs that nobody had ever taken the trouble to clean. Propped up against the pillows he'd been, the poor old chap, the tassel of his nightcap bobbing against his stringy neck, and his old hands trembling on the patchwork quilt, and the old voice trembling in his tired throat...

Don't sell the shop, Nicholas, it's needed.

Needed! When for days on end no one had pushed open its dusty door except to buy a bobbin of thread, or a packet of needles, or maybe a paper of rusty pins. Needed!

Well, now they were tearing out its bowels! Plate-glass windows the new shop would have, and polished mahogany to do honour to the latest offspring of the Co-operative Stores. The Co-op would do better for the village than old Nicholas had ever done. It would give better variety, better quality, lower prices and inducement to save. Everyone better off. Except maybe old Shuttle, who had cheated long enough with his dusty tea and his sanded sugar. And he deserved all he got. Penny's needed! He, Nicholas, had done the village a right good turn — owed him by rights, it did, a vote of thanks.

He crossed the narrow road and, went into Pillsden's.

"Eh, Nicholas, lad!" Pillsden jerked his meat-saw in the direction of Penny's. "Th'owd man'd just ebowt turn in is grave. Ah niver thowt mesen, ter see th'day when Penny's were sold." He dissected out a piece of fat with concentration and skill worthy of a surgeon. "Fowks is rare finnicky these days, stomach turns, seemin'ly ovver a bit o' fat th'way yo'd not credit! Ay, an' then wantin' it slipped in free, gratis an' fer nothin'." He placed the offending fat upon a piece of greaseproof paper. "Th'owd man niver thowt so, neither," he added, coming back to his first point.

"Got to move with the times," Nicholas said, his nose wrinkled against the smell of meat.

"Ay, that yer have — even if, mebbe, th'times i'n't fit ter move wi'. Bob Shuttle 's roarin' mad at yer, he is that! Says 'e'll 'ave yer blood!"

"Shuttle'll have to move with the times an' all!" Nicholas said comfortably. "Ay, and at the double, too, if he doesn't want to lose all his custom! That old trick of an extra ha'penny here, and an extra farthing there, and never being sure of the exact price — highway robbery, I call it! Time he mended his ways, old Shuttle. Why you folk have put up with it all this time I can't think! If you want to know the truth —" Nicholas bent confidingly across the clean scrubbed counter, "I'm the village benefactor!"

"Whativer's that?"

"They benefact. Do good to all and sundry!" Nicholas elaborated his statement with a wave of the hand.

"Ar!" Mr Pillsden ran his fingers along the knife's keen edge. "I get yer. But will Bob Shuttle? That's what I want ter know, will Shuttle?"

"That's his look-out! How's old Ellen these days?"

"Ar, there's another wain't git yer meanin'. Very low, she is, poor soul, very low. No work. Nothin' comin' in an' all goin' out. Livin' on 'er savin's. It's mortal 'ard yer can't but say! Th'owd man did ought t'ave left 'er sommat, so he did! No offence, Mr Nicholas! But then — theer's some born to be driftwood as yer med say!" And Mr Pillsden sighed.

Nicholas echoed the sigh. "Poor old Ellen. Nobody's enemy but her own! Where's she living now?"

"Same place. Down by th'bridge."

"I'll go along for a word with her."

"She'll not be ovver glad ter see yer!"

"I'll chance it!"

Nicholas swung down the muddy lane leading to Ellen's cottage. The wind was keen, but he whistled as he strode, enjoying the nip in the late September air. He was pleased with himself. He was going to do the old thing a good turn — he was going to give her a job when she believed no job possible; he would give her back the power of earning when she had looked for nothing but the slow wasting of her poor savings. . . and the workhouse. Kill two birds with one stone, he would! Do them both a bit of good! Get for himself a worker who dursn't demand too much in the way of wages, a worker who dursn't complain at hours or conditions of work, a worker who knew well enough that if she let this job slip, the miracle would not happen again. No, nothing then but the workhouse! Nice to do someone a bit of good — and do it cheap!

He found Ellen's cottage at the bottom of the lane, so low-set, so almost covered with autumn creeper, that though he had been there before he all but missed it.

He knocked upon Ellen's door. He liked the sound of his fist falling with heavy portentous raps. He heard the slow movements within, the shuffle of spiritless feet. The door opened.

It was difficult to distinguish Ellen's dark form in the darkness of the narrow passage. She peered forward, closing her eyes against the clear autumn light. Then, with a sudden fierce gesture, she flung the door to. Nicholas's shining toecap stopped it from slamming.

He pushed his way through the narrow passage, driving Ellen before him.

"Not going to ask me in, Ellen?" he asked reproachfully. "That's not so nice of you! And I've come all the way to see you an' all!"

Ellen began to shake, not only her head, but her whole body.

"Get out and stay out!" she screamed suddenly. "You've done your worst, you rat, and I'm not afraid of you no longer!"

"Shut your gob!" he commanded. "It'll not do you any good going on that way!" Then because his dignity could not regard her outburst as that of a sane person, he said in a kinder tone, "You're not well, Ellen. Why don't you sit down?"

"It's my house to sit or stand as I choose!" She turned on him her defiant face — grey like a creature who has lived long without light, hollow and stained beneath the eyes as one who has lived without food, without sleep.

"You —" the breath failed in her throat. She tried again. "You —" She stood there, voiceless, trembling, the difficult tears running unchecked down her sunken cheeks.

His pity, genuine though it was, was pricked with annoyance because she hindered him at his business.

"Ellen —"

"I don't want to hear your voice," she interrupted fiercely, "no, nor the lying words that come out of your mouth. False you are, false through and through!"

"Look here, Ellen, it's no good going on at me like a madwoman. It's not my fault, it's the way things turned out. I never meant you any harm. . ."

"You did. You always did, from the minute I found out about you — and Stella. You meant to hurt me, you meant to punish me. . . Oh, my God — all my young days wasted in that shop! All the strength I had, poured out into that shop! And then, when I was old and tired and nobody wanted me, you turned me out like a dog, to starve!"

He put compulsion upon himself. "You don't understand," he said. "It's the times. Times change. You can't hold them back!"

"Evil men don't change!" she flung at him. "It's them you can't hold back!"

"Steady now —" Nicholas began. But she was beyond all restraint.

"Not content with that —" the trembling of her head had become fantastic, indecent, "you hunted me, hounded me, stole away my chance of earning a living. Job after job I tried for — I tried Griffin and Spalding, I tried Jessops, I tried Pindars and Pages! Not one of them would give me a chance, not one! Queer, wasn't it, Mister Nicholas Penny — big shops like those, with lots and lots of assistants, and not one would take me? Not so queer though, when you come to think about it, not so queer after all! Why was it, eh, Mister Nicholas, why was it? I'll tell you! Because you blackened my character like you said you would. It ought to have counted, my experience. It *would* have counted, only you chose to backbite me, to persecute me. . ."

It was as much as he could do, not to tell her that no one had as much as applied for her reference; that no one in his senses would employ a grim-faced virago when he had simply to pick among bright and smiling youth. But he held back the words.

He said again, "Times change. That's your answer, the whole answer. But I didn't come here to quarrel with you, Ellen Bird. And it's none too clever of you to quarrel with me!"

He let the shadow of the threat reach home.

"You see I came —" he spoke slowly, drawing out her suspense to bring her to obedience, "to offer you a job!"

"I wouldn't work for you, Nicholas Penny, I'd rather starve. I'd rather die, rather go to my grave, rather. . ." She pressed back the wild grey hair with trembling hands. "A job?" she faltered, unbelieving, "Did you say a job?"

"I did. But since you feel the way you do, I'd best be going!"

Her trembling head craned forward, peered into his; her trembling hand pushed forward a chair. Smiling Nicholas sat down.

"You're cruel!" Ellen screamed at him, "Bad through and through! You came to have a bit o' fun with me, didn't you? Didn't you? Well, I hope you enjoyed your laugh! Me — in the lace-trade! Head cook and bottle washer for Nicholas Penny! Trotting round after the machines! Doing the jobs the kids used to do, me at my age, with my experience. Pity you still can't get 'em young — the very young and the very old — those are the ones you get cheap! Me — winding bobbins, watching threads, sweeping floors, mending your lace maybe. . . all the jobs nobody else'd do! Besides —" she added sullenly but in a quieter tone, "I couldn't do it — even if I wanted to, I couldn't. My hands tremble and my eyesight's none too good!"

"A bottle of medicine and a new pair of specs! Don't you *make* difficulties, Ellen, you've got enough of your own without that! Let's talk plain. It's my way. And a darn good way when you come to the end of polite parlyvoos! Not that *you've* been over polite!" he grinned. "Look here, Ellen. You said just now that you'd tried for job after job, didn't you? Well — and it's God's truth I'm speaking — not one of those shops so much as took the trouble to ask me about you — not one! Why? Go look in the glass! The answer's plain! What they want is bright eyes, a fresh young smile, a good figure. Experience? You can pick that up as you go! The other things — once gone, gone for ever! This is your only chance of a job, now — your *last* chance! Take it or leave it! It's all one to me!"

He stood up to go. "Take your choice!"

"I haven't any choice! You've put that plain enough! But I'm all of a muddle, Mr Nicholas, all of a muddle!" Her hand fluttered crookedly to her head. "You haven't said — I mean — I don't know what I'm going to get or where I'll have to live, or nothing. What are you going to pay me, Mr Nicholas?"

He said pleasantly, "Well you're not a skilled worker, yet, you know! What d'you say to seven-and-six a week to start with?"

A faint smile trembled on her lips. Mr Nicholas was being pleasant! Now he'd got his way he was ready with his little joke! Still smiling, she said, "I can't live on that, Mr Nicholas, you know I can't!"

"Thousands do!"

She stared at him, the smile frozen on her mouth. "Maybe! Those with the bright eyes and the bright smiles you were telling about! Young things with a home they can turn to. Or a sweetheart, maybe, so's they know they're not going to be sweated all the days of their lives. But me — I'm different. I'll never get another job — like you say. And I haven't got a soul to help me out. I *spend* more than what you offer me, now — a lot more. And I live right down to the bone, Mr Nicholas, right down to the bone — I have to!"

There was no change in the pleasant smile. No pity, she thought, none. . . She hung grimly to her slipping self-control As he said, railing wouldn't serve her purpose. Desperate, she tried again. She said, almost conversationally, "Know what your uncle gave me? Thirty-five shillings!"

"You were worth it — to him. You had years of experience behind you. Now you've got to learn a new job, learn it from A to Z. And you're not so young as you were! Eyes not so good. Nerves bad — like you said. Look here —" he was beginning to feel aggrieved that she, the miserable scarecrow, should bargain with him. "I can't sit here all day! You mentioned lace-mending before. D'you think I'd let you touch that? Lace-mending, it's a skilled trade — one of the best-paid in the lace business. Know what a skilled lace-mender gets? Fourteen to sixteen bob a week — and that's top-price! But I'm sorry for you — the Lord knows why! Look here, I'll tell you what I'll do! Down in the basement of my mill there's a room. Used to be the kitchen. Got a sink and a tap an' all! A bit dark, maybe, and a bit on the small side. But you're not so very big, yourself, are you, Ellen? It's warm and it's snug and you can have it rent-free — till I need it. How's that? You get your room and your heating thrown in! And you're on the spot — no getting up in the dark and trudging miles, no. . ."

He was playing the gentleman benefactor and enjoying it.

"And what do you get out of it, Mr Nicholas?"

Her voice spoiling his pleasure, shrivelling it to nothing.

"Knowing I've done you a good turn!" *You damned old crow!* "Besides, you can do something in return — keep the steps and the stairs and the windows clean — little things like that!"

She looked at him. She could not for her life speak. For seven-and-sixpence a week and a rat-hole in a basement, she was to leave her home — home where she had been born, where she had lived her life-long. She was to wind bobbins, and watch machines, to scrub and scour, to take on jobs no one else would do, to be charwoman and odd-job man, at her age, she Ellen Bird!

He said mildly, "There's many would give their eyes for the job!" She was getting on his nerves, the old scarecrow, standing there with her spiteful face and not as much as offering to say *thank you*. "I offer to pay you while you're learning a new job, I give you a room and heating for a bit of cleaning any char would be glad to do for sixpence, and you haven't the decency to say *thank you*! If you don't want the job then don't take it! And good morning to you, Miss Bird!"

She cried out at that, a skinny hand hooked upon his arm. "I'll do it, Mr Nicholas, of course I will. And," she choked upon the word, "thank you!"

"That's the way. You'll find the work light enough, and when you get a bit used to it, why then we'll see!"

"I don't work of a Sunday, Mr Nicholas!"

"If you can afford your little holidays, take them! The work's there, and if it's done, it's done! You ought to be downright happy, Ellen! Nice little room and money coming in regular. I mean to say you don't want champagne suppers! My word, you're in luck! You won't have to rack your brains thinking where the money's coming from! I may lose pounds upon pounds a week — after all, I'm only a beginner myself. But I have to pay for my mistakes. But what I lose won't worry you! Upon my word, I envy you!"

She sent him the oddest look from her shifting eyes. She said no word as she went with him to the door. She stood at the low door of the cottage, watching him stride away, her hatred following, following Nicholas, debonair, well pleased with himself.

Chapter 16

John Ware was angry — angrier than he had ever been in his life. It was different from his usual, easy-flowing anger; it was cold and contained and a little cruel. He sat there, finger-tips lightly touching, looking at Heriot, deliberately keeping her standing, deliberately reducing her to the level of a disobedient servant or a naughty child.

"You must be lost to all sense of decency! Welcome that guttersnipe —" his voice quiet and cool pointed the insult, "into my family! A man without principle, without sense of responsibility, without any basis of truth in his whole nature —"

She reminded him in so low a voice that he strained to catch her words, that he did not know Nicholas.

"*Know* him! No, not I, nor you, nor anyone else! Because he doesn't mean anyone to know him, he takes very good care of that!"

"What do you want to know? What is there to know?" And then, throwing caution to the four winds, "There's one thing you might know, anyhow! Nicholas was one of your workhands. That," she added bitingly, "speaks for itself! Salt of the earth — as you always say!"

"Cooking salt. For the kitchen — not for the dining-room! One of my twist-hands! Oh, Heriot," his voice softened, "you little fool! Can't you see how utterly impossible it would be!"

"I love Nicholas. I love him and I trust him — in spite of what you say, I trust him."

"Trust!" Ware's cold anger deepened. "Can't you see? Isn't the writing on the wall clear enough? The fellow uses that beastly charm of his to pick up whatever's worth picking. He'd suck you dry — if you'd let him! He'll see he's all right, never mind who else lands in Queer Street! That night for instance — the night he first came here — there he was sitting there so innocently, with his *yes, sir* and his *no, sir*, leading me on, discussing the trade as if it were an intellectual question. Sitting there and listening and agreeing, agreeing! And all the time picking my brains! And then, having agreed about the iniquity of taking machines out of Nottingham, knowing full well that it means starvation for still more people, he goes straight off and hires his machines and takes them out to Long Eaton! Disgusting!"

I don't see that it's disgusting!" Heriot said. "Nicholas can't afford to set up in Nottingham — the rents, the rates, insurance — everything, it's all beyond him! Besides — his two machines won't make or break anything!"

"Every machine taken out is a nail in our coffin! What I can't forgive myself is that *I* put the idea in his head."

"You needn't distress yourself about that, papa. It's the obvious thing for a beginner with very small capital. He'd have thought of it himself — he couldn't help thinking of it!"

"Then he ought to be doubly ashamed of himself! How any right-minded citizen can bring himself to steal his city's trade, to destroy it, destroy it utterly. . . it's beyond me! The city has rights, I tell you, it has rights!"

"Nicholas has rights," Heriot said obstinately, remembering how few those rights had been.

"No man has the right to work against the common good, to make others suffer!"

"Others made Nicholas suffer. Conscience wasn't so tender when Nicholas ran about barefooted and hungry! But what's the use of *talking*. . . Nicholas is not a child, he cannot be dictated to by you or me or anybody else. He must do exactly as he thinks fit!"

So! She had caught the ugly infection! She denied the right of elders to guide the young and the ignorant! She was a foolish child led by the nose by romantic notions! Always she had inclined to romantic notions but he had let her be. He had been certain that her extravagant ideas would calm down with time. But instead they had become a danger to her — she was admiring ruthlessness in that young man, admiring it because she didn't relate it to everyday life — a mean ruthlessness which she glorified into courage and strength. She hadn't the imagination to see how this ruthlessness would affect her once — *if* — they were married!

It was a terrible thing to see one's child, one's only child, bent on a path that could lead only to misery.

He tried again, his heart sore for this foolish child of his.

"Heriot, I am not angry now — I have stopped being angry, so listen to me. You must listen to me. No one has the right to advise young Penny, you say! Well, maybe you're right. But what about you? I'm still your father, my dear! Can't you see, isn't it plain enough, that this young man will never make you — or anyone else, happy? It isn't in him. It just isn't in him! He hasn't a thought save for his own plans, his own self. What he wants to do he will do, regardless of anything, of any person. Regardless even of you, Heriot — more than anyone, perhaps, of you — once he's got you! He has charm, I grant you. But don't be led away by it, Heriot, don't be led away! I tell you again, that young man is utterly selfish, utterly ruthless to the last degree. You can't see it at this moment because you don't have to depend upon him for anything. But how would it be if you did? How would it be in the future, Heriot, answer me that?"

She said obstinately, fearful of his gentleness, "I don't know about the future — no one does. I only know that I love Nicholas."

"And does Nicholas love you?"

"Why else do you think he wants to marry me?"

"A hundred reasons — and all of them good. There is, for instance — Heriots."

"He doesn't want Heriots. He wants me."

"So he says — now!"

"Now — and always!"

"Just as well! For he'll never dip so much as the tip of his finger in Heriots!"

He saw by the set of her mouth that he had lost what little ground he might have won.

He began again. "I know you wouldn't marry without my good will, you're too much my daughter for that!"

"My own good will comes first!" She looked at him with steady eyes.

John Ware lost his temper. She ought to be whipped, the impertinent child, standing there and defying him! Since he could not whip, he let fly his words.

"I'm warning you — warning you both! Marry without my permission — which you can whistle for — and you don't get a pennypiece, understand, not a pennypiece! We'll see the strength of our young friend's devotion once he understands that!"

"Yes, we'll see!" Heriot agreed and went quietly from the room.

Mamma was even more difficult than papa — for she never spoke of the matter. She ignored it entirely, as if no problem existed. Only the iciness of her manner betrayed her.

And then, as if things were not difficult enough, Edward Jebb must reappear on the scene. It was not exactly a reappearance, for Edward had never been definitely off the scene. He had always been more or less hanging about, as though staking a claim he was too lazy — or too indifferent — to demand. But now it did look as if he had suddenly awakened to the fact that someone else was stealing his bone. Not the prettiest way of putting it, Heriot thought, but exactly what Edward made her feel like!

Mamma on the warpath was not lightly to be hindered. Penning Heriot into a corner of the drawing-room, whence, short of violence there could be no escape, she opened the attack. . . Edward was the friend of her childhood. They were of the same class, the same upbringing, they spoke, naturally, the same language. Nothing more important — mamma's tone was significant — than equality of class in the making of a happy marriage. To which, Heriot, stung by mamma's insinuations, retorted that Andrew Heriot's granddaughter was nearer Nicholas's class than Edward's. For when had the Heriots ever been landed gentry?

"But you played together as children!" Mamma ignoring Heriot's point, returned grimly to her own. "You know each other through and through!" To which, the thoughtful Heriot replied that if from their rather casual meetings she really knew Edward through and through, then surely there could not be much to know!

But mamma would not take *no* for her answer, could not, indeed, consider the possibility of *no*. She dealt affectionately upon the advantages of being Lady Jebb; she touched with horror upon the impossibility of being Mrs Penny.

Heriot listened quietly. Let mamma talk! She owed mamma that! Anyhow there was no stopping her!

And mamma talked. She dealt faithfully with the theme of ingratitude — stupid, criminal ingratitude. Until, Heriot, stung by the assumption that Edward, dull dilly-dally Edward, conferred honour where Nicholas conferred none, lost her temper. And, what is more regrettable, enjoyed the sensation. She shouted at mamma, she, Heriot Ware, model of ladylike propriety! It is more than a question that had Edward seen her, then, he would have dilly-dallied no longer, but would have taken himself and his offer elsewhere.

"I'm sick, sick, sick to death of hearing about Edward Jebb! I'm sick of hearing about the pretty way we played together as children. We never played — never! He was too stupid and I was too bored. . . and we haven't changed a bit, either of us! A good basis for married life I must say! No, thank you, mamma, I mean to have a husband I can respect! I'm done with Edward Jebb — and everything that goes with him — done, done, done! So," she added by way of anti-climax, but none the less rudely, "you can save your breath to cool your porridge!"

And she burst out of the room with a slam of the door that set the fire-brasses a-rattling.

She was contrite afterwards. Her temper! She sighed at the thought of it! Tempers were unpleasant, but — they were useful. They served to shut the other person up — if you were quick enough, and angry enough! She would never let Nicholas know she had such a temper, never even let him suspect such a thing! But then — she would never want to be bad-tempered with Nicholas. . . he was so charming. And she loved him.

And anyhow, she would apologise to mamma.

Against the inflexible will of their daughter, the Wares were helpless — even Ada Ware, grim of lip and eye, helpless. Who would have thought it of Heriot, of Heriot their own child? A certain obstinacy, Ada had long recognised, but not this rigid will, neither to be bent nor broken. One weapon, indeed, they might have tried — acting upon the best principles of melodrama they could have forbidden Nicholas the house and locked up their daughter. But — to become the centre of meaty gossip, to allow the Ware name to be ridiculed, the Ware dignity tarnished!

There was nothing for it but to appear to accept the state of affairs. They rationalised their fear by telling each other that Heriot's resistance would be further stiffened by any threat of violence. Idiotically romantic, she would delight in the new conditions; it was the certain way of throwing her into that creature's arms!

"Nothing for it," said Ada Ware, distaste bitter upon her tongue, "but to allow the affair to wear itself out. The little fool has lost Edward. If we give our consent we should be in a position to insist upon a long engagement."

"I say, No and no and no again!" John Ware was white with passion.

"A long engagement —" she smiled wryly, "merely a more tactful way of saying *no*. The creature is undeniably good-looking, but when the glamour wears off — as it must — there will be little to attract, and a great deal to disgust, a girl like Heriot!"

"I don't like it. I don't like it at all." But he bowed, as always, to Ada's judgment.

So Heriot, a little frightened to find that she had won her first real battle, was prepared to take life on the wing. Life was marvellous!

Life was marvellous — maybe! But — it didn't seem to be getting any easier. She was engaged to Nicholas, certainly. But no girl, she was sure, whose engagement was sanctioned, had ever been made to feel so little like a bride and so much like a criminal. Her parents' studied coldness to herself, their all-but-rudeness to Nicholas, first wounded and then gradually hardened her spirit.

She took a leaf from Nicholas' book!

For Nicholas would take no offence, would see no offence. He was John Ware's future son-in-law and be took care that everyone knew it! Almost unlimited credit was his for the asking — and even without asking. He was treated with deference wherever he went. Young Mr Penny might be a dark horse — but if John Ware accepted him as a son-in-law, it was security enough! So Nicholas went often to the Wares' house. Apparently he did not see that cold inattention bordering so nearly upon downright rudeness. Enough warmth radiated from him to thaw the chilliest greeting. But there was anger — and to spare — in his heart.

In making their enmity so plain they had been too clever — they had defeated their own end. Nicholas found the stick with which to belabour them.

They were sitting all together in the drawing-room, for Heriot and Nicholas were not for one moment left together. As if, thought Nicholas, grinding his teeth, I should suddenly fall upon the girl and rape her! He sat barely enduring the atmosphere of suppressed irritation. Suddenly it occurred to him that he had put up with this clumsy rudeness too long. Why did he sit there, time after time, and allow this insult?

His anger burned. Here they sat, time after time, and always he endured their intolerable rudeness! And then, suddenly, a gift from heaven, the stick to beat them!

He turned to Heriot, where she sat, the smile of patience cold upon her face.

"Heriot," he said, his voice calm, his speech careful, "our engagement has lasted long enough. As we are all together," he smiled charmingly upon Ada and John Ware, "could we not fix the date for our wedding?"

They opened their mouths, John and Ada, rigid with refusal. But he waved them aside. "This is as Heriot wishes!"

And what Heriot wished he had no doubt. She was heartsick of this treatment. She suffered, she said, more than he, since she suffered for him, feeling the indignities he endured, wounding her own spirit. No, her desire he could not doubt, but — her courage?

He almost loved her when she said, "As soon as you like, Nicholas!"

Nicholas stood in the Wares' hall shaking the rain from his coat. He knew well enough, though he gave no sign, that the manservant no longer hovered. The fat man knew that Nicholas was no welcome visitor. A damn bad servant, Nicholas thought, a good servant never lets on. . .

John Ware came out of the smoking-room on the left. "Hey, Penny," he called abruptly, "I want a word with you!"

Nicholas thought, following him, I've learned to be a good servant to myself — I never let on! Nor did he so much as move a muscle of his friendly face, though Ware made no movement of even formal politeness, even though he did not invite Nicholas to sit, nor sit himself.

The two men faced each other. But it was the old man, trained from childhood to social usage, who gave himself away. There he stood, obviously hostile, obviously embarrassed, facing the cool and pleasant young man.

Ware said, "So you think this ridiculous business is going on?"

"I don't understand you, sir!"

"You understand perfectly!"

Nicholas raised an effective, much-practiced eyebrow. Then, quite deliberately he dropped into a chair, crossed his long legs and absorbed himself in the crease of his trousers.

Ware, still standing, felt his temper slipping. He clung desperately to his formal manner.

"I disapprove absolutely of my daughter marrying you, and I have never disguised the fact from either of you! I have made an effort to countenance my daughter for appearance's sake — and also because I had hoped she would herself have seen the folly of this affair. I had hoped that she would have seen for herself the kind of man you are!"

Ware's glance of distaste travelled Nicholas slowly, from head to foot.

"But you are clever, far too clever for that! And now that — that" he stumbled a little upon the words, "the wedding day is so near, and there is no longer any hope, I must warn you again that I shall give her nothing, nothing at all! I have said it before, but apparently you have not believed it! So I say it again — if she marries you, Heriot will be penniless, And that is not comparatively speaking. I mean completely and entirely penniless. Does that interest you?"

"Not a great deal!" Nicholas still wore his pleasant smile. "You must do exactly what you please with your money!"

"Very heroic. Very heroic indeed! But it won't work. Don't care about money — and all set to marry an heiress! You're a liar, my man — and a foolish liar at that!"

Nicholas said, still pleasantly, "Not very complimentary to your daughter — are you? Listen, once and for all! I want Heriot. That's all I want from you! As for saying I don't care about money, I'm not such a fool. And only a fool would misunderstand me. I'm not interested in *your* money. . . I can make all I want for myself, thank you!"

"And for your wife?"

"And for my wife!"

"No doubt," Ware's gentle tone was an insult, "you don't know how much it costs to keep a lady!"

"My wife will teach me. And now, if you don't mind, I'll go and find Heriot, so good evening to you!" In the doorway he turned. "You're wise," he said, "not to fling your money about!"

And closed the door gently behind him.

Chapter 17

A drab basement house with a leprous stretch of land running down to the sluggish canal — but to Nicholas, a delight to the eye. He could never look long enough. Penny's mill. There it stood, its two machines already set up in the basement. How easy it had been to get them! As soon as his engagement to Heriot Ware had become known, he could have had a dozen machines for the asking. It had been a temptation. He had imagined himself carelessly inviting old Ware to come over and look at his eight, nine, ten machines. But he had known well enough that he could hardly afford the wages even two machines would entail, to say nothing of the fact that the upstairs floors were too flimsy to take the weight of a machine... Besides, John Ware was still sore, he would never have come!

But patience. A little patience. If all went well he would have more and more machines. He would pull down this high and narrow house with its useless floors and put in its stead a long low building — glass and steel and brick. And after that, there would be more and more buildings rising from that stretch of sour field, running down to the banks of slow-moving water. And when he asked John Ware, John Ware would come!

All in good time. Patience, that was all, patience!... and the sense to keep one's desires within the bounds of commonsense.

Yes, he had been wise to limit himself to two machines! Three or four capable folk could run the place — if they put their backs into it! Why, he himself could do the work of three! He knew how to set out a machine and how to design, ay, and how to make a working drawing an' all! Not that he was above using another chap's design — if it was good enough and cheap enough to work. Put in an extra thread here, leave out a thread there — just to keep on the right side of the law. That was how they dodged the copyright. He knew the game as well as anybody — it was a game everybody played.

And he'd got Betts. Not much Betts didn't know, from the buying of yarn to the disposal of finished goods. And the final stroke of luck — if luck you could call what really amounted to sound common-sense, he'd got Barton. What would old Ware say when he knew he'd lost his chief fitter? Hurt his pride as well as his convenience, that would! Barton hadn't wanted to leave Heriots. But you'd dinned it into his ears, you and Betts together, that Heriots was none too safe. Stiffish price, he asked. Thirty-seven and sixpence! It would make a hole! Still, the more you spent on the fitter the less you'd spend on the machines!

Pity they didn't allow kids to be employed nowadays. Damn sentimental nonsense! Nice easy job pushing bobbins into the carriers — when you got the knack of it! Still, that was where old Ellen came in. She could learn to fill the bobbins an' all. And she could examine the yarn for faults. And she could do, mebbe, some of the simpler jobs of mending. But a first-rate mender he had to have. The tiniest hole, a hanging thread — and he might as go and hang himself! He'd got hold of a lacemender for the time being, but she wanted a damn sight too much! Seventeen-and-six. Never mind about union rates, the workers knew how to look after themselves! Suck you dry if you'd let them!

No good trying to push the work on to Ellen. . . her hands were too shaky. Pretty hands Stella had. Used to mend up the job-lot collars at Penny's. Flick, her fingers would go, flick, flick, quick as butterflies. And the collars would be mended so fine you couldn't see the fault. . .

Stella. . . why, it must be all of a year since they drove her away, Ellen Bird and the old man together. He himself, he hadn't seen her since that day he'd been helping old Ellen with the boxes — Stella standing there in the dark doorway, standing there, and looking at him out of her white face. . . He'd thought of her, sometimes, though — thinking maybe he was a father now, thinking maybe it was better he didn't know, thinking maybe he was well out of that business.

But. . . he'd like to know how things were with Stella. Had she got a job? She'd find that none too easy with a kid tacked on to her! Maybe she'd be glad of a job! She wouldn't expect top wages, neither. She'd have the sense to see that beggars couldn't be choosers, and that she'd be doing herself a bit of good — learning a good trade, ay, earning and learning the same time! But — how could he get on to Stella? He hadn't the slightest idea where she was. Maybe the old bird could tell him something. . . she hated Stella but she was nosy enough to find out! Yes, she'd know something. . . better not rush matters, though, better think it over careful, weigh it up from all sides.

From the basement came the sound of low whistling. Weighing his problem, Nicholas went down the dark stone steps. Barton was bending over a machine dusting it lightly with blacklead.

He lifted a black and smiling face. "Niver laid hands on such a bewty, niver," he said. "An' th'way yer can change ovver from narrer ter wide wi'out losen time! A reg'lar marvel!"

"Cost a fortune!" Nicholas said, a loving hand on his machine.

"Mek a fortune an' all!"

"Fortunes aren't that easy made! Too many overheads, I'm thinking. You know, Barton, I've often thought what a waste to send lace out to be finished — starching, bleaching, gassing, to say nothing of cartage! Easy jobs all! Why can't they be done under one roof?"

"Too many irons in th'fire, that's why! Some on 'em's boun' ter get a cold place!"

"Can't have too many irons in the fire — if the fire's a good one! You wait and see! I'll show you how to run a mill, I'll show everyone! One of these days I'll have the yarn come in and the lace go out — bleached and stretched and stiffened, ay, and boxed, ready for the counter. You'll see!"

"Can't be done! Nob'dy iver done it afore, nob'dy niver will!"

"I will!" said Nicholas.

Something had broken in Ellen. It was as though in forcing her to obey him, Nicholas had taken a vicious pull and the worn elastic of her mind lacked the power to contract again. But though he had robbed her of a certain amount of initiative power, he had by no means robbed her of the power to suffer. And suffer she did when she took her last farewell of the cottage.

Wandering from room to room, a candle flickering in her shaking hand, flickering and sending spots of grease to harden upon the stone floor, she thought how odd it was that after tonight, she would never sleep under this roof again. Odd. . . because every single night since she was born she'd slept here. No, every night bar one. The night mother died Mrs Pillsden had come and taken her back to sleep; and then, the next day, Margaret had come home.

It was then she'd come to hate Margaret. For before Margaret had come to spoil things, she had been happy — as happy as a bird in the green trees in summer. For she had landed the most coveted job in the village. Round about thirteen she'd been when Nicholas Penny first set up shop..

Wandering ghostlike, the candle in her trembling hand, her shadow witchlike on the walls, she remembered the excitement down in the village.

A draper's. Of their own! A shop where you could buy not only needles and thread — you could get those down at Shuttle's — but real things, dress-lengths and gowns and hats. . . and bride veils and babies' caps. It had been a long time before the child Ellen understood that bride veils and baby bonnets were not for her and never would be! She hadn't learned that till Margaret came back. . . Margaret, and the boys' eyes following her as she swung down the street. It was because of that she had come to hate Margaret. Because Margaret had put her out in the cold, had left her to shiver in the cold for the rest of her life.

Ah, but before Margaret had come, when she had got her job! Yes, she'd got it, even though Ann Sparrow and Kitty Bates would have given their eyes for it — and both of them pretty as paint! But it was she; she, Ellen Bird, who had got it because of Mr Penny saying she'd got her head screwed on right. She could see her now, little Ellen Bird, with her long black frock and her black alpaca apron and her mousy hair piled high above her child's face — Penny's saleswoman.

Three years... three happy, happy years learning her job; learning how to measure and cut without giving away a fraction of an inch, how to reckon and how to make up a bill; learning how to talk the way a young lady in a shop should talk, And all the time, a little queen among the big black treasure-boxes, boxes of stockings, wool and cotton, black and white and brown; boxes of shining ribands, and boxes of gloves; and best of all, the collar box, coarse lace and fine; narrow collars and wide, and all of them pretty as pretty. And Mr Nicholas himself, so tall, so handsome...

Walking aimlessly, grease dripping unheeded upon the stone floor, it came to her for the first time, that old Nicholas had not really been handsome or clever or kind... A dull young man — that was the truth! A little kind, a little stupid, a little generous — all his qualities on the little side. But she had found him wonderful, beyond words wonderful. Now why was that? Because — she faced it now — because he was her master and she obeyed him without question; because in his hands lay her fate, to dismiss or employ as he willed. But greater than either of these, she knew it now, because she had been young and wild for a young man's kindness — and he not too ugly a man!

Happy days before Margaret came back, happy, happy nights, when falling to sleep she had forced herself awake to think of Nicholas Penny — thinking not hopefully, but rapturously, as one tells one's self a fairy tale that moves always to its appointed end. And then, falling asleep and dreaming.

Those dreams...

Morning. And rising like a bird and hurrying through her dressing and through her breakfast. And running, running down the cobbled street, skirts lifted high, not to be late.

And then Margaret. And after that she had not to force herself to wakefulness, for they had begun then, the long sleepless nights of twisting and turning and blind misery.

Margaret swinging down the street, chin lifted high as though the whole world belonged to her. As it did! It did! Margaret pushing open the door of Penny's and standing in the sunlight — standing in the sunlight and bringing in the darkness. Margaret.

And Nicholas looking up and seeing her stand there in the middle of the sunlight... and staring as though he saw a vision.

And that was the end.

Not quite the end. Wounded she'd been to the heart, but she'd set her lips, denying the wound. But Margaret had taken the knife and twisted it about right inside the wound, twisted and twisted. Innocent? Maybe.

But none the less devilish. Margaret laughing at Nicholas with the warm ringing laugh you'd come to hate, laughing at his clumsy ways and his slow speech; making his would-be lover's ways ridiculous, flicking him away with a snap of the fingers — Nicholas for whom you would have died.

Margaret so grand, so secure in her beauty, laughing away with the careless laugh of hers.

It was for that she had really come to hate Margaret.

And then, when things got so bad, she couldn't bear them any longer, Margaret went away. Just as simple as that! She said she was going — and the next day, she went. She said she hated the village. It stifled her with its spiteful old women, and its spiteful young women, who couldn't forgive her, any of them, for being pretty. And she was stiffled, too, she said, with the oafish young fellows who pestered her till she didn't know which way to turn.

Yes, Margaret had gone. But it was too late. Too late — because Nicholas never looked at you or any other woman again.

And the slow years passing over your head. And Nicholas sometimes kind, but oftener irritable. And sometimes generous, but oftener mean. The long slow years. . . and you passing from girlhood into womanhood. And then quietly, so quietly you hadn't noticed it, you were middle-aged. It was queer. Although you'd seen Nicholas get grey and fat, although you knew Margaret was dead, proud, laughing Margaret, you hadn't realised what the years had done to you! You hadn't known that youth was over and done with till you'd looked up one day and there was Stella standing in the sunlight, as her mother had stood long ago.

For one moment you had thought, Margaret, this is Margaret come back. And the hatred you had forgotten, came rushing back with a beating of wings.

Stella, turning you again to bitterness, Stella more cruel even than Margaret, because she took away the last thing you had — your peace.

Yes, you had built up a sort of contentedness, knowing yourself useful and respected — and then Margaret's child had come and taken it away — even that she had taken away. All the world set to rob you — Margaret of love and Stella of peace. And now, young Nicholas who had sold the shop, sold away her life's work, and at whose command she must leave her home!

She was seized by a passion of hatred for young Nicholas because she must leave this place that had known the young girl in the black frock, hair piled unchildishly upon her childish forehead, the child dreaming of a young man handsomer and kinder than old Nicholas had ever been.

Her head shook in violent duet with the shaking candle.

Ellen looked about the small dark room. The clatter of the machines broke and rumbled in her head, so, she thought fretfully, she couldn't listen to her own thoughts, couldn't hear what they said to her, the way she could back in the cottage. It was hot, too. You could feel the air hot when you breathed. And the smell of oil was making her sick!

She stood on tiptoe and rubbed a hand against the small high window. The hand came away streaked with dirt. She wiped it fretfully upon her dark skirt.

Everything was dirty here. It came from that blacklead they put on the carriages to make the machines run easy. It got everywhere, in your clothes and up your nose and down into your lungs when you breathed. Mr Nicholas said that was her imagination. There wasn't enough blacklead, he said, to clog the hind-leg of a fly! Clean and healthy, he said. Much he knew! Let him say when he pleased, this wasn't the sort of air she was used to!

She was taken with nostalgia like a sickness for the clean air of her home.

This is your home! In the dark close room she knew how the hunted feel. She leaned against the wall, closing her eyes against the tears.

. . .Down in the hollow under the trailing blackberry her cottage stood. When she stood at the open door she could see the clean river running, throwing back sunlight between water and sky. And behind her, the dark tangle of the wood, cool on the hottest day. And in summer, the little patch of green where the trees came down to the river was blue with forget-me-nots and red with ragged robins. And now it stood empty, her cottage. And no-one would live in it again, because of it being damp from the river — so they said. Empty, quite empty! At least, when she thought about it in the daytime, she knew very well it must be empty. But when she thought about it at night she wasn't so sure! You couldn't live a lifetime in one place and not leave something living behind, could you? No — she wasn't at all sure!

Well, that was all behind her now! Now she must live as best she could with the mean and scrubby bit of waste and the canal that went slow and heavy, as though it were oil and not water. . .

Nicholas came in noisily, bending his tall head.

"Cosy, isn't it?" He stood there handsome and full of good cheer. She wondered whether it were possible to hate a person so much that they could stand together in one small place and he not know it, not feel it!

"Want some help to get this straight?" His eyes despised the mess of junk.

She shook her head. She thought, if he so much as touches with his finger anything that belongs to me, I'd want to kill him!

"Can't manage this stuff by yourself!" he pressed her kindly, "I'll send in a man to give a hand!"

She mumbled something that might have been thanks. *I'll send in a man!* Not so long ago he himself had been at everybody's beck and call! She choked back her hatred because he played the master!

He turned to go; at the door he paused. "Seen anything of that niece of yours?" he asked carelessly.

"She and I don't meet," Ellen said. She could feel her head beginning to tremble.

"That so? Know how she is?"

"She's all right! Her sort always is!"

He resisted the temptation to take her by the shoulders and shake a reasonable answer out of her.

"Know where she is now?" he asked.

She hesitated before giving her answer. "Yes."

"Let's have her address. We were friends — once. I'd like to help her!"

"It's ovver late for that!"

"Never too late to mend!" Nicholas said cheerfully. "Come on, Ellen. Out with it!"

She turned her back on him. "I'll think about it!"

"You'd better! And double quick at that!" He made no further attempts to hide his irritation as he flung from the room.

Ellen dropped down on a corner of the bed. All round and about her possessions were piled where they had been thrown. She made no attempt to make herself comfortable, even though the sharp edge of a picture-frame cut into her shoulder. She sat there, lost to the world, her whole being set upon her problem.

Which would harm him more — tell him? Or not?

Suppose she didn't tell? Then he would forget Stella — as he had so long forgotten her. He would marry the girl, the thin girl whose picture was in the paper. And if she didn't fill the bill — and she wouldn't, Nicholas liked them plump and hearty — he'd take up with another, and then another. If he never saw Stella again, no great harm done!

But if he were to see Stella again! Once, once only — and then, misery and jealousy and muddle and confusion. And bitterness. Yes, there would be bitterness and to spare! And fear, too, fear spoiling his life and Stella's life and that other girl's life, ay and the lives of their children after them. Stella's child too... no end to the misery... Because Ellen Bird knew what she knew, they were delivered into her hands, all of them into her hands, her empty, despised hands. And she would sit and say nothing. Like God. Only she would laugh and laugh and laugh!

Chapter 18

Heriot lay still in the darkness, trying desperately to sleep. Tomorrow was her wedding-day and she must look her best. She wasn't pretty, she knew that well enough. But she could look pretty on occasion — and if one's wedding-day didn't count as an occasion, then what did?

Why couldn't she sleep? Why was she lying here worried to death? Tomorrow was her wedding-day and she loved Nicholas, loved him with all her heart.

But does Nicholas love you? papa had asked that, too, echoing the question of her own heart.

She was an idiot. If Nicholas didn't love her, then why was he marrying her, in spite of all unpleasantness, in spite of all difficulties, marrying her? Not for Heriots, as papa had suggested. Nicholas wouldn't look at it as a gift, wouldn't even pretend to care about it to please her. Not for any money he might get; papa had been clear, devastatingly clear about that from the beginning. She was a fool upsetting herself in this ridiculous way. The truth was that Nicholas was not the person to let himself go in easy words. When he said *dear*, it really meant something; it meant more than *darling* and *I love you* meant from anyone else. Nicholas loved her. And that was enough!

But did he? Did he?

Oh, she was stupid to lie here doubting. This time tomorrow she would be lying in the big brass bed that took up most of the front bedroom in the little house in Scarrington Drive.

She pressed her hot cheek into the cool pillow.

Lovely. But rather frightening too! Better not think of that — it certainly wouldn't send her off to sleep! They would be starting their new life right away — no honeymoon. Nicholas said the factory needed him. But she knew that he simply hadn't the money! She didn't mind. It would be fun settling down in her own little home.

Perfect little doll's house... mamma to her friends! But the coldness of her eye might have warned anyone not to be taken in by warmth of her tongue. Heriot had been made to feel, very clearly, that the little house was an insult to mamma. Mamma had not minced matters when she had expressed her opinion of the row of hateful jerry-built boxes, growing like hideous toadstools upon the dignity of The Park.

Mamma hated it so much that she had even suggested that you and Nicholas should live here at home till he could afford something more suitable, This, from mamma who disapproved of the marriage to the point of loathing and never troubled to conceal it!

But Nicholas had had enough of Ware hospitality! He was quite capable of supporting his wife, he had informed mamma, without even troubling to add *thank you*. For Nicholas was proud of the Scarrington Drive house — pathetically proud. The very latest, he had said. Bathroom with hot and cold once you'd lit the kitchen range. And tiles all round the sink. And a pump for rainwater, too! But what did one do with rainwater? "Of course it's not as big as the house you've been used to! But then your grandfather didn't mind about a little house, nor your granny! I bet your mother wasn't born in a house half as good — though maybe she forgets it!"

"She doesn't forget it. She just pretends to forget because things were so bad. It hurts her to remember."

"You've got to start as a poor man's wife!" Nicholas had said. "But you'll not end that way, neither! I promise you'll not end that way! Still — if the start's not good enough." He'd shrugged the rest of his sentence.

Now again, lying in the darkness, she felt the fear she had known then, fear of losing Nicholas. She couldn't live, couldn't even try to live, without Nicholas.

She sat up in bed, turned her pillow, and rested upon its fresh coolness.

Life with Nicholas. Pots and pans hanging neatly upon hooks in the little scullery. A life of pots and pans! And once she had believed that she and Nicholas might work together for Heriots. And then — if not for Heriots, why then for Pennys. Pennys — the new factory, starting humbly, starting carefully, as Heriots had once started. Nothing she wouldn't do to help Nicholas there, work her fingers to the bone if need be... Well, there wasn't need, she'd come a long way from those dreams; and if it was pots and pans and Nicholas she was satisfied.

Yes, in spite of pots and pans and the rather horrid little house, she was glad Nicholas had refused mamma's invitation — which was no invitation at all but a royal command to save mamma's dignity. She'd had enough of that pride that sought day in, day out, to feed upon Nicholas. *Live with you! No, thank you, mamma!* But she had kept her thoughts to herself. "It's very kind of you, mamma," she had said politely. "But after all, we shan't be so very far away!"

"Further away than you think!" mamma had said tartly. "Nearness doesn't depend upon distance. You'll be further away from our kind of life in that wretched house of yours, than you would be in Timbuctoo!"

Heriot turned restlessly. Mamma's sort of life? Living well. Comfort. The best of everything. Giving a dinner-party. Going out to dinner. Whist. Sitting on a committee as earnest of higher things. She herself would be bored to death! As long as she had Nicholas, she wanted nothing else — nothing!

Then why did she sigh as she tossed sleepless upon her pillow?

In the big front bedroom along the corridor, Ada Ware turned her back on the moonlight that slipped through the chinks of brocaded curtains... Violet had drawn them very badly, very badly indeed! She would speak to Violet in the morning. If it had not been for those wretchedly drawn curtains she would have been fast asleep by now, instead of tossing and turning and wishing it was daylight. Odd to be wishing for daylight — it would come soon enough, Heriot's wedding day!

She sighed deeply, remembering her hopes for Heriot. Tomorrow would see the end of those hopes. Tomorrow Heriot would throw herself away on that man — that man without family, without money, without principles. A man who could be depended upon for nothing — except to make his wife unhappy!

Oh Heriot, Heriot you *fool*! She heard her heart cry so loudly in the darkness, that it was a wonder John didn't stir in his sleep at her side, nor Heriot run in barefoot to see what ailed.

Heriot, you don't know what you're doing — you don't know! And I can't stop you! Time was when parents locked up children who didn't obey! Wise, how wise! That little time to think... I wish I could lock you up. I'd rather break your spirit for a little than your heart for always.

He doesn't love you. He doesn't love anyone but himself, his fine handsome self! But even if he did love you, even then? You don't know what it is — the mean life in the mean house. It's prison, just as much as if the door were locked behind you. It's worse even. For some time or other you're free of prison, but the mean life gets you for ever...

I remember... I remember...

Ada Ware lying in the soft bed, her mind moving back among memories she hated.

...The scullery dim beneath the volume of copper-steam; the peculiar smell, the sickly smell of washing, boiling. Even as a child who had known nothing better, her heart had cringed at washday. Mother scrubbing, standing on the cold stone floor, thin with undernourishment, white with fatigue... And the nagging tongue, the bitter tongue! And then, the swift repentance of the over-driven woman battling against time and lack of money and lack of nourishment, and all the aches and pains of her worn out body.

She herself had been so small, she hadn't understood to the full the bitterness of her mother's life. But small as she was, she'd known what it was to go always a little hungry, a little cold. She'd known, too, that she feared her mother, shrinking from the hard hand, the harder tongue; finding her own refuge in the easy lie. And later, when she had been old enough to understand, it had been too late. Pity she had found for her mother, but no love — love had died of fear.

Wealth when it came had come too late for Andrew's wife. Set in that mould to which life had shaped her, unable to take her ease when ease had come, Mary Heriot had found rest only in the grave.

It was because of this that she, Ada Ware, would never willingly let her mind go back to childhood, would never talk to Heriot about her grandparents. Not through pride — as Heriot must think — but because the pain and the bitterness were all too near.

And Heriot, herself — how would she stand up to that sort of life? The life she would lead might not be so cruelly hard — but she had not her grandmother's training to hardship. Heriot had been bred soft. Sheerest of linen, lightest of wool, thickest of silk. Her hand had touched nothing heavier than featherbrush or clean duster. How would she cope with the cooking, the scrubbing, the mending — all those duties that fall to the lot of the one woman in a poor home.

A doll's house, my dear. . . a doll's house. . .

But Heriot was no doll. Her soft and cared-for body would bruise and scratch. Frost working upon cold water would cut her hands — Heriot's long fine hands — they would be cut and ditched with dirt.

And if her young body would suffer, what of Heriot herself, what of her mind, her soul?

She was suddenly wild to shake her husband from sleep, to urge him to rise, to do something, anything — anything at all! But — what could he do? He couldn't stop this marriage. . . but he might make it an easier sort of marriage, he might help them! It had been in her mind a long time now, that idea, pricking and worrying away; but she had been too hurt, too angry to deal with it. But — Heriot's wedding day was tomorrow, and it could be left no longer. If Heriot would not live with her husband in her parents' house, then John must make it possible for them to live decently in their own. He must make them a reasonable allowance, he could afford it.

But — the question was at her before she was aware of it — *could* he afford it? Was she so sure about that? John never spoke much about money, he was always generous. But — lately — hadn't he been just a little over-careful? For instance, when she'd been talking about replacing Rose by another housemaid, he'd asked, he, John, who never interfered with household affairs, whether one housemaid wouldn't be sufficient, since Heriot's marriage would leave the household smaller. When she had explained that a maid's work depended less upon the number of people in a house than upon the extent of her duties, and that if she added any of Rose's work to Edith's list, Edith, too, would rise up and go, he had said, *of course, of course!* But she had thought, even then, that he hadn't sounded wholly convinced.

And now, lying here, she wondered again, as she had wondered once or twice lately, whether John was worrying about money.

Nonsense, arrant nonsense! As if John Ware could bother about so paltry a thing as a housemaid's wages! She was letting her imagination run away with her, because she was distressed about Heriot's marriage.

Heriot's marriage. How often she had pictured it! St. Mary's; and outside the crowds, twist-hands and strangers waiting to see the Ware bride. And inside, the heavy scent of lilies, and the choirboys singing in their pure young voices. And the waiting people, handsome well-dressed people, people of wealth and worth, as became an alliance of Wares and Jebbs. And then, Heriot, shimmering in satin and pearls, her veil a rosy cloud behind her. . . your own wedding-veil with its great border of true-lovers' knots, blush-rose to flatter the pallor natural to a bride. . .

How it all came back to you! An American millionairess had wanted it copied, but papa, with the queer pride that went so oddly with his real humility, had refused. The veil had been designed for his daughter. It was hers and hers alone — his wedding gift. And although the dollar princess had begged and prayed and had offered the most fantastic price, he had still refused. Let her get it elsewhere — if she could!

Her wandering thoughts came sadly home. Tomorrow there would be no St. Mary's, no bridal satin and rosy veil, no cutting of an immense frosted cake. A quiet visit to the registry office; a neat travelling costume for the bride — not that Heriot would travel very far. And yet — how far?

Ada Ware felt angry and cheated. But more than anything she felt frightened, badly frightened, as she tossed restless in the warm soft bed.

Stella Wade had long given up trying to sleep. How could she sleep when every sly minute was taking Nicholas away? She would not let herself sleep if she could! She *had* to be awake to count the minutes before Nicholas was lost to her for ever.

She had tried to make herself believe that she didn't care, that she was well rid of Nicholas, tried and tried. Useless. . . useless. In spite of everything Nicholas had done or still might do, in spite of everything she herself had done, or still might do — he was Nicholas and she, Stella. . .

She lay there, unsleeping in the darkness, wounding herself with hopeless hope.

The enclosing walls of the attic room she shared with the other maid seemed to close in upon her, so that she could hardly breathe. If only she might fling off the bedclothes, throw wide the window, lean out into the moonlight and take great breaths of the cold air into her lungs! But she must lie still, quite still, lest moving hand or foot she touch the other woman. Surely, this was the last horror, to be so little free that you dare not put out hand or foot for fear of touching someone, someone strange to you, body and mind. . . two live people shut together in a dark tomb.

Yes, it was a tomb, this little black room. But she stretched out, unmoving, was not dead. She was alive. She was suffering as the dead do not suffer, for they have been laid to rest. She thought that she would be well content to be dead if she might sleep untormented by desire for Nicholas.

All these nights lying sleepless, sleeping and tormented! She had not slept properly since she had parted with the child. If only she could feel his warm little body, his kind little body curled against hers — then she might sleep!

She pressed her hands tight over her bosom to still the pain of the breasts that rose obedient to the thought of that little seeking mouth.

But to keep that little body warm she must work. And who would give her work with a young baby pulling at the breast? It was queer how she longed for the child! But she hadn't wanted him. She would have been glad if he had died — she had prayed, even, for him to die! But now there was nothing she wouldn't do for him — go through fire and water for him, fight for him, yes, fight Nicholas himself, if need be!

A clock struck below in the darkness of the house. She counted three solitary strokes.

It was morning — the very morning that Nicholas would marry Heriot Ware.

Stretched out in her narrow place, staring into the darkness, she tried to force her mind to accept the fact. But her mind refused it. Not passionately, not even in revolt, but quietly, simply.

Nicholas would never belong to Heriot Ware, never in this world. Nor in the next. Let him protest, let him struggle and strive and strain against the bond — still the bond held. Though she herself were willing to set him free, it was useless. The thing had passed beyond their willing. They two, could never be free of each other. Though she herself married, still she would belong to Nicholas — as he, in spite of Heriot Ware, would belong to Stella Wade. She might die. Or Nicholas might die. But that, even that would not be the end, for they would still be bound, one to the other. If she died, her spirit must always turn to him, drawn beyond its will to his presence; her spirit turning his thoughts towards her, shaping his dreams. . . and if Nicholas died, then he would come for her. . .

Would she be frightened of the ghost of Nicholas? Surely not. Nicholas dead could not harm her as the living Nicholas had done.

Nicholas and Stella — Stella and Nicholas. . . and there was nothing any of them could do about it, neither he, nor she, nor Heriot Ware.

Heriot Ware. Take life gently, or take it fighting, Nicholas's wife would never get happiness out of her marriage. Again Nicholas would play the cheat — taking all, giving nothing. Nothing? Heriot Ware nothing? She would lie beside him night after night. Her children would bear his name. . . But he would never turn to her with passion and take her because the love in him was too great to endure. And the children born of that feeble mating, how could they be strong and beautiful as the children of lovers? Heriot Ware — what could she ever have from Nicholas, that she, Stella, could not take, with a mere glancing of the eye, take?

Heriot Ware had security. One couldn't win that with a glancing of the eye. One had to force one's body down to work — and even then, maybe, not find security. But — being in a man's blood was better than being married in church — it outlasted security. Nicholas would come back. He would come back not because he wanted to, but because he had to. He would come back to take what he had to have!

Well, she had learned that lesson! *Take!* She loved Nicholas, but she would never be soft with him again. She had lost him that way once — she would not lose him twice! Back he would come, and she would show how well she had learned her lesson! Get what she could out of Nicholas, take and take again. She loved him. She had made him the free gift of her body. But Nicholas had taught her that the free gift is a worthless gift. A hard and hateful lesson. . . but still she had learned it. And learning it, she would hold Nicholas even more strongly. They would belong to each other for ever.

Stretched upon her narrow bed, sleepless in the darkness, tormented because of what this day must bring, Stella a little pitied Heriot Ware.

But Nicholas slept peacefully — smiling in his sleep.

Chapter 19

Stella opened the back door and shut it quickly. But Nicholas was quicker. It was a trick he had learned, to thrust his foot against the swiftly-closing door, a trick that would serve him all his life.

He looked at Stella standing there — lovely Stella with her bright curls and her bright mouth. The fool he had been to stay away so long — the fool! For a whole month he had known where to find her! For a whole month weighing this, weighing that, blinding himself! Telling himself that he would get Stella cheap for his mill since jobs were hard to come by these days — and for such as her, hardest of all!

But standing there and drinking her in, feeding on the sight of her passionate eyes, on the throbbing breasts his fingers had known, he understood that whether he got her cheap or whether he didn't, he wanted Stella. Heriot with her thin body and her prim and childish ways... He shrugged the thought of Heriot away. Stella was his. She was his woman. She was in his blood and he could never be free of her again!

He said, "Don't run away from me, Stella. I've been looking for you — looking everywhere!"

"You didn't have to look far. Thought I'd keep in cold storage, maybe, till you thought fit to take me out again!"

He thought her tongue had learned the trick of bitterness; thought, too, there was a carelessness in her speech, a slight coarseness, almost, that he had not noticed before.

She said tartly, "You'd best be going. You lost me my job, once, I won't have you lose it me again!"

It's Nicholas, Nicholas... If I put out my hand I can touch him, touch Nicholas.

"I came to offer you a job," he said.

"I don't want anything to do with you, nor your job!" Stella said. "And I'm not allowed visitors, neither! In case you don't know, I'm slavey, here!"

I've starved for the sight of him, wept myself blind to see him again... but the very sight of him drives me wild... smooth and prosperous, the very words that come from his mouth sleek and prosperous... a different language taking him away from me, away.

"Slavey! You! You weren't ever meant for a slavey, Stella, not you!"

"What else then?" Her hand went out in protest. He noticed how cracked and soiled it was, the fine skin chapped and raw. He could have wept over Stella's hands, though he had not wept at deeper wrong done to Stella. That had not touched his understanding, but her hands, her cracked and roughened hands, those he could understand. He was suddenly wild to get her away — not because he desired her, not even because she would prove cheap and useful, but only that she might cherish her spoiled hands back to their one-time beauty.

"Jobs aren't none too easy come by — specially for me! Let me tell you I didn't find it too easy to get this! And I'm risking it now gossiping with you! I've got more'n myself to think of — there's the child!"

She lost some of her brightness standing there and her secret out! The fool he had been to seek out Stella, to drag her back again into his life — there was no place for her any more! He had been lucky with Stella. She was the kind who asked favours of no-one. When she'd understood that he was in no position to help her, she'd gone away — shut her mouth and gone away! Lucky! He'd say so! Any other girl but Stella — and where would he be now? Slaving his guts out in some other chap's factory; Sunday afternoons pushing the go-cart. . . coming home to napkins steaming round the fire of their one room. . . trapped, caught, done for! But she was sensible and she had set him free. And now, fool that he was, he had dragged her back again into his life!

Of course, he had thought about her — often. . . dropping off to sleep unsatisfied because Heriot was not Stella; or seeing a woman who carried herself a little like Stella he had wondered whether it had ever been born, his child and Stella's. . . hoping it had not been born, but thinking, too, he would help Stella and the child. . . one day.

It was queer standing there, and knowing quite certainly, for the first time that he was a father. But there was no pleasure in the thought — only a foolish wonder that the thing had happened. . . and he did not know whether it was a boy or girl.

"Boy or girl?" He had the grace to be ashamed that at this late hour he had need to ask.

"Boy," she said quietly enough. And then, as if she could not trust herself but must still bully herself into anger against him, cried out, "But it's not your business, not any more. Go away and keep away!"

Release. Freedom once more handed to him — a gift! Without knowing fully what he said, but because he could not endure to be thrust out of her life, he answered, "I could make it my business — if you'd let me!" And when she made no answer, added humbly, "what's his name, Stella?"

At this unlooked-for humbling of Nicholas, she softened.

"Pen. That's what I call him, Pen!"

Pen! Pen? A warning of claim to come?

She stood there knowing his thoughts, despising him for his thoughts. . . Same old Nicholas. Even now he did not know her, did not understand that she would never have sought him out, never have made claim either for herself or for the child. If he wanted her, then he should pay for any favour he might receive. If not — then let him go his way and never trouble her again! If he did not know this without telling, then let him puzzle over the child's name, worry, suffer a little, just a little...

"Pen," she said again, her tongue caressing the sound.

...And he should never know, either, how ill and sick at heart she had sought to drive away loneliness with some friendly thing, and there had been nothing, nothing at all except a name — a mere suggestion of a name...

Her anger rose because he was selfish and stupid and ignorant.

She said, steadily, "A woman's well rid of you, Nicholas Penny!"

...But if you so much as crooked your little finger, I'd follow, I'd follow...

"I can't stand about here all day," she added sharply, fearful of her own weakness. "Goodbye — Nicholas!"

In spite of herself her voice softened on his name. He caught at her hand. Even while he held it, he thought, Let her go... for all of us, wiser... for Stella herself, wisest of all... But she is going... going...

He said, "You can't go like this! I've got to see you again!"

"Why?" she said, the softness gone from her.

"There's the boy!"

"The boy isn't your concern!"

"Isn't he, Stella? Isn't he?" *But I am mad, quite, quite mad.* "Not Pen, whose name is almost my own?"

She thought, why do I push away help for Pen? Is there so much kindness that I can afford to push it away? But... this is not kindness, there is no kindness in Nicholas... there is no help in him either for me or for Pen...

"Go away!" she cried. "Go *away*!" And made to thrust him off with her hands.

At the sight of those spoilt hands his last defence went down. He said, "I'm going, now, because you ask me to go. But I'm coming back. I'm coming back because there's too much between us to be left!"

She looked at him again. She thought, If I take him back now, I'll never be free of him again.

"When shall I see you, Stella? When shall you be free?"

Free... never again if I say yes, never again... She could not speak, could not think the words, even, that would set her free. And yet, facing him, seeing him, knowing him, she wanted to be free, wanted it terribly... but all the time, just as terribly, she knew she couldn't be free of Nicholas, couldn't even want to be free.

Her voice came out without her volition. It was, she thought, the voice of someone else, someone quiet and cold, and, as it might be, dying.

"Wednesday. Nine. The old place."

It was finished, finished for her! She had chosen. All the loneliness, all the hardship she had endured, wasted... all the new decent life she was trying to make for herself, wasted...

"You won't be sorry, Stella, I promise!"

She watched him swing away down the road... His promises! His easy, useless promises! She was crazy to listen to him, even for a moment to listen!

She took a running step forward. She wanted to call after him that she took back her word, that never, never would she see him again. Her mouth opened. But no sound came out. Her step slackened... *Pen whose name is so nearly my name. ...* A faint smile lifted the corners of her mouth.

Nicholas disappeared round the bend.

It was quiet down in the hollow. He could hear the brook in the darkness slipping over the pebbles, falling with a soft splash where the level suddenly altered. He could see the long bare branches of the alder falling dark against the pale water.

....Soon he would look up and see Stella moving towards him, coming towards him in the darkness, as she had done over and over again more than a year ago... But now he was married to Heriot Ware, and it was no longer right that Stella should come to him in the darkness. It was different now... but he didn't *feel* different. Here in the darkness it was as if the long year had not been. Surely it was only yesterday that Stella had come to him under the alders.

He moved impatiently.

Fool that he was! And liar as well as fool! He knew well enough that the year had been; that if it had brought dissatisfaction in his marriage-bed, it had also brought the golden hope of prosperity. Well, he had expected both — and his golden hope he wouldn't barter for an eternity of Stella.

Then by what right did he pace mad in the moonlight, because soon Stella would come? No right... no right at all except the remembered feel of Stella's breasts moving beneath his hand...

His hand made a half move outwards.

Stella was his woman.

But Heriot — Heriot was his wife...

He knew the half-impulse to run, to run as fast as he could, to leave this moon-drenched place that had belonged to Stella and himself — leave it to Stella alone. It was no longer his. He had lost his right... And when Stella came and found him not there! Why then she would set it down as one more unkindness — a little unkindness after so great an unkindness could hurt her no longer.

He heard the rustle of her cloak dragging upon the dewy grass. His heart was leaping in his throat. There was the oddest taste in his dry mouth. He felt the pulses hammering madly in his forehead, in his neck. He wanted to run across the grass to meet her, to draw her close into his arms.

He stood dumb and brutish, rooted to the ground.

She was coming nearer. . . nearer. She was standing there, standing before him. . . Stella.

He ached for her, his body ached. All these long months lacking Stella. How had he lived? How?

She struggled against him. She cried out fiercely to him. "Have done! Have done!" she cried again and again. And then, when he would not, "I'll have no more of your tricks!"

He still held her and she struck out at him, hitting him wildly across the mouth. His arms loosened, then fell to his sides.

They stood there, staring at each other.

It was odd, he thought, that he was not angry. Had any other in the whole world struck him, he would have had blood for the blood that trickled from his cut lip and down his chin.

Suddenly her face worked. He could see it twisting in the moonlight. He wanted to comfort her — Nicholas who had done her so much more hurt than this and never thought to give her comfort.

She put out a hand and touched his wounded lip. She spread her fingers in the moonlight, looking in wonder at the stain. She was crying quietly, heartbroken as a child. "I didn't mean to hurt you," she said. "Oh Nicky, I didn't!"

Their feet stood in the cold October dew. The cold moonlight was on their white faces. Nicholas, driven by his body's unease, said irritably, "We can't stand about here. Isn't there somewhere we can go?"

She said no word; she only went on staring at him out of her darkened eyes. Her moon-whitened hand slid into the dark pocket of her gown. Still unspeaking, she held it out, palm outwards. A key lay upon the palm. A shadow, in her dark gown, she went before him. A shadow he followed. Two dark shadows slinking in the moonlight.

They stood in the dark passageway of Ellen's cottage. It struck damp and chill. But neither of them noticed it. They were together — alone — and in a house. For the first time a roof sheltered them.

Stella trembled. She was shaking with cold, but more, much more, with the knowledge that no good could come of this. But most of all she shook because of the tremendous uprising of her desire for Nicholas.

She moved into the deserted scullery, her mind, unthinking, set upon his comfort. In the shadow of the copper she found a few sticks and some oddments of dampish paper. Only half aware, because of her body's clamour, she gathered them up in her dark skirts.

She knelt by the forlorn hearth. Dead cinders lay among the yellow ash. Her hands were patient with the damp wood. He watched her fingers moving in the moonlight. The moonlight made them whole again. He was glad of that — he was desolate because of her blemished hands.

A tongue of flame went up, flickering yellow in the dark room, throwing odd shapes upon the wall of such pieces of derelict furniture that Ellen had been forced to leave. One yellow flame, and then another. . .

The fine shape of her body, the rounded swell of her breasts stood out black against the yellow flame.

Physical unease rose in him like a tide.

Chapter 20

Stella stirred. She sat up abruptly lifting a white face towards the dead fire. Her fingers moved nervously over her disordered gown.

"It's late," she whispered, "awfully late! What's the time?" She held her breath awaiting his answer. Nicholas slanted his watch to the moonlight.

"Two o'clock!"

"Oh God," she breathed. "*God!*"

"Take it easy, Stella. It's not the end of the world!"

"For me it is! You don't understand. You never did!" Her voice rose.

"Stop that! No good shouting now! You wanted it as much as I did or it wouldn't have happened. Whatever you were when I first had you, you're no blessed innocent now! It's your fault as much as mine!"

"*Your* fault! *My* fault! Who cares? Who *cares*? It's happened — that's all that matters. And I'll do the paying!"

"You usen't to shout before you was hurt, Stella!"

"That's the only time you get anything, by shouting — I've learned that! Besides — things are different, now. I've got my responsibilities now. I've got Pen!"

"What about — Pen?" The child's name — had she brought it in as a threat? If she reckoned that way, she reckoned wrong!

"Don't play the fool, Nicholas! I've been out all night. It's goodbye to my job!"

He shrugged. "Plenty of other jobs!"

"Not for me. She'll turn me out without a character. Couldn't expect one, neither."

"To hell with your character! See here, Stella, don't get across me! Let's talk reasonable. Know why I came here tonight?"

"Clear, isn't it?" she said bitterly.

"Don't get across me, I said. I came here to offer you a job!"

"A job! You could have written — if it was decent. I don't want your sort of a job. I want a job where I can work honest and work regular — a decent job!"

"Please yourself! In that case I'll turn over and get a bit of sleep. It's a long time till morning!"

The broken springs whined beneath his shifting weight. She was on her knees beside him, shaking him fiercely.

"The job! Quick, Nicholas, the job!"

"You don't want my sort of job!"

"Don't drive me any more or by God I'll do you an injury! I mean it,

Nicky, I'm desperate!"

"All the more reason to keep a civil tongue! Damn cold in here!" He shivered, obviously dismissing her and her troubles.

"It's not a hotel!" she answered fiercely. "The job, Nicholas, the job."

He said, playing out his game, "A chap can't think in this ice-box!"

He got up, sulky in his turn, and went over to the fireplace. He knelt, cheeks grotesquely puffed, blowing upon the dead coal. Stella rose drearily, and rummaged in the empty scullery. She was half sick with anger and with fear. Her fingers slid along the dark and dusty floor, closed upon a few faggots left unnoticed in the hollow of the copper door. Unhopefully, she brought them back to the dead fire.

He judged the moment ripe.

"See here," he said. "You know about my mill — I expect Ellen told you about it! Well, I still need a couple of hands — folk that won't mind putting their backs into a job and aren't particular to an hour or so; folk that know when you start in on a new business, that's the way it goes. I've got to have folk who trust me and who I can trust..."

"Think you can trust Ellen? The only thing you can trust her with — as far as you're concerned — is a bottle of poison!"

"And that's why I'm offering you a job!" He ignored her remark. It was silly and it was spiteful and he wouldn't even give her the satisfaction of knowing that he was aware of her mean prick!

"Me? In your factory?" She stared at him. Was he stupid? Or clever — cleverer than a simple person like herself could guess?

"You're sure you can trust me, Nicholas? Why are you so sure?"

"Because my interests are your interests, that's why! If things go the way I want, I could help you a bit... I always wanted to help you, Stella!"

She moved impatiently. "I don't want to hear fancy-talk! What's the job and what's the wages?"

"Lace-mending. It's a good trade — skilled."

"*I'm* not skilled —

"You soon could be! Dainty hands you've got, Stella —"

"*Leave* fancy talk, I said!" She was fierce, snatching her spoiled hands from his sight.

"You'll grow like your auntie — if you don't watch out!" he grinned. "No, but serious, Stella, listen to me. You've done a sight of mending. Many's the time I've seen you. Used to pick up no end of job-lots, the old man. Didn't sell them as jobs, though, not when you'd been at them. When you'd finished, no-one could say where the flaw was! And what you don't know, you'd learn — you'd learn quick. There's a woman I've got now could learn you. A good trade, Stella. You needn't be beholden to anybody then. You'd be free, independent —"

"What do I get?" She ignored his rhapsody.

"Three ha'pence the hour."

She knelt there, staring up at him as though she had never really seen him before.

"You swine," she said softly, "oh you swine."

"Don't lose your temper," he said. "And don't show your ignorance, neither! Fifteen shillen the week — that's what a skilled hand gets! Now you — say you work twelve hours a day, and why not? Light work. Sitting all the time! There's many does a sight more — and glad to do it! You'd get nine shillen clear. Do a bit of a Sunday, and that makes, let's see, ten-and-six. Not much to grumble about there!"

"And how d'you think I can live *and* keep a child on ten-and-six? Sell my body? If they all pay as generous as what you did —"

"Shut up! Haven't you any shame talking that way?" The thought of Stella selling her body made him see red. "You shut up, I say, and listen to me! I'm treating you fair — more than fair. Besides, there's nothing to keep you from working more than twelve hour. What's twelve hour to a young woman like you? If you wanted to *work*, put your back into it, like I said, there's no end to what you could make — and you not even skilled. And what's more — look here — I'm an easy man, you can share Ellen's place, if you like, I wouldn't make any charge!"

"Thank you for nothing. You've got me where you want me — under your thumb!"

"Don't talk like that, Stella. It doesn't help and it's not even true!"

"Isn't it, though? Who helped me lose my job, knowing full well I'd not get another in a hurry!"

"That doesn't help — like I said. Why can't we be friends? Mine's a good offer, as you'd see for yourself — if you took the trouble to think about it. Listen." He was driven beyond caution by the misery in her face, "I'll give you a hand with the child. I don't admit any responsibility, mind! But because we've been — friends — and if you swear not to tell a soul, I'll give you two shillen every week towards his keep."

"I won't tell," she said. "I'd be ashamed for anyone to know I'd sunk so low. I wish I could throw your fine offer back in your face. But I can't. Pride, decent pride, costs more than what decent folk can afford!"

Your fine offer! She'd said that, scorning him and his offer together. . . two shillings trickling away from his profits, his hard-won profits! And if at first there were no profits, still two shillings. Even if he lost week by week, still two shillings. Every week, every single week. . . And fifty-two weeks in the year! Eight shillings a month! Five pounds the year! And how many five pounds had he got? With five pounds he could buy. . . Quick, let him get away before he repented of the offer she hadn't even the grace to accept decently. . .

Daylight was cold in the little room, cold about Ellen's bits of derelict furniture, about the blackened choked-up hearth, about those two standing there and hating each other.

He said, not looking at her, "It'll be full daylight soon. Goodbye, Stella. When the kid's old enough he can come into my mill."

"When d'you want him to start?" she asked mocking. And she could have killed him! "Eight? Or seven? Or maybe five? But I forgot — it's not allowed to start them that young, not any more! Rotten interfering law, isn't it! Greedy, lazy little Pen! Eating up your precious two shillings and no return!"

What in hell's name had got hold of Stella? Used to be so sweet, sweet and gentle. Now she couldn't open her mouth but she dropped gall! He said sulkily, "you don't give a chap credit for nothing! I was only thinking to help. I was thinking, Let him come into the mill when he's old enough. I was thinking he'd take his place there natural and I could help him."

"Your help!" She checked herself with violence. He could see the working of her full white throat as she forced back the word! She went over to the window and looked through the grimy glass. "Ay, it's morning all right!" she said drearily.

She swung the dark cloak about her shoulders and turned towards him. "It's all so simple to you, isn't it, Nicholas? Simple as that!" She snapped her fingers. "But it's not so simple for me!" She turned again to the window, staring out at the thin trees, paper shapes against the grey sky.

Simple, she thought, gritting her teeth over the nastiness to come, simple! Getting back and facing her. Swallowing all the insults she'll throw at me, taking them in silence so as maybe she'll let me take my clothes! Arranging about Pen, trying to borrow a bit of money to pay for him in advance, to show I won't run away. . .

She turned swiftly about. "What is it about you, Nicholas?" She came close, her dark eyes searching his face. "I don't understand. I don't understand — anything. You love me — in your way — I swear you do. But you're hard as nails and mean as Judas!"

"Easy as A.B.C. A man's got to have something in his pocket before he can take anything out!"

"A mean man's mean, even if everything he touches turns into gold. He'll be careful not to touch too much in case he sends the value of gold down!"

"Why don't you watch your tongue, Stella? It doesn't help — all this bitterness!"

Suddenly he was sick of Stella, sick of the bickering, of the unpleasantness. He said again, "No, it doesn't help. It might even hinder!"

She said, "Trying to threaten me? Because it won't work. I know you too well, Nicholas. You didn't leave your comforts on a night like this for nothing — no, not even," her voice was thin with contempt, "to take your pleasure out of me! You came for me like you came for Ellen — because you thought you could get something for nothing!"

"You're too clever by half! Where's your sense to take kindness for anything else? What d'you think I get out of Ellen, halfwit that she is! And what d'you think I get out of you that I couldn't get out of a dozen women?"

"Ellen — she can work. Mechanical — like a machine. And she doesn't cost what a machine costs. When you've finished with her you can throw her out. As for me —"

"As for you!" Suddenly he lost control of himself. "If yer don't want my help, then do wi'out it and be damned to yo'! An' if yer want it — take it and shut yer mouth. And what's more, I'll not have *Nicholas* on yor tongue — not when there's any to hear. It's not fitting and it's not —"

"Safe!" she mocked. "Thank you, Mr Penny, for taking your pleasure of me, just now!" and she dropped him a curtsey.

"Yo' devil!" he shouted. Quite suddenly, he smiled. "You *are* a devil," he said with a return to his more elegant manner, "but I like devils. There's no-one to touch you, Stella!"

She said wondering, "If you'd asked me to marry you — after the first, I'd 'a said *no*. I've got my pride. But I've got my curiosity, too. If you think all that of me, why didn't you want to marry me!"

"A man can't always do what he wants!"

"You can, Nicky! You always do. You always will. . . until something bigger than you comes along and says *no*! And then you'll crumple up, because of not knowing how to stand up to *no*. Funny —" a half-smile lifted the corners of her lips. "I came out tonight, hating you. Then I loved you. Then I sort of despised you. And now," she opened her hands and let them fall, "now I'm empty. I don't feel anything — anything at all!"

"You can't go on playing on top-note all the time. You'd be wore out. But you love me all the same. You *do* love me, Stella."

"What's that got to do with it? You're married. What we did last night — it was hateful. I'm ashamed. Because what you said was true — it was my fault as well as yours. It's no good asking you to believe I'm decent — not after the way we've been together. But listen to me — and believe me, for it's God's truth I'm speaking. I'm coming to work for you, because I need work, need it desperate. And I don't see where I'm to get any other. Work — that's all there'll be between us now. Everything else is finished. If I thought I'd come to you again — the way I did last night — the way animals do, I'd want to die. And yet — I know very well I wouldn't die. However much I'd want to die, I'd still go on living. . ."

"Nothing to get all that tragic about. Things'll be all right. You'll see!"

"Yes, I'll see. I'll see all right!" She was silent for a moment. Then she said very softly, "what's wrong with you, Nicholas, isn't that you're bad — not really bad. It's just that you're stupid. Your eyes don't see, your ears don't hear. You're for yourself only. That makes a man stupid, Nicholas!"

He could have struck her full in the middle of her white faintly-smiling face. She, ignorant alike in books and in the ways of men, with nothing but the fine body he'd taken and would take again when he wanted it, she, to stand there calling him stupid!

His teeth locked together in the effort for control; but he, too, was smiling a little. "Never you mind all that!" he said. "No need for further discussion!" He was consciously using his careful speech, emphasising that with sun-up, all was different — he was the master, and she, the meanest of his servants. But in spite of his care, the old Nicholas broke through. "Yo' tek care o' that tongue o' yourn," he said roughly, "or yo'll land in Queer Street!" The wicket gate slammed to.

Stella stood perfectly still in the empty cottage, hands hanging loose against her dark cloak. She thought, It didn't ought to have happened. I didn't ought to have let it happen. That first time. . . down by the brook, I didn't know. I didn't know anything. . . But this time. . .

Her glance moved towards the couch, so old, so broken, that Ellen had not found anyone willing to take it away for nothing. She thought, fit bed for a shabby love. . . She laughed a little at that, shivering in the cold room, pressing her knuckles against her mouth to stop the dreary noise. She thought, what will become of me? Of Pen?

Her soft mouth took on an ugly line. Don't worry, Pen, I won't fail you. He's stupid. It's God's truth. And I only just saw it. He's stupid and I'm clever. And things'll work out right. You'll see, Pen, you'll see.

Chapter 21

Heriot frowned a little, carrying the breakfast things into the scullery. Caught off her guard her face wore a dissatisfied look. It was not wistful — the chin was too firm, the mouth too strongly set — the face of a woman who is not satisfied and means to do something about it!

She thought, easing her tray so that its edges didn't scrape against the door-jamb, that the house was tiresomely small, and that as the days went by, it seemed to get smaller. It was almost as if, when you weren't looking, the walls crept slyly nearer.

Of course that was all nonsense. Naturally the house seemed smaller because it was getting more and more cluttered with things. Nicholas loved things. He had an almost childish love of piling up possessions — if only they cost enough. He admired the minute hall, though you couldn't move without brushing up against its plush portière or its jardinière and palm, or the bronze lady with the extremely low bodice and the tiny pinched waist and the short frilled petticoat smiling naughtily beneath the pink-frilled lampshade. As for vases, clocks, candlesticks, whatnots and knick-knacks that crowded every available niche, Nicholas declared that they were objects of art and he wouldn't part with one of them! So there they remained, cluttering the tiny rooms and trebling her work as she lifted this, lifted that, clearing this, that and the other out of her way before she could so much as begin.

She thought, sometimes, picking a careful way among the rubbish, that her own life was growing like the house — cluttered with cheap things. She had not married Nicholas to get a poor imitation of the life she had left. She wanted something different — real things to think about, real things to do. And Nicholas — most of all she wanted Nicholas.

Now, picking her careful way with the heavy tray, she thought, But Nicholas doesn't love me. He never did, I suppose — in a way — I've known that always. But, it doesn't make sense. Why did he marry me? Not for my beauty, certainly. Not for money — he knew I shouldn't get any! He's got a certain respect for me — but you don't marry a girl out of respect! Or — do you?

She put the laden tray down on a corner of the scullery table.

If I had to choose all over again, knowing Nicholas, knowing he doesn't love me, would I choose the same?

She began to unload the china onto the table.

Yes. Because I love him. And I don't believe you can go on loving a person as I love Nicholas, without that person coming to love you back again. . .

She poured the water from the kettle into the white enamelled basin and added soap and a knob of soda.

. . .Not true. Not true at all. No good being sentimental. Loving a man is no sort of guarantee that he'll love you in return! The world would be a different place if it were! Let's face it. Nicholas doesn't love me. But he does respect me. One could build on that — I suppose. . . a chilly sort of foundation!

Her fingers shrank from the cold wet dishcloth, but she seized it boldly.

Silver first. . . Nicholas. He's quite, quite different from what I used to think. It's been, in a way, rather like marrying a stranger and learning all about him. Eight months ago I knew nothing, really, about Nicholas, I only thought I knew. . . sweet, attractive, frank, kind and clever. . . I used to count up his virtues on my fingers.

Sweet? She watched the iridescent bubbles dissolve and break. Who but an ignorant creature like me would have labelled any man that? But he did encourage me to think it! He *has* a certain sweet ingenuousness — when it suits his purpose. . . A wiser woman might have been misled. . .

Attractive? She reached out for a greasy plate. Certainly attractive with his handsome face and his oh, so frank eyes! He deceives you deliberately with those eyes — he never means to let you know what he's thinking, he deceives you even more with that smile of his — he uses it as a mask to his secret thoughts.

Kind? She turned the plate upside down on the drainingboard. He has a certain careless-seeming kindness — only there's no carelessness about it. He makes use of it quite deliberately — sweets handed out to a child. But come up against Nicholas, want something that he doesn't want, disagree with him ever so slightly. . .

Her clear eyes clouded.

. . .then you learn something about Nicholas — the real Nicholas! Hard. Disagreeable. And more than disagreeable — cruel, downright cruel. . .

I've seen that once or twice and over the smallest things — so small, I could hardly believe it! That time he wanted me to call on Mrs Brain because she was a customer's wife, and I wouldn't. I didn't like the woman. I'd do a great deal for Nicholas, but there's a certain — integrity if you like — that one can't sacrifice. Besides — why should he mix business with his private life? Papa never did. . . After all, even if I'm not Heriot Ware any longer, I'm still papa's daughter!

How furious Nicholas was! His mouth set hard. . . that pleasant voice of his gone slipshod, common. He said. . . he said. . . I prefer not to remember what he said. I hated to see him like that! I nearly gave way... anything, anything to bring the old Nicholas back. But I remember how it came to me, standing there and looking at Nicholas, that if I did give way, the old Nicholas would never come back... I knew quite certainly that on this point I must never, never give way because I'd lose Nicholas. For what have I, after all, of Nicholas, but a certain respect?

She reached out for a greasy frying-pan, wondering a little helplessly what was the best way of dealing with it.

...If respect's all I'm going to get from Nicholas, I'll hang on to it like grim death!

She hung the imperfectly cleaned pan upon its hook and reached out for a scrubbing-brush. Attacking the kitchen table, she thought, It's hateful to have to plot and plan to grab every scrap of advantage. But there it is! If I'm not careful I'll be just another object in his home — and not an object of art, either!

She picked up a curl of bacon rind from the sink.

Doing maid's work and not doing it well — that's not the way to keep his respect... and when I've lost that, I've lost everything!

She picked up a broom, and stood leaning upon its handle.

...That first time we sat together and we talked up in the Long Gallery, it was. And I told him about Heriots and what it meant to me, and what I wanted to do for Heriots, one day. And he let me go on talking, and all the time he nodded as if he agreed — and all the time he was thinking his own thoughts, thoughts he wouldn't let me reach.

And then we used to meet by the machines, time after time by the machines... And I thought he understood my passion for the machines... but he didn't care, he didn't care. And afterwards, when I knew there would never be any place for us at Heriots, I still thought, *Nicholas and I working together... working for Pennys*. And I thought. how it was more exciting, more satisfying, really. I thought, Pennys starts small. Pennys will grow and grow like Heriots... Pennys with the machines going, filling the air with their grand noise...

She was suddenly wild to hear the voice of the machines, to smell the heavy exciting smell of oil.

The broom fell from her hands, measured its length across the floor. She left it where it fell. She was upstairs, pulling on her jacket, her hat, snatching up her gloves.

She was hurrying down Scarrington Drive, hurrying through The Park, short-cutting through the new, as yet unnamed boulevard, half running, wholly panting on her way to the station. Running, actually running, long skirt lifted high; she had not the faintest notion how the trains went. She only knew that somehow a train would be there and she must catch it.

...Pennys. Noise of the machines. Warm thick smell of oil. Bustle and movement — purposeful movement. She needed these things as she needed air.

She ran as she had never run — even for Nicholas.

The mean and dingy street struggling down to Pennys mill, wore, she thought, an adventurous look. Even the poor bleached grass on which the mill stood, took on something of colour, as if among its dried-up roots, new life might even now be stirring. She stopped short, staring at Pennys. She saw it with her father's eyes, comparing it with Heriots, knowing it small and poor, of no importance; then seeing it with the eyes of Nicholas, she knew it dynamic, of immense importance, holding within itself the power and will to grow, rich with the promise of untold possibility.

She thought standing there, standing outside, I'd like to help. I'd keep books, mend lace, wind bobbins, nothing I'd be too proud to do, if Nicholas would let me.

She picked her careful way down the narrow dark stairs.

Standing in the doorless doorway, she wondered for a nightmare moment whether she had wandered into a dream.

One, two, three, four, five, six machines. She counted them again. Yes, there were actually six machines clattering away in the yellow gaslight. And the basement room itself... an entire wall had been removed. The great room stretched out over the yard and into the levelled field beyond.

The smell of oil was hot and thick, drawn upwards in the gaslit room.

Nicholas had done this! Nicholas had extended his premises, he had levelled the field to take the length of the new room, he had bought four new machines. Four new machines — and she had not known, she whose heart was set upon machines.

Why had she not known? Was it because struggling with the unfamiliar, the tiring duties of her house, she had heard, unhearing? Had Nicholas spoken and her dulled mind remained shut? If that were so she pitied Nicholas. She did not deserve his respect, even, let alone his love!

But it was impossible, quite impossible! Nicholas talk of machines, and she not hear! It must be that Nicholas had not seen fit to mention them — he did not set great store by the opinions of women, no, not even when he respected them.

Whichever way it had happened, she felt a pang of loss that Nicholas had done this big thing and she had not shared, had not even known. She put her regret on one side. She was here now, and she would make the most of it!

There were a couple of men and a little old woman, all intent upon the machines. They had looked up at her entry, and then had gone on with their work, as though they had not time, even, to tell her that she intruded and must go away. Nicholas, she thought, had them well in hand!

She would have liked to come right into the room, to linger by the machines watching the swift play of the bobbins, to ask questions about these newest machines. What width of lace did they turn out? How long did it take to change over from broad to narrow? How many racks per week could one make on them?

But this was an unwelcoming room. The little old woman crouched in upon herself, chin out-thrust, sharp nose out-thrust, intent upon stacking empty bobbins, seemed to embody the spirit of the place. Her absorption, intense, almost bitter, warned you that this was no place for idlers.

Heriot stood there, trying to hold her ground, trying to smile as she used to do at Heriots, to show her friendliness. Her smile broke against their blankness.

She turned away.

She had not meant to go. But still she went, driven by their will.

She went slowly up the dark staircase; the summer sunshine did not reach it and the glimmer of gaslight did little more than reveal the dirt and fluff upon the treads.

She pushed open a door on the first landing and found herself looking into a largish room. It had obviously been the drawing-room of the house, but the folding doors had been removed. The room was darkish, for the windows at each far end did not admit much light.

Close up against one of these windows, a band of dusty light streaming in upon her bent head, a woman sat bowed over a cloud of lace.

The first thing Heriot noticed was the woman's hair, titian red in the sunlight. Lovely, vital hair, running into bubbles of curls. The next thing that struck her was the expression on the face when, for a brief second, the woman had lifted it from her work.

. . .Unfriendliness. Quickly hidden beneath blankness. *But you can't hide it, not with those eyes!*

Heriot thought, but why should this stranger be unfriendly? It was she, herself, who was unfriendly. Because she had come here uninvited, because at the back of her mind lay the thought that Nicholas didn't want her here, she was ready to fancy everyone and everything unfriendly!

She was ready to be ashamed of herself.

Heriot came right into the room. The young woman went on with her work and made no sign, not so much as the lifting of the eyes.

. . .But this isn't natural. She must guess who I am! You'd think curiosity alone would make her *do* something. . .

She knew now that it had not been fancy with her — that both the old woman in the basement and the young one in the sunlight, hated her.

She tried to shake off the unpleasant knowledge, advancing with hand outstretched, knowing her friendliness already rejected. She wanted to talk to the young woman, to compliment her upon her obvious skill, but the words dried on her tongue. She was an intruder — and they meant her to know it, meant her to know that she was disliked, distrusted, unwanted. . .

She stood staring down at the lace-mender, feeling surprisingly like crying. How pretty the girl was — and how tired! She was lovely and pitiful, with the full red lips brilliant in her white face, and those dark-ringed eyes.

Slowly, against her will, the lace-mender raised her head and stared at Heriot. There they were, the two of them, stiff with distrust, when Nicholas came in through the open door.

He was not pleased to see her. She knew that because of the switched-on quality of his smile; it had an intensified charm that warned her. She was beginning to learn Nicholas, to recognise each mood, to gauge its quality by the register of his smile.

He took an arm possessively, introducing to her the handsome, haggard woman. "Mrs Wade —" and the smile dazzled more than ever, "queen of lace-menders!"

Mrs Wade barely uttered *good morning*. The sombre eyes were down again upon her work.

Of course her manner's odd, thought Heriot. Her arm still held by Nicholas, she found herself being led from the room. And all the time she felt the Wade woman's unfriendliness going with her.

Picking her way up another steep and dirty flight, she thought she would like to ask Nicholas about the woman. Was she always so unfriendly? And so unhappy? Did Nicholas know why? Was there anything one could do to help? At Heriots one had always helped. . .

But this is not Heriots. . . This is Pennys. She guessed the answer. Besides — she had, she found, the strangest reluctance to asking about the woman.

She followed Nicholas into another large room — three attics thrown into one, with a great north window added. The sunshine poured in across the drawings on Nicholas's desk.

Hanging over the drawings, she forgot, for a moment, the woman downstairs. The designs delighted her. Granddaughter of Andrew Heriot, she recognised a piquant freshness spicing their traditional design.

"Nicholas," she said. "Oh Nicholas!"

"Like them?"

"*Like them?* They're lovely. Who's your designer?"

He bowed with mock humility, one dark lock romantically fallen.

"They're lovely!" she said again." Oh Nicholas, you're clever, you're awfully clever!"

"Seems like I haven't sweated in vain. Of course, I've a natural gift to start with!"

She picked up another. "Oh Nicholas!" She was smiling over a pattern of picotees, their grouping traditional, their demureness all their own.

"Got that idea from that picture of yours — that bit of old French manuscript. . ."

"It's lovely. So fresh!" Her heart was singing because it was from her that the inspiration had come. She remembered showing it to him thinking how charmingly it might be adapted. He had barely glanced at it — so she had thought. She had forgotten all about it, but not he, not he! But he had come back to it, he had turned it to fresh beauty.

"A good seller, I should say!" Heriot said.

He shrugged. "Can't put it on the market. Not yet. Can't afford the risk. The trade looks to Nottingham for its novelties and its fine work, and to Long Eaton for same old patterns done cheap. It pays, too! Still," he began to gather up the drawings. "Give me time! Pennys designs. Everyone'll know 'em, everyone'll want 'em. A little time, a little money — and then you'll see! You can't keep a good man down!"

She felt her pride warm in Nicholas. Wrong she might have been believing him kind and frank, but believing him clever — there at least she had made no mistake.

She handed him the drawing she held as though she hated to part with it. "Oh Nicholas," she said, foolish with pleasure, "I didn't know you *could!*"

"Lots of things you don't know!" He said it lightly, bantering; but some of the sunshine went out of the morning. Her thoughts flew back to the new machines, to the handsome unfriendly woman downstairs. She looked half-heartedly at her watch, expressing surprise at a morning flown. He made no attempt to keep her, did not even offer luncheon, explaining that there was no place fit. He took her downstairs, a hand solicitous upon her elbow. The stairs were steep and dark; the guiding hand, natural. But she could not escape the thought that he was making sure that she actually did depart.

He stood at the front door, smiling his farewell. Walking down the long and narrow road, she looked back once. There he stood, guarding Pennys against all intruders.

Pacing up and down the little station, awaiting the slow arrival of the train, she was conscious of depression; she struggled against it, but the depression remained.

The new boulevard, her best way home, stretched away past the Castle Rock. She walked slowly where so short a time ago she had run. Was the day sunless? Was it grey? It matched her mood, anyhow!

Suddenly she felt she could not face the little house — not yet those tiny rooms with their vulgar jumble of meaningless things, not yet.

She took a short cut up the steep and narrow road that climbed towards the castle gates.

Meeting-place of lovers once... But he didn't love me. Even then he didn't love me.

The gay lawns, the great flower-beds in brilliant carpet-patterns, mocked her.

...Here we sat... and here. Here we leaned looking down to a world remote... but he didn't love me... he didn't love me.

She got up from her bench and followed the path round to the front entrance. Through the dim hall and down the shallow steps into the great basement, where the old machines stood, silent, useless. Looking at the wheels that would run no more, she felt the strangest sense of kinship.

Useless... useless...

A passion of rebellion seized her. In their time they had been used. They had served their turn. Now they were old and worn with service, they rested. It was right they should rest. But she — she was young and strong, she was unused. But she was useless... useless. She served no purpose.

Now that the machines reminded her of her uselessness, she could not endure to look at them.

Hastening away up the stone staircase, she stood for a moment, rooted to her step, her gaze averted... She would not look, she would not! For the dark eyes of the Magdalene in the picture, the full red lips, the pale face set about in reddish curls, reminded her... reminded her...

Oh, nothing at all! thought Heriot Penny decidedly, and head high, descended the portico steps.

Chapter 22

Dull dishevelled hair — and no wonder! In the morning so many jobs clamouring to be done! And at night one was so tired — tired to the bone! One's arms refused... Had there been a time when you had so little to do that you could just sit in front of a mirror and brush your hair — for so long as a quarter of an hour, sit quietly and brush? Had there really been a time when — if you didn't feel like exerting yourself, Edith would come, or Violet, and do it for you? Sitting in front of the mirror and watching the silver brush rise and fall with long sweeping movements, and feeling the pleasant tingling stirring the roots of your hair, and watching the gloss come up as bright as the polished silver...

Heriot staring into the looking-glass did not at all like what she saw there. She spread her fingers fanwise, bending towards the mirror.

...Dreadful hands. So dreadful that she had pleaded a violent cold to escape mamma's whist-drive. She simply could not have gone! When one picked up one's cards, when one held them fanwise, everyone would see her hands, they would all see...

She was desolate about her hands. Nicholas had admired them — once.

"It won't do!" she informed herself in her high authoritative voice. "It will not do!"

"It certainly will not!" Startled, she faced her mother in the mirror.

"The party?" Heriot faltered.

"Over long ago!" Ada Ware plumped down onto the bed, not minding how she crumpled the white coverlet... Only a rich woman can do that, Heriot thought wearily, I'll have to iron it again...

"Don't you know the time?" Ada asked sharply. "It's gone seven!"

"Late as that?" Heriot was disturbed that mamma should see no sign of a cold. She took out her handkerchief.

"You can put that thing away!" Ada Ware was not one to beat about any bush. "Now — why didn't you come to my whist-drive?"

Without a word Heriot held out her hands.

"Dreadful!" Ada said. "Quite dreadful! And so is the rest of you! Wispy, untidy... the only thing one can say for you is that you're clean!"

Wispy... untidy... barely clean! It was true. Those things true about Heriot Ware! Pretty she was not — she remembered that every time she looked in Nicholas's eyes. But carefully dressed she always had been, spruce, stylish — and maybe that would hold Nicholas longer than mere prettiness.

"I expect I have been a bit careless —" she faltered.

"Careless! Careless!" Ada Ware's voice was acid. "Don't flatter yourself, Heriot! It's worse than that, far worse. *Mary Heriot bent over the steaming copper, Mary Heriot crouched scrubbing the cold stone floor...* You've been stupid, criminally stupid! You are allowing the hateful drudgery of the house to steal away your rights — your rights as a woman — more important, believe me, than the rights those foolish women are clamouring for!"

Heriot said lightly, though her eyes were troubled, "It isn't the actual work — there isn't so much of it, really. It's just that I'm not clever at it. But I'll learn, I'll manage."

Worn and bitter of tongue, Mary Heriot coughing her heart away...

"Manage! You can't afford to manage! You're no beauty, my dear! You can't afford to drag yourself down to the level of the working-man's wife! Your husband has no respect for the working-woman!"

Heriot stared. This from mamma whom she had thought stupid! Mamma had flown unerring to the heart of the matter. Nicholas *had* no respect for the really poor — he had seen too much of them! He didn't appreciate the heroism of the working-woman. He'd swap the seven virtues for a smart shoe or a chic hat!

Ada said quietly, "He's got an odd sort of respect for you — don't look so surprised, my dear! Of course he's never said so — he'd die rather than admit it, but it's there! It comes out in the sort of thing he says — if you listen — and I do listen, Heriot. I listen for anything that might help you!"

"Help!" Heriot said a little proudly, but a movement of the hand betrayed her.

"I said help. And I mean help! You took on a hard job when you married Nicholas Penny. I warned you — but you didn't listen. Well, crying over spilt milk never helped anyone — though it's sometimes useful to analyse it! What you've got to do now is to tackle that job and make as good a thing as you can out of it!"

"I don't know what you mean," Heriot said. "Nicholas and I —"

"*Don't* tell me how you love each other! The love is all on one side and well you know it! I'm here to help you see straight — not to blind you with fine phrases. Respect — it's the only hold you've got on that husband of yours — and that won't last long if you go on the way you are going! And God help the wife your husband despises! Respect — you've got to build on that! And you're going to start by getting a maid!"

A maid... could one's happiness depend upon so little a thing, so outside a thing? Heriot, a little obstinate, said, "We can't afford it!"

"You can afford it, perfectly well! It's just that your husband drains every farthing away into that mill of his! That's a mistake, Heriot, the most expensive mistake a man can make. I've seen it and I know!"

Heriot thought, She's right. But Nicholas will make a fuss, I know he will. Well, I'll just have to be clever. She thought, surprised, Everything I want I'll have to be clever about — cleverer than Nicholas! And then a thought even more surprising, *Is* Nicholas clever?"

She turned to Ada with the question.

"Clever? I don't know — I don't know! He's got what I should call a single-track mind. Shrewd rather than clever, I'd say! He knows what he wants — and every act, every thought, goes into the job of getting it. He means to get on, that husband of yours. And get on he will! He started with two machines — how many has he got now?"

"Six. Six of the newest and biggest! You never saw such beauties!"

Ada waved this enthusiasm aside. "He started with three hands — and now?"

"A dozen — working double shift!"

Ada nodded. "Nothing your husband does in business will ever be wrong — from a business point of view! Ten years — five perhaps — there'll be nothing you can't have. Everything yours for the asking — except, maybe, what you want most!"

. . .*But it'll be too late then. Too late!* She heard the thought scurry round and round the emptiness of her mind.

"You've got to be clever for both of you!" Ada said. "Because your husband isn't clever at the thing that really matters — he's not clever at the business of *living*. . . and he needs to live, and live fully! Money, success — those things will never really satisfy him. In his way" — and her tone was grudging — "he's too big. Power — that's what he needs, and that's what he's got to have! Give him power and some greatness may come with it. Without power, he'll sink to mere bullying. Power to direct, to command the lives of others, dignities, honours — all those things he needs as he needs air. And he isn't clever enough to get them by himself. When he leaves the path he knows — business — he'll fall and hurt himself."

Heriot rejected the notion of Nicholas fallen, hurt, ridiculous.

"That's where you come in, my dear! It's for you to look ahead, to see the difficulties, to move them, to get round them, to make the way smooth. It seems a lot — but it isn't so bad when you get used to the idea. I've been doing it all my life!"

Ada Ware rose — and the room seemed smaller for her rising. "I must be going," she said evenly, just as though she had not sent Heriot's world trembling about her ears. "Your father does not like to be kept from his dinner! You need not come down with me, I shall not lose my way!"

Her tone said all that need be said about Heriot's house. The very staircase seemed to shrink with her passing.

Heriot came back to her chair by the mirror and took her chin in her hands. . . So that's where I come in! Not among the machines. But here — in this house, looking ahead, moving difficulties, making the path smooth. . . Does Nicholas, I wonder, realise his limitations, ever so dimly realise them?

She smiled to herself in the mirror. Not Nicholas. There's nothing he couldn't do, nothing he couldn't be — so he thinks! But — suppose deep down inside him, so deep down that he can't really be sure, mightn't he suspect that maybe he isn't such a fine fellow after all? Mightn't that be the secret of his rather noisy ways. . . and perhaps the secret of his respect for me, too. . .?

She went over to the bed and twitched off the white coverlet.

What Nicholas needs from me, I can give him. It's little! And yet, in a way, it's a lot, too! Life isn't what you want it to be — it's what you *make* it be! Here am I, not a year married, and I find my husband doesn't love me and never did. But I don't dissolve in tears. Don't even tell myself life isn't worth living. Because it is! Very much so! I agree with Grandpapa Heriot — life's more exciting when you've got to fight!

On his new safety bicycle, Nicholas pushed gloomily homewards. He looked well on a bicycle — knickerbockers suited his well-turned leg; and besides a bicycle conferred a certain social air. But it was damn tiring! All very well to pretend he liked exercise — he did, when there wasn't a day's work behind him! But what man in his senses would cycle all the way to Long Eaton, put in enough work for three, and then cycle all the way back again? In spite of that air of being a gentleman-at-large he'd take the train — if he could afford it!

Money. Always one was hampered by lack of money! The mill was going well enough — but he needed more room, more machines, more men. . . more money! Pennys all set for prosperity — and held back by lack of money!

Turning down Scarrington Drive he looked about him with contempt. . . .All the little front windows, all the little front doors exactly alike! Strange to think that so short a time ago the road had pleased him by its newness, its air of gentility. After the back bedroom looking out onto Preen's yard, it had seemed luxury indeed. How ridiculous he had considered the Wares' objection to the house. Well — one lived and learned — and it didn't take long to learn!

Money. If he knew where to put his hand on it! If he knew! Maybe another heart-to-heart talk with his bank-manager? Here he was at his wits' end, and there was Stella — damn her — acting as though he were made of money! Some folk didn't know when they were well off! Giving her two shillen a week, he was, regular as clockwork. And she earning as much as twelve herself! And no rent to pay, neither! But still she wasn't satisfied. Wanted a place of her own! Could you beat that? Stella who was dependent upon his goodwill for the very bread she ate, Stella having the sauce to make demands!

"I'm sick of sharing that filthy hole with Ellen," she said, her voice quiet, but hard with bitterness. "I'm sick of being without Pen, And I'm sickest of all of the hole-and-corner way us two go on! I'm sick to death of creeping out to meet you in some godforsaken spot, sick of looking round to see no-one's coming, sick of stuffing the old woman up with lies the next morning. But I'm done with all that! Finished!"

And while he was wondering what had so suddenly changed Stella, she herself had provided the answer.

"It's been in my mind a long time, now! It isn't that I don't care about you any more, Nicholas. I do. I suppose I will till I die. Only — I've never been happy with you — that way — not since that night you came back. . . that night in Ellen's cottage — remember? And then — it was seeing your wife just about finished it! Before then she wasn't a real person to me. I expect I wasn't thinking clear. Anyhow, it didn't seem like sharing. And then I saw her. . . she's a real person, Nicholas. . . and I don't share you with any woman any longer! But — I've got my rights same as she has! I never asked much and I don't ask much now! A place of my own. That's what I want and that's what I ought to 'a had long ago. A place where I can have my own child along o' me, and let him know he's got a mother — even if he hasn't got a father!" And then she'd looked at him with those big eyes of hers, very steady. And she'd said, "You've got to give it to me, Nicholas!"

"Blackmail?" The word had frightened his heart before ever it reached his tongue. He'd spoken quiet and smiling, though he was filled with black anger against her.

But she'd not been ashamed, not she! Nothing could shame Stella when her blood was up!

"Call it what you like," she'd said, and she was smiling too! Actually the nerve to smile! And then, quite suddenly, she'd stopped smiling. "If you weren't so mean," she'd said, "I wouldn't ever have had to ask. You'd 'a done it of your own free will long and long ago!"

And when he'd asked her, not hiding his disgust at this shameless blackmail, just what it was she wanted, the answer had come pat.

"What do I want? I might say I wanted a lot of things — a house like your wife's, for instance, with a gas-cooker and a tiled kitchen and hot and cold. . . But it's no good crying for the moon however low she hangs! So I'll just say I want a place of my own, ne'er mind how small! Two rooms'd do. But they've got to be decent. They've got to be where a child won't have to take in foul air, no, nor foul words, neither! And you've got to put in a bit o' furniture an' all! That's what I want, and that's what I'm going to have!"

And it had been clear by the squaring of her chin that she'd meant it — every word! And all this at the moment when he hadn't a bob to spare! Here was he cycling all the way there and back from business because he hadn't the brass to spare, and here was she shrieking for rooms full of furniture! Couldn't she understand, damn her, that every shilling went to feed Pennys? Hadn't she the patience to wait a bit? Women were greedy — all agog to kill the goose for the sake of one golden egg. If Stella were not such a damn fine worker, he'd put her out in no time. . .

He almost believed it as he pedalled along.

He wheeled his bicycle round to the back. Though the kitchen door stood open, he came round again and let himself in through the front. No back doors for Nicholas Penny — not ever again.

The lavish furnishing of the tiny hall pleased him. What if it was a bit crowded — it was crowded with things that cost money! His house might look the same as everybody else's outside, but you come inside and he'd show you something very different. This portière, now, serge in every other house, or maybe bamboo and beads, but this — He enjoyed the feel of costly plush beneath his hand; he stroked it as he might have stroked a woman's soft hair — Stella's hair.

Heriot came from the kitchen at the end of the passage. She wore a long white pinafore, but her hair was elaborately dressed; its high coils of pale gold shone under the gaslight. She took off her pinafore and he saw that she was wearing a tea-gown lavishly looped with ribbons.

"Visitors?" he asked, half-pleased, half-vexed at such extravagance.

She offered her cheek. The texture of her skin was pleasant, fresh, he thought, and innocent of device — like herself.

"No. Why?" She was nice when she smiled. But — she wasn't pretty — and never would be! He found it difficult to reconcile himself to the fact that he had married a not-pretty woman.

"I don't know!" Not for worlds would he confess that he considered her too fine for himself alone.

She smiled again, knowing his thoughts and pleased that she found him so simple to understand.

The table was elaborately set, rich with satin damask, glittering with silver and cut glass; scarlet carnations nodded in the épergne from a nest of feathery green.

He was dying to ask her why this sudden alteration in their humble ménage — but he would die rather than ask. Nothing was too fine for Nicholas Penny!

"I'll have a bit of a tidy!" was all he said.

"Do! I'll go and dish up." She heard him upstairs in the bedroom. That was the water jug set down. . . that was the clink of the ewer on the marble. Washing under the bathroom tap didn't go with carnations and cut glass! She smiled to herself! She smiled still more as she dished-up. It was a very badly cooked dinner. Even Heriot in the earliest days of their marriage had never cooked worse. But she smiled serenely upon the hard and burnt potatoes, the watery cabbage, the dried and leathery meat.

In spite of his handsome table, Nicholas ate gloomily. A day's grind — grind so hard that he didn't even stop for a midday meal, but snatched a sandwich as he worked — and then, to come to this!

Heriot looked at him over the nidding-nodding carnations, her eyes young and round. She said, faltering, "I'm sorry, Nicholas, I'm very sorry!"

He thought, proud, even while irritated by her incompetence, poor kid, she does her best! Mustn't forget she does all the work of the house without complaining — in spite of the grand way she's been brought up. Many women, who haven't been brought up to luxury, the way she has, would demand a good deal more than she does — if only to make their value felt. But she, poor kid, not only does she work without complaining, but she tries to keep up to the standard set by her father's house. . .

He was sorry for Heriot sitting there in her fine gown and doing her best. And her best so poor!

Heriot rose and shook out her silken lap. "Let's go into the drawing-room. I've got a fire there!"

Bit wasteful, he thought. One fire in the house was enough — two, if you counted the kitchen! Besides — a chap wanted to put his feet up and have a smoke!

"I was thinking of having a bit of a smoke," he said, remembering the Ware code of manners.

"Smoke in the drawing-room then." She picked up his pipe from the mantelpiece and held it in her slender hand. "Do come!" she coaxed. "I know you can't bear to look at these dirty plates a minute longer!"

It was cold in the drawing-room. From the black grate sulky coal sent out sulphurous fumes. "I'm not very clever at fires — yet!" Heriot said regretfully, "but I've got all the winter to learn in!"

All winter! And did she propose to spend night after night in this cold and smoke-filled room?

Heriot leaned back in a yellow satin chair and swung a beaded shoe. Filling his pipe, he thought that she had a lovely foot. If he had to choose a woman by her foot — say they were hidden behind screens and only their feet sticking out — why then he'd choose Heriot. She had the perfect foot of the perfect lady — even Stella couldn't hold a candle to her!

"I've been thinking," Heriot said cheerfully, "that we've been getting rather careless. Me, I mean! Having a lot to do — sweeping, dusting, washing-up, cleaning —" she gave him the whole catalogue, "doesn't excuse a person for getting slack. After all, there *is* a certain standard, and one ought to keep it up. And we have been pigging it rather — like sitting on in the dining-room after a meal, because I'm too tired to light a fire. Well, there isn't going to be any more of that! You're going to have a decently-run house, I owe it to you! And this *is* a lot nicer, don't you think?"

She shivered in her silk gown. Herself she desired nothing pleasanter than to sit by the fire in the warm dining-room, in a thick frock, her back comfortably turned to the littered table.

"You know," she went on sweetly, "living the rather careless way we have, isn't good enough — it isn't fair to you, Nicholas! You work so hard all day long and when you come home you're entitled to a little comfort."

Her tone postulated that he was, and always had been, used to the elegancies of life.

"But —" he was bewildered, though gratified, "won't that be a lot of work for you?"

"I'll manage!" Heriot promised bravely.

And manage she did! Day after day, a little more weary, a little more pathetic, valiantly keeping up to the standard she had set herself. Heriot "managing". While in a house daily more dusty, more untidy, Nicholas, irritable with the pangs of indigestion, besought her to find help. Heriot, patient, and oh so grateful, shook her head. She knew how very careful they had to be! He was not to worry. She'd manage! She was so plucky, with just the tiniest quivering of the underlip to betray her pluck — till Nicholas in a rage at this obstinacy in the most unselfish of women, flung out of the house.

He took himself round to the Wares' house. He visited them as little as his diplomacy allowed — but this was, after all, women's business. Let Ada Ware settle this affair.

And settle it she did! He never stopped to consider, clever Nicholas, that no sooner had he poured his annoyance into Ada Ware's ear, he should be informed that without a doubt he was right, and that she could put her hand on the very girl for whom they sought — a good plain general servant, and own sister to Sarah, her kitchenmaid.

It was pleasant to go straight back home and inform Heriot that he, a man weighted with his own affairs, had yet found time to settle her domestic problems. While she so childishly refused to consider a maid, he had been up and busy — and the new girl was coming in on Thursday.

Very curious. And very fortunate. Very fortunate indeed!

Book 2

Chapter 23

Five years. Five years of planning, of grim and concentrated work. Five years of growth, of prosperity — Pennys forging ahead, its name assured — a force to reckon with.

Five hands, twenty, thirty, forty, fifty, a hundred hands, two hundred — yes, two hundred hands, working double shift to turn out Penny Lace.

Clean patterns. Quality yarns. And a reputation for value. No wonder Pennys could not turn out their stuff fast enough!

Keen value. Nicholas could afford to smile — now; though even now his smile was grim, remembering those early years. He had sold always on the very closest margin of profit — and often enough with no profit at all. The price of his lace had been a wonder and a marvel — and he himself the best-hated man in the trade. From Derby, from Heanor, from Beeston and from Nottingham they had come, trying to spy out his secret; they had bribed his hands, trying to get at the secret. But the secret was so simple, so entirely not a secret, that though it lay under their very noses, they never saw it.

The truth was that he had sold at so low a price by drawing upon his small resources, drawing upon them again and again; and those gone, he had piled up an ever-increasing overdraft to the limit of his bank's patience — and the manager, a man of insight, had been very patient indeed. Often enough, towards the end of the week, Nicholas had not had the price of a meal upon him. He had known what it was to sit resplendent in his office — the master — his belly crying out for a square meal! But who was to guess that, looking at his hand-made boots, and the good stuff of his well-cut clothes? He had thought, in those days, that his mill was like a bubble, handsome and shining, but that the merest breath would shatter it to nothingness. And how easily that breath, the breath of rumour, might have breathed upon his fortunes!

But he had gone on taking the risk. At the end of the week he had been satisfied to thrust a hand into an empty pocket — and wait for the next week. He had been glad enough of his bicycle those days. A man ought to get all the fresh air he could — he had said that so often his soul sickened at the mere sound of the words. For in fog and snow and driving rain, still he must seek fresh air — he would have been hard put to it, at times, to find the price of his railway ticket.

But no one had guessed — ever. Certainly not the Wares, when he appeared, elegant, in their Sunday drawing-room; certainly not those men he met in the way of business — a cigar, or a brandy-and-soda was never lacking — if they were worth it; those were business expenses. Only, perhaps Heriot, brows drawn over the housekeeping accounts, wondered why Nicholas was not always prompt with the money. But even she did not wonder very long, for if not this week, then certainly next, with a little bit over by way of a douceur.

But whatever difficulties, whatever his own personal privation, he had kept his prices low. He had built up for Pennys the reputation for keenest value in the trade. Yes, now he was established. Now he had made his name. His carriage bore him proudly. Once his bicycle had conferred a certain little distinction; now his carriage cried aloud the stability of Pennys.

Leaning back in his well-sprung seat, he looked with quickening pride at Pennys. However often he came, his pride was new and shining as the mill itself. There it stood, stretching long and wide and low, to left and right of the original house, the red-bricked building with its continuous band of windows. He had not wanted to destroy the old dark house. Sentimental, the architect had grumbled, since the house was not so old and certainly not beautiful. Sentimental — well, why not? But in his heart Nicholas had known that it had been more than mere sentimentality. There had been an almost superstitious fear of destroying it. The keystone of his business it had been, and the keystone it should remain. So the old dark house had been gutted and new and handsome staircases put in, new and handsome windows. And now it stood, its intimate look contrasting curiously with the business-like severity of the rest of the factory. Nicholas cherished the old house — it had become his mascot.

He thought, as the carriage bore him swiftly up his private road, that he had done well with his property. Two years ago, when he had acquired the rest of the wasteland that adjoined his own, old Ware had let off his penny crackers of wisdom. . . Nobody but a fool would buy acres of sour waste so far away from the town, no, not even if it were going for a song!

And it had gone for a song! And now, witness his new mill that took the eye with its shining bands of windows. In spite of its magnificence, it had not been as expensive to build as the old several-storied type.

He thought, staring out of the carriage window, that one of these days he would set up a finishing works. Why not? Old stagers, hide-bound and timorous, had warned him that it could not be done. If it could be done, why had no one ever done it before? That was the sole argument, finishing with the statement that a lace-maker was a lace-maker — neither more nor less. His job was simply and solely to make the lace. Let him take on the finishing process, and he'd find it was himself that was finished!

Nonsense. Sheerest nonsense! He'd show them whether it could be done or not! He had the space for the plant and the money to buy it — and he had the water at his doorstep.

Gassing and bleaching and stretching — simple processes all. Simple enough. And cheap enough. But they lost him forty per cent of his profits. Forty per cent of his profits thrown to those sharks that called themselves finishers! Well — once he got his plant going, he might even become a shark himself! Why not? Why not do the finishing for other Long Eaton mills? Why not rake in his share of their profits? They'd find it cheaper — there wouldn't, for instance, be the same cost of transport. He'd gain. They'd gain. Everyone would gain — except Nottingham — and Nottingham must look after itself!

He would like to put the proposition to old Ware, just for the fun of seeing the old boy go up like gunpowder. Rant and rave he would, stamp about and swear that Nicholas was trying to steal Nottingham's last bit of the trade! Well, why not — if the trade was as easy as all that to steal? Not that one need take the old chap seriously — Heriots was not doing all that well, by some accounts!

But even if the old boy's opinion *was* worth anything, even then it didn't matter. A man should go his own way, always. Keep his own eyes open. Jump to his opportunities! In Nottingham the lace-makers were asleep — so fast asleep that they'd actually ignored Jardine's new power bobbin-presser! Turned it down, in spite of the fact that Jardine's had offered to install the new pressers in any Nottingham factory free of charge. Ay, and to remove them, also free of charge, at the end of six months, if they weren't a success! There was faith for you! And well-deserved too! Foolproof the new presser was! Impossible to spoil the bobbin. And it did the work with one-tenth the labour and in a quarter of the time! Time and labour saved — and a perfect job! He'd had a couple put in at Pennys, ay and paid for them an' all, paid top price! But the Nottingham masters — they'd opened one eye at the astounding offer and then gone off to sleep again!

Penny's luck, they said. Luck! What was luck but work and sweat? Work and sweat — even that was not enough! They didn't understand that, the fools who envied what they called his luck. Penny's luck! It wasn't luck. It was a question of ability, of using it to the last fraction of a fraction; of keeping every bit of your brain alert — watching, waiting. And even that wasn't enough, either. You had to bring your imagination with you, force it down to serve you, you and the machines.

Imagination — he had not failed in that! In his mill was housed the largest machine, and the smallest in the world, ay, in the whole world! David and Goliath, the men called them. And he had designed them both, ignoring the advice the makers bad sought to give him. He, Nicholas Penny, knew what he wanted. He would take no man's advice!

On David, the miniature machine, all the new designs were tried out. No-one before had ever had the sense to think of so simple, so obvious a thing. Even Betts had not realised the beautiful economy of the thing. No, he had actually protested against the wastefulness of so small a machine. But David had been fashioned. And on David every important design was tried out. One could correct that extra thickness of thread that hadn't been obvious in the working drawing, adjust this, or that, balance the pattern. He had a pretty good eye for a drawing himself, but you couldn't be really certain about a design until you saw it before you — lace.

And Goliath, his shining giant that stretched the full length of the great shop — Goliath turned out lace seven yards wide. And once a machine was set out — wide lace or narrow, the labour entailed was the same. So it cost him very little more to make seven yard lace than five yard lace! Two yards out of every seven for practically nothing!

He smiled again, recalling Jardine's warnings — earnest, oft-repeated warnings. The thing would be useless. Even if a floor could be reinforced sufficiently to take its weight and a man be found strong enough to work it, even then the thing would stand useless — a white elephant. They, the most important makers of lace-machines in the country, had warned him. They had warned him and he had not listened.

And there it stood. The largest machine in the world, clattering away, never silent except when the finished piece came off. He needed no man's warning, neither needed nor heeded! All he needed was his own eyes, his own ears, his own imagination. A man had to think for the future — remembering the present.

A man should go his own way, always. His own way! It had brought him his up-to-the-minute factory, the light and airy rooms filled with his machines, his workers, his cotton, his silk, his stock... Everything brought into being by the brain and will of Nicholas Penny, everything belonging entirely and without question to Nicholas Penny.

Queer to think how he had begun... that narrow dark house. If he'd searched the world over he could hardly have found anything more inconvenient. But it had been dirt cheap and he had been glad to put up with its inconveniences. He had even added to its inconveniences by allowing old Ellen living-room. That was odd to remember when you looked round Pennys now, Pennys the high-water mark of modern efficiency.

But it had been worth it at first — she had cost so little. Old and feeble though she was, she had worked, ay, for two-and-a-half years she had worked! But after that. . . the work slackening, slackening — and then ceasing altogether. For six months the old woman dragging out her sick life, her useless life, in that dark hole. And that cough of hers! Hack, hack, hacking away in hateful spasms, so that when she lay like a sick mole in its burrow, he could have sworn to that hack, hack rising above the whirr of the machines.

Maybe it had been Ellen's coughing that had hurried him on with his building plans. He was a kind man — but even Ellen herself must see that there could be no more place. . .

He had not enjoyed telling the old woman she must go. He was a kind man and he had not enjoyed it.

Two years ago. . . There she had stood, coughing and blinking and almost falling to pieces in her fusty black. And it was not only her head that trembled, but her hands and her knees and her whole wretched old woman's body. She hadn't looked quite human standing there like a scarecrow hatefully endued with life. It had made him uncomfortable to look at her. He was a kind man!

"But where?" she had asked in that toneless old voice. "Where?" He shrugged now, as he had shrugged then. Not his affair! Any sane person would understand it was not his affair. He ran a lace-mill, not a home for lost dogs! He'd been good to the old creature, given her house-room long after it had been decent to have her in any house. But now, he needed the room and she must go!

Reasonable. . . but it hadn't been easy to forget old Ellen understanding. . . at last understanding and crawling away. He could see her now — dusty grey face, dusty greyish garments, dusty grey head shaking, shaking. . .

And then, as if he hadn't had enough, Stella bursting into his private room, daring to intrude into his privacy, daring to take him to task, him, Nicholas Penny, whose lightest word, unquestioned, ruled all his workfolk! Stella wild with passion and shouting, shouting that he had dragged the old woman from her own home, that he could not, must not, dare not, throw her off now!

It had been as much as he could do not to take her by the shoulders and put her outside. But he had controlled himself sufficiently to point out that the old dame could go where she damn well pleased — to the nearest workhouse for preference. He would meet all future responsibilities for the old thing by paying his rates — and high enough they were! If the old bird fancied herself too fine for public institutions, let her pay for her fancies — if she could!

Stella had wanted then to take the old woman home with her, Stella who so short a time ago had complained of the old woman's coughing and spitting, who had used it as a lever to extort from him a place of her own! Ellen had been unkind in her time, Stella owned, but she was old now and sick — and blood is thicker than water!

He had let fly then! He was a patient man, but it had been more than flesh-and-blood was called upon to stand! He had let her have it! Did Stella really think he'd stand for that! Did she really think he'd have that stinking bag of bones chaperoning him and Stella? By God, women were damned unreasonable — all of them — except Heriot.

He had thrown Heriot's name at her — a none-too-gentle reminder — a reminder that Stella was doing what she had sworn never to do — sharing.

That had done the trick. She had dried up at that, the high colour dying in her cheeks. She hadn't said another word. Only she had gone quickly out of the room shutting the door behind her.

But the problem had settled itself — though not quite as pleasantly as one might have wished. For Ellen had been found dead a few days later, frozen to death upon the doorstep of her old home. And the dead feet thrust through the old boots, broken and heavy with mud, had told their own tale... no... not a pleasant way to die!

But Nicholas was wrong. It had been pleasant — in fact a very pleasant manner of dying. For old Ellen, a flush on her grey cheek bright as that of a girl hurrying off to meet her lover, had gone home. Had her feet trodden all of those long and weary miles? Did some kind soul give her a lift along the road? Or did angel hands bear her strongly aloft, spurning the cruel ground? Angel hands. She was certain of it! And why not? Such a little thing for God to arrange, such a little thing...

Exalted, bemused, she wandered the long road, obedient to the call that came from the old cottage, calling her home.

She had stood at last, swaying on her feet, whispering to herself, peering in at the grimy windows. She had lifted a hand to smear away the dirt. She had stood there, wondering a little at the grey dirt upon her grey hand. Then she had looked through the window again — the window rosy with light that streamed from the fire, the welcoming fire.

And then she had seen him, from the dark corner stepping — the young man who was like what old Nicholas had once been, but handsomer, kinder, than old Nicholas had ever been... But the girl... hadn't there been a girl? There *must* be a girl... She felt frightened, standing out there in the cold, quite, quite frightened because there was no girl... because if she could not find the girl, then she herself must stand out in the cold for ever and ever...

She had tapped upon the window, tapped and tapped again, She must make him understand that he must find the girl. She could not make him hear, even. He was turning his head this way and that — as if he, too, were looking, looking for someone... *Oh, find her, find her quickly... It is so cold out here, so very cold and soon it will be too late... I tap once more upon the window, once, and then no more...*

He was turning his face towards the window... his eyes were smiling. Her heart was suddenly so full of gladness that she felt it must burst. Fool, fool, foolish that she was, she was the girl, she herself! All the time she was the girl hidden under the dusty, fusty clothes...

His hand was on the window-latch, the stiff and rusted latch. Those windows were hard to open always, one opened them so rarely... the door! *Quick, quick, the door!*

She turned her eyes towards the front door.

It was opening... opening... quick, oh quick. An ever widening patch of welcoming light... He was standing there in the ever-widening light...

A very pleasant way to die, compensation for that hard frustrated life. Almost.

Chapter 24

In his bright and pleasant office Nicholas stood and drummed upon the window-pane. In the next room his secretary waited. Let her wait! Let everything wait. For once! He could think of nothing but that at this moment Heriot was in labour with his son. That it would be a son he did not doubt. The luck that had held in everything he had set his mind upon, could not fail him now. . . His son!

He looked at his watch.

How were things with Heriot now? Hard or easy? With Heriot you couldn't tell — physical or mental distress, it was all the same! She never let on. And the same if she were happy — she never let on. So quiet, so calm she moved about her business, you'd think neither pain nor joy ever touched her! Queer to think that only five years ago, four even, she had been the girl with the quick eager ways, the girl who, that first time they had ever talked, had poured out her hopes and her fears and her joys and her griefs. She had seemed then the kind of person it might have been easy to hurt. But now she had turned so quiet, so, in her way, not caring, you'd think you couldn't get at her at all.

What had happened to Heriot? Was it, maybe, the soft life she led sort of wrapping her round so that you couldn't get at her? But then she'd always led that sort of life. Was it just that she had grown up? Or was it that he hadn't really known her — that she had never been that eager, easily hurt sort of person at all? Well, whichever way it was she was lucky living the soft, easy sort of life she did!

Soft. . . easy. . . he'd say so! No expense spared in this business! The most expensive doctor, the finest nurse — the best all round money could buy! Had things begun to move a bit? Would today see the birth of his son? Or had he arrived already, the heir to all his planning, all his hopes? The doctor thought today. So did the nurse, brisk and bustling. Only Heriot, a little paler than usual, had said nothing. She had simply smiled that thoughtful, rather sweet smile.

Well, Heriot had taken her time over this business. Not that he liked children — children were untidy and noisy and tiresome. But they could, he supposed, be kept in their proper place. A man in his position ought to have children — they added to his importance, gave his work and his ambitions meaning. . . Heriot ought to have seen that for herself. And maybe she had. Sorry she might have been not to have had a child, or relieved, or merely indifferent — you'd never know!

Stella. . . by now Stella would have given him a nursery full of children. Stella — she hadn't been backward. Better for both of them if she had! Not that Stella's child was any sort of drag on him — he never even saw it. Never had! Stella seemed pleased enough to keep the boy out of his way. Only at odd moments he couldn't help thinking here was the child living and growing — growing maybe into a responsibility he had no desire to shoulder.

He paced up and down the sunny room.

He hoped things weren't being too bad for Heriot. She wasn't a big strong woman like Stella. She was tall but she was narrow, finely made. But she was having more help than Stella ever had — the best that money could buy!

He looked again at his watch.

Patience, patience! Everything comes to him who waits. And by God, he'd waited long enough for this! He was doing no good here, this morning, why not cut everything and go off home? It was too soon, far too soon! He'd be useless there, as here. He couldn't rest. Couldn't sit or stand. Couldn't eat. And anyhow it wasn't lunchtime yet! This business of becoming a father! He'd toss for it who was more comfortable at this minute — himself or Heriot!

Restlessness drove him. Up into the draughtsmen's room, peering here, peering there at working drawings, altering this, countermanding that, finding fault where no fault was. Down to the shops where the hands bent yet closer to the machines — Penny was no easy master.

They thought him a hard master, did they? He knew it and was glad of the knowledge. Hard he might be. But his machines were at work, every one of them, while in Nottingham more than half the machines were silent. His men filled their bellies with good meat and bread, while the Nottingham workers filled their swollen bellies with wind. Work and wages — did they think that both fell from the sky, the fools who called him hard? Didn't they know that if he had not spared them, still less had he spared himself?

Standing there, his eye filled with the machines, his brain filled with the knowledge of his own power, he almost forgot Heriot. This, this he had planned for, worked for, sweated for! And it was worth it, worth the spending of a man's power, worth all his work, his sweat!

A wonderful year this might be! The salvation of the lace trade if only the trade had the guts to see it! This new process of making embroidered lace. . . a new opportunity, a unique opportunity. Down in Nottingham things were going from bad to worse, more and more hands going on outdoor relief. If only the masters would wake, wake and shake themselves, rise up and grasp their great chance — then the good times would come again . . .1895. He wouldn't be surprised if this year weren't long remembered, the year that brought new life to the dying trade.

1895. He himself — he'd remember it all his life. The year his son was born. The year that saw the new burnt-lace process.

Pennys had never touched embroidered lace. He had always disliked the crude process, the ugly clumsy patterns embroidered upon net. No scope for the designer there! The flimsy net wouldn't stand much, For him, the only lace had been twist-lace — the swift movement of the bobbins, the play and interplay of threads weaving the pattern into the fabric itself; the smooth movement of the jacquard band, the brain of the machine, carrying out perfectly the designer's plan. He had found it ever-stimulating, the unlimited possibilities of twist-lace.

And now this new process. It was cheap and it was simple and above all it was effective. He had seen the most delicate, the most complicated pattern carried out by it. Mightn't burnt-lace become a bit of a menace to twist-lace? That made a man stop and think!

No man could foresee the future, but this one thing he was certain about — nothing, nothing at all, should ever be allowed to become a menace to Pennys! And after all, why should it? If burnt-lace was going to be the craze, why shouldn't Pennys have a whack out of the new cake?

1895. The birth of a new Penny. A new process. A new venture. He had his Goliath and his David, and now he would have his first Schiffli. . . he would christen it Young Nicholas!

He caught sight of his foreman and called out to him, "What say we try out a bit of burn-out? That new process — remember I was telling you? A couple of those new Schifflis wouldn't cost a fortune!"

"Whativer for? Us down't want no foreign machines!" Nicholas had never seen a man so bewildered. "Yer niver could abide that there embroidered stuff!"

"I know. But this is different. The new burnt-lace. It's got me! Can't stop thinking about it! It's cheap and it's good and it's simple!"

"Ay — till yer get down t'it!"

"Don't whittle, Betts! It's so simple a child could understand it! The whole thing boils down to this. You strengthen the net with some animal fabric — silk or schappe or wool even. Schappe'd be best to my mind! Then you embroider your pattern. Or you can embroider straight on to your schappe — you would for guipure — just depends on the pattern. The Schiffli — it's a marvel. No sort of pattern it can't turn out! Heavy or fine, it's all one! Makes me itch to get down to designs — new types of designs! When the lace comes off the machine you pop it in a bath of weak acid, and the background, the animal stuff you know, dissolves out. You can see it dissolving, actually see it — and no effect at all on the cotton. Fascinating! I can't tell you how fascinating to watch the pattern come out bold and clean!"

"Mebbe! But whyiver should Pennys tek it ovver? Us is doin' pretty well, i'n't us?"

"Ay — but we can do better! I'll tell you why, though — and you can keep it to yourself! Because in ten year, five year, even, all embroidered lace is going to be made on a Schiffli. It's cheap and it's beautiful — and it's going to be a rival, and a damn serious one, to twist. So, if there's any pickings, why not for Pennys?"

"Yo' want ter run afore yer can walk, Nicholas! It's not ivery man dare ter face yer wi' the truth. But ah've known yer long now. Yo' keep yer nose in yer own dish!"

Nicholas laughed outright. Betts never forgot that once he had been foreman over Nicholas Penny, twist-hand. And he was the only man Nicholas allowed to remember it. There was the comradeship of work between them, a comradeship that Nicholas had never achieved with any man of his own standing, and did not want to achieve. He stood alone — worked alone, and trusted no one. Except Betts.

"Yo' ought ter be a Nott'n'ham mester yersen, that yo' ought!" Nicholas said. "Yer've got th'reight sort o' brain!" With Betts he would let slide his fine speech, slipping back into the comfortable speech of his youth as a man thrusts his feet into old slipper. "Th'writin's plain on th'wall — if yer've got eyes ter see! Know how many firms are usin' Schifflis in Switzerland? Three hunderd, justabowt! Know how many in Plauen alone? Three thousand — and ovver! Know how many's bein' used in Nott'n'ham? Not one — not a single one! And the Nott'n'ham sits down on her arse an' grizzles because she's losen trade! By God, if she lets this chance go by, she *deserves* to lose, ay, every little bit of it!"

"Mebbe yer right!" Clearly Betts was doubtful.

"Mebbe I am!" Nicholas was dry. His shrug dismissed Betts.

Up and down and round about, his eye alert, his judgment sure. The clamour of the machines drove out all thought of Heriot.

But back again in his quiet office set high above the clamour, his agitation returned.

How were things with Heriot?

His secretary rapped upon the door. There was no trace of disturbance in his voice as he ordered her to come in, no trace of disturbance on his smooth face as he bent over his letters. He was as efficient, as impersonal as ever. He wasted no smile, nor any word in greeting. Geniality and charm he kept for occasion — senseless to waste it upon those who were paid to carry out his wishes!

How were things with Heriot?

He put a hand over his correspondence. His nod dismissed the girl. Alone, he got up, and began again to wander about the room.

How were things with Heriot?

He'd go and see for himself. Too soon, was it? Who said so? Who was to tell him, Nicholas Penny, whether it was, or was not, too soon? It was his house, wasn't it? His wife? His child? His money paid the doctor and the nurse. Never mind how grand they might be, once they took his money they became his servants... yes, they were as much his paid servants as the meanest hand in his mill. He'd go now, if it pleased him — and be damned to the lot of them!

Striding heedless down the corridor — let whoever would get out of his way — he all but knocked over a child and stood staring down in amazement. A child — a little boy! At Pennys! A hallucination? An omen perhaps? He stared again... A handsome boy... shabbily dressed... the face was familiar, it reminded him... the child was like... He knew which child this was...

Brow black he stopped at the porter's office. "Tell Mrs Wade my mill's no place for brats!" he ordered.

The carriage clopped along the road.

...Pen she had called him. Pen! How could she have been such a fool! Well — if she was a fool, so was I... so was I. I should have finished with Stella long ago... Stella and that child. There's another child to think for now... Pen... Pen. A proper little lad. I wish I hadn't spoke so sharp. Pen... a millstone round my neck if I don't look out...

Heriot... how are things with Heriot?...

At Long Eaton station he dismissed the carriage. The train took him swiftly... Heriot and the child she bore, Stella and the boy Pen... his thoughts raced and ran.

They had been on the watch. Before the hackney carriage had reached his house, the door was flung open and mamma-in-law Ware stood on the doorstep.

"Nicholas!" she said, and caught her breath.

He thought, damn the woman, why doesn't she *speak?*

"Oh Nicholas!" she said again. "It's a girl!" And wept a little. Through his most cruel disappointment her words came slow, disjointed, so that he had to make them whole in his mind, endue them with meaning.

"She had a bad time. Such a bad time. She was brave. She was so very brave. Not a sound, Nicholas, not a single sound — even when it was hardest. It made me proud — oh, Nicholas!"

There she was, weeping away, as though she, and not Heriot, had borne the anguish of the body; as though she, and not he, had borne the anguish of mind.

He said, in the pleasant voice he always used to her, the voice that hid alike irritation and dislike, whose pleasantness, as she well knew, meant exactly nothing, "Don't cry. It's all over now..." *And she ought to be ashamed of herself slobbering away at her age. Ugly women shouldn't cry... ugly old women...* "It's all over now!" he said again. "Just think — you're a granny!"

She heard his footsteps overhead, moving to the left, and not to the right, where Heriot lay... *But someone ought to remind him that he's a husband!*

He stood by the window looking blindly over the tree-tops that fell away beneath him.

...Over, all over. A girl. For this he had fought and planned and sweated and slaved — slaved more desperately than the meanest hand in his mills.

He was desolate at the thought of his wrongs...

He looked about the handsome room, its walls lined with a library picked up complete at a recent sale — but none the less effective for that!

... A girl. Heriot had given him a girl. He didn't want a girl. A girl was no use to him... no use at all. He wanted his heir... he wanted his son...

His son. His own self in little. His own self bigger and finer, maybe. He was well enough — but he wasn't perfect. All the best of himself in his son. All the things he had never had — for his son. He had made himself a gentleman, learning to speak gentleman's speech, watching his every word, watching his thoughts, even, for his son, all for his son...

He was conscious of such cruel disappointment that the tears came pricking — he who had not cried even as a child, no, not when he had been cold and hungry.

He was suddenly furious — furious that he, the strong, the successful, should have been given cause to weep! He knew the moment's impulse to seize these quiet books and hurl them through the window, to take the brasses from the hearth and send them hurtling through the window, to take and break, to smash and destroy...

But these things had cost money... and it wouldn't help, it wouldn't help!

He wandered about the room, beating one hand upon the other.

...Everything he had undertaken, everything in which he had had to rely upon himself and himself alone, had turned out as he had planned — ay, better than he'd planned! But in this one thing, this simple common thing that almost every twist-hand at Pennys could call his own, he had failed. Heriot had made him fail!

Again that impulse to hurt, to destroy. He was taken by longing to burst into Heriot's room, to berate her with the full strength of his tongue — to scold, swear, storm, bully — to rid himself in words of this most cruel pain.

He would say... he would say...

Rehearsing what he would say, the impulse died. He came back drearily to a more reasonable frame of mind... Better luck next time! Next time a boy. A man ought to have a family even if he didn't care overmuch for children. Yes, better luck next time. Leave it at that!

He stood for another moment staring out over the tree-tops. Then he went slowly along the heavily carpeted corridor to his wife's room.

The right gesture. It was expected of him. Well, he would not disappoint them! In spite of his bitter disappointment he would play his part. He knew well the value of the right gesture — it accentuated one's picture of the gentleman.

His bedside manner was perfect. He kissed his wife with the right expression of tender gratitude, admired the baby and was pleasant with the nurse. But neither that, nor the handsome diamond ring she wore that night — Nicholas's thank-offering for his first-born — comforted Heriot. She knew her Nicholas!

Well — to know one's adversary is half the battle!

One's adversary... the battle! Must one fight? And fight? And go on fighting? All these five years she had fought — fought against the slow tarnishing of her passion for the machines, fought against her hot sense of injustice. She had sought, with what energy remained over from the efficient ordering of his house — and what that efficiency had cost no-one would ever know — to keep her interest fresh with books borrowed from the library; she had followed in her daily paper every word on the ever-changing conditions in the trade. She knew of every patent, large or small, that had been taken out. She listened with enthusiasm while Nicholas talked about Jardine's new bobbin-pressing machine, although — in theory — she knew as much about it as he did. She had known for years about the new Schiffli, following its progress in Switzerland and Germany; she had taken the trade papers regularly in order to miss nothing of the new process of making burnt lace.

She had once tried to talk to Nicholas about it. But he hadn't been interested — hadn't even pretended to be interested. All right in theory, he had said, but it wouldn't work out commercially — nothing would come of it.

Nothing would come of it! And in less than a year, a new wing at Pennys given over to Schifflis!

She was tired of her second-hand interests gleaned from trade papers, tired of trying to influence Nicholas — an unrecognised and unwanted good fairy whispering in his ear! There was so much she wanted to do, so much she could do! She wouldn't mind how humble the job, not as long as she could get down to the machines, feel her own brain working directly on the machine, her own fingers firm on the stuff of lace...

This life she led wasn't enough. It wasn't enough!

She raised herself on an elbow and looked about her. Her room... mamma, with her passion for what was proper, had turned it into a setting appropriate to young mother and child... muslin crib, smothered beneath frills and ribbons, silklooped bed-jacket for herself, pale ribbons in her plaits; and flowers, flowers, everywhere.

...But all the same it's a battlefield. And I'll fight... But not now. Not just now. I'm tired. I'll call a truce till baby's weaned. Make do with being a cow till then.

He took the news that there could be no more children so badly that she turned away her eyes. She could not look at him. She was ashamed for him, ashamed that anyone, herself even, should catch him without his gentleman's armour. She was thankful that no eye but her own had seen it — that complete indifference to her own disappointment, that maudlin sentimentalising over "my son", that horrible self-pity — her own self could hardly endure it!

And she was angry, too, with an anger that refused to be still. How dare Nicholas behave like this, how dare he? He was not childless.

But she was Heriot. Her anger was wild but she had learned to give no sign. When he came to her with his demand for sympathy, her voice was gentle. And she smiled. Only her eyes she kept hidden. One can order one's mouth, but one's eyes one cannot command.

With his natural elasticity Nicholas was over the worst of his disappointment. Soon he would forget it altogether. Soon he would be certain that he had not wanted a son, that a daughter was and always had been the sum of his desires.

His child. He thrust from him the thought of another child — a child with Stella's eyes... Pen... Pen... Penny...

There was no child in the world but one.

She was christened Nicolet. Heriot's wish to call the child by her own name, he pushed roughly aside. He would not even consider it as a second name. Heriots, he said slightingly, was at this moment not much to shout about! He wanted his own name as near as possible. Nicolette, he agreed was too fancy and frenchified — it reminded him of cheap hair-oil. But Nicolet was neat and fine. Yes, Nicolet it should be.

He would think, sometimes, how he was reduced to a makeshift — a Nicolet and a Pen together did not make the sum of a Nicholas Penny. Two half-pennies — he smiled at the whimsy — don't make a penny!

It was a good joke and he told it to Stella. But Stella, like all women, lacked a sense of humour. She didn't think it at all funny! Indeed, racked by jealousy on Pen's behalf, a jealousy she had not reckoned with, she flew at Nicholas, so that he flung out of her little room, to consider the question of breaking with Stella altogether... She was no pleasure to a man any more. She had a filthy temper and she wasn't so much to look at neither. Getting as thin as a bone... no pleasure to a man any road!

And Stella, supporting herself against the door, sick with jealousy and fear, looked after Nicholas, wanting desperately some assurance of his kindness — and wondering whether to call him back or let him go. Which would help Pen more?

Nicolet throve. She laughed, cried, ate and slept at the proper times. Model baby — as the child of Nicholas should be.

Day by day he searched her infant features. Was she growing like him, just a little bit like him? She was fair-haired like her mother. And she had blue eyes. But surely, surely, there was something of himself in the tiny indeterminate face?

Useless. Even he knew it was useless. It was far too early to guess anything about this child whom he willed to inherit her mother's breeding and his own handsome face.

He questioned the nurse for the hundredth time, hanging about the luxurious nursery and distracting her so that she pushed the powder-puff into the infant mouth and snatched it out again, wishing she could as effectively close his own. And for the hundredth time she told him that all babies are born with blue eyes... "As for the hair, it's like I say, you can't ever tell! It rubs off in a month or two and then maybe it'll grow out different. Light when you thought it'd be dark; and then, often as not, t'other way about. There's many a tale..." She broke off to cluck at the infant Nicolet, pitying her for having so tiresome a parent.

Week after week, One month... two months... three...

But the eyes remained obstinately blue — old Heriot's deep blue eyes. The hair was as bright as ever. And she had her mother's wide sweet smile. He could encourage himself no longer... Her mother's child.

But looks are not everything. It's character that counts. In character she must take after me... plucky, strong-willed... clever. Eye skinned, not allowing anyone to cheat her of the value of a farthing. But generous — at the proper time. Like me. Not a bad sort of a chap to take after. She could do worse, a lot worse.

Chapter 25

There was no end to his pride in his daughter. He no longer regretted her lack of resemblance to himself. She had her mother's air of breeding, the sweetness of her smile. Something of him she inherited in her features — her brows were arched and delicate, her mouth full and beautiful. She was pretty... she was beautiful... she was altogether perfect. And she was his!

The child was the centre of his life, with Heriot hovering, detached, on the circumference. Heriot was there, and he took her for granted — an essential part of the pattern he had planned. When he thought of her at all, it was to congratulate himself upon having given his daughter so useful a mother — in every social circumstance, Heriot would prove an asset.

Planning the infant's magnificent future he would ask himself whether at long last he began to understand something of the Wares' dislike of his own marriage with Heriot. Would he, himself, allow this child of his heart, this heiress to all the wealth he should create, marry a man without family, without money? If the man were such as himself — yes! But only such a one! Then he might as well say no at once — for there was only one Nicholas Penny and no other! And for the Wares there was no excuse.

Heriot handed the baby to the nurse and went slowly upstairs to her own room. So it was over, at last over, the long, tiresome, tiring business of breast-feeding, and she was free — a free person!

At the open window she stretched her arms, taking in deep breaths of her new freedom.

Well... why wasn't she pleased? She could go ahead, now with her own plans, she could carry on the fight she had planned those months ago. The truce was at an end... But instead of wanting to fight, she felt surprisingly as though she wanted to cry. No use pretending she'd enjoyed turning her mind out to grass! Why... she knew well enough, why! In spite of the tiresomeness of it all, she had delighted in feeding the child; she had delighted in it because for these few months she was more to Nicolet than Nicholas could ever be. For this brief period of her life she was essential. Nicholas was destined to be the sun that shone — that was the part he seemed to have cast for himself, but for these few short months, from herself alone, Nicolet drew life.

Well, now it was finished... the close, satisfying, animal life that had enclosed her with her child. Over... the word that should strike warm, struck cold. And no wonder! Commonsense, banished by those heroics when she lay weak in bed, had returned with a challenge.

What did she propose to do? Did she suppose for one minute that Nicholas, who from the beginning had shut her out, would, suddenly, for no reason at all, alter his mind and welcome her into Pennys? And if he did? What then? What would she do there? She — face it — *face it!* She was stale, spoiled for practical work, rusty with long neglect.

She would not, could not, face the truth.

But the passion is there... She beat her two hands together... The passion is there...

Is it? Still the old clear passion?

She searched her face in the glass... The face of a woman settling into her ordered way of life... Calm. Perhaps a little inclined to let things slide... a little lazy. The desire keen but the will slack. Now when she took up a technical book or a trade paper, didn't she find it a little difficult to follow... as if in emptying her breasts the child had also emptied her brain...

It was terrible standing there and knowing that it was dying... dying, her desire that should have grown in strength, increased in vision. And Nicholas had done this to her! He had denied her, starved her... he had forced her wide ambition down into the housewife's coffin.

Standing by the window, arms fallen to her sides, she thought, Nicholas knew what I was and what I dreamed of. And it would have been easy for him to give me what I wanted... so easy. But he didn't care... Though just at the first he pretended he did. He didn't care ever...

Standing there by the open window there came to her ears the sharp passionate crying of the child. Her useless breasts rose to the sound... No more to console... no more...

The sharp crying deepened into rage, She could imagine the red and crumpled face, the clenched and waving hands, the small feet violently thrusting... The temper the child had! She smiled, remembering her own helpless childish rages. But — she stopped smiling — Nicholas encouraged the child. It amused him. While she tried to soothe and quieten, he would stand there laughing, intensifying the small creature's rage. He liked to see a girl with a spot of devil, he always said!

It was not fair, it was not fair to the child. This was the time for discipline. She could not wish her child to be restricted and restrained as she had been, forced down, rebellious, to a meaningless pattern; but sensible guidance, strengthening the child's will, strengthening and not exciting it — that was tremendously important.

Nicholas, with his constant petting, his delight in the small thing's rages — and truly they were comic — was going to make things hard for all of them later on — harder still for Nicolet — and if he wasn't careful, maybe hardest of all for himself!

But he didn't care. He was crazy about the child. He thought her perfect. And as long as he was satisfied — who mattered?

She mattered. It was her job to matter. *Nicolet is my job...* It was the first time she faced the fact clearly; always it had been obscured by her own ambitions. To watch over Nicolet... to keep her unspoiled! Fighting. That means fighting, again and again fighting with Nicholas. Battle after battle — though he won't know it. I won't let him know it... all day, every day, fighting my secret battle alone...

To Nicholas, remembering his own pinched childhood, it was enough that one spent lavishly. It was enough that a governess should be expensive; expense was his guarantee of quality. Whenever she thought of it — and it was often — Heriot would smile ironically. It was a never-failing wonder to her that so hard-headed a man could be so foolish. Watching Nicolet, she never for one moment underestimated the forceful will that lay beneath the pretty childish ways. Not that there was much opportunity for displays of will, for nurse and governess both hastened to satisfy the child's lightest wish, to anticipate it even. More than their mistress's disapproval, they dreaded the quiet, *I shall tell my papa...* Keep the child satisfied at whatever cost — so they pleased the master.

But not the mistress. The life Nicolet led provided the worst sort of forcing-house for character. The child must learn obedience — and she would learn it only from those who had no nest to feather! A spoiled and only child, she must learn to give and take, to share, without undue prominence, in the life of an equal community.

Nicolet should go to the new High School.

Heriot did not consult Nicholas. If he could be obstinate, so could she — certainly she could be obstinate when the child's whole future was at stake. She meant to get her own way, but she preferred it without the noise of argument. So governess and nurse had both departed and Nicolet entered as a pupil at the Nottingham High School for Girls, before Nicholas was aware that there had been any question of change.

Nicolet herself was the first unconscious bearer of the news.

Upon his own doorstep he met a strange but somewhat familiar little girl, wearing an unfamiliar dark blue uniform — a severe workaday little creature, this, shorn of the frills that marked his own small daughter. Beneath the absurd stiff straw hat, Nicolet's eyes danced.

Nicholas's anger raged. His voice could be heard booming from top to bottom of his big house, so that Annie up in the attic tidying herself to serve at luncheon, and cook down in the basement, wondered what had bitten the master this time! He stood at the head of his table refusing to sit down, refusing to see that Heriot was already quietly seated and ready to begin the meal. His fist crashed down upon the table so that silver and china rattled. A gladiolus leaped from the épergne and landed with a shower of water-drops upon Nicolet's blue serge lap. Nicolet giggled.

Heriot sat still and said nothing.

Nicholas continued to storm. Annie continued to stand, black skirts pressed against the sideboard, waiting to serve; cook continued to stand above her pots awaiting Annie's summons from the lift.

. . .Let them wait! All of them! He had been fooled and his will set at naught. In his own house he had been belittled and ridiculed. Everyone in the house knew it! Everyone of them knew that the prim pussy-cat who sat at the foot of his table looking as though she couldn't count two, had taken the law into her own hands and flouted his authority. Cook knew it. Annie knew it. Nicolet herself knew it! So let them wait, all of them wait, while he showed them who was master!

He continued to storm. Heriot continued to sit quietly at her end of the table. Nicolet continued to stare at him with round interested eyes, Annie, expressionless, continued to press herself against the sideboard, enjoying the show and pretending she wasn't there.

". . .Yer must be fair daft, that yer must, like all th'Wares, ter think fer one minute I'd let my dowter hobnob wi' any kid whose feyther can scrape tergither two farthens ter pay th'measly fees. *My* child rubbin' showders wi' th'brats of any Tom, Dick an' Harry! Yer've gone beyond yersen yo' 'ave! Bin too sharp an,' all! Cut yersen wi' yer own sharpness if yer down't look out. . ."

Nicholas shedding his painfully acquired gentility, reverting to the words, the accents of childhood — and perfectly aware of it! Aware, but too angry to do anything about it. Nicholas enjoying his freedom from the stilted tongue and vaguely conscious that somehow or other it served Heriot right!

It was Nicolet who put an end to the exhibition — it had been funny at first but now she'd had enough of it; she was hungry! Besides, she had enjoyed her first morning at school. It had been a pleasant novelty to meet other little girls — to meet them not on the painfully polite ground of visitor and visited, but on perfectly neutral ground. Such a thing had never happened before! It had not been unpleasant, either, to find herself dressed like any other child. After the first hour, she yearned no longer to show off her best frock. It was even possible, she considered, that others possessed Sunday frocks with as many flounces as her own! Meanwhile bloomers were comfortable after the starched frills that scratched your legs, and you could rush round without catching on to things. And — it was terribly exciting to find out about people — what were their names and how old they were and where they lived and what they liked to eat and how many dolls they had and whether they had Christmas parties as well as birthday parties even when their birthdays came near Christmas... all sorts of really important things! Besides, it was interesting at school. There was always something to do! She was suddenly aware that she had often been lonely; that the long days up in the nursery had been dull, hatefully dull. She was not going to allow papa to drag her away from all the fun!

So Nicolet's quiet little voice broke in upon the noise, informing papa that she intended to go to school — every single day there is — she added, so that there should be no mistake on the subject.

For a moment, Heriot quiet at her end of the table, Annie quiet against the sideboard, thought he would have a seizure. The blood rushed violently into his face; when he tried to speak he could not get his breath...

Then quite suddenly he laughed — a good hearty laugh and no pretence about it. It pleased him to see this small scrap setting herself against him.

"Papa knows best," Nicholas said, "papa will do exactly what he thinks fit!"

But Annie springing to attention, and Heriot quietly waiting, and Nicolet, smiling at papa, knew that he would do exactly what Nicolet thought best.

For Nicolet, young as she was, was no fool. She knew all about "managing" papa. She knew with unchildlike certainty that when you want your way in big things, you give way pleasantly on those things that do not matter. Among the things that do not matter, she included doing those things she actively disliked or even feared. She understood perfectly that as long as the essential Nicolet was not challenged, dislike and fear, even, could and ought to be overcome. But she knew, also, that as soon as she was asked to accept something that might challenge, however remotely, her essential self, she must take up arms and fight.

These things she knew not so much with her mind as with her blood.

There was the question of her daily ride. To Nicholas the child's riding was the symbol of the more spacious life. For Nicolet, no gentle pony but a mare, swift and fine and strong-willed like Nicolet herself. And Nicolet must learn to master her. His pride was strongly set. His daughter might break her heart, or her neck, even, but master the mare she should!

Nicolet hated the mare. In plain truth she was terrified of it. It stood so high and its eyes were fierce, and fierce its glinting teeth; its iron-shod feet shining in the sunlight, restive in the sunlight, filled her with terror. Into the quietness of lessons the horse came prancing — and there was no more quietness; into the stillness of sleep — and there was no more stillness, only a hateful, tossing nightmare of wicked hooves and wicked eye and wicked teeth.

Nicolet knew very well that she had only to go and tell mamma that she was frightened — frightened of dreadful eye and shining tooth... *all the better to see you with, all the better to bite you, bite you...* Yes, she had only to go and tell mamma and the riding would stop. Or if she didn't tell — if she just hinted enough to let mamma guess, there would be no more riding, no more huge and hateful teeth bared all the better to bite you with.

But safety she knew might be too dearly bought. She realised, in her childish way, that there was more to this than the mere question of riding. What that more might be, she was not at all sure. She had no clue to the pride that poverty had nurtured; she only guessed that she would lose some of her power over papa. That she possessed this power she must have been blind and deaf not to have known. It was an open secret in the household that Miss Nicki could twist the master round her little finger.

No, let her break her heart or her neck, but let her not lose any of her power over papa.

Every day, waiting with fear, hollow with fear, she would remind herself that never, never would she disappoint papa by being a coward. So she would steel herself, heart shrinking and thumping. But for all that, chin firm, hands steady. She had built for herself, out of her own need, an unchildlike self-control.

Soon she was surprised to find herself not quite so fearful. And then not fearful at all. She was even enjoying it. Yes, she was enjoying it very much. It was pleasant to sit high up, feeling the great muscles obedient to her lightest touch, the fierce spirit submissive to her will.

It was her first real lesson that if you set your will firm enough, there was nothing you could not do, nothing you could not get.

She never forgot that lesson.

Nicholas was never really happy without his daughter. It was as though his happiness, his peace, even, lay in her small childish hands. It was, he thought, as if the most precious, the most ambitious parts of himself had been renewed more finely in her. He must have her always near him. She must take her breakfast with him; she must, in spite of Heriot's protests, sit through the long and elaborate dinner; she must be there to reach on tiptoe and pretend to help him off with his coat. If he arrived home and she was out, he felt aggrieved and showed it. He was jealous and possessive and uncertain in temper. But young as she was, Nicolet had learned to handle him. She knew the storm signs when even she must make careful going. She learned to choose the right moment for her requests so that however extravagant they might be, he rarely refused her anything.

Heriot looked on and said nothing. The child had a disturbing subtlety which she used deliberately to reach her end. Nicholas knew it — to a certain extent; but he did not recognise its depth. It amused him. But it did not amuse Heriot. This subtlety — it made for peace, certainly, for they never quarrelled, those two, never argued, even, Nicholas was too fond and Nicolet too — subtle. But what would happen, Heriot wondered, if one wanted something that the other was not fond enough, or not subtle enough, to grant? What would happen if it came to open conflict? Which would win — her husband's overbearing obstinacy or the child's deliberate subtlety? Why worry? Why? There might never be any conflict at all! After all, Nicholas *was* fond and Nicolet clever.

Cleverness, subtlety — was it of Nicolet she was thinking, Nicki five years old? Yes, it was Nicolet. Clever she might be, subtle she might be, but how far was that removed from plain unvarnished slyness? But — subtle or sly, Nicki must learn to obey. And her mother must learn to watch and seize, as it arose, each opportunity for wise discipline.

Nicolet's first visit to the Penny mills — a day almost as thrilling to Nicholas as that first day of all, when he had stepped through the dark front door of his own mill — the master. Ever since the child could walk, almost, he had longed to take her to Pennys. But always he had restrained his longing. . . She was so small. She wouldn't understand. The great machines might frighten her — make her cry! He could not endure the notion that Nicolet would not admire Pennys.

But now she was old enough — surely old enough to appreciate the power, the beauty of his great mill. Today, the two things he was proudest of in the world would make contact.

Heriot watched them go. Neither of them so much as thought she might be interested — Nicholas because he had long forgotten the girl who had met him years ago among the machines. She was his wife and his housekeeper, she did not belong to this part of his life at all. Nor did it occur, even remotely, to Nicolet that her mother might be interested since she herself was so bored — but of course it would not do to let papa guess that! She was much more concerned about being back in time to go shopping with mamma. Mamma had promised her a new frock for the school party. But papa wished it — and it was always worth while humouring papa.

Heriot stared out of the window, listening until the sound of the horses' hooves died in the distance. Then she shut down the window — and it was as if she shut it down upon her own loneliness.

. . .A new frock. Natural at five years old to be more interested in a new frock. But she, at Nicki's age, shut in by the silly circle of her home-life, how she had craved for the sight, the sound, the smell of the machines.

One remembered. . . how one remembered that first visit to Heriots, long and long ago when she had fallen in love with the machines — and had never been heart-whole again!

Five years old she had been — Nicki's age — and dressed in her best — since her best, papa had said, was not too good for Heriots. A white piqué jacket she had worn, with white muslin plaitings on the sleeves; and a grey mohair frock flounced and piped with royal blue; and blue bows on the flounces and blue kid boots to match. And, yes — a blue feather in her funny three-cornered hat — but she had not thought it funny then? Five years old! And holding tightly to papa's hand, and craning her head backwards to see, so that the three-cornered hat slid backwards and the blue plumes tickled the back of her neck. But she hadn't minded that — for there were the great machines towering above her, like houses, like hills, like mountains. And the great warm voice of the machines; and the twist-hands moving neatly, moving rhythmically. . . and in the middle of them all, papa who cared for everything, papa who was like God.

And night after night, dreaming about the machines, sick or well, dreaming about the machines. And every day looking at yourself in the glass, to see if you were growing bigger — big enough to work for Heriots. And licking the spoon because Nanny said that cod-liver oil would make you grow. . . Day after day, nothing, nothing but lessons and walks, and now and again a tea-party, or perhaps, even, a real party — but Heriots, Heriots only, a special treat. . . And then school. And leaving school. And nothing, nothing but the intolerable round — tea-parties and shopping and now and again, a ball!

But for Nicki it was different. The world was different. Women were waking to their responsibilities, to their chances. Nicki, if she wanted it, could take her chance — chance to work and breathe and live among the machines. Nicki's chance — which she would never take! Nicki's chance, for which you would have given your soul! Ah well — no good crying for milk long spilled — for milk that was never yours to spill! Nicholas and Nicki — they looked to her for their comfort. Hers not the honest job of loaf-making, hers the silly task to put the tinsel on the ginger-bread!

She sighed a little, shrugging away her thoughts. . . The fish, would Willis remember to call in at Burton's on the way back from the station?

She settled herself to quietness before going down to interview cook.

Nicolet was not impressed by Pennys. Even its size meant nothing to her... naturally one expected everything connected with papa to be rather grand! She disliked the clatter of the machines and the hot smell of oil; and more than anything, she disliked the drab workers... they were poor and they were ugly and they made her feel miserable. But one thing she did enjoy. She enjoyed knowing that all these people, these hundreds of people, were obedient to her father's will — and more than that, there was a definite mingling of fear with the obedience. Child as she was, she could feel the nervous tightening of attention whenever he appeared.

Nicki passed through the great noisy shops, head up, playing the princess and enjoying it thoroughly, from the ostrich feather in her green velvet bonnet to the white tips of her kid boots. Heriot, had she seen the performance, would have abandoned her principles and slapped her daughter. But Nicholas found it perfect.

At the door of the menders' room, Nicholas stopped short. But it was too late. Nicki was inside, Nicki playing the small princess among the lace-menders, playing the small princess with Stella.

He saw Stella jerk abruptly to her feet, caught sight of her face as she stared down at the child — a white carved face, the eyes blazing. But for all her anger she looked lost, helpless. Then he saw her deliberately turn her back — a slap in the face for the small princess.

Nicholas gave no sign. He stood there, smiling pleasantly, explaining to Nicki that every inch of lace must be carefully examined, perfectly mended. One flaw — and who could say what loss might result? He watched, as though he had no other interest, while Nicki examined a piece of mended lace, and joined in her laughter when she could not discover the flaw.

Standing aside for the child to pass out — he delighted in these small courtesies to Nicki — he heard Stella's voice, low and clear, and meant to carry... *Factory's no place for brats!*

He was surprised at the violence of his own anger. She had the cheek, the blasted cheek! She had taken his own words into her mouth! She had the nerve to use his own words against him! She had the bloody sauce to compare her brat...

He tried to quieten himself... After all the boy was his boy, too! But he could not appease himself... The boy had no place, no place at all. He and Stella between them had robbed the boy of his birthright. What was done, was done — and he could pretend to no interest in a child he never saw. The boy had no place, no place at all...

Fury seethed long after Nicolet, passing down the line of smiling workers, made her triumphant exit.

Chapter 26

He waited for Stella, sitting remote and forbidding at his great desk. He thought, as she stood before him, that this was no longer Stella. Thin as a bone she was, with a waxen pallor on her cheeks, the mouth even — Stella's mouth — pale. Only the splendid eyes were left, eyes darker and more brilliant, even, than they had been. And her spirit, the spirit, that too, remained! Look at the way she stood before him — the master — with just a hint of swagger, recalling the lovely pride of her youth!

Youth. Why, she wasn't much above thirty now! And look at her! Lines scored in deep about her mouth and eyes; cheeks fallen above the bone; hands thin, the tendons like rope. How they let themselves go, these women! Queer to remember that this woman and Heriot were the same age! Heriot, in spite of that quietness of hers, bore the signs of youth on her smooth cheek, her red lip. Yes, as a woman, Stella was done for!

He said, using her surname to show his anger, "You were insolent just now, Wade, and I won't have it!"

She said obstinately, "I can't see that I was insolent, Nicholas. What I said — they were only your own words!"

"I'm master here, and what I do is right! Get that into your head and keep it there!"

"You may be master —" and she was quiet enough standing there and fighting down the sickness that came so often to trouble her, "but you're not God Almighty, Nicholas, though you like to think you are! And you act wrong, sometimes, and you know it! Pen —" she faltered a little, "Pen's just as much a child as what she is!"

He brought his fist down upon the desk so that the papers fluttered and slid about the room. She made no attempt, as in other days, to pick them up. She stood quietly, looking into his angry eyes.

"I don't want to hear that talk!"

"Hear it or not," she said steadily, "it's all one!"

"I'll not stand for this!" he shouted. "By God, I will not! It's time we parted company. You'll have to go, Stella!"

She half smiled, leaning heavily upon a chair-back. He had never asked her to sit in this room, nor did she expect it.

She said, and her smile was crooked, "You're right, Nicholas. I'll have to go!"

He looked up sharply. . . Submission?

Her hand was at her mouth. He watched it come away again. The fingers — he followed their downward movement, were a little flecked. . . red. . . they were red. . .

She said, still smiling, "I got it from Ellen. It was that room you know. . . sleeping together, breathing in her breath, and no proper window. But maybe —" she shrugged, pitying the horror in his face, "it's in our family — I'd 'a got it any road!"

Truth stronger than compassion broke fiercely through.

"But not if you'd 'a treated me right, I wouldn't, not if you'd 'a treated me right!"

She coughed a little, fumbling in her apron pocket; and with a handkerchief to her lips, stood half-fallen upon the chair, her body shaken with coughs. She crumpled her handkerchief in the palm of her hand. He wondered in horror, whether the white hand would take the stain.

The colour had risen in her cheeks from the strain of coughing. Her eyes were brilliant with fear.

She's lovely, he thought. And wondered that he had thought her done for. But he was aware of something frightening, repellent almost, in this new strange beauty. And all the time he was hollow with pity for her because she was young and so soon must die.

He wondered at his own blindness that he had not seen the mark of death upon her. He was taken with admiration, too, of her courage that she faced the grave so quietly.

Pity for her, and admiration. But no kindling of love. His love had always been for her fine body — and now her sickness repelled him. And at the bottom of his heart — fear, the hateful fear of her accusation.

Was it true, what she had said about his share in her sickness? It was not. It was not. . . How could it be? He had treated her well. Given her work. Given her a house to live in. It was simply her sick woman's fancy. . . bitter against those who are well — sick folk were like that!

He wanted to cry out, *It's in your family. Ellen had it. You said so yourself. . . you said so. . .* He wanted her to unsay her words, to take away the scarifying suspicion. He was afraid to cry out to her, lest she should look at him with those dark eyes of hers and brand the fear into his life for ever.

He sat there playing with his paper-knife, not looking at her.

She said, "I'm glad you know — now. I didn't want to tell you. I —" the red colour stained her thin cheek, "I was ashamed — being sick! I'm glad you sent for me — even if it was only to row me, Nicholas!"

They smiled sadly at each other.

He said, "Sit down, Stella!" and pushed forward a chair.

It was the first time he had asked her to sit in his office. She thought, Now he knows he isn't going to be bothered with me much longer, he can afford to be kind.

He said, "We ought to talk — about things."
She made the funniest little mouth as though she were going to cry.
He said slowly, "I know what's on your mind, and I'll do the talking. It'll save your strength a bit. It's the child — isn't it?"
The child... She stared at him with her great eyes, willing him to know, to understand how she lay awake at nights, racked with terror because so soon she must die; because she would never see another spring, but must lie in the cold earth where there is no more sun nor wind nor bird song... in the cold earth — and there would be no one to care for the child. And how at the thought of Pen, so young, so defenceless, so unfriended, she must sit up in bed holding trembling lips with trembling hands that the wailing should not burst through... *Pen... Pen... who will care for you when I am gone.*
"It *is* the child?" he asked again. "It's," he hesitated over the name. "It's Pen — isn't it?"
She nodded. She could not speak. To hear her son's name upon those lips, to hear Nicholas for one moment consider the child as something to be guarded, something precious!
He said, "I'll take care of the boy. It's a promise, Stella!"
...You said you'd take care of me — once. That was a promise, too! Stella sitting there and holding him with her mournful eyes, and by her silence reminding him... reminding him.
He was shaken by a gust of annoyance. What more did the woman want? He had paid for his pleasure — all these years he had given her work, given her a home...
His annoyance passed. She was ill. A woman as sick as she must be allowed her fancies... But all the same he was not going to be her victim..
"Listen!" he said. The tips of his fingers pressed lightly together; his chin rested upon their apex. His eyes, steady and hard, held hers. "I'll look after the boy. I promise. On conditions."
"Conditions?" She fixed him with eyes steadier than his own... only her hand, traitor to her will, fluttered oddly towards her heart, fluttered and dropped.
He nodded. "How old is the boy?"
"You've forgotten!" she said. "Even his age you've forgotten!"
"There's a lot to remember!" Must she ravage him with this nonsense. "I don't always remember my own!"
"But you remember hers — the little girl's —"
He brought his fist down with a crash. "Enough o' that! That's no concern o' yourn! The boy now — how old did you say?"
"Ten, Nicholas, have you forgotten — everything?"
"Ten!" He ignored her question, looking at her coldly above his joined

finger-tips. "Ten!" Going to school of course! Well, there he must stop till he's twelve! "Good Lord!" he looked at her half-humorously, "how they pamper kids' nowadays! Cotton-wool and silver spoons! I was working before I was ten, myself! This lad now," he was impersonal, as though he discussed some other boy, not Pen — not Pen. "As soon as he leaves school he can come into my mills. Of course, he'll start at the bottom — same as any other lad!"

She looked at him. There was an expression in her eyes he did not care to read. She said, "What are you offering Pen you wouldn't offer any other lad — any lad with no claim at all?"

For a moment she was silent. Then she said, very slowly, as if speaking words she hated, but must none the less speak, "Your son... Nicholas!"

He said violently, "For God's sake don't start that, this time of day!" The old Nicholas burst through. "It's ovver late fer all that! Th'lad ha'n't bin browt oop as my son. I down't even know as he *is* my son... I ha'n't seen him above once in my life!"

"You wanted it that way, Nicholas!"

"Drop th'past, I say, drop it! It's th'future we're talkin' abowt!"

He stopped, waiting on self-control.

"For God's sake use your brain, woman, unless —" he was being deliberately brutal, reminding her of her helplessness, her ever-increasing helplessness, "you're too sick to use them! What do you want me to do? Take the boy into my own home? Send him to a school for the sons of gentlemen? Label him bastard?"

She thought wearily, You've changed your clothes and you've changed your speaking — sometimes. But you haven't changed yourself. Still the old Nicholas — mean as Judas. And all the time pretending, pretending it's for the other person you act so mean... All right, go on pretending... Pretend it's for Pen's sake, for my sake, for anybody's sake — except to save your own face!

"I don't want a scandal," Nicholas said smoothly, "naturally I don't. It wouldn't help anyone — least of all the boy. Can't you see? If he comes into my mill, same as any other lad, no-one will think twice about it! And there's a lot I could do for him — keep my eye on him, see what he's fit for, help him along — if he deserves it. It's a perfectly natural position. Natural, that's what everybody'll think, knowing you worked for me..."

Worked... worked... All is past... past... She bowed her head. She wanted to weep, to weep tears of blood, because all was finished — over and done with!

"I'll have him taught, Stella..." Her thoughts came heavily back. "If it's the machines he cares about, machines he shall learn, study the whole thing from A to Z. If it's designing — and it may well be — I'll have him taught designing. He'd work here during the day, learning the practical side, and he could go along to night classes at The School of Art."

"No more than a work-hand, Nicholas?"

"No need for him to stay a hand. Depends upon himself. No knowing where he'll end. Foreman, manager, owner even — like me. I didn't stay put! As I say — depends what he's got in him!"

"He's got it in him all right! He's got the brains, ay and the hands, too! He draws — he draws like an angel! And why shouldn't he? He — he gets it from his father, Nicholas!" She was looking a little sly.

. . .*Your son*. . . *your son*. . . She was bringing it home to him again, at this late hour, pressing it home! All those years she had been content to forget the fact. Now she was ill and needing help, she found it useful to turn round. . . but hadn't she the sense to see it was over late to try and turn him?

She thought, What he promises — it isn't much. It's less, so much less than he could do — and never know he'd done it. But that's Nicholas — always do the least. . . and it's something. . . it's something. A little help while Pen's so small and he'll manage. But who can trust Nicholas to do even that little? *How* can I trust him?

She said, "Nicholas — if I could believe you! If I could!"

"You can trust me — why not? I give you my word. But I want your word, too, Stella!"

"My word? Whatever do you mean?"

"I'll tell you what I mean! Does he know — the boy, I mean — that I'm. . ." He stopped. He could not bring himself to say the word. Only one child in the world should have the right to call him *father*.

"About — us?" Stella said. "How could I have told him, a little chap like that?"

"Anyone know? Anyone at all?"

"No one in the world. Ellen knew. She found out — remember?" She was smiling a little crookedly. "But you managed to shut her up — and I wasn't exactly proud!"

"Then you've got to swear he'll never know, you've got to swear now!"

Her eyes narrowed. The sly look came back. . . She hadn't intended to tell Pen. She had her reasons! But what was Nicholas playing at? What dirty game?

She said, "Why should I swear? Maybe he *ought* to know!"

"I should have thought it was obvious. It's little enough you have to leave him, nothing at all really — except respect for his mother's memory. Do you want to rob him of that?"

"I'd risk that — maybe! I could leave a letter for when he's older. He'd understand. You see, Pen loves me. You wouldn't understand the difference that makes, would you, Nicholas?"

By God, if she were not sick, he'd take her by the shoulder and shake some of that damned sauce out of her! Whether she promised or not he'd see the brat didn't starve — but all the same she'd got to promise. She'd got to! After all these years he wasn't going to have all that muck raked up! He'd got others to think for, besides her! No good putting her back up, though — not when she was in this mood! The devil was in her! He knew her of old... Gently now, gently...

He said, "But think, Stella, think! What good would it do the lad, what good at all?"

"I don't know. I'm not clever. I never was. And I'm too sick to think, maybe — like you said. I don't know anything for certain — except I'm going to die. That's why I've got to help Pen, because there isn't anybody else. Right and wrong — wise and foolish! They're all muddled up in my mind. Maybe that's the way when you're ill — ill and frightened, the way I am, because of the child you've got to leave behind... such a little child..."

"It couldn't help, telling him, it couldn't help at all! Believe me, Stella. It's bound to unsettle him, make him dissatisfied, lazy, maybe!"

Quite suddenly he lost his temper. "Anyhow I won't have it! I won't have it, I say! You tell the boy — and I'll deny the whole story. I'll say you were mad. I'd say women with your complaint — dying women —" he brought out the word brutally, "have queer fancies! Who'd you think would believe you? *Why didn't she say so before?* they'd ask. *All this time and never a word...* They'd say that an' all! *Sick woman's spite*, they'd say. And so it is, Stella, so it is, though you're not well enough to know it! Now take it quietly and listen to me! I'm in earnest — dead earnest. You try that game and I wash my hands of thy boy. He can starve. Or go to the workhouse for all I care — very likely he will!"

She stared at him with dark wild eyes.

He went to work deliberately, "Yes, he'll go to the workhouse, that's where he's bound for! And that'll be, the end to all your fine plans! He'll be a workhouse apprentice — tinker or sweep, maybe... dirtying the fine skin you've kept so clean. Or maybe a butcher... those artist's hands of his can do artist's work with the meat saw! And maybe he'll be beaten, and certainly he'll go hungry."

She began to cry at that, all the spirit broken at the thought of Pen hungry, his tender body beaten. Her sobs hardened into short dry coughs — her mouth and chin were flecked with blood.

She said painfully, "What kind of man are you, Nicholas?" And then half-laughing, half-crying, "I asked you that once before, but I never got an answer — I never got an answer!" She fell silent, huddled in her chair, flecked chin dropped upon flecked bosom.

Your word... your word... He sat there, forcing the pressure of his will upon her. Weak she was and hollow with sickness — she could not escape his will.

She said, without raising her fallen head, "I promise." She looked him full in the eyes. "And if you break your word, Nicholas, I'll come back — I'll come back. If there are no ghosts, still I'll come back. I'll come back as a thought, Nicholas, a thought in people's minds — in your wife's mind, in the little girl's mind, but most of all in your mind... in your mind for ever and ever. You'll never be free of me again, Nicholas!"

He said, pleasant, now that he had gained his point, "Don't threaten, Stella. And don't talk nonsense! You've no need and it does no good. You've done very well out of me — if you had the wit to see it. But you haven't the wit — you're too sick, maybe!"

A smile widened on her pale stained lips. She said, slowly, "Yes — I've done well enough — now. And I have the wit to see it. Thank you, Nicholas!"

He said kindly enough, since he could afford his kindness now, "Go home, Stella. Don't come back today. Take a rest,"

She cried out, "There'll be rest enough in the grave. Work I must — now. It's got into my blood, the need to work. I can't help myself. While I breathe — even if my breath is choked with blood, I must go on working... working..."

Oh Nicholas, while the eye can see, the ear hear, I must see you, hear you. While I breathe, it must be the air you breathe...

She said, struggling with speech, her whole will set to speak for this last time, "The way things turn out! Working for you — first it was my cross. And then it came to be my crown. If I could go on, sick as I am, just as I am... only to work for you! Once I thought I was fit for something better than sit in a corner, mending, mending... And now, if I could pick and choose, out of the whole world, choose, I wouldn't want anything better — not if I could see you, sometimes — just now and then, Nicholas."

She pressed both hands to her breast, as if to help out the words.

"I was a pretty lass once — remember, Nicholas? I'd like someone to remember the way I was before I got ill. Those days... after you left me, Nicholas, I could have wedded. And maybe I should. Given my boy a father. But I couldn't, Nicholas. Whatever I might have done, I wasn't light with my love — you know that, Nicholas. You did know that, didn't you? You took me. And when you took me, you made me yours for ever. And when you didn't want me any more, I was still yours. I didn't want to be. I hated myself — but I couldn't help myself. Whatever I thought, and whatever I did — whatever I did, Nicholas, I was still yours. And so

I will be — for ever. I'm thinking —" she was smiling now through the tears running down sunken cheeks, "if there's a heaven, and if ever I get there — and maybe I will, for if I've done wrong, I've paid for it — heaven would be a poor place, wanting you, Nicholas! I haven't always been kind, Nicholas, I'll own. But them that fight can't afford to be soft. But now it's the end, and plain speaking won't harm anything any more!"

He said, open to pity, because he had had his way, "Maybe things aren't so bad. Maybe if you rest — get a good doctor, feed up! Money's no matter, Stella!"

She stood up and she was smiling. "I'll rest," she said, "and money's no matter, any more! But you'll remember Pen, you *will* remember, Nicholas?"

"I promised. And you promised. I'll look to the boy."

At the door she turned, searching his face, trying to fill her eyes, her mind, her heart, with the sight of him; trying to carry away that which must content her to the grave.

She said, "Pen — he's so little and he's so good — so *good*. Nicholas! Help him to grow the way he ought! Goodbye, Nicholas. . . oh Nicholas, this *is* goodbye. . ."

Chapter 27

She was right. It was goodbye.

Nicholas frowning upon his drawings, knew that Stella was dead. Never more would he see her bright head bent over her work, never more would she lift following eyes as he passed. Resentful eyes, he had thought; eyes, he knew now, that followed to hold his image as he passed.

Well, she was dead — and that part of his life was over and done with! Was it, though? Was it? What of the child he had promised to befriend? What of the boy Pen?

He frowned more heavily awaiting the child. Why must his life be cluttered with old responsibilities because once, of a summer's night he had loved Stella? Surely, young as he was, he, too, had been betrayed, betrayed by his blood, just as certainly as Stella herself. But for that betrayal Stella had paid. And now she could pay no longer and it was his turn.

This boy. The thought of him didn't bring a quickening of the blood. And why should it? All of five years since he had seen the child standing in the corridor of Penny's mill. Stella's eyes. That was all he remembered about the boy — but for that, surely for that, he would want to help... Yes, he was willing to help the child because he was Stella's son, not at all because he was his own... Queer!

Fatherhood. There was no sure instinct of fatherhood. If there were, he would be waiting, heart beating, for this child of his... Not the faintest quickening of the heart-beat! Face it — he didn't give a damn for the boy!

Fatherhood — a rum business! He'd go through fire and water for Nicki. To help Nicki he would see Pennys, yes, even Pennys, go up in flames. But towards this boy, empty, quite empty...

Well, and wasn't that natural? He'd never seen the boy but once. Stella had been satisfied, careful even, to keep the boy out of his sight... I've never talked to the lad, never thought about the sort of person he is, never watched him grow... That's it! To love a thing you must know it. To know it you've got to watch it grow. Like watching a seed you've planted, watching it bud and then come to flower. Poetic. But true. Maybe when you got down to it you'd find a bit of truth in all real poetry... Now that was a queer idea for a man to have — a successful hard-bitten business man... ay, but he was not an ordinary business man, he was Nicholas Penny!

At the timid knocking upon his door his thoughts came swiftly from himself, back to Stella's boy.

. . .Suppose after all fatherhood would not be denied? Suppose after all his heart went out to the child — his child!

"Come in!" he called out sharply.

. . .Nothing but surprise that he had fathered this child. Not the faintest flicker of warmth! He was conscious of relief. It kept things simple. . . Great resentful eyes the kid had, full resentful mouth. . . The boy was all Stella. But — against his will he admitted the thought — Stella's young eyes, Stella's young mouth had harboured no resentment. That had come later. . .

Someone had attempted to make the brat presentable. Cleaned him up and hadn't made a good job of it! Dirty marks round the eyes marbling the white skin. And his clothes — his best obviously — his poor best, flapping about his childish body. A man's suit cut down. Bought second-hand and cut down. Stella, so dainty-fine when he had first known her, so careless of the future, Stella had learned to dress the child she loved in this grotesque fashion that the hideous clothes might last!

For the first time he began to understand something of what life had done to Stella.

"Come here!" Nicholas said sharply. He was not going to be trapped into false sentimentality. And then, remembering that the boy had, after all, lost his mother, added more kindly, "what's your name?"

"Pen. Pen Wade, sir!"

"Queer name — isn't it?"

"My mam called me after a place she knew — her mam's mam came from there."

"Ever see your father?"

"No, sir. My dad died afore I were born."

"So you're all alone now?" *Ever see your father? See your father? Your father?*

"Ay, sir!"

No telling what kind of voice the boy had. At the moment, toneless with grief, it did not remind him of Stella's voice. . . he was glad that the voice did not remind him of Stella.

He seemed colourless, this child — with sorrow, maybe; or maybe it was fear of the master — voiceless, mindless, standing there, his eyes upon his boots, grotesque boots, weighing clumsily upon his child's feet. He had — Nicholas knew the look — the look of a child that went barefoot most days.

Barefoot. . . but this was his son! Surprisingly that stung his dignity.

Nicholas said, "We'll look after you — if you're a good lad, till you're old enough to look after yourself. Not every boy has your luck! But mind, you've got to do your part! Work hard at school. Learn all you can, while you can. No idling, no loafing, just because folk are sorry for you!"

The child winced. His eyelids fluttered as though each word of wisdom was a blow. The sight annoyed Nicholas.

"Understand?" he asked sharply.

The child nodded. He seemed physically unable to speak.

"Who's looking after you now?" Nicholas was growing impatient at this interruption of his morning.

"Mrs Greenhalgh. Her says I belong of her now!"

"Like it there? All right. I'll get someone to see Mrs Greenhalgh and arrange about your keep. Now remember, the only way you can pay back is by being a good lad and working hard and doing as you're bid. That's all!"

The boy hesitated, shifting forward a little on his hideous boots.

"I said, That's all!"

As the child fumbled with the handle of the door, something moved in Nicholas. He wanted to call the boy back; he wanted, for a brief moment, to take in his own strong hand that childish defenceless hand; to put his arm round those shrinking shoulders, to tell the child that here was a friend.

So brief the moment.

. . .Not wise. Not at all wise. Put ideas into the brat's head. . . into other people's heads. . .

He was suddenly angry — with the child for disturbing his work; with himself because he had allowed the disturbance. His face went bleak. Rigid he waited for the closing of the door.

The door closed.

He turned irritably to his work. A man's work ought to be kept clear of complications! He took up the drawing again. With a sudden movement he rejected it, Damn bad design. Not only florid and clumsy, but worse still, impracticable! Too much work in it for the price. Seemed like he could trust no-one but himself to work out the simplest design!

His pencil hovered. Clean up the design a bit — simplify it. His pencil moved surely, moved cleanly. Thus it should go. . . and thus. . .

Time flowing evenly, flowing peacefully. Ups and downs in the lace trade. Old established houses crashing to ruin. New houses rising to fortune. But more ruin than fortune. And in the midst of the heartbreak and uncertainty, Pennys all set for prosperity.

Penny's luck. A byword in the trade. They didn't see, the fools, that Penny made his own luck, that he planned, worked, sweated for his luck.

Nothing too great to be attempted, nothing too small to be considered; nothing too old or too new to be pressed into service. And above all, Nicholas brooding, thinking, creating — making his luck.

On Pennys' waste, housing his finishing plant, stood the new buildings refuting the wisdom of all who had sought to dissuade him. *It cannot be done...* Betts with his accumulated knowledge of years. *It cannot be done...* Stapleton of Queen's Mills and Ridgeway of Short Cut, knowledgeable men both, echoing the parrot-cry. *It must not be done...* Old Ware grumbling, helpless, at this further threat to the remains of Nottingham's industry.

It cannot be done. It must not be done... And yet it had been done.

Nicholas had not troubled to argue, had not bothered, even, to justify himself. His justification was there in the smoking chimney-stacks — and in the profits they brought him. Forty to fifty per cent saved on each rack! And not only was he finishing his own lace, but as much lace as he liked to handle from other Long Eaton mills — he saved them time and cartage... Pennys gathering in most of that forty to fifty per cent profit that had gone jingling along the road to Nottingham.

On the east side of the main block where the twist-lace was made, stood the smaller, newer block, turning out burnt-lace as fast as men could work.

Right. Again right. In the teeth of all wisdom, all advice! Obstinate for his own way, he had carried his plan triumphantly to success... Old Betts protesting that by trying to manufacture the two types of lace he was cutting his own throat. Old Ware warning him that in the manufacture of twist-lace it was better to specialise, otherwise you split your market. Heriots had specialised always. Heriots had specialised in finings always, Heriots had not been tempted into making anything else — not even when flounce lace had ridden the crest of fashion.

So much the worse for Heriots. Old Ware giving advice! What did he know of present-day demands, the old man who ruled Heriots? Heriots had been the finest factory in the Midlands — once. But now it was sliding with its tired old guardian down to ruin.

He hadn't listened either to Betts or Ware. What had he, Nicholas Penny, to do with the maunderings of old men? He thought for himself, acted for himself. What had he said to Betts five years ago? *In ten year, five year, even, nine-tenths of the trade will be burn-outs*. And so it had happened. In less than the five years it had happened. Less than five years ago he had bought his first Schiffli machine because he had seen there was no limit to the beauty, the intricacy of pattern it could turn out. Within a month he had bought his second, and then his third. Within six months he had built a whole wing to accommodate his Schifflis. Once more he had beaten Nottingham at its own game!

But it had not been all jam — of course it hadn't. Only a fool expects all jam — and a fool would get sick on it! Fortunes aren't built up on prophecies alone, however brilliant. A man needs common sense and the eye to see that there is no wastage by cheating, by carelessness.

Raw silk, for instance! Silk from Italy, silk from Japan, you'd think it fell from heaven the way the silk-washers were allowed to steal it. Time-honoured custom? Maybe! But not at Pennys. For this past year he had had the silk washed in his own mill — not given out to be returned weighted with soap to make up for stolen silk! He paid for silk, not soap! From the very first he had saved one third of his usual outlay on silk. One third! Silk cost gold. And gold cost sweat! Let others deal with raw silk as they chose — Pennys would prepare its own!

And the winding of the silk. Why should Pennys give that work out? Custom again! Then to hell with custom — the trade was lousy with custom! The warping-mill had been costly — but not nearly so costly as paying year in, year out for the work to be done outside — to say nothing of yet further loss through silk-stealing!

All the processes carried out under one roof! He had promised himself that years ago — fifteen years ago when he had first started — and he had kept that promise in spite of the snarlings and the yarlings of the others. The best-hated man in the trade! Of course he was! And proud of it! And he was also the most feared, the most respected. He didn't give a damn for their feelings — not as long as he saw his success in the respectful eyes of his fellow-masters, in the obsequious back of his bank manager!

Good times and bad times. But by his own effort, his own watchfulness, his own sweat, he had made the good times outweigh the bad — far, far outweigh the bad.

'Ninety-eight! A bad year that had been! A terrible year. Worst in the trade for a generation. A year of toppling fortunes, of bankruptcies, of the closing down of famous houses. But Pennys had come through — it had come through, though he was still paying for that new wing of his — the Schiffli wing. Heriots had come through too. But it still trembled from the shock. Everyone knew it, even the old man. Ay, he knew it right enough, or why was he wearing last year's overcoat, old Ware, once smartest of the dandies? And there was no carnation any more in his buttonhole. Old Ware blaming the Spanish American War, blaming the bad spring, blaming everything — except his own incompetence. The war! Enough to shake you, maybe, but not enough to break you, not if you were sound. . . It did not even shake Pennys —

Old Ware — like all Nottingham masters — half-asleep the lot of them! They'd waited a year, a whole year of misery and despair, before even thinking of putting things right! Yes, a whole year slipped by and the trade all but finished — and then they'd called the men together to decide how to lock the stable door!

Well, and even then, they might have coaxed back the straying horse — if they'd had the sense. But they hadn't. While they'd argued and quarrelled, other folk had ridden the mare away!

Eighteen-ninety-nine that was! Masters and men meeting before that Board of Conciliation. Conciliation! Masters and men jabbering away and getting nowhere. The masters out for a twenty-five per cent cut in wages — and the men — at first — out for no cut at all! The men couldn't see, wouldn't see that it was the high rate of pay that was helping to strangle the trade. Why should they expect to be paid by the width of the lace? They put the same amount of work into wide as into narrow lace — or just about! Why wouldn't they face the fact that if they agreed to a cut in wages, a good stiff cut, they could set the machines going again — would earn something instead of nothing!

He himself had come into this business — he had been invited by the precious Board to put forward his views. So prosperous a man, they had thought, might well point out the way. But it had been useless. They wouldn't listen. Neither masters nor men. The men — because he was a master, with master's privileges nearest his heart; the masters — because his ways were not their ways, and because coming from Long Eaton, he must necessarily be their rival.

Fools, fools all! The good of the masters and the good of the hands — it was one. Neither could prosper at the expense of the other. If he himself had prospered, his men had prospered with him. Why wouldn't these fools be content to learn?

The cut, the cut alone could save them, but the men had put forward the most fantastic excuses to reject it! They had not been ashamed to argue that the suggested cut would result in a forty-two per cent cut for those who worked on silk lace!

God, the stupidity, the incredible stupidity! They talked as if the silk-lace trade still existed in Nottingham! Didn't they know that in the whole of the city one factory alone still made all-silk lace? Didn't they understand that while they quarrelled and argued and starved, the silk-lace trade had long departed to Heanor and Derby?

He had urged them, urged them with all his heart. Were they going to let a great trade die out while master and men quarrelled? And then slowly, slowly, he had brought the men to agree to a fifteen per cent cut. And from that they wouldn't budge!

And the masters had refused — naturally they had refused.

Speaking for them Old Ware had risen in his place to explain, to make a last appeal to the men. He said his heart bled for them and looking at his sick and worried face you could believe it!

"But listen to reason," he had urged, "you must listen! Figures speak louder than words! In this town, bobbin-finings made on a twenty-quarter machine cost one shilling per rack. Even with the fifteen-per-cent reduction which you concede, the cost would be tenpence-farthing. But these very finings, the identical patterns made in Long Eaton on an identical machine, cost sixpence-farthing! How can we carry on hampered like that, how do you expect us to carry on?"

You'd have thought those figures would have spoken for themselves! But looking round at the obstinate faces of the workers; Nicholas had realised that they were deaf to reason — the hunger in their bellies made them, maybe, hard of hearing. But if they didn't listen now, they'd be a deal hungrier than they were at present — and when they were willing to listen it would be too late!

He had stood up then, forgetting in his urgency the speech of the gentleman, speaking to them man to man, trying, before it was too late, to make them understand.

"Afe a loaf is better'n no bread! That's a fac', i'n't it? *I'n't it?* Yer just abowt clemmed now ent yer? Tak th'cut while yer can and set th'machines goin'! If yer down't set th'machines goin' now, some of yer, mebbe, wain't niver 'ear th'voice o' th'machines no more!"

And when he had seen it was useless, quite useless, he had lost his temper and shouted, "Come to Long Eaton an' see th' hunderds o' young chaps all grimy wi' honest work! Ay, an' th'hunderds o' young lasses — an' all of 'em jinglin' th'brass in their pockets. An' then if yo're so damned obstinate, hand us ovver th'rest o' yer trade an' starve!"

And he had flung out of the room. And he had been nearer to tears than ever before in his life — he, Nicholas Penny, to whom Nottingham's lost trade was so much golden fish in his own net!

Penny's luck, they said. Penny's luck! He didn't trust to luck, not he! He trusted to his own eyes and to his own ears, and to his own common sense. . . And yet, he had been lucky, too!

Young Wade. There was a piece of luck! Fifteen now, but he'd paid his way, more than paid it, ever since he'd left school three years ago. Pen Wade. Draws like an angel, Stella had said. And by God, it was true! And that wasn't the end of it, neither! He'd had his doubts about young Wade at first — too handsome by far with those dark thoughtful eyes, and the long fine hands! Too much the gentleman! The lad had been put right away to mind the machines, and then it had been clear that those thoughtful eyes missed nothing, that no work was too dirty or too heavy for those fine hands moving with clean quick movements.

Artist's hands. The boy was a born designer. And finding it out so soon — that had been a bit of luck and all!

Passing through one of the Lever's shops, Nicholas had seen the boy take his dinner from his pocket, and flick out with it a crumpled piece of paper. He had thought no more of it at the time, but returning later, through the almost empty room, and finding the paper still there, he had stooped to pick it up. After all, any little bit of information one picked up about one's hands might come in handy!

With one glance, his own designer's eye had seen where the boy's gift lay. The little pattern had quality. It was a trifle complicated for the narrow lace for which it was intended — a beginner's error. But it had quality!

In a moment his pencil was out. It flicked here, there. That was better, Perfect now. Quite perfect!

In the midst of his pleasure at the find, he thought uneasily, his birthright! We couldn't steal that! He was uneasy but he was hardly surprised. *If it's design — and it may well be...* He had said that to Stella all of five year ago!

He sent for Pen Wade, awaiting him, as once before, at the great desk piled high with drawings.

The same room, the same Nicholas — but not at all the same Pen Wade. This was a lad who carried his handsome head high, though there was still something of sadness in his eyes — maybe a shadow of that shadow Stella had carried those last unhappy years. But in spite of his pride, he was shy — not with the tender shyness of childhood, but with the agonising, pitiable shyness of adolescence.

Nicholas said heartily, "Well, young feller, how goes it? Like the work?"

"Ay!" Pen was not enthusiastic. But quick to see the frown upon the master's face, added at once, "Thank you, sir!"

"Like the shops?"

The boy hesitated. He must not explain to this hard and hearty man how much he hated the noise and the heat and the greasy feel of black-lead upon the carriages. *You must not offend the boss...* You might lie or cheat or steal — if you got the chance, so they said, but you must not offend the boss!

He said lamely, "I like to see how the pattern comes, the way it blocks itself in on the thread. I like patterns. Like making them, too!"

Nicholas, hunting among the drawings on his desk, noted the pleasantness of the boy's speech. *Too*, he had said, instead of *an' all!* The *i*'s, too, were clear and sharp.

He found the drawing for which he sought and held it out to the boy.

"Like it?" The design was his own, one upon which he had lavished care. He waited, with absurd anxiety, for the answer. It was an experience he had not known these many years — this waiting upon the judgment of another.

"Ay!"

That — and no more. He was disappointed, he, Master of Pennys, because a raw lad could find no further word of praise.

Vanity pricked him on to try again.

"Why!"

"Because it's right. Simple and clear, the way a pattern ought to be. Not one line too much, nor yet one too little!" The boy was speaking now of something he knew — something he knew almost emotionally.

Nicholas did not smile. He was not one to give himself away. He sent the boy back to the shop.

All work thrust aside, Nicholas considered Pen Wade. Here was a find! Something to add to the resources of Pennys. The boy was a natural designer. He had a heaven-sent gift!

His first impulse was to take Pen from the machines and send him as a day student to the School of Art.

But Nicholas did not believe in giving way to impulse. That matter had to be considered, to be considered all round!

Take the lad from the shop when he might be earning! The surest way to start gossip. Not that he, Nicholas Penny, cared about gossip, he was above that sort of thing — now! But he didn't want to spoil the boy — and another thing, the practical work at the machines would be of the greatest help to him as a designer. Besides — no good making things too easy for the lad! Every man who meant to make good had to learn to sweat first! He himself had had to sweat! Let young Wade show whether he had guts!

A week later Pen was enrolled as an evening student at the school — upon terms. Nicholas sent for him to explain those terms. The fees to be paid by Pennys — and Pennys to have the first option upon his services. To put it clearly — the boy must undertake to work at Pennys for five years after he had finished at the School of Art, the work to be paid for at a fair rate — the rate to be fixed by Nicholas.

Eyes luminous, eyes of the young Stella, Pen, all gratitude, accepted the conditions.

Yes, that had been a piece of luck — in its way. Nicholas wouldn't deny it. But his handling of the situation, that had not been luck, it had not been luck at all — it had been smart work!

Chapter 28

John Ware was angry. He sat very upright, looking at his son-in-law, while anger burned in his thin cheek. Away from them stretched the long expanse of table, crystal and flowers and fruit mirrored warmly in its shining depths... Inexpensive flowers, cheap fruits, as Nicholas's experienced eye did not fail to note; but on the whole, he had to admit, making a good enough show.

Ware was so angry, he was finding it difficult to speak. Yet, he reminded himself, it was for the very purpose of speaking that he had sent for Penny. No — he corrected himself with bitterness — one did not *send* for Penny, one *asked* him, asked him with deference — the fellow who had once sat humble and penniless in this very room.

He swallowed on his bitterness.

Nicholas helping himself to a glass of port was amused. He could afford to be amused. With one strong thumb pressing into his walnut, he waited for the little crackle of broken shell. The nut-cracker lay despised at his hand.

Nicholas waited. It came pleasantly, the sharp breaking-noise. He found pleasure, always, in small trials of strength, no less than in big ones. He thought, sitting there very much at his ease, that John Ware looked old. But then hang it all, the chap *was* old! Just looking at him made you feel, well, if not positively youthful — at any rate in the prime! Made you appreciate your own energy, and the way you were able to get enjoyment out of everything... you enjoyed a good dinner as much as the youngest — more, because your palate was educated! Sight as good as ever — especially if there was a pretty woman about.

He took the bouquet of his wine... The old chap still had a palate!

"A bad position, bad all round!" Nicholas picked delicately at the white nut and crunched it between strong teeth. "But I warned you, long ago I warned you! Six years ago I warned the Board of Conciliation that nothing but a forty per cent cut would save the situation — but the men wouldn't listen and the masters couldn't make them! I said then, that you'd all find yourselves in the soup! Well, now it's happened, and the soup is maybe hotter than even I thought! But I don't see I'm called upon to scald myself, I don't see that I come into this at all!"

"You came into it," Ware said slowly, "when you took your machines out of the city — took them where there was no union rate."

"Sound arithmetic, wasn't it? I'm a business man, not a Don Quixote!"

The old man flushed painfully. With his thin face, hollow blue eye and thin beard, the gibe seemed pointed enough. But Nicholas went on pleasantly, "A man's responsibility is first of all to his family!"

His eye wandered about the handsome room — silver massive upon the great sideboard, huge pictures of still-life opulent as ever. But every time he entered this room, the expensive embossed wallpaper looked a little dingier, the thick silk curtains more faded; and, when you looked at them closely, they were frayed, ever so slightly, at the edges. Nothing new ever came into this room nowadays. . . How, with all his inherited wealth, had John Ware provided for his family?

John Ware, watching, interpreted the glance. His left hand lifted from the table, with a slight regular movement began to saw the air. He looked at his hand. . . Mustn't get excited. Take it easy, Ada had said, take it easy. . . He laid his hand carefully upon the table.

But Nicholas noticed nothing. He was enjoying the sound of his own voice — voice of a man whom events have proved right.

"Stop blaming me — and put the blame where it belongs! Union rates of pay, it's still strangling the trade. Ay, even the revised rate! The cut wasn't enough, it wasn't enough to serve any real purpose. I said it then and I'll go on saying it! Union rates have ruined plenty — and — believe me — they'll ruin plenty more!"

"Maybe!" John Ware said, "but it didn't help us, taking the trade away from the city!"

"It helped me!" Nicholas grinned and reached out for another walnut. "The trouble with you is that you don't see straight! Let me tell you that the men themselves did more to strangle the lace trade by trying to hang on to union rates, than I did when I built my mill outside. If they'd taken that cut twenty year ago, ten, six even, you'd all have done a damned sight better! But it's too late now! You owners, you've been chucking your money down the drain, trying to keep your heads above water. You paid away money you couldn't afford in high wages, when you ought to have kept the money for new machines. You knew well enough, you masters, and you should have forced the men to know — that with those old narrow machines, and payment reckoned by the width, you couldn't compete with us, couldn't begin to compete. Because the truth is this — never mind how hard a twist-hand may work, let him sweat by night and day — if the precious union allows it — if he works at union rates, he'll starve in the end. Ay, and you masters with him! Because — I'll say it again, I'll say it as often as you like — you can't compete, you can't begin to compete against us at Long Eaton, with our new wide machines, and our way of reckoning pay, irrespective of width. Well, it's too late to bring all that up now! If you ask me, there's only one thing to do, as I see it — and my sight's reckoned damn good! You get out of it while you can! Close down Heriots. Live on what you've got — while you've still got it!"

Close down Heriots... joking, the fellow was joking. His sort of joke, silly, a little cruel...

Watching the younger man's face, he thought. But he means it... he does mean it... Close Heriots... *Heriots!* But Heriots is more than a mere factory, it's the hope of its hundreds of workers — in these bad times, their only hope of life... What would old Andrew have thought of closing down his factory?

He raised his eyes to old Andrew's portrait — Andrew who looked like pirate turned poet. His mind, moving backwards, rejected the suggestion.

Old Andrew... And then himself coming into Heriots, not so much for love of Heriots as for love of Andrew's daughter. A young man, coming into Heriots and learning from the old man — and learning to love the old man and the place together. And then, in fullness of time, himself taking up the guiding reins, himself the master... Watching the workers grow old — himself growing old along with them; watching their children take their places, and their children's children growing... watching those children as he had watched his own child grow...

You knew well enough, you masters, you couldn't compete...

His problem was at him again. There was no refuge in the past.

Yes, he had known... but he had known, too, the hard and bitter lives of the workers. How could he have joined in with the cry for lower wages? He couldn't — knowing that working at cut rate on sixteen-quarter machines, they couldn't live, couldn't exist, even!

Close Heriots! Heriots' men along with all the others, hundreds upon hundreds, wandering the streets... No work... no work... Even now it cut him to the heart to see the fine able-bodied men wandering the streets, good workers most of them. He could pick a good worker at a glance — he'd been an employer of labour long enough! And how would he endure to see Heriots' men, men he had known and loved all his life, wandering frightened, hopeless, bitter, belt tightened in upon famished belly.

No work...

You ought to have forced the men to see... To see what? To see that if they took the full cut they'd starve, and if they didn't take it, they'd still starve.

Close Heriots? Not while the breath of life remained in his body! There was a way out, a way he'd thought of during the long and sleepless nights, when he'd lain wakeful in the darkness, turning the question this way and that. It was because of that way out he had asked Penny here tonight.

He said, as if the suggestion to close Heriots had never been made,

"There's a way out. A good way. The only way! And that's machines. New machines. If I had ten new machines — ten only — I'd save Heriots. I'd show others the way. With new machines we'd bring the trade back, back where it belongs!"

"Nice for me!" Nicholas said and grinned.

"You or me — what does it matter? It's the trade that counts. The trade — and the men who live by the trade, and their women and their children. . ."

"Ten machines!" Nicholas ignored Ware's outburst. "Ten thousand pounds! It's a devil of a lot of money — even for me!"

Even for me. . . even for me. . . Did he mean to whip you, pointing the difference, the well-fed young man sprawling in his chair? All his money didn't gild him, didn't hide the base metal. But he was a success as men count success. . . just as you were a failure as men count failure, as you yourself counted failure. Once you could have raised the money. Heriot credit. It had been as safe as the bank. But nowadays, when house after house went crashing, when others hung on, like Heriots, by the skin of their teeth, there was no more credit for anyone.

But Penny had money. Penny knew how to make money. Penny knew his way about! How you had laughed at him for buying that scabby bit of land that went down to the canal! Well, Penny had let you laugh! But it was he who laughed now — and he didn't trouble to hide his laughter, either!

Yes, Penny had the money! But — he wasn't the sort of person one wanted to ask favours of! Not that he'd refuse — he rarely refused — he enjoyed the sense of power it gave him. But he had a way of granting a favour so that it turned sour on you!

. . .That time you'd asked help for old Coates — broken leg and down on his luck after twelve years' faithful service at the club. You'd asked for one pound and Penny had given ten! But he'd let you know it — let everyone else know it, too! At the time you had actually asked, you and he had been alone in the cloakroom, and he hadn't his purse on him — so he said!

But later, when you had been dining at the Borough Club, and every table crowded as always on a Wednesday, Penny had taken his sovereign-case out of his pocket. There on the tablecloth he had built up a neat little pile. . . one, two, three, four, five, six, seven, eight, nine, ten. . . ten golden sovereigns — and all eyes following, giving each sovereign its full importance. Penny's strong fingers neatening, straightening the little pile. . . and then, the pile stacked to his satisfaction, he had pushed them across the table at you, announcing in that loud voice of his, that he was heading a subscription for old Coates.

Generous. . . of course generous! It was you, yourself, that had not been generous. You had unaccountably wanted to pick up the money and throw it back into the man's too-handsome, too satisfied face. And then, Penny, sitting back, red with feeding and good wine, bullying the others with that damn superior look of his to go and do likewise — though he knew well enough there was hardly a man in the room that could afford it!

Penny's generosity! Damn good advertisement for Penny! Cheap! More ways than one! You'd been ashamed of him!

No, you couldn't ask Penny!

But you had to ask him! It was part of the payment one made for being a failure. You had to have the money. You had to show both masters and hands that there was still a way! You had to keep Heriots on its feet!

But suppose it didn't keep Heriots on its feet? A loan of this size might bring Heriots back to full working power. Or — if things didn't work out, Heriots might be pushed into bankruptcy...

Nicholas, intent upon his dessert, watched his father-in-law. He knew well enough the thoughts — if you could dignify them with the name — that went on in that muddled head.

Ware, eyes closed, wondered what, in these same circumstances, old Heriot would have done... Queer, after all these years, to be sitting here, and missing the old man, and wanting the old man! Heriot would have risked everything for an idea. Walking by his own light, he had called it... And his light had always led him the right way. Vision and good Scots common-sense — that had been old Heriot.

You yourself, you were only an ordinary man without vision, with only the tremendous desire that the lace trade should come back to the city, that a living wage should come back to the hands, the empty hands of the workers.

Empty hands. Could a man turn his back on those; for the sake of his own dignity, his own safety, turn his back?

He said abruptly, knowing his resolution might fail, "I must have ten new machines to start with!"

"Ay, and finish with! You'll not get men at less than union rates, not in Nottingham. You'll find yourself landed with enormously expensive machines and a wage bill you can't meet. Heriots —" He cracked a walnut with sudden sharp explosion to demonstrate, without words, exactly what would happen to Heriots.

"It won't be the finish, I tell you! It'll be the beginning — it'll point the way!"

"Ay, so it will! But maybe it won't be a way you'll like! Until the union allows the men to take lower wages, you can't afford even one new machine!"

"Until we've got new machines," Ware was obstinate, "the union daren't allow another drop. Machines come first — and someone has got to lead the way!"

"Why you?" Nicholas's tone was contemptuous beyond the point of rudeness.

Ware ignored the rudeness. "Why not?"

But he knew the answer — he knew it well enough; knew, equally, that it was useless trying to make Penny understand. Penny was too clever to understand so simple a thing as loyalty to the place where a man had been born and where he had lived his life long.

His town. His own town. He knew its every stick and stone; he knew its history — warm homespun shot through with the dark doings of kings.

His mind, taking its brief release, went back. . ..

That time he had been taken to Sherwood Forest for the first time. Sherwood Forest — the very words were music! A little lad he'd been, seven, maybe — or eight. A long drive it had seemed. . . legs dangling, cramped legs. He had wriggled the toes inside his boots, trying to drive out the cramp! He remembered it — as he remembered everything that had happened that day. Not that there was so much to remember as far as actual happenings go! But it was the sort of experience that goes deep. . .

. . .A fine summer's day with the sky very blue and. the sun making rainbows of light in front of your eyes, making rainbows of light in your heart, because you were going to Sherwood Forest, home of your heart's hero.

And then the disappointment, so that you had refused to believe you were really there, even though you'd left the dog-cart and were walking, both of you, in the green grass — disappointment because the trees were thin and scanty — birches on a sort of sandy common. This was never, never, Robin Hood's Sherwood. You had tugged at father's hand. You had wanted to go back to the dog-cart and go home and not see any more!

But father had led you on. Deeper. . . deeper. The trees were growing closer and there were oak trees now as well as birches.

And then — Robin Hood's Oak, Robin's own tree!

And maybe he had stood where you stood, his feet on the very spot, his eyes looking where your eyes looked. . . And then, quite suddenly, the wood had come alive. Robin and his men. You could have sworn to the clear note of the horn.

And all the time you had known it was more than that — much more. It had come to you, though of course you hadn't fully understood — the enormous unbroken power of tradition, the linking of life with life. A tremendous thing, really, for a little boy to guess at, even if guessed never so faintly.

And then, quite suddenly, you had turned and run. That was because of the tears in your eyes — though you had pretended it had been for a quite different reason. You had been ashamed of those tears. But now, perhaps because of them, you had to do what you were going to do!

Well, Penny wouldn't understand that — he certainly wouldn't understand about the tears — it would take a wiser man than Penny to understand that! But, if you brought things down to their simplest, then, maybe, you might make him understand — something.

"I suppose," Ware said, "it's a way of saying *thank you.*"

"Rather an expensive way!"

"Thanks ought to cost something!"

Nicholas sat tight and said nothing. After his first instinctive rejection of Ware's appeal, he was beginning to see a very possible advantage in it to himself.

"Listen, Penny — will you lend me the money?"

There it was out! John Ware sat rigid, his eyes fixed upon Nicholas, his whole will bent upon the effort to make him say *yes*.

Nicholas could have laughed outright. The idea of old Ware forcing his will upon Nicholas Penny! But his face was grave as he said slowly, "I'm not what you'd call a wealthy man, though I don't advertise the fact. What I have," the shrug of his shoulders flicked away so insignificant a sum, "has come to me through sheer hard work. I began with nothing — *you* know that!"

He paused to let it sink in, to remind the old man of his opposition to the marriage, of the lack of any marriage-settlement.

"And I have my family to think of — my wife." He paused again. Heriot would have been a rich woman in the not-too-distant future, if her father had run his business with guts! Now she had little enough to look for from her father — maybe nothing, at all! Let the old chap put that in his pipe and smoke it!

"And now you come to me and ask me to lend you ten thousand pounds for —" his tone made of the word an insult, "an ideal! Well, ideals are all right — in theory. But in practice they hardly ever work out. And I, as I say, have my family to think for! What security do you offer?"

"There'll be the machines."

"Maybe! But I've all the machines I want. Second-hand yours would count as — parts worn, spoiled even. Why should I saddle myself with them? I can get all the new machines I want!"

The arrogance of him! Pointing out the difference, the difference between himself and you!

"I don't propose to cripple myself to buy new machines for the purpose of handing them over to you!" Ware said with spirit. "I'm proposing to pay you back in cash!"

"I've no doubt you intend to. But suppose circumstances are too much for you? And they may well be! To put ten thousand in machines with trade at a standstill — it's asking for trouble!"

"I've never been afraid of trouble. Besides — there's Heriots."

"To send Heriots bankrupt wouldn't give me any pleasure. Nor would it help me in the least. If Heriots credit were — well, what it was once — you'd get the money anywhere!"

Ware felt his temper rising. He'd asked for a loan, not for cheap sneers. He'd borne with this fellow long enough! Even Ada with her counsels to patience would agree with that! Steady now, steady. He wanted this loan, wanted it more than he had ever wanted anything in his life. He wanted, with all his might, to have a hand in bringing the lace trade back again. He wanted, with every power within him, to help the men, those good fellows who walked the streets, idle hands upon tightened belt. He wanted to show the way, to risk everything, yes, risk Heriots even, to revive a dying industry. The good things of life — he had had them so long! They were old now, Ada and he, they wanted so little. As for Heriots, if it served in any slightest way the needs of the trade and those who lived by the trade, let it take the risk! If he failed — then Heriots would make a good end.

He said proudly, "The new machines — and Heriots. Those are my securities!"

Nicholas said, masking his pleasure, "It's a serious step. Take your time!"

"I have taken my time. I've thought of it day in, day out, for months, years even. What I'm going to do is the right thing to do. Others will see, others will follow. The trade will come back again, back where it belongs, back to us in Nottingham. You'll see!"

Nicholas cracked another walnut.

Ten thousand pounds to bolster the failing fortunes of Heriots, the moribund fortunes of Heriots. Ten thousand pounds! But good security given!

Nicholas said nothing about the transaction to Heriot. He did not believe in discussing business with women. Besides — he had the uncomfortable feeling that she would not be pleased.

He was ready to be annoyed at this further demonstration of Ware unreason. Why should she not be pleased? He was lending money at little more than bank rate. He had covered himself, as any reasonable man would do, by accepting security. Did Heriot, by any chance, expect a free gift? There was no end to the Ware foolishness — foolishness they called idealism and thought to make all well! Ten thousand — what was a mere ten thousand to serve their foolishness? Nothing. . . nothing. . .

If Heriot knew of the transaction, she said no word. She went quietly about the house, as if her interests had never ranged beyond its four walls.

He had not meant to speak of the matter. He had not meant to! But the sight of the new machines filled his mind, as fine machines always must. He had gone down to Heriots to look at them. Shining steel, infinitely delicate, infinitely strong — beautiful beyond words in their massive grandeur. Quite frankly he had envied Ware — though he could match them any day. He had not recognised his feelings as envy. He had simply told himself that it was a futile waste to put such machines in a mill like Heriots. Heriots was doomed.

But — he had counselled himself to patience — he had only to wait, to wait a little, and they would come to him in the end.

He had not meant to speak. But to Nicholas, a fine machine was a never-ceasing wonder — and speak he must.

Heriot said, quietly, "I know. I've seen them." And then, with sudden passion, she, the quiet, the controlled, "I wish he hadn't bought them! Oh, I wish, I wish, he hadn't. You can't stop the tide from going out, no-one can!"

He had a sudden disturbing memory of the young Heriot, eager and impulsive, in her funny smart clothes. Nothing then had been too good for Heriots, no machine too fine, no hope too extravagant.

He said lamely, knowing the lameness, "your father thinks the tide will turn!"

"*You* know it won't. *I* know it won't. Everyone knows it won't. Except father. Why didn't you stop him, Nicholas? Why didn't you stop him?"

"I tried. It was no use. I couldn't stop him. No-one could. He wouldn't listen. His mind was set!" He tried to lighten the misery in her face, to speak the language she could understand. He said, "In his way — he's rather fine!"

"Fine!" She had forgotten her own language, the bitterness in her face showed him that. He thought how oddly things had come about that he must play idealist to her realist — and she not even understand. "Fine! When Heriots is smashed! I haven't mentioned Heriots, oh, for years! Why should I? I was out of it, quite out of it — no place for a woman! But I've thought about it a lot. . . the men and the machines. And how everything was sliding away from safety. And how we could have brought it back again, you and I, brought it back to safety. I've never stopped thinking, really. Sometimes this house — your house, Nicholas — and the things I do in it, seem thin, like something out of a dream. And Heriots is the only real thing. All the years of being silent, of brooding, of hiding my thoughts — they're curdling inside me. I've got to speak of Heriots, speak just once, and then no more, Nicholas, no more!

"Heriots was my grandfather's life work, a thought in his mind that he made come true. All his life he kept the idea of Heriots in front of him. All his life — a working life that began so young, so awfully young. Six years old when he went out to work! Can't you see him, Nicholas, stumbling out into the frosty moonlight? Or maybe there wouldn't be a moon at all, and he'd be frightened of the dark. Children are, you know! And maybe it would be winter and he wouldn't have enough to eat. Not enough warm clothes, either. And his hands and feet — baby's hands and feet — would be swollen with chilblains. And he'd be tired, taken from his sleep, so terribly tired. He'd lean against a bench out of the road of the machines, wanting to sleep — and not daring to sleep; and propping his eyes open with his fingers. Or lying down on the cold and dirty floor, and the draught blowing under sharp as knives, and trying to snatch a moment's rest.

"But it didn't down him, and it didn't make him bitter. It made him strong and it made him wise. In spite of everything he was able to keep in front of him the idea of Heriots — the great factory where men could work and live. Live, Nicholas, not scratch out a bare existence. Heriots gave fair wages, Heriots gave fair hours, long before the law demanded it — before the law thought of demanding it. Heriots was a light in the darkness, and now it's going out. . . it's going out, Nicholas. . ."

A long speech. And an odd speech. But it was only once in a way — as she said. He wouldn't grudge it. These Wares! Their thoughts ran thin and sweet as sugar-water — and just about as useful!

He said good humouredly, "it's a little late to be weeping over old Heriot. And in any case you haven't got it clear! Your grandfather went to work at six, not because he'd got Heriots in his infant mind, but because he had to! And all his life he worked, not because Heriots was a dream he had to make come true — though it's a pretty notion — but because he had to work or starve! He had courage and he had strength and he had will. And so Heriots came about. It wasn't because it had been a sort of vision in a poet's mind as you seem to think, but because it was inevitable in a businessman's life — and that man Andrew Heriot. Make no mistake, Andrew Heriot was a first-rate business man and that's all there was to it!"

Heriot said, stiff, bitter, "Haven't you an idea in your head but pounds and shillings and pence?"

"Thousands of pounds! Tens of thousands! If I hadn't, what would become of you and Nicki?"

Suddenly he dropped his bantering tone. "See here, Heriot, it doesn't do to mix sentimental notions with work. It doesn't pay. One or t'other's got to go under. And if you let the work go, what becomes of the worker then? Wrapping the worker in cotton-wool — that's the mistake the Factory Acts made. I tell you the lace trade was in danger the minute it was brought under the Factory Acts. By some miracle it hadn't been included and so it flourished. And then soft-headed sentimentalists got busy and they started shouting for lace to be included. Well, they got their way — and that was the beginning of the end! For Nottingham at any rate. Factory Acts at one end — union rates at the other! High wages and short hours. No trade can survive on that. The result is always the same — less and less work for the workers. And soon, no work at all! There's an old saying about having your cake — and by God, it's a true one!"

Heriot said, "What sort of cake? Men and women working in the noise and the smell and the filth — yes, the filth, Nicholas, breathing in black-lead from the machines, breathing death into their lungs."

"Don't get sentimental, Heriot. Black-lead never hurt anyone!"

"Maybe not the stuff you use now — but it did, Nicholas, it did, horribly. That's why the Factory Acts came in — not to put money in your pockets, but to save the lives of thousands upon thousands of men, women and children. You don't read old reports, do you, Nicholas? I do — it helps to pass the time. I know them by heart — almost. There was one in eighteen-sixty — I told you about it once, long, long ago — you thought it mattered then — or you pretended you did! Grandfather's friend was responsible — Mr Charlton — remember now, Nicholas? That report had some interesting things to say about black-lead, how it destroyed eyes and lungs. That was happening every day — lungs and eyes eaten away — happening not only to men and women, but to the children, Nicholas, the children!

"And it wasn't only their bodies those Acts had to think about — there was worse than that, far worse — the damage done to their minds. I won't annoy you, Nicholas, by sentimental talk about souls! Boys and girls turned out of bed at nights, hanging about in the dark streets waiting for the work to come off the machines, and learning hateful, vicious habits while they waited. Hanging about in the dark where no-one could see them, and trying to make the cold darkness bearable with their hateful habits! And then, those children grown to be men and women, their shameful habits grown stronger and unashamed. The marketplace on a Saturday night! Ask my father, ask anyone who remembers. Maybe you remember something, yourself, Nicholas, even though you were too little to understand. Do you really think it better for that sort of thing to go on, do you really think so, Nicholas?"

"Special pleading, Heriot, that's what I think. And I also think it doesn't matter what I think, because the Acts are old history —"

"What you think today makes the history of tomorrow!" she flashed with yet another disturbing glimpse of the young Heriot.

"Exactly. Today your father thinks new machines will save Heriots — tomorrow —" he shrugged, "finished!"

"As bad as that?" Her eyes, not her voice asked the question.

"Ay! It's losing money hand over fist!"

"That's just it!" She spread her helpless hands. "That's just what I don't understand. How did Papa get the money? Where did he get it from? Heriots has been losing steadily, oh for ages — I've known that, but I didn't know it was so much! And now — ten machines at something like a thousand pounds each! Who would lend him the money? Who *could* have it to lend? There's no-one, no-one with all that to spare, no-one we know, unless —" her hazel eyes narrowed, "unless it was you, Nicholas. It *was* you, Nicholas, wasn't it?"

He shrugged.

"Was it, Nicholas? *Was* it?" The old high voice of authority coming so strangely from long-meek lips.

He said, marking his patience, "My dear, what *do* you want? A moment ago you condemned me for not having an idea above *£.s.d.* You contrasted me, not at all favourably, with your father, who is, apparently, the shining example of what a businessman should be! And now, I, the money-grubber, lend ten thousand — and it took some grubbing, believe me — to the sentimentalist to carry out his sentimentalising, and even then you're not satisfied!"

She looked at him without speaking, knowing the hopelessness of speaking. . . *I know you, Nicholas. I love you, but still I know you! If you lent ten thousand it was because you thought it worth your while. Nothing counts with you when it comes to money, nothing at all — neither flesh nor blood nor sweat nor tears. . . Careful, I must be careful. The wrong word now — and he'll remember it against papa all his life. . .*

She smiled, but the sweetness was lacking; the mouth twisted a little. She said, "Women! In business! What do they know? I'm such a fool, Nicholas!"

So she denied her life's dream.

He smiled, patting the outstretched hand.

. . .Heriot fools! Thank God their foolishness was not inherited by Nicki! She took after him. *His* girl! Sound as a nut, and as properly hard. She saw clear — did Nicki, her eyes were not sticky with dreams!

At Heriots the new machines stood ready — ready for the press of work that would never come. Sometimes bar and bobbin throbbed and danced, and the longed-for clatter went echoing through the quiet factory. But oftener the machines stood silent, testifying dumbly that the tide had not turned. . . not yet turned.

And how, Nicholas thought, had old Ware expected it to turn? Can the river flow backwards? But apparently that was exactly what old Ware did expect — the miracle to happen for him, because he was a Ware.

Chapter 29

Nicolet swinging along from school was thinking — she was thinking about mamma. She had a long walk in front of her, for she was going to tea with grandmamma — and plenty of time to think in. She turned down Arboretum Street and into the Arboretum. It was a clear day in early summer with a warm honey-scent in the air. The great flower-beds were crammed with wallflowers of different colours, so that they looked like an immense Turkey carpet, thought Nicolet, stopping and wrinkling her nose to smell.

She came past the little refreshment kiosk and stopped to consider the advisability of buying some chocolate-cream. But there would be a row if you were caught eating out-of-doors, and your school hat on! Besides, it would be a pity to spoil the good tea grandmamma would undoubtedly give her.

Down by the ornamental lake the willows hung grey young leaves to the water. She leaned her elbows on the iron railings and watched the ducks fussily waggling their way under the absurd Japanese bridge that seemed to begin and end nowhere.

The wind stirred the hair beneath the absurd straw sailor. It felt hot and tiresome pressing upon her head. She would have liked to jerk it off, to let the wind cool the red mark she could feel coming round her forehead. . . but the headmistress had announced suitable penalties for that girl, who, lost to decency, should walk in a public place, her school-hat dangling. She did tug at her gloves, though, and push them viciously into a corner of her satchel. Now one could think better!

But why, she thought, am I worrying about mamma? Mamma is as she always was, there is no difference, no difference at all. . . then why do I worry?

Worried? Not worried — exactly! Interested. Maybe because I'm growing up. When you grow up you don't go on accepting things, you begin to question, to ask yourself why? I suppose that's why I'm beginning to think that perhaps I don't understand mamma, don't *know* her. . . One has, sometimes, the oddest sort of feeling that it isn't mamma at all, moving about the house, but a stranger, or, more than that, the shell of mamma carrying on mamma's business.

Odd. Very odd. Because to look at mamma is pretty much like any other mamma — she dresses nicely and she's kind. Nothing ever seems to go wrong at home, and you never hear her voice raised. She never complains, no, not even so much as a comfortable little grumble. She never seems to express the slightest wish — and that isn't because she has everything. I have everything — but I can always think of something more. It isn't that she isn't interested. She listens to everyone, to me, to papa, to the maids, to the boot-boy, even, with the closest attention... all the time listening quietly, not missing anything in spite of being so quiet... perhaps because of being so quiet. That's what's wrong with mamma... too quiet. She smiles sometimes, of course, but not very often. Pity she doesn't smile oftener... that smile — seems to light her up from inside.

But smiling now and again — even if the smile's lovely, isn't good enough. For the rest of the time mamma isn't there, she just isn't there!

One goes on all these years, thought Nicolet, accepting things. I suppose I've accepted mamma — but have I? Have I accepted mamma? Mamma isn't as easy to accept as papa. Papa... her mouth widened into an unconscious smile — you know where you are with papa. He's jolly, he's kind, he's quick to laugh. Quick to be angry, too — but not with you, never with you! When papa comes into the house, the whole house seems to wake up and live... except mamma, except mamma.

But papa, bless him, isn't a thinking sort of person. He always expects you to listen to him — he never seems to have time to listen to you... it's a pity! Only the other day you'd tried to explain to papa that you weren't really satisfied about mamma. But he laughed and pulled your hair and told you not to be a fanciful puss — romantic like mamma.

Nicolet tossed back the bright curls beneath the ribboned sailor-hat... papa oughtn't to treat me like that, and I shall tell him so! I shall say, I'm fourteen and grown-up... nearly!

Is mamma fanciful, though? Would that help to explain the thing you'd heard mamma say years ago? You'd worried over it a lot...

It was that time you'd fallen from your horse — ten you'd been... just before your tenth birthday and there hadn't been a party because of it. Lying in bed...

The stiff straw hat, pressing upon her head, was bringing it all back.

...The bandage pressing, pressing... It hurt... it hurt...

She turned her back upon the pond and came into Waverley Street. But she was not in Waverley Street. She was lying, miserable, in the dark with a hurting head. Whenever she tried to turn her head to find a cool place on the pillow, it was as though someone hacked at her with a knife — a blunt and rusty knife...

She was whimpering a little with the pain; and because she wanted papa. She wished papa would come. She was miserable lying there in the dark with her hurting head... Over there, in the greenish light where the dusty sunshine crept in at the edges of the dark blinds, mamma and grandmamma stood, heads bent together, talking... talking the secret way grown-ups do — all of them except papa. She didn't want them, not either of them. She wanted papa. She wanted him terribly to put his hands on her forehead and stop the pain.

Papa, she whimpered, papa. . .

Over there by the window, they couldn't hear. When she moved her mouth to speak, the pain in her head was worse, terribly worse. She tried to forget about papa, to think of something else.

Yes, in spite of the hurting pain, her head was clear. She could call her thoughts and they would come. And they would stay, too, they would stay as long as she pleased. They didn't go sliding away into the dark as they had been doing. . . How long had her thoughts been behaving in that odd way? She didn't know. . . she just didn't know. . .

She spread her thoughts in front of her.

. . .I am Nicolet. I am ten years old. I go to school. Yes, they were sensible thoughts, they were behaving properly.

Nicolet was pleased.

. . .I fell off my horse. When did I fall? I don't know. . . this year, next year, sometime. . . there was the answer, sometime. . . Why did I fall. . . I don't fall off horses! I fell because that boy threw a stone and Polly shied. Papa won't be disappointed about me falling, not when I tell him how it happened. I'll tell him it wasn't my fault. I'll tell him I wasn't afraid when I fell. . . there wasn't time to be afraid, really. . . but I won't tell him that. Brave, I'll say, ever so brave. . .

Papa. . . she wanted him, she wanted to tell him now. . .

Papa! she said. Papa! And began to cry. The tears were making the bandage wet — they were smarting the cut places on her head and on her cheeks. It made her cry more.

Mamma came softly from her place in the greenish light. "Be a good girl," said mamma, "papa will come soon!" But Nicolet didn't believe her. Mamma sometimes didn't like the fun she and papa sometimes had. Mamma would stop it if she could — she'd say something about being kept up too late, or missing lessons — or a word called dizzyplin. That was a word they used at school, too, and it wasn't a nice word. Nicolet didn't believe mamma, now, because she was speaking in her dizzyplin voice.

"Don't cry, darling," said mamma still in the dizzyplin voice, "because you'll make the sore places wet and then they won't heal up nicely!"

Nicolet wanted to go on crying — but it hurt her head to cry. She turned her head very carefully upon the pillow. . . she closed her eyes. . .

It was then she heard the thing that had been worrying her all these years. They thought she was asleep. She could hear them talking in quiet whispers. She heard grandmamma say, "why haven't you sent for her father?" She strained her ears for mamma's reply — she needn't have strained them, though, mamma's voice, though quieter than grandmamma's, was beautifully clear. "Doctor's orders. Nicholas is no earthly good in an emergency. He'd simply lose his head — and the doctor knows it! He'd upset her. If the temperature goes up any more, we shall really have trouble. . ."

. . . Funny about papa losing his head. . . there wasn't anything wrong with papa's head. Mamma had made a mistake. . . it was Nicolet's head. . . Nicolet's. . . But it didn't matter. . . nothing mattered, except she wanted papa.

She cried a little for papa before she slid back again into the dark. Nicolet looked about her a little dazed. She had come out of the Arboretum by the funny little lodge and down Waverley Street past the School of Art, and into Goldsmith Street with its shabby shops and shabbier houses — and she hadn't realised it.

Had mamma said that, really said that, about papa being no good in emergencies? It made her angry whenever she thought about it. It was wrong and it was unkind and it was untrue. . .

Was it untrue though, absolutely untrue? Was it? Was it?

The question mocked her as she came round by the Theatre Royal and across the Theatre Quadrant. She was blind and deaf crossing the traffic-laden Quadrant — she saw nothing, heard nothing. She was not there at all.

. . .She was sitting up in her rocking-chair; it was the first time she had been allowed out of bed since the accident. Her legs didn't feel at all nice and the bandage was still round her head. She was nursing the new doll papa had given her. There were at least twenty dolls over there in the cupboard, but this was the newest and it had cost the most. . . the most expensive doll in Nottingham, papa had said — so, of course, it was the best!

She was sitting there, and she wasn't enjoying the rocking-chair, nor the doll, nor being up, nor anything. Because in a minute they were coming to take the bandage off — mamma and the starchy-nurse. She was frightened, because the bandage had stuck. It would hurt, hurt hatefully. She knew that because she'd tried to get it off herself, she'd given it the gentlest of tugs, and it hurt. . . it hurt worse than ten thousand sharp needles sticking into you all at once. . . it hurt like hell. . .

But it wasn't the hurting she minded. . . so much. It was the fear, the horrible fear that when they pulled off the bandage, they'd pull the bad place open again, make a hole, maybe, in her head. And the pain would all come back, and the darkness. . . lots and lots of dark days, and each one of them without papa. . . and perhaps her brains would come creeping out through the hole, and she would die or go mad... and in any case they would take her away from papa.

The door opened softly and mamma came in, mamma and the starchy-nurse. She was frightened, so horribly frightened that her heart stopped beating... almost. She remembered, though, that papa was proud of her when she was brave, and she sat still as a statue.

The starchy-nurse dipped the sponge in water. The disinfectant stuff stung... but she didn't make a sound. The starchy-nurse went on bathing. Suddenly, she gave the bandage a tug.

Nicolet hadn't expected that. It was like the starchy-nurse had taken a long sharp knife, and dug a hole in her head... a deep hole... a dark hole... Nicolet said to herself, I'm bleeding... I'm bleeding to death. She saw the hands of the starchy-nurse come up from the basin. She caught them with both her own. She cried out, I won't let you touch it, I won't! She kept on saying, *I won't*... and every time she said it, her voice getting louder and louder. When she heard herself screaming she got more frightened than ever, because she knew very well she wasn't the sort of person to scream...

Mamma asked the starchy-nurse to stop. She said in that dizzyplin voice of hers, "Be sensible, Nicki!" And suddenly, Nicki knew by her eyes that mamma meant to do it herself!

She screamed out for papa then... Let papa do it! She'd be as good as gold, she wouldn't murmur, she wouldn't stir even, if only papa would do it.

Papa came in. But papa didn't do it. He looked as if he were going to be sick. He couldn't do it because he loved you so much, yes he loved you so much he couldn't bear to hurt you...

But mamma had done it. Mamma didn't care about hurting... mamma's fingers were suddenly icy-cold against your skin. There was a tearing sort of pain... and the bandage was off... No mamma didn't care about hurting... she was a cold sort of person — like her fingers.

"Your mamma is brave!" the starchy-nurse said, grinning all over her face like the cat in the Alice-book. Brave! What did she mean? Did you have to be brave to mind hurting someone else... it didn't make sense...

Nicki, crossing the Market Place, smiled to herself... That's what one thought at ten! But at fourteen you knew that it does need a sort of courage to mind about hurting people...

And of course, mamma had minded... only at ten, one couldn't be expected to understand! For years, she'd treasured it against mamma that mamma had not loved her enough to mind about hurting her... Yes, she understood now... but it rankled a little still — unreasonable — but true!

She glanced at the gay stalls beneath the bright awnings. She thought, Everything looks nicer here than at home, the oranges are solider, the apples redder, the cabbages greener.

Walking up Friar Lane, towards the castle, she thought, They used to meet here, mamma and papa, meet in secret. *Romantic like your mamma*... you couldn't think of quiet, cold mamma being romantic. And yet, she had married papa in spite of them all, papa who had been poorer than any churchmouse... Yes, but papa is *papa*... nobody could resist papa...

She swung past the top of her own road and turned down Cavendish Crescent North. She thought, I'm glad it's tea with grandmamma, I can pump her a bit... Life's awfully *interesting*...

But she was still disturbed at the idea of mamma, a stranger living her strange life in one's own familiar home.

Ada Ware held out a plate of Nicolet's special cakes. She would never, she knew, have spoiled Heriot like this. But then, one's grandchild — it was different. One had no sense of responsibility about a grandchild, only pleasure; one could relax, be pleasant, take one's pleasure! Besides, when one's grandchild came to tea, one had the agreeable feeling of being complimented.

It was curious, really, the difference between Nicolet and the young Heriot. They were alike to look at — though Nicki was far prettier than Heriot had ever been. Nicolet knew exactly what she wanted. Heriot had known too. But Heriot had fussed her way there — she had known that, of course, one must occasionally tread upon people's corns — but she had always stopped to apologise. She hadn't known that that sort of apology is more exasperating than the injury! But this child was different. She lived in a different sort of world, a world of opportunities for women. Votes for Women — it would never come of course — unless the world turned upside down. But shouting for the vote, fighting for it, dying for it — had cleared the way of quite a lot of old lumbering obstacles. Nicolet was the child of her age. She was not gentle. She would never stop to apologise. If your feet were in the way she'd tread on them — and be damned to your corns!

You knew where you were with Nicki. Restful, Ada decided grimly.

Nicki chose her cake swiftly and looked inquiringly at her grandmother. She had asked, surely, a simple question, and she was waiting for her answer.

Ada Ware arranged the sugar in an elaborate pattern in the sugar-basin.

"Well?" asked Nicki with a shade of impatience.

"Your mother?" The child was all Nicholas now, sitting upright and impatient and severe. "Your mother — an ordinary little girl I used to think, ordinary in lots of ways. A good little girl — but sometimes she had a violent temper!"

"A temper! *Mamma!*"

Ada nodded. "She learned to control it — that's all! Life taught her that lesson, and whether it's a good thing or not, I don't know. We used to think it was... *Self-knowledge, self-control... You* know... unless Lord Tennyson like so much else, is out of favour! But how far it's wise to bottle up steam, I don't know... I don't know."

Nicolet picked daintily at the curled chocolate upon her cake. She wished grandmamma would get on with the information and not start on her frightful bits of philosophy.

Ada, watching the fingers nimbly picking, thought, I'd have punished Heriot for that — rapped her over the knuckles, or sent her out of the room!

She felt Nicki's will pressing upon her, relentless for her answer.

She said, "Yes, ordinary — so we used to think. But we live and learn — but sometimes we learn too late! If I had my time again I'd do differently — if I understood as I understand now. I wanted Heriot to be happy..." There was a note of appeal in her voice, "of course I wanted her to be happy. Every parent wants that for a child. But I was so certain my way was the right way, the only way. I didn't see that a person's happiness comes only from his own way, I didn't see that till I was quite old..."

And it was too late... too late. If we'd given Heriot her way, let her go into the factory, we shouldn't have driven her into the arms of Nicholas. Nicholas who is cheap for all his success... a disappointed life, empty...

Nicolet coughed a little to bring grandmamma back to the point. Old people were tiresome, you'd think they had all time before them, the way they rambled.

She stretched out a hand for the second cake.

...I should have lectured Heriot for that, pointed out the need for self-denial, even if there were no need, even if nobody else wanted the cake, even if in the end it were to be thrown into the dustbin... cluttering up life with silly rules we thought were moralities...

"Your mother," Ada said, "is, in her way, rather a remarkable woman!"

Nicolet stared at her grandmother. Over the chocolate cake, her eyes were startled.

Ada nodded. "None of us ever does your mother justice — no-one ever did! She's quiet — and we take her at her face value. The truth is, if you can understand it, she's nothing like what her face tries to make you believe — she's a woman born out of her generation — no spiritual home!"

"I'm afraid I don't understand. . ." Nicolet was so interested that the cake remained half-way to her mouth.

"Why should you? I didn't. Nor her father. Nor her husband. And we," she smiled her grim smile, "are a little older than you! You see your mother wasn't ever interested in the sort of thing one expects girls to care about. Her heart was set on the factory. From the time she was tiny she was crazy about machines. When she was good, her treat was to be taken to Heriots. When she was naughty, we threatened her with no more Heriots. When she was sick we coaxed her well again with the promise to take her to Heriots. Her books — when she chose them herself — were never fairy-tales or even school-stories, they were books about lace, about yarns, about machines. Many's the time the maid brought me down one of your grandfather's trade-papers from your mother's pillow, the pages crumpled where she had fallen asleep."

Nicolet nodded. She knew. . . she knew. In mamma's own room you might find the newest novels — but they remained new. . . and at the back of the shelves, books on machines, on lace — old books read and read again.

"But we didn't think it would last, we didn't think it *could!* Unnatural — that's what we thought! You see we'd never come across a girl like Heriot, never even heard of one!"

"To want to do things — even if it's only machines — not *so* wonderful!" declared Nicki.

"Thirty years ago it was different! Even you ought to understand that!" Ada was tart. "Just think! Every teacher in your school has been to college, everyone has got a degree — hasn't she? Well, when your mother was a girl, you could count them on the fingers of one hand, the women here in Nottingham, who'd been to college. And even then, when they'd done the actual work, no-one gave them degrees! I don't blame anyone for that — not suitable — but there it is! I say again, your mother is a remarkable woman — not because she'd a passion for machines and an understanding of lace, not even because she might have been the first woman-owner of a lace factory in the world — that wasn't the remarkable thing, though at the time we thought it was. No, what was remarkable — though you're too young to know it — is the way she put her ambition away and never let it sour her. She put away the work she wanted to do and could have done well, and took up work she didn't like and couldn't do at all — and with never a word of complaint, she taught herself to do it perfectly!"

"She couldn't have wanted it so terribly much," said Nicolet, "When you really want to do a thing, you've *got* to do it — or burst — and sensible people *don't* burst!"

"You Pennys!" Ada shrugged. "You let other people do the bursting!"

Nicki laughed outright. "It's the best way! It's no good being sentimental," she unconsciously aped papa. "But really, I think the truth is, that when you get to be old, old like mamma, you don't care much about anything!"

"Is that so?" Ada was tart. "And what about your papa, miss?"

"Papa isn't old — and never will be! When I say old, I don't mean years. . . I mean. . . well, it's that quietness inside old people, that makes them never want to run, hardly ever smile even, not care much about anything. And mamma doesn't care, she doesn't care about anything really. Nearly everything papa asks her, she says, *As you like dear.* Or *I really don't mind!* Only last night papa asked her about our summer holidays, and she said — as you might have guessed — *I don't mind.* Skegness or Timbuctoo — it's all one to mamma!"

"And where are you going?"

"Skegness of course! And that makes it all so silly — because she didn't even have to choose, she only had to say. . .

Skegness again? Don't you ever get tired of Skegness?"

"No, we love it! Papa likes the golf and there's pretty good riding, and lots of my friends are there. It's fun. We wouldn't want to go anywhere else!"

"And where are you staying?"

"Taking *The Crofts*, as usual!"

"It's a big house."

"We need a big house — we know such a lot of people."

"Do we indeed! And the servants? They go with you of course? And you take your own linen and your own plate?"

"That's mamma's job!" Nicki was a trifle impatient.

"And the housekeeping, and the meals — and the entertaining?"

"Mamma sees to that, too!"

"And don't you think mamma might like a change from plate and linen and housekeeping? Pictures in Italy, perhaps? Or dresses in Paris? Or even," Ada said softly, "castles in Spain!"

"Then she ought to say so!" Nicki said sharply — she disliked the uncomfortable feeling of being somehow in the wrong. "No, the truth is, mamma's grown comfortable — she likes things the way they are!"

"Then everyone's satisfied!" Ada looked at the clock. "Getting on for seven, time to go, my child!"

Nicolet moved over to the bell. "You could fetch them yourself," suggested Ada with a ghost of a twinkle, "it isn't so far!"

Nicolet came back again into the room, tugging the straw hat down over her curls. Ada Ware looked at her grandchild as though she wanted to say something. Something not to be easily said.

"Listen, Nicki," she said at last. "I'm going to say something that very likely I shouldn't say, something that very likely you won't understand. And it's right you shouldn't understand — now. But the time may come when its important you should understand, it may make a difference to your whole life — and there mayn't be anyone then to tell you!

"It's your mother's the strong one. Not your father — your mother. If you want anything with all your heart, and you're not strong enough to get it for yourself — then go to your mother. In the end it's your mother that counts!"

She nodded into Nicki's unbelieving eyes.

"You think she doesn't care because she doesn't nag and whittle whether she goes here or there, whether she does this or that! And you're right — in a way! Skegness or Timbuctoo, it *is* all one to her! You see, she sets her mind on essential things — and those things she follows, she follows them to the end, and nothing or nobody will ever turn her aside. When she cares, she cares tremendously. Ordinary things — they don't matter. But come up against one of her essentials, and not even you, Nicki, strong though you think you are — will so much as move her. She's quiet outside, cold even — but inside, inside, Nicki, she's flame. Remember, Nicki, it's your mother that counts!"

Nicki went running down the street, swinging her satchel. She ran for the pure joy of movement this young summer evening. . . It was old in grandmamma's room, old and tired and anxious, run, run away from it, run as fast as you can!

Ada standing by the slightly-shabby brocaded curtains, watched her and sighed a little.

. . .Now whatever had possessed her to talk to the child like that? Nicki hadn't understood, nor could one expect it of her! It was not dignified to have dissected Heriot like that for the child, not healthy! And yet — She turned back from the bright evening, one had a sense of guilt about Heriot. By one's own obstinacy one had pushed her into a cheap, unsatisfactory life with Nicholas. Somehow, at this late hour, it was as if one wanted to vindicate Heriot. . .

Nicki went on running and skipping and swinging her books. She was trying to run away from grandmamma — but grandmamma pursued her.

. . .Pity mamma was not easy like grandmamma. Grandmamma could hit out when she wanted to — and quite often she did want to! That was why she was easy — she came out into the open with whatever she wanted to say! She didn't go about smiling and not caring — or pretending she didn't care. Of course, lots of the things grandmamma said were nonsense, she was old, she was sentimental — a sentimental Ware. The truth about life was, decided Nicki, if you wanted a thing enough — you went all out to get it! The business of being all ice without and all flame within was nonsense — Ware nonsense. . . *Your mother's the strong one. . .* that had an odd sort of sound — and yet, wasn't it, in a way, familiar, too? Who was it that had sent you to school and kept you there, in spite of all papa's noise? Who was it that had tackled the bandage when papa stood sick and sorry? Who was it on half a dozen occasions you could think of right away, who had quietly and — you could see it now — oh, so cleverly put in the deciding word, just the very word to set papa firm in his purpose; or to make him turn in swift answering annoyance from a cherished plan of which mamma did not approve. . . mamma smiling and pretending to approve — and then, at the right moment, the irritating word, the perfect word, sending him in spite of himself the way mamma wished him to go. . .

Gracious! She was catching the Ware foolishness! Infectious! Mamma was all right. . . mamma was, maybe, stronger than you'd thought! But the idea of mamma living her strange life in your own ordinary home, the idea of a mamma enormously strong, enormously secretive! The idea of any grown-up person eating her heart away in silence! It was sickening, sickening and silly!

When I want a thing, thought Nicki, running up the glittering steps of her home, I won't suffer in silence, and I won't ask anyone to help me, I'll raise all hell till I get what I want, myself.

"Papa in?" The man nodded. Nicolet flung her satchel at him, and then her hat and coat, and flew along to the study.

Mamma and her problems were forgotten.

Chapter 30

Penny's luck. A byword in the trade. Still a byword.

Luck! Nicholas thought contemptuously. A man had no luck but what he sweated for! Luck, they said, as it might be the brushing of the good fairy's wings! Luck — there was no such thing! If you wanted to have and to hold, you had to make the leap to the circumstances. You had to have the courage to chance the loss of all you'd gained, all that through the years you had laboured to gain, agonised to gain. So a man made his own luck!

Nineteen hundred and five! What a year that had been for Nottingham! Common knowledge that never in the story of the lace trade had things been so bad. Nineteen hundred and five — five years ago — the year he had lent ten thousand to Ware. A useless loan — from Ware's point of view. And precious little for himself so far. Ware could hardly scrape up enough to pay the interest, let alone anything else! Well, you weren't surprised! You'd warned him!

And over in Nottingham, things were going from bad to worse! *There is no lace trade in Nottingham*, said the *Nottingham Express*, quoting the experts, *you will find it all at Long Eaton.*

Ay, at Long Eaton! And the pick of it at Pennys.

Pennys had first pick always — pick of orders, pick of raw materials — the finest cotton, the purest silk found its way to Penny mills. And no wonder, for in the ups and downs that so regularly shook the trade, Pennys demands were certain; Pennys payment, sure.

In the Penny mills, the Levers and the Schifflis were going full speed. Penny's "luck"! How long, though, would this "luck" hold?

Quiet in his high office above the noise of the machines, Penny himself sat pondering the chance of survival of twist-lace in the Midlands. In Nottingham it was almost dead. Nottingham had lost nine-tenths of her counter trade; and worse, she had lost the great American trade. Yes, Nottingham had let that last chance slip. Straight to Long Eaton came the American buyers — and of all Long Eaton mills, to Pennys first.

Pennys — first to attract American trade to Long Eaton. And Penny would never let go. Never — if he could help it! But suppose he could not help it? Suppose outside circumstances paralysed his grip? Suppose American buyers cut out England altogether? How if they went straight to the continent — to Calais? to Plauen? to St. Gall? The choice was wide enough... And there were indications. Yes, there were signs enough to set a man thinking. A wise man leaps to the circumstances, makes his own circumstances — his own luck!

Suppose it did happen — mightn't this new fashion for wool-lace help fill the gap? Let old Ware say what he would, wool-lace was more than a mere craze. Women, once used to its lightness, its elegance, would never let it go. It would be used not only for dresses but for underwear, yes, more than anything for underwear... there was a revolution coming in women's underwear and wool-lace would play its part! Yes, he was ready to bet that wool-lace would become more and more a settled demand. Let Ware and the rest of Nottingham masters give wool-lace the go-by! Pennys wouldn't quarrel with that!

Wool-lace... new machines. Of course it could be made on the Levers, but the change-over would take weeks — a loss of trade he could not for a moment consider. Whatever the future demand for Levers-lace, at the moment Pennys was selling every inch it made. He would make that hay while his sun still shone!

New machines...

He turned over the specification of the new Barmen machine. How history repeated itself! A second time John Ware had been offered a Barmen, a second time he had refused it. It had not interested him, he said. No, it didn't matter to him that the new Barmen was finer, swifter, full of infinitely more possibilities than the machine he had refused twenty-five years ago, that with wool-lace he could build up a new, a certain trade. What he knew, that only he trusted. And so, in spite of that ten thousand pounds, in spite of a new untapped source of trade, Heriots was slipping down the dusty path to oblivion.

Barmens. If one began with half a dozen... But where to house them? They were small — they wouldn't need much room. But there wasn't a corner in Pennys hive that wasn't a-buzz. One would have to build... Well, that could be done! There was space enough between the bleaching works and the canal. How old Ware had sniggered when you'd bought that land! Ay, he'd laughed once too often.

Building and buying — that was nothing. The process of making the lace, there was the question. One would have to start learning from the beginning. One would have to learn all those things about wool that one had known about cotton by instinct... Qualities of wool. Suitability of grades of wool. Dyeing... and all those thousand-and-one technical difficulties that would find him entirely at the mercy of his manager, his foremen, his very hands, unless he, too, knew something of the job!

Learning... There would be so much to learn! Ultimately one had to trust to one's experts — but there would be policies to determine, decisions to make! Already he had more on his hands than he could cope with!

Had he, he wondered, contemptuous of himself, caught something of old Ware's complaint? Was old age infectious? *Worth while?* Not only was it worth while — it was essential. As long as there was even the faintest possibility that the future might see a drop in the demand for twist-lace, so long must he be ready.

But it was much for one pair of shoulders. . . too much.

Suddenly he felt tired, discouraged. A man grows older. A man working at full speed grows tired. He may be young in years — why he himself was barely forty-three — he may wear the bright look of youth, but he is like an old machine, bright on the outside, but whose fine inner parts are worn.

He should have had sons now, sons growing up to take some of the weight from his shoulders. Heriot had failed him in this. Failure. . . he hated the sound of the word, he could not endure that it should have the remotest connection with him, with Nicholas Penny! But for all that, through Heriot, he had failed. In all his vast works, there was no-one with intelligence quick to match his own, no-one whose right it was to help with his burden.

Not true. . . not true. There was one. . . one young and untried but rich with promise. Nineteen-year-old Pen Wade — he'd be quick enough to take a burden, to make of it no burden at all. . . but he, himself, had taken the boy's right away. . .

My son. . . my son. . .

He turned from the thought, and meeting the boy later, treated him with cold roughness, to cover his own pain.

Penny's luck! The stream of gold he had dreamed of once, standing empty-handed in the castle garden with Heriot, stream of gold hopping and jingling and leaping to his hand — it was coming true. He was making it come true!

Penny's luck. Two years since the first Barmen had been installed, and now thirty machines clattered away in the long low factory between the bleaching-house and the canal. There had been, so far, no drop in the demand for twist-lace. No machine at Pennys was ever silent, save when the finished work came off and the new went on. Wool-lace, burnt-lace and twist-lace; washing of silk and winding of silk; making of jacquard cards; bleaching the lace and gassing; mending and stretching and stiffening; making of boxes, even. All processes and ramifications of processes carried on in that vast assembly of buildings known as Pennys.

Had he ever thought the demand for twist-lace would fail? Pennys designs were known the world over. Pennys designs travelled not only to America, but to Africa, to Japan. And in Europe you would find them too, in Italy, in Germany, in France — yes, even in France whose own mills turned out Nottingham lace — Nottingham patterns on Nottingham machines. But still the smartest shops in Paris sold Penny lace. Nicholas had seen his own lace in Paris, priced at four, five, six times its worth.

He had a story about that!

It was last year, when Nicolet, aged fifteen, had been on her first visit to Paris, and he had promised her a gift in honour of the event. Anything she fancied and money no object! Nicki had chosen a lace scarf. Four-hundred-and-fifty francs it was priced and very pretty it was! Nicki hung over it enamoured, but Nicholas refused to buy — surprisingly refused, since it was his pleasure to spend lavishly on Nicki. He offered her instead an ostrich feather cape, a gold mesh handbag, or a fan whose ivory had been carved long ago by a Chinese master.

But Nicki, unaccustomed to not having her own way, refusing this, refusing that, left the shop pouting. They marched side by side along the Rue de la Paix, Nicki sulky, Nicholas grim at her unreasonable behaviour. Quite suddenly he burst into chuckles. "You don't need to come to Paris for Penny lace!" he explained between chuckles. "When you get home you can have that identical scarf — at one-tenth the price!"

Penny lace, made on Penny machines by Penny workers!

Penny lace encircling the world — shipped across the sea to India, to Japan, to China for modern girls aping the West, to Africa to deck the calicoes of dusky ladies.

He was always ready, was Nicholas, to leap with the times. His eyes, his ears were always open, his imagination always at work — his common sense always at hand to curb his imagination. No item of news that might have the faintest bearing upon his work went unconsidered; no idea appeared too fantastic to think upon as a sober plan of enrichment, to think upon, to weigh with the most scrupulous judgment. That spark of imagination to seize upon the fantastic, to cage it in sober common sense, to watch the cage that the bright bird neither flies nor dies — there the secret of Penny's luck!

From such a caging of the fantastic came a new venture, a new source of wealth.

Grumbling a little, but flattered at having been asked, Nicholas took Nicki to a film entitled *Darkest Africa*. Half-asleep in the darkness, he could only wonder at the popularity of this fashionable but tedious form of amusement. Suddenly his eyes opened upon a scene depicting African bucks, nodding frizzy heads grotesquely neat and flat.

Common or garden hair-nets, explained the commentator. And very fashionable, very much prized. A stolen hair-net would certainly mean a broken head — if nothing worse. For makers of hair-nets — he threw out the frivolous suggestion — did they but know it, a fortune!

Nicholas was suddenly wide awake. The half dozen figures on the screen multiplied themselves, became thousands upon thousands of dusky warriors beauteous in hair-nets.

A fortune. . .

He tried to laugh at himself, but he could not drive the idea out of his head. They haunted his dreams, those thousands upon thousands of dusky warriors chic in Penny nets.

Hair-net, twist-net. . . the same process. So simple, so sure, so untapped a source of trade. A fortune. . .

He had awakened early from his tantalising dreams, and now, in his high quiet office, he sat, twirling a hair-net upon his hand. *Human Hair*, said the card upon which it had been mounted. *Made by hand*. He unravelled a bit of the net. As he had thought — just like twist-lace! The process was fundamentally the same. He unravelled some more. Yes, it was exactly the process of twist-net. Then — hair-nets could be made on a Levers — if you could find the way — hundreds upon hundreds at a time. You had to find the way — that was all!

Difficulties? Of course difficulties! The thing bristled with them! But whoever tackled anything worthwhile without finding difficulties?

. . .Betts was his man — sharp as a needle, quiet as the grave! Nothing would ever leak out through Betts.

Betts stood and listened, and smiled at this childish nonsense — Betts at sixty, a little more bent, a little more grey, but the same Betts with the same pugnacious eye, the same unbeatable chin.

"Th'idea's fair daft! Yer can't string 'uman 'air on a Levers!"

"Is that so? But — what about silk? Ay —" he was wholly triumphant, "silk, that's it! Finest of silk — what about that?"

"Aw reight — in theory! If yer can mek bobbin-net, yer can mek 'air-net — in theory. Ay, an' on th'same machine an' all — in theory. An' that's as far as it goes! But wot abowt th'finishin' o' th'edges? Hev yer thowt o' that? When yer come ter cut up th'piece, it'll just abowt ravel ter bits."

"Find a way," Nicholas said, "and you'll not lose by it!"

"Nowt but me sleep!" grumbled Betts who was a good foreman and an old friend, and the only man among them all who said what he thought to the master! "Aw reight! But I've got t'ave a machine to muck abowt wi', ay, an' a place ter keep it private an' all!"

"Take David. We're not putting on new patterns just now!"

Shifts were changed and the day-workers departed, but Nicholas and Betts worked together in the room with the locked doors. . . Day by day working, and far into the night, trying to wrest the secret of the process from the machine. Nicholas would hang over David while Betts adjusted the bobbins, slipping in an extra one here, an extra one there, adding the carefully calculated warp thread to make secure binding edges when the net should be cut. Together they would watch the net grow, rolling up, patterned with individual small nets. They would take the length of silky net from the rollers — they would cut through the binding threads. . .

Always it was the same. Always the cut net would fray. Quickly, or slowly, in the end it would fray. . .

But they were two good men on their mettle. Betts, his whole pugnacious nature aflame to the challenge, set his reputation upon finding a way — a way to make hair-nets upon a Levers machine, a way that should be quick and cheap and good. And Nicholas — a hound upon the scent was no keener than he when out to capture a new source of trade!

If they could find the way! If only they could! The thing could be done so cheaply. Nottingham had had yet another bad year, and good machines were going two-a-penny. If only they could find the way! He could buy up second-hand machines for his nets, pick them up for a song. . . besides. . . those machines of Wares, by all accounts they ought to be available soon. If only they could hit on the process, Pennys would pile up yet another fortune!

All through the hot summer weather they laboured. For Nicholas it was no longer a mere question of another fortune, it had become a need to down difficulties that threatened to down him.

Again and again. . . setting out and resetting the machine, thickening the warp-threads this way and that, to make a sure edge, trying it out more carefully than the most complicated lace-pattern — circular, hexagonal, square. . . They had accumulated shelf upon shelf of useless jacquard cards.

Again and again, taking the work from the machine they were certain they had found the way — this time they were certain, they could not fail.

But they did fail. Again and again as the scissors cut through, the net spread — ravelled.

The long summer evenings began to draw in, there was even a nip of frost in the air — but they were no nearer the solution of their problem. They seemed nearer, so often they seemed nearer, the shining net was perfect — in the piece. But they cut — and it splayed, frayed.

They were no nearer than at the beginning.

Betts had an idea. It was evident in the excitement he tried to cover beneath a solemn face. He would say nothing. He knew nothing, thought nothing — except it was just abowt time to chuck th'whole damn thing!

But his very solemnity gave him away!

Nicki's seventeenth birthday and the Pennys giving a party. Windows blazing with light; music falling upon the dark garden with its fairylights of blue and yellow and red. And then, suddenly, from the study, shrilling out its summons for the master — the telephone.

It was Betts. His voice came over the wire, vibrant with triumph. *Ah've done it!* Just that and no more. And all the answer Nicholas received to his tumbling questions was, "Yo' come ovver an' see fer yersen!"

He was on his way, overcoat thrown carelessly upon dress-clothes. Party or no party, he couldn't wait!

The motor moved steadily along the dark road; hedges and trees leaped black into the light of his headlamps, slipped backwards. He could see a rabbit, its ears laid back, its belly flat against the road, as it flew madly for safety! It would have to learn to fly a damn sight faster, Nicholas thought, with all these motors on the road, ay, more and more coming every day! He was glad he had listened to Nicki — she'd been at him for a motor for ages! Twenty-five miles an hour, could you beat that? Why he'd be there in no time... soon he would be hanging over the machine... The car lurched a little... if the damn thing didn't break down first! Soon he would hold the net, the perfect net, in his hand...

Betts was waiting, standing in triumph before the machine. He twirled about his fingers a finished hair-net. Nicholas snatched it from him, turned it this way and that, searching for fault. His eyes, his fingers, examined the edge. The edge stretched, contracted again...

Betts chuckled. Nicholas was holding the net to the light... A perfect edge! He looked again. Was it possible? Elastic, hair-fine, not merely binding the edge, but forming the edge.

Betts' other hand came forward dangling what looked like a long garland of bleached seaweed. "Yer've nobbut ter cut!" he said.

Nicholas spread the limp garland upon his fingers. At regular intervals the exquisitely fine elastic formed a warp thread. An interlocking of threads defined the top and bottom of each individual net.

"Yer've nobbut ter cut!" Betts said again as if repeating a ritual.

"Man, you're a wonder!" Nicholas said. "How on earth do you do it?"

"Simple as kiss yer 'and! On'y marvel is us di'n't tumble to it afore. Ah've got David ready ter show yer!"

Betts stepped aside and Nicholas saw. Instead of the usual one spool, two supplied the warp — one wound with silk and the other with elastic. A thread of elastic formed the edge at regular intervals of fifty threads.

"Simple! Like ah said!" With a sudden upwelling of excitement Betts seized the strip from Nicholas, flashed his scissors across and across — twirled two more nets upon his fingers. Nicholas snatched the scissors, and like a schoolboy, for pure pleasure, cut and cut again.

"When yer spread 'em on th'card, they mek a perfect round," Betts said with pride. "Not a thread o' waste!"

Nicholas went on cutting. He must make some movement, do something, anything, to hide his leaping jubilance.

. . .Snip. . .snip. . .snip. . .keeping time to his thoughts. . . Perfect! Strong — but not too strong! Neat. Pretty. Novel. . . ay, *novel!* No more twisting up of edges, tucking in the screwed-up bump to fit a too-small head. The elastic took care of that! Fit all heads these nets would. No more scrabbling about in boxes by shop-assistants to find the right size. *Penny nets fit all heads.*

To the tune of snipping, his mind played with advertisements. *Penny nets fit all heads*. . . his slogan — his trademark! The patent first — of course the patent — immediately! Before the slightest hint of rumour could get about. But — he could not keep his mind from his advertisements. . . convenient. . . simple. . . handsome. . . cheap. . . novel. . . He played among the delightful words.

The snipping ceased. He had come to the end of his nets. He turned to Betts. "Man, you're a fair wonder!" he said again, putting forth the charm he used so consciously, so sparingly. "You'll not lose by this."

And he kept his promise. As he always did — when it suited him.

Pennys growing, growing. More land acquired for new buildings. More and more land, more and more buildings. Pennys hair-nets not limited to African bucks, but finding their way to countless English homes. Every word of those cunning advertisements was true — the nets were convenient, and simple and handsome. And they were novel, too! They were of glossy silk, not of dry and brittle human hair — they were strong and they were decorative. They caught the feminine taste. Though few of the wearers looked as seductive as the charmer that formed the trademark, women went crazy over them; they worked in them, slept in them, set out to dance or dinner in them, Pennys nets carefully adjusted lest the wind disturb elaborately dressed heads.

Pennys nets. Should the inconceivable happen and Pennys follow the misfortunes of other lace mills, still Penny nets would go on catching Penny fortunes.

Property in land, in houses, securities in the bank piling up. Did Nicholas ever remember that first bank-book, that first cheque?

And did he smile to remember? He was too busy to remember anything but work — far, far too busy.

Pennys safe as houses, safe as the Bank of England. Other firms might suffer lean years in that curious rhythm that caught the lace trade — ten years of prosperity, maybe, and then, from the peak, the sharp drop; and after that; from the depression, the swift upward rise. In that unaccountable but ever-recurring rise and fall, mills went under, famous mills some of them, but not Pennys. Not Pennys.

Pennys safe as houses, safe as the Bank of England. Penny's luck!

Chapter 31

Nicholas moved his family into its third house — a house in keeping with his exuberant fortunes. A country-house in town, Nicholas explained — he did not care for the country. The finest house in Nottingham, he told Heriot over and over again, recounting its many distinctive features — its Corinthian pillars, its mediaeval studded doors, its shrubberies, its lily-pond, and its minute waterfall, to be lit, upon occasion, by coloured ever-changing lights — the only waterfall in Nottingham!

When he passed the Wares' house, he smiled to see how small it seemed. On the rare occasion when he visited the Wares, he noticed the increasingly evident signs of economies, of shabbiness, even. . . Well, he had come a long way from the time when this house had represented the peak of good living!

Twenty-three years since he had first set foot in that house, twenty-three years since the Wares had presumed to try their trick of making him look small. It made him laugh now, when he thought of it. But it made him angry too. He would never really forgive the Wares — though they had changed their tune. By God, now they had changed it! Old Ware no longer presumed to give advice — instead, he sought it, leading the conversation humbly round, slipping his question unobtrusively into the conversation. Mamma-in-law Ware didn't like him any better, it was clear, in spite of her efforts at charm. But at any rate her front seat high-and-mightiness was no longer visible. And no wonder! Ten thousand pounds was a lot of money! Ay, and twenty-three years a long time! A lot of water had flowed under the mill since then — and it was his turn now to call the tune!

He walked restlessly about his study; the library, it was called now, and the room showed clearly the rise of his fortunes. The furniture was antique, each article a museum piece selected by a famous London firm; and the books, no longer picked up wholesale, had been chosen either for the fineness of their binding or the rarity of the edition. Nicholas could talk quite knowledgeably about first editions. It was effective, this room, and beautiful, in its impersonal museum-like way, but not nearly so comfortable as the old study with its hide chairs and its big roll-topped desk and the miniature knight in armour that in his steely entrails obligingly concealed the fire-irons.

He went over to the gilt Florentine mirror; that ill-fated Isabella of the house of Medici had studied her features where now Nicholas studied his own.

. . .Twenty-three years. It *was* a long time! And yet he hadn't altered — much. Not to look at! Under fifty a man was still young! Hair a little grey — it lent him a distinguished look. Wrinkles at eye and mouth — they showed character, a character of which he had no need to be ashamed! And the self — his own self, hidden beneath hair and eye and cheek? The same energy to leap to an idea, to pin down an idea, to plot and plan its fruition. But. . . he tired more easily. No good trying to cheat himself with vain excuses — he knew that well enough! He found it more difficult to hide his anger, to wrap it about, when necessary, in that charming smile. When he was angered the rough speech of his childhood would break through, driving everything before its fury. It had cost him many a humiliation in his time, but he didn't mind now — was even proud of it. He was Nicholas Penny, he could afford to be "a character".

Twenty-three years. Heriot had altered. . . how she had altered! She who had been quick and impetuous, was now quiet and sober. Yes, Heriot had altered more than he had. He had developed along his own lines — he was the same Nicholas grown older, stronger, wiser. But she — she had grown into a quite different person. It was as if that young Heriot had died, or had never been — something, maybe, in a dream. . . And just as well! The young Heriot with her eager excitements, her fierce sense of justice, had not been a comfortable person to live with. . . Curious, how from the first he had set his mind upon her! She had not been pretty, she had not been comfortable, but she had been the first girl of her class, the first "lady" to talk to him with human friendliness.

. . .No, she had not been pretty, she had not been quietly comfortable, she had none of those pretty graces he had thought a young girl should have — but she had been honest and brave and — in her own way — kind. . .

Well, whatever his reason, it had been, on the whole, a good choice. Love, he thought, what is it? When you are young, you think it's the breath of life! And so it is — for a little while. But love goes swiftly, and once gone is gone for ever — but you go on breathing all the same! Try to recapture love — as he had done — to hold it, and you get nothing for your pains, nothing but distaste and bitterness!

Yes, he had done well enough with Heriot. She had worn well. . . there was a certain handsomeness in her maturity. There was no disturbing quickness in her now — all was calm and peaceful — as it should be at her age! Forty-two and settled down; content, as she ought to be, considering that he had given her more than she, more than he, even, had ever dreamed.

Yes. . . he had given her everything a man can give a woman in this world — but he had never loved her.

Love? What practical man took that into account?

Stella. He thought of her so little now. It was odd, wasn't it, that even when he looked at Stella's boy, he barely remembered his young love. How should he! He was a man and living. . . and she so long dust. Now and again he had taken a woman with easy liking — why not? He was a man, and Heriot something less than a woman. . . but he had allowed himself to love no more — a wise man does not make the same mistake twice. Domestic life makes one sort of pattern — passion another. Never again would he risk that violent pattern tangling itself in the quiet threads of his home life.

Love is violence. Married life a mere quietness. . . and he had chosen well. Heriot, too peaceful for passion, had been the right wife for him. . .

. . .He had done well with Heriot — except in the matter of child-bearing. Nicki was his heart's darling, but Heriot should have given him sons, sons to help him with his increasing burdens. Heriot herself — she was up to sample, good quality all through. In all these years he had never known her slip from her standard of behaviour — damn ladylike behaviour he called it when it irritated him. There had been times — and still were — when he would have liked a good set-to — with Heriot, that perfect lady, letting off steam and not being over-nice about the words she chose! He would have liked her better, perhaps — and yet, he would have lost something, too — the fine glaze chipped, spoiled for ever!

Yes, he might have liked her better, but he wouldn't have admired her so much! After all these years, he still admired, still respected Heriot. . . It was queer, whenever they went anywhere together, to a civic reception, or to a public dinner, or to a ball, wherever there were crowds, his eye would go seeking, seeking Heriot. He, Nicholas Penny of Pennys, handsome Nicholas, successful Nicholas, needing to reassure himself with the sight of his wife, his quiet, not unhandsome but rather colourless wife. . .

He grinned wryly at himself in the flower-embossed mirror.

He and the chap in the mirror, they knew the truth!

Nicholas Penny, so sure of himself in his own world, the world of men and machines and money, was never really at home among the crowd — the social crowd. It was as if he must talk loudly, lay down the law, make himself certain that it was all really real — till the sight of Heriot confirmed its reality. He still admired a pretty woman, of course he did, he was a man, wasn't he? But he needed Heriot — needed the assurance that he, too, was authentic, that he, too, had his own proper background. . . Heriot had first-class written all over her. Like that mother of hers, she expected a front seat — she had been brought up to expect it. But unlike old Ada, she took it with a sort of graciousness — and she had always an eye for those with no seat at all!

But what he admired most about Heriot was the way her manner never changed. Always the same from day to day — and pleasant with everyone. The same Heriot whether she talked with her charwoman or with a duchess... one solitary duchess to be truthful, but it proved the point. He had to respect Heriot because she did what he could never do. When he spoke to his social superiors, he either flattered them or was rude — he couldn't help it! But she — she never altered her manner or speech by a hair's breadth from the normal.

He came away from the mirror and looked down over his vast garden... A garden like this almost in the heart of the town! Why the land was worth... it was worth...

...Twenty-three years ago — and not a penny in his pocket. And now this! Penny lace — twist-lace, burnt-lace, wool-lace; Penny nets; Penny bleaching and dyeing... and this great house set in its vast grounds. But he had worked for it! How he had worked! How different his life and Heriot's!

His admiration for Heriot was salted with annoyance — as it so often was.

...How easy everything had always been for her! Without the lifting of a finger she fitted perfectly the life she led. Without the lifting of a finger everything fell into her lap — everything! But he — to gain all this he had had to toil, to sweat, to endure. She — had just to be!

Heriot was restless. How could one settle in quiet of the spirit when one's spirit had no home? This great house was not home — no house of Nicholas had ever been home. Always he had cluttered it up with things. In the Scarrington Drive house, cheap and common things. And now — the things were priceless — priceless and meaningless. They were only things, nothing but things...

And Nicholas expected her to be grateful, grateful for cluttering her life with useless things, grateful for being allowed to play housekeeper in his over-big, over-ornate house. What it had cost her to put away her ambitions, to quieten the spirit that still rose fiercely, to clog her mind with the thousand and one cares of his great house, she whose heart had been in the machines, he would never know — and she would never tell him! He complained sometimes that his work was exacting, never finished... and it was true, because he delighted in his work, could never leave it alone! But in all his success he must have something to complain about — a flick of salt in his porridge! He would really be surprised, if she told him right out that his own life had been easy, kind, since every day saw his dreams fulfilled. But she — what had she — she had put away her desires to live his alien life, a stagnant life beyond his reckoning!

He wouldn't believe... because he wouldn't understand. He understood so little — so very little more than he could see and touch and hear and smell!

She looked about her large, light room — the only spot in all this house where she could breathe freely. There was a feeling of space about it, almost of emptiness, that gave an illusion of freedom to the spirit.

Nicholas had been angry about this room. It was to have been in keeping with the rest of the house. He had arranged for gold mosaic walls and gold tissue curtains, with carpet and furniture to match. It was then she had taken matters into her own hands.

She smiled, looking about her pearl grey room with its touches of warm Venetian red, at her floor of honey-coloured wood, at her pale hand-made rugs.

Nicholas had been away — fortunately. But when he returned! His loud and senseless anger! Bare rooms! Empty rooms! No need for her to qualify for the workhouse, he had shouted for anyone to hear. All very well for her parents — they would come to it, no doubt — but he had saved her from that!

His hateful vulgar anger! She had taken herself away from him, withdrawing her spirit, standing there a hollow, rather humble Heriot. To make one's self empty — it was the only way of dealing with Nicholas...

The only way? The easiest way, perhaps! But not the bravest way — not even a good way. A way that makes for peace... but it makes for failure, too.

I have failed... failed so badly. Failed with Nicholas, failed, even more, with Nicki — failed most of all with Nicki.

I tried. I did try. But Nicholas was the obstruction... always he liked to obstruct, to set himself against me — to set himself on the other side, with Nicki. There should never have been an "other side". The only side for parents is the child's side... But always that partnership, that unspoken, perfectly defined partnership — those two against me. And all the time, I watched, working quietly, working secretly, trying to rush my small disciplines, before he could stop them, trying to help Nicki before it was too late... fighting over such simple things as the right bedtime, the right food... and all the time Nicholas obstructing, and Nicki remembering, remembering it against me.

Nicki, so pleasant — when she isn't crossed; so ruthless. And so subtle! Nicholas such a fool in spite of all his shrewdness, Nicholas thinking that if Nicki stands up hard and determined for what she wants, it's because he allows it... thinking like the king in the old story he can say *thus far*. . . and the sea will hear him and turn back. . .

And Nicki lets him go on believing it!

Nicki, Nicki my dear, I never had any illusions about you! From the first, before you could speak, even, one saw it — that selfishness, that determination, blind determination. I tried — I tried to make Nicholas understand, but he laughed. He always laughed. . . when he wasn't angry! He laughed at the very idea — even with the evidence clear before his eyes, he would laugh. All children are selfish, he would say, they wouldn't be children, otherwise. Of course children are selfish — but we are not children always. . . children must be helped, taught. and it is parents that must do the helping. But not Nicholas! He hated a pappy-natured child — he used to say that too, say it so often, I could have screamed. He couldn't see, wouldn't see, that discipline should strengthen, not weaken.

. . .And those times when he wouldn't laugh — he'd be angry, furiously angry, trying to shout me down with his loud voice — that voice gone back to his childhood's tongue, voice I used to love and then got to hate and despise, because I only heard it brawling. Nicki not perfect? His child not perfect? And always, always that unspoken partnership. . . shutting me out. Nicki never trusted me. . . All those times I stood out against Nicholas for discipline adding up and up. . . And then that time with the bandage — how she hated me. Never forgave me. I knew it would happen like that — but I had to do it! Nicki never trusted me. It coloured all her relations with me for years. . . maybe it does still. . .

And so it went. . . and so it goes. . . Nicki — selfishness deeper and deeper-cored. Determination so blind, so unyielding it will survive all reason, all decency, all disaster. Talk of right and wrong and Nicki will laugh at you. . . no, she wouldn't be bothered to laugh at so stale a story — she'd hardly bother to smile even. . . But there *is* a way with Nicki — when desire doesn't go too deep. You'd never win her with the moral appeal, but you might on the score of expediency — she has a lot of common sense, has Nicki, and a wholesome regard for expediency. . . .Not much to work on, but still something. . . something. . .

Heriot watchful for the present, fearful for the future, when by their very nature, self-willed man and self-willed child must be forced into open conflict. How it would come, or when, she couldn't guess, couldn't guard against — but come it must! Fear for the future — it crouched ever-present beneath the calm eye, the pleasant smile.

Chapter 32

Twenty-three and a force to reckon with. Pen Wade. And he was handsome. Women were ready to love him because of those dark eyes wide-set and confident beneath the white forehead; and because of that sensitive mouth, half-sulky, denying a little the confidence of the brow. Yes, it was the mouth that drew them, that wholly appealing, wholly misleading little-boy mouth. Women's eyes followed him — he knew it, he was no fool. He cared nothing for it — certainly he was no fool. He had his gift to use, his way to make.

Pen Wade was an artist and knew it. He was not proud of it, any more than be was proud of his two hands or his one nose. The gift was there. . . He had a genius for design — how could he help but know it? And he had the ability to translate his ideas into patterns of practical utility; he could combine the most elaborate pattern with the utmost economy in costing — though he would never sacrifice one thread of a design to mere economy, he never lost sight of the selling price. In the trade a Penny design was recognised everywhere by its strength, its beauty, but more than anything by its originality. There was no attribute Pen could not weave into his pattern — fantasy, humour, grace — he made use of all.

Wherever he went, whatever he saw, transformed itself into patterns of beauty — curve of a snail-shell, twist of an old candlestick, leaf in the margin of a flowered missal. All of these remembered, all by some magic of his own blended with the traditional forms of pattern. At the School of Art, they had declared that in designing they could teach the boy nothing — the gift was inherent. There were no principles he need acquire, he had the matter by instinct.

He had insisted upon learning the technique of working drawings. He had been told that it was a sheer waste of time. His job was to design; working drawings were not, and never would be his concern. He had not argued — but he had had his way. He had known even then, that he would never blindly trust his designs to the hands of another. He must be able to check for himself — that the working drawing did his design no wrong. How often had he seen a design spoilt by clumsy simplification — orders from above, to save a ha'penny on the rack! With his designs — never!

So he had found pleasure in learning to make technical drawings. The tiresome counting of infinitely fine lines to be translated into terms of bobbins had not been tiresome to him. It was the means by which his pattern would take on the life his brain had conceived.

Nor would he ever abandon this principle. In spite of the call upon his time he would allow no-one to relieve him of this responsibility. . . and the call upon his time was tremendous. But the time — in Pen's opinion — was not wasted. No work bearing his designs had ever to come off the machines in order to put the pattern right, no, not even off David — though it had happened time and again with Nicholas's designs. Pen saved time and money and labour — and what mattered most, he guaranteed the integrity of his own designs.

Pen's attitude infuriated Nicholas. Although the hundreds of machines working at double shift filled the air with unceasing clamour, Nicholas would have no other designers but himself and Pen Wade. In theory, they two were responsible for all new patterns; but because of the ramifications of his enormous business, the new designs were almost entirely in Pen's hands. Pen knew perfectly well that in other mills, once the drawing had passed out of the designer's hand he was finished with it. But it made no atom of difference to him! He, himself, must examine every working drawing, his initial must check it before the jacquard-band was prepared. He had even been known to check every hole in a band when a pattern was peculiarly elaborate. Every design was, and always would be to him, a living thing to be made or marred.

This idea of Pen Wade's that no-one at all could be finally trusted with the translation of his designs into working drawings, exasperated Nicholas. He understood the feeling — up to a point — he was an artist himself! But he was a business man, too. He paid others to do routine work. To insist upon doing what others could do as well as oneself was a stupid and conceited waste of time.

He had expressed himself strongly upon the subject more than once, but the young man hadn't listened — hadn't even been polite enough to pretend that he listened!

It was infuriating, this independent, unlistening attitude. It was unreasonable. It was ungrateful! Two holds he ought to have upon Pen Wade — the respect due from a son to a father; and the gratitude of a foundling for a benefactor.

The first he must not expect. . . must never expect. It was curious, Nicholas thought, that nowadays he barely remembered Stella's part in the boy. Once the boy had seemed all Stella — and Nicholas had been content. But now, whenever he saw Pen, whenever he turned over a particularly striking design, he would think, *my son. . .*

It was not at all that his heart yearned over Pen — Nicki had the whole of his heart. But Pen was his — his own possession which he must not claim. Yet how clear that claim. Pen's gift — his unique gift — there was his birth-mark. But he must not make that claim! Pen recognised no allegiance — he was his own man.

Why had Heriot never given him a son — a son he could take pleasure in, a son he could acknowledge? She should have given him sons — sons like Pen Wade. Nicki, Pen... so handsome, so clever... Salt of the earth both! Half-a-dozen sons would not have been too many...

My son... my son... He longed sometimes to tell Pen Wade the truth, to put the seal of possession upon him, to make Pen recognise the seal. But he knew it was madness. It could do nothing but strike at the present relations between them — the boy would be no happier for knowing himself a bastard, and he, himself, would lose the best designer in the country.

And it would not stop there. The truth dragged out at long last would stink like a long-buried corpse. It would dirty Stella's memory — all she had left her son; it would distress Heriot, destroying her peace; and it would shock Nicki — her idol would come tumbling! All, all of them, would turn upon him, blaming him for this long concealment, blaming him because it had happened at all! Ignorant, they would still take it upon themselves to judge! He would never make them understand that he had done what Stella had wished, that he had acted in the best possible way for them all! He had kept Stella's memory clean for her son; he had protected that son, nurtured his talent, brought him up to a good livelihood. And he had protected his own womenfolk... What more could any man have done? But it wouldn't satisfy them! Wise after the event, they would consider themselves competent to judge, Even Nicki — little green Nicki... Most of all Nicki...

The truth must remain as it was — decently buried.

Yes, that first hold on Pen Wade, he must keep to himself. But the second? The second the young man refused to acknowledge. He had made his attitude in the matter clear as daylight. He had actually declared himself to be the best judge of what was necessary for his own work! And when Nicholas, disliking his manner, had touched, quite naturally, upon the theme of gratitude, Wade had said, "If it hadn't been worth it to you, you wouldn't have done it!"

And he had not been ashamed to add the final insult, "And it *was* worth it, too!"

Even he, the ungrateful young man, had dared go no further. But what he thought was plain in his face. *That contract I was too young to understand, it paid for my training and everything else over and over again...* And that his attitude had not changed, young Wade showed by his assured, his even slightly arrogant, bearing. Infuriating... still, what about looking into that contract now? Be better than the contract before it came to an end. Being generous never did anyone any harm — not if it was sensible generosity!

But the thought that sooner or later the contract must come to an end, that Pen Wade would be free, free to go, free to leave Pennys, to offer himself elsewhere, gnawed at Nicholas. The desire to label his own possession pricked so roughly that he would turn savage, savage with Heriot, with Pen himself, with Nicki, even. He would be crude, violent, pouring forth cheap sarcasms in the broad tongue of his youth.

Heriot received the attacks as though they concerned her not at all. Only a faintly-lifted eyebrow warned him that should he go too far, he would destroy the fine image he had made of Nicholas Penny.

Nicki soothed and flattered and comforted... Of course he was tired, and of course he was cross! People had a way of being utterly and entirely stupid. Nothing was so wearing as stupidity! Only she — she intimated, in the whole world, understood the wear and tear of stupidity upon a nature as fine, as sensitive as that of her dearest father.

But Pen met these outbursts with an indifference masking a temper dangerously like Nicholas's own.

Nicki leaned back in her own small car. Her idle eye registered the countryside streaming past. Divine! It was an almost mechanical reaction; her mind was turned inward on her own affairs...

...Lovely having a car of her own! You could get along in this twice as quickly as in the big Daimler. Three times — if no-one was looking! She'd urged that when she was persuading papa to give her her own car. But he had laughed in that rather steamroller manner of his. Go twice as far in half the time, she, with all time on her hands! What for, in God's name?

Dear papa! He wasn't speed-minded — not yet! He had a tendency, hadn't he, to get just a little left behind in things that didn't actually concern his business! Fortunate to have an up-to-the-minute daughter to save him from so horrid a fate.

Nicolet stopped the car at the main entrance to Pennys. She removed her goggles and motor-veil, flicked a powder-puff over her nose and tucked in a stray curl. Her thoughts ran on.

It hadn't been really difficult to persuade papa. Papa was easy — if you knew the way! A motor of her very own, she had intimated, would be very pleasant — but of course, it wasn't necessary — and motors, as she knew, cost a great deal. She wouldn't be the only one among her friends without a car... things weren't too good in the lace trade just now, were they?

She looked at herself in the tiny silver-framed mirror opposite, catching her face at this angle and at that. From any angle, she was pleased to observe, completely satisfying!

...Yes, that had certainly fetched papa. And here she was in her very own motor! And she had come to drive papa home herself — Dawkins could take the big car back. . .

White skirts daintily held she stepped from the car. Pretty foot! Pity there was no-one to admire it!

She ascended the stone steps.

. . .Straight up to papa's room! Papa would be delighted to see her! Funny papa! He'd always been a little disappointed because she didn't go mad about Pennys. But why should he have expected it? Because long ago he and mamma had sat together and had heart-to-heart talks about the machines! And much good it had done them! Leave Nicki alone with a handsome young man and she'd find more exciting things to talk about! She — she came to the virtuous conclusion, was more interested in people than in things! She would never grow like mamma who cared so little about people. . . Born before her generation, grandmamma said! Grandmamma was sentimentalising — a true Ware! The truth about mamma was that she would probably have been the same in any generation — not caring. . . accepting everything, desiring nothing. . . only half a person. . . No, she would never, never grow like mamma.

The lift now. . . To the left? The right? The right of course — same side as her bracelet hand.

. . .Dear papa, how delighted he would be! She would fling open his door, without knocking, and he'd look up scowling and furious to see who *dared*. . . and then the scowl would simply melt into smiles like that other time she had surprised him.

His birthday. . . and she had brought him an orchid for his buttonhole. The exotic flower — the journey specially made — she had guessed that would please him more than the conventional gift presented at home. And she had been right — as she was always right in her guesses about papa. His delight had been quite touching. It was then she had decided that she must come again quite often, to give papa pleasure — and to make the handsome young man who had come into papa's room with a drawing look at her, really look at her as though she were Nicolet Penny and not one of the chairs that stood against the wall. Very handsome chairs she was ready to admit. Real Chippendale, and cost a fortune. But he could come in and look at them any day of the week!

Now — what was the young man's name? Why pretend, even for a moment, she couldn't remember it? The name was short enough, the name of that very good-looking young man!

Papa had introduced young Wade — and papa hadn't seemed pleased. It was then, she had thought, that his emotion of delight had definitely watered itself down. . . *This is Wade — my designer*. . . papa careful to give the young man no chance of getting above himself by allowing him a handle to his name. Papa, bless him, was a bit of a snob!

Then papa had taken her by the arm and had quite obviously propelled her from the room. Dear, clumsy papa! He had gone the right way to work if he had wanted to arouse her interest in the very handsome young man. Good thing handsome nobodies weren't her style!

Nicolet stepped into the lift and shut the door carefully according to instructions. She hoped she hadn't been too venturesome! Suppose the thing stuck half-way and she had to shout until she was rescued! Not a very dignified procedure for the sophisticated Miss Penny!

The lift rose slowly, smoothly.

. . .Papa would so enjoy the drive! She must remind him to transfer his motor-helmet and goggles from the big car — it was rather dusty along the road. . . She really was a very thoughtful daughter!

Then why did the heart of this very thoughtful daughter beat so hard beneath the lace insertion of her fine muslin gown? Surely one so young, so light as Nicki, could not be breathless from so brief an excursion in a lift!

She was smiling in anticipation of papa's delight as she turned the handle and walked in.

But papa did not seem nearly as delighted as she had thought! He was standing looking over the shoulder of a young man — a tall dark young man. Could it be, could it really be, the same young man? Unexpected, was it not, since papa did not, as a rule, encourage young men in his office? Exceedingly unexpected — and amusing!

But papa did not seem to find it amusing. He nodded quite curtly, and he was even frowning a bit! As for the young-man-with-the-short-name, he too looked up and threw her another of those glances he might have reserved for one of the famous chairs. It was clear that he was more interested in his wretched drawings!

A flurry of irritation ruffled her calm. She wanted to snatch the papers from that odious smug young man, to pull his attention quite violently from something he could look at all day — if he were silly enough — to something he could see but rarely and would be wise to look at as long as he could!

She held out a hand for the drawing — a friendly hand, showing a polite and pleasant interest. But, if you could believe it, he was quite unwilling to pass the drawings! It was clear that he wanted her to go away and leave him to get on with his work.

But her hand was waiting — a pretty hand, as she very well knew. An implacable hand — as she knew even better.

The hand holding the drawing moved unwillingly, moved definitely towards her. At the touching of fingers, Nicki enjoyed a most pleasing and stimulating sensation.

An exquisite design. Even Nicki's unappreciative and not very interested eye could see that — convolvulus, the perfect bell curved inwards upon its tendrils.

She exclaimed with pleasure, lack of interest quickened by the presence of the good-looking, completely indifferent young man.

She must have this for herself! She was urgent, voluble, with a widening of blue eye, a pouting of red lip, with indeed that complete and hitherto fetching impersonation of the kittenish young thing.

. . .Yes, she *must* have it! The design must be hers and hers alone! It was her very own already, because she loved it so! He must alter it a little, of course. He must introduce, somehow, an *N* into the pattern. It must be reproduced in two or three widths. She would use it for her handkerchiefs, she would use it for her — She dropped modest, pussy-cat eyes. But he must understand, this design must be kept for her and for her alone. . .

He wasn't even listening. Not even listening when you might have expected him to be bowled over by the compliment. Nicolet Penny didn't make a habit of running round and dishing out compliments — least of all to her father's work-people! But he was frowning — actually frowning — straight brows drawn together, as he explained, none too graciously, that the pattern was right as it was — on that question he was perfectly satisfied.

And in any case, the jacquard cards had already been punched!

Well, what did that matter? She was Nicolet Penny. If she wanted a pattern altered, if she wanted it kept exclusively for herself, she had only to say so, hadn't she? She was Nicolet Penny!

. . .But the young man with his talk about the importance of the pattern didn't seem to understand the importance of Nicolet Penny!

There pricked within her the desire to show him, *show him*. . .

She turned to Nicholas with appealing blue eyes. Those eyes had never failed her yet!

"Why, certainly, if —" She was already tasting the sweetness of her little triumph, when the young man interrupted, actually interrupted papa! And not too politely, either!

Nicolet fixed her eyes upon papa, watching for the crimsoning of the face, the twitching of the blue vein in the left temple; waiting for the familiar loud, nerve-shattering outburst — for those who had nerves to shatter!

Yes, there it was — flush sweeping hotly upwards, blue vein leaping. . . *Look out young man, look out!*

But there was no loud violence to shatter the young man — no violence at all!

"I will not alter one line of the pattern, not one single line! The thing is right as it stands!" declared the creature as though there were no fury signs to warn him.

Now she, even she, was holding her breath.

"I," said papa, unbelievably meek, though the vein twitched and jumped more than ever, "I am the best judge of that!"

"I," answered the young man with perfect calm, "am responsible for this design!"

. . .*Well you won't be much longer!* She'd bet on papa's next words.

But nothing came. Nothing at all! The young man, as if the interview were over to his complete satisfaction, and without at all realising that he had done an unspeakably shattering thing, was proceeding to gather up his drawings.

Nicki bubbled with inward laughter. A mere employee, a nobody, standing up to papa! Amazing! But more amazing still — why hadn't papa turned and rent this impertinent young man?

Because — the young man, impertinent though he might be, could not be a nobody! No mere nobody could stand up to papa like that! Because although papa, bless him, looked ready to burst with rage, it was clear that something about the young man put papa — she forbade the fleeting smile — into his proper place.

What hold had he got on papa? He didn't look a blackmailer standing there and looking at papa with those honest, indifferent, and oh, so handsome eyes. Besides — there was nothing to blackmail in papa's dull and blameless past! No — the truth was that somehow, miraculously, papa had at last met his match!

The bubble of laughter broke. Papa, perhaps! But not Nicolet Penny, not Nicki! As far as she was concerned the clever young man had made a slight miscalculation. It would take more than any young man, however clever, to get the better of Nicolet Penny!

Meanwhile she had asked for that design — and that design she would have!

She pouted up at Nicholas, the underlip red and dewy. "Please, papa!" she coaxed in her most little-girl voice.

Nicholas hedged. "I'll see about it!"

See about it! *See about it!* She, Nicolet Penny, demanding something here and now, and papa would see about it!

She had not fully recovered from her surprise, even after papa had taken her by the arm and gently but unmistakably led her from the room and into the lift and down the entrance steps and into the motorcar.

She sat back among the cushions and she was fulminating. Yes, fulminating was the word — and a good word, too! Fulminating at the colossal impertinence of the young man, who calmly and quite indifferently opposed her wishes... didn't even bother to oppose them! Just behaved as if she had expressed no wish at all! Impertinent. Insolent. Outrageous! Not worth wasting a thought on! And she wouldn't be thinking about him either, this nobody — if he hadn't behaved so disgracefully! No, she wouldn't be thinking of him at all — with that queer lock of hair falling across his forehead into his dark eyes, and that sulky bad-tempered mouth — no, not if he were twice as handsome!

She was angry but hardly surprised when papa told her that evening that the new pattern had already gone into manufacture and that it was impossible to recall it now! She was also a little amused. He had won the first round, Mr Impertinence. Well — the fight had only just begun. Let him look out!

She ate her dinner not knowing whether it was clear soup or thick; whether it was mutton or beef. But she found out, oh so tactfully, oh so indifferently, the young man's Christian name... Wait, Mr Pen Wade, wait! She'd get even with him!

But — how did one get even with a young man one would never see again — never wanted to see again? One's own wishes didn't come into it. It was obvious, wasn't it, that things couldn't remain as they were? She could not allow an unknown young man in her father's employ to get the better of Nicolet Penny! She never wanted to see him again — that was clear! But it was equally clear that in order to get even with him, she must see him! And private feelings couldn't be allowed to count!

She tossed about in the darkness, she whose habit it was to slide away into sweet and dreamless sleep. More bitterly than the pea beneath its twenty mattresses, the thought afflicted her of that young man, that utterly unimportant, utterly despicable, utterly unworthy-to-be-thought-of-young-man.

She felt surprisingly that she wanted to cry, she, Nicolet Penny, with her enviable reputation among young men more worthy of note, for hard riding, hard flirting — and no bones broken.

She sat up in bed suddenly.

Refuse her, would he! Set his will against hers! *I will not alter one line, not one thread...* Let him not! Let him not! She didn't want that design — not now! He had spoiled it for her with all that unpleasantness! More fun to be got in other ways! Why not admit that honestly? Well, she would admit it! Admit, too, that she knew all those ways — every one of them! He'd started the game and she would play it — according to her own rules! He should make a design specially for her, yes, for her and her alone! Papa should order it. And then let him refuse — papa's work-hand! And she would lead him a dance! Let the design be fit for the angels — still he should dance! He should alter this, alter that, alter the other, before he had the pleasure of seeing her fling it into the wastepaper basket. She would fling it — not scornfully — the thing was not worth scorn — but carelessly, as if it were of no importance!

I am the designer here... Are you indeed, Mr Impertinence? But I am Nicolet Penny! You may have got papa somehow or other under your thumb, but you've yet to learn, Mr Insolence, what it means to set yourself against Nicolet Penny... Penny... Pen... Pen.

Chapter 33

Pen Wade was at his work. But he was not working. He was looking at the design Nicolet had admired a week ago. And he was frowning. The design was finished, the work already on the machine — his part in it was over. He had not meant to think of it again. Then why was he wasting his time over it, when there was work to be done, and a pattern in his mind clamouring to be set upon paper?

But still he bent over the little design.

. . .A good design. Simple and bold. Cheap to make and effective to sell! He'd have been a damned fool to alter one thread to please her ladyship! Silly little madam! What did she know of lace-designing? Girls like that hadn't any business in places where men worked. Her place was twittering away at some damn silly party. . . *I want it altered. . . I want it for my own. . .* Twit, twit, twitter. . . though you had to admit she did it prettily — if you liked twittering! Ay — and if you liked damned sauce and all!

Twit, twit, twitter. . . blue eyes she had — a sort of warm look in them. Chinese blue. . . clear and warm. Warm! He'd say so! Too warm — when she was in a paddy! Hell-of-a-paddy she'd got, the mardy madam! *I want my initial. . .* Do you now? Is that all? *N. . .* she said. Now what did *N* stand for? She wasn't a Nora nor a Nell — nothing so honest-to-God! She should be something French and fine! Come to that he'd heard the old man call her something French — what it was he disremembered — he hadn't been listening all that! *N?* Bother the wench! He'd something better to do than worry himself about her precious name!

He pushed the hair impatiently from his forehead, as if with the movement he pushed away all thought of the tiresome creature.

But for all that, his fingers played with the pencil, worked with the pencil. He could no more forbid his fingers than he could forbid his mind. Unthinking, unknowing, the design grew. Forget-me-nots, exquisitely fine, lying where they dropped upon the net — and a tiny lovers' knot joining them, the ends curving into an *N*, an *N* so discreet you might well miss it.

His eye took in his drawing. Damn it, he'd done what she wanted, done it after all! But she wouldn't like it, the silly spoilt girl! She'd want something to express what she called her personality. A great *N*, sprawling all over the place — no missing it!

Designed for me. . . specially for me. . . You could almost hear her, twittering away as pretty as you pleased! The airs she gave herself!

You'd think she was a princess at very least!

He smiled, unknowing. Unknowing his pencil drew a minute crown, seven-pointed. And beneath it, an unmistakable *N*.

. . .Pretty. Silly pretty design. Just right for the silly pretty girl whose name began with an *N*, the girl whose name he didn't know — and didn't want to know. . .

He frowned over the delicate drawing. Her design indeed! For what single person should the twist-hands stand through long days, eyes vigilant upon the machines, fingers swift upon the machines? Not to serve her whim, the pert young girl, the spoilt young girl!

He crumpled the paper with swift nervous fingers, and shied it at the wastepaper basket. It hit the plaited edge and bounced upon the floor. He let it lie. One of the cleaners would pick it up and throw it away!

Nicolet, breathless, all eagerness to surprise, looked in at papa's empty room and rang imperiously. His secretary, answering the summons, greeted Nicki coldly. Mr Penny was somewhere about the building. Her tone expressed the conviction that his whereabouts concerned neither of them. Questioned further by an unimpressed Nicolet, she volunteered that Mr Penny had said something about finding him in the shop — burnt-lace. And if not there! Urged further by a smiling, determined Nicki, she added that he might be with Mr Wade. And then, dragged forth by a silent, grimly undeclared battle of wills, added grudgingly, "Third door. Second floor."

She sent Nicki's gay back an unfriendly look. It was not fair that that girl should blow in whenever she pleased. Ay, and dressed up that way and all! Fine feathers. Let her have all the fine feathers she chose — but let her flaunt them elsewhere! She wished, as she sighed her way back to her desk, that she had not mentioned Mr Wade.

Nicolet, peeping in through Pen Wade's door, found this room also empty and stepped inside. Why not? Papa might drop in here any minute. If she went chasing him through this conglomeration of buildings they would find themselves playing at Box and Cox. . . Those papers scattered about on the desk — they were very untidy! She'd got a minute, so why not put them straight?

. . .Drawings. Pretty. Quite pretty.

She flicked them through with unconcerned fingers.

A screw of paper lay upon the floor by the paperbasket. It had obviously just missed its goal. And that young man had been too lazy, too untidy, to pick it up! Nicolet stooped to the crumpled paper, smoothed it absently, looked at it carelessly. . . and then looked again.

There she stood bent upon her treasure, eyes bright, cheeks bright, little murmurs of delight coming from soft lips.

Pen Wade found her like that, standing in the middle of the room — his room — as if the place belonged to her! And, by all that was holy, messing about with his papers, his own private papers! The whole damn place might belong to her — but not his room. Let her learn to keep herself out of his room!

Resentful, his underlip full and sullen, he stood in the doorway; his fingers itched to take her by the slim puffed sleeve and thrust her outside.

He took a half step forward.

She lifted her head at the sound. He saw the fine colour run from her cheeks, from her lips. She was a white girl, standing there. Her eyes were darkened — he thought irrelevantly. . . blue flowers; but the sun's gone in. . .

His anger went abruptly. He felt the blood rise, pricking beneath his skin, flooding into his cheeks, making hot his forehead, confusing his thoughts. He felt a fool standing there, all a blasted crimson, in front of the white girl. He felt the oddest, strongest impulse to run away, to fling open the door of his room, and run, run anywhere at all. He didn't want to get himself mixed up with this girl. For all her white cheeks and her frightened eyes, she was dangerous. Penny's daughter. When you'd said that, you'd said everything!

But she was sweet — in her way, standing there so white, so quiet, looking at him out of her darkened eyes. Dangerous! How? Why? He didn't know. And he didn't care! She was the old man's daughter. That was enough!

The tears, crystal bright, gathered on the dark curve of her lashes; the clear upward sweep was a delight to him. He did not want to look at them. . . he could not take his eyes from that fine strong curve.

Damn it all, what did it matter that she was the old man's daughter? She was only a girl, for all she played the mardy madam, only a girl — like any other girl. She was frightened. She was unhappy. She needed help, comfort. Someone ought to comfort her. . . but not he. . . not he. . . She was the old man's daughter.

Like a trumpet-blast shrilling through his head, came the knowledge that only he, himself bewildered and a little afraid, could comfort her.

The old man's daughter. . .

Danger sounded its last warning, went unheeded. She was in his arms, the girl whose name he didn't even know, her tear-stained cheeks hot against his, her fingers still clutching her treasure as if she could never let it go.

She hadn't meant it to happen like that. She hadn't meant it to happen at all! She had meant to play a little with the young man, to amuse herself at his expense; from her high place, her safe place, leaning down to punish his insolence. And then, quite suddenly, her high seat, her safe seat, had tottered, and she had been flung down from her place, flung headlong, flung dizzily. And his arms, his open arms had received her.

It had been like that — just like that. And if his arms had not received her, then she must have fallen to her death. For without Pen Wade, she could not, would not, live. . .

Thus Nicolet, wild-eyed at her dressing-table, smoothing and re-smoothing the crumpled piece of paper.

. . .His love-letter, his poem, beyond all letters lovely, beyond all poetry, poetic. The little design, so silent, so secret — to eyes that see, revealing all, to ears that hear, saying all, all that can ever be said. . . all that can never be said. . .

Forget-me-nots. He will never forget. The lovers' knot. I am knotted to his heart. And the little crown. I am his queen. . .

Nicolet, the hard-bitten, laughing and crying by turns, head on the gold-and-crystal littered dressing table. Nicolet the fearless, at every distant footfall, hand flown to heart to defend her secret.

She lifted her head, jerking the bright curls back from her hot cheeks. Why did she cringe and cower as though she were guilty? What had she done?

What had she done? She might well ask! She had without papa's permission, without her own permission even, fallen in love. She had fallen suddenly, headlong and for all time in love.

That was the whole story.

Not quite the whole story — not as far as papa was concerned. The young man was in her father's employ; he had no fortune to match her own. That was all papa would see. . . But he has his own fortune, he has his gift, his matchless gift. And. . . he is himself. But papa will not understand that. Papa understands nothing but what he may touch and handle — concrete gold, concrete silver.

But mamma will understand. Mamma is quiet, but she is strong. . .

She thought amazed, How do I know mamma is strong, mamma who gives way so easily?

It's your mother's the strong one, not your father — your mother. In the end it's your mother that counts.

A tea-table and a little girl, a disbelieving little girl who thought she knew everything. . . and an old woman. Grandmamma long ago. . . But I didn't believe it. I didn't care. Because I didn't *need* to care. But it's true. I know it's true. I see it now. Everything mamma needed for me, mamma brought about. Big things. And little things. School. And proper bedtime when I was small and time after time papa wanted to keep me up. And suitable food, in spite of papa, papa wanting to take his six-year-old through the whole length of his dinner... Grandmamma was right. Mamma does not waste her strength. She does not set her heart on little things. She gives way on all the things that don't matter. But touch her on the thing she cares about — she's stone, she's steel.

If you want anything with all your heart and you're not strong enough to get it for yourself, then go to your mother. It's your mother — your mother that counts.

So long ago. I thought I'd forgotten. But all the time the memory was there, waiting... waiting...

But — she sobered to a thought. I must not bring mamma into this. It would not be fair. We have never been friends, mamma and I. I have not given her one thought that counted, ever. Papa and I — that is a different story. Between papa and I, this must be fought!

Can I fight papa who is strong and ruthless? Always I have fought for the things that don't matter. Unlike mamma, I wasted my strength. Now it has happened, the thing that is my whole life — and I am afraid.

On a deep breath she steadied herself. *I am Nicolet Penny. I do as I please!*

And since that was not enough, for the first time not enough, added, *I am Heriot Ware's daughter. I do what she did!*

She was back again, with surprise at the thought that her mother would count in this — would count in the long run more than her father.

Yes, it was mamma who would count, mamma about whom she knew so little! Mamma who was a stranger, who in the midst of the familiar home things, led her strange and lonely life...

She was taken with the poignant regret that she had allowed her own indifference to stand, a wall, between herself and mamma.

...As for papa, he was easy. Nothing much to be known there! He was a ranter, a raver, letting out anger in hot words — in easy words. And then, talked out, he would grow mild as new milk. She had calculated upon papa her life long — and she had made no mistakes. He had refused her nothing — her whole life long, nothing. Would he refuse her now, her life's happiness?

Yes. He would refuse. She knew him. Let her be never so meek, so dovelike, still he would refuse. Because happiness was something he could not hold in his hands, weigh in his hands, he would consider her heart's need a child's whim; would offer her, maybe, an expensive gift — something you could touch and hold and put a price upon. Because of his pride, his enormous, impossible pride, he would refuse.

Well, let him wear himself out with ranting...

You can't stop me. Nothing in this world can stop me. Nothing.

But she must not say that to him, must not let him guess, even, she was thinking it! She must handle him carefully — more carefully than ever in her life, watchful not to affront his aggressive, his monumental dignity. She must woo him, flattering his power with her sad eye, her down-dropped mouth, her silence — a sweet all-enduring Grizelda. Yes, that was the way with papa — patience, sweetness and the considered word!

Suddenly it came to her that she was no longer free to act alone — Pen had his part in this! Curious, disturbing, the thought that one could no longer press forward obstinate for what one's self wanted... one must consider another's good, equally with one's own — more than one's own... Pen and she stood together in this.

But — her heart suddenly dropped. *How* do we stand? He did no more than kiss me. Only a fool would read a man's heart into a kiss! I am Nicolet Penny who has kissed and been kissed! But that kiss was different. For the first time I know what a kiss can do... I know it can pull the heart out of your breast, turn your blood to water, weaken your every limb so that hands hang lifeless at the wrists, feet stand helpless upon the floor, helpless to save you from falling, helpless...

But he — Pen Wade? Had he, too, felt these things? Or had be kissed and laughed and kissed again — the cool young man, the insolent young man? Whether he had ever kissed and forgotten and kissed again didn't matter — it didn't matter. This time he had not been cool — his heart had beat as wildly as her own... this time he would not forget...

She came back smiling to the dressing table and stood smiling at herself in the flower-wreathed mirror. And well might she smile. Red lips, flushed cheeks, bright eyes!

She picked up a comb and fluffed out the bright curls. She thought, I'm lucky. I'm terribly lucky! Suppose I hadn't met Pen! Suppose I'd thought I was in love... married someone I could never love as I love Pen. I wouldn't have known — not until it was too late... I've never been in love before...

At the thought of her tremendous escape, her rosy cheek paled.

I'm a hard sort of person, really — I know it. Deep inside me a hardness nothing could melt — not papa, not friends, nobody! And now I've met Pen. And I want to be kind, I want to be kind, not only to Pen, but to everyone — to everyone for Pen's sake...

She leaned forward. The comb teased out a curled fringe upon her forehead.

....If I hadn't met Pen! Going on, getting harder and harder. Shoving my way through everything — like father. Or, maybe, smiling over emptiness, like mother...

There came to her a sudden swift understanding of what life had been to her mother. Her heart was scalded with pain.

. . .A disappointed woman — as all women must be who are born out of their time! Beneath that unspoken strength, that voice of authority, beneath that elegance, beneath that charming smile, beneath the comfort that folds her in to snug living — emptiness, coldness. . .

She thought with sudden real terror, I couldn't be like that — ever! I'm not strong like mamma. I couldn't live with emptiness. I should go mad! I *need* Pen. . . And I'll fight!

She thought of Nicholas, chin out-thrust, lock-lipped with obstinacy, her softened mouth set into Nicholas's own line. . . I'll wheedle, coax, lie, shove, kick, thrust — fight with any weapon, clean or unclean, to save my soul alive!

Pen Wade paced up and down the narrow room at Mrs Greenhalgh's — a queer incongruous room. Upon its walls sprawling with faded buttercups and daisies looped horribly with blue ribbons, he had pinned a few black and white drawings. He had a passion for elegance in form; he distrusted colour as an irrelevance, obscuring the clear rhythm of pattern. Amid the sickly medley of faded flowers a drawing cut from an art journal enchanted him with the perfection of its line — a woman's figure, drawn, so it seemed, in one magnificent careless curve by an artist with a foreign name — a name unknown to him — Rothenstein; near it, one of his own designs, minute, intricate, the perfection of applied art; another drawing, audacious and swift by a man called John, was all pure rhythm.

A small Queen Anne bookcase, picked up cheap in the Sneinton Market, held his books — they showed the deep but limited quality of his interests. Books on drawing and design, books that reproduced the works of old masters, *Felkin's History of Lace*, a rare but tattered copy of *Mrs Palliser on Lace*, with here and there an old number of *The Yellow Book* picked up on a bookstall and treasured for the charm of the drawings. The little case that held them was quite perfect. Whenever he came into the room his eye leaped to it; his fingers would caress the warm and shining wood — perfection!

His own property, scant and slowly acquired, was beautiful. He would buy nothing unless it reached his high standard of beauty. Once bought it became part of him; he could no more consider parting with it than he could consider parting with an arm or a leg. But the hideous wallpaper, the yellowing lace curtains fallen into holes, the iron bed with its fly-blown knobs, distressed him not at all — they were neither his property nor his choice. All the years he had lived here they had never existed for him; he never saw them, never had seen them. His treasures — they alone were his home.

But now there was no more pleasure in them, not even in his beloved little bookcase. His absent fingers smoothed the shining wood; his absent eye flickered over his Rothenstein, his John. But neither hand nor eye carried pleasure to his senses. To his excited mind, working irritably upon what had happened this morning, every ugliness stood out, every crack, stain, speck upon the fly-blown knobs assaulted his senses.

The ugliness of the room seemed suddenly overpowering. It was odd, he thought, that he had lived here, year after year, and had never really seen this room. His mind, refusing his problem, escaping his problem, went back to that day when, scared and sick at heart, they had taken him from that other room where his mother had died.

His mother. . . His mind went back, remembering. Beautiful she had been — and sick, and frightened; gentle and loving and brave — but still frightened, horribly frightened. No-one had ever told him so. But he had known it with his child's intuition; known it beyond all question when he had stirred in his sleep, disturbed by the low coughing, sounding so sadly, so full of omen, in the dark room. . . And sometimes she had wept. He had not known till then that grown-ups could weep and the sound of her anguished weeping had stiffened his heart with fear; for he had known without any telling that it was for him she wept.

He stopped abruptly in his stride. Now why did he think of his mother long-dead — even in memory, long-dead? Because something had happened today that he hadn't wanted to happen, had never dreamed could happen. Because he wanted desperately to share his disturbed, uncertain mind with another. Sure of himself, he had always shrunk from sharing any of himself; now, for the first time, he felt the need to share, to ask; to give and to receive.

He did not accept this new need easily. He was angry, humiliated. A man must not lean upon others, a man must settle his own difficulties.

He forced his mind back again to its problems.

That girl. . . No good deluding himself further, without any forewarning, without any desire on his part, *that* girl had become suddenly, inevitably, *his* girl. . . the girl whose name he didn't even know!

Life was odd, he thought irritably. You went on doing the same old thing — it was like working on an old, a familiar pattern. And then, suddenly, without any warning, everything jerked, everything tangled and twisted, and the pattern was broken. It was like a faulty thread in the machine. . . but it wasn't at simple as that! You could remove the knot, mend the threads, carry on with the pattern. But life wasn't like that. With the unforeseen twist, the pattern was utterly, inevitably and beyond all question, changed.

His fingers drummed fretfully. It irked him that a pattern should be broken and a new one started — and no mastermind to direct, to guide.

He was dissatisfied with his crude metaphor. He thought, life isn't like a machine that once set, runs smoothly. Life is moulded by every circumstance, every wind. Life works unceasingly, works violently, works secretly. From the most secret depths unknown thoughts rise slowly upwards, unguessed emotions are thrown... a man can do nothing. He may watch and think and plan, but the moment finds him defenceless. He can do nothing. Nothing.

He paced the narrow room, trying to hammer out a philosophy in his young untutored mind.

If a man can do nothing, then what use character? What philosophy? What religion? But a man can do something... a little... but only a little. By standing up to circumstances he enlarges himself. But though he may enlarge himself, he doesn't alter the essential pattern, no, not by one hair's breadth alter the pattern.

The thought appalled him. He had been so confident, always, of his own strength, his own power to make whatever pattern — whatever reasonable pattern — he wished of his own life.

The narrow room seemed to stifle him. The sick flowers on the wall were suddenly flowers faded upon a tomb.

He paced the streets. In the market-place yellow flares lit up the shining globes of oranges and apples, fell upon the deer-dappled bananas, the purple bloomy grapes. In spite of himself, his eye drew him. His problem became less urgent. He lingered at a fish stall... the delicate whorl of a whelk, it should go so, rhythmic as water... He saw the completed pattern. And the fine-drawn sole, so... standing and curving upon its tail, its foolish mouth agape with fishy curiosity upon an unknown world... and the twisting eel, its convolutions curious as a burlesque dancer... curtains for a fishmonger's palace — they would make the world laugh!

His own mouth widened to a grin. He didn't know a millionaire fishmonger, so he'd sketch out the design to make himself laugh!

Up and down the flare-lit alleys. Leeks tossing white hair like Lilliputian fates: pineapples opulent as councillors; pots and pans, saucy teapots and grave coffee-pots; portly tureens — councillors again.

He came through the market and wandered up Market Street. Nothing to spice the imagination there, nothing beyond a vague distress that shop windows could be so dull. In the dullness that the shop windows made, his problem was at him again.

...He didn't want to get himself mixed up with that girl! She wasn't the type he admired. She was pretty enough — bright as fresh paint — and just as easily scratched to show the cheapness underneath. Hard and bright and brittle — he'd met her sort before! She was unsuitable, completely and utterly unsuitable. And the most unsuitable thing about her was that she was the old man's daughter!

The last thing in the world he wanted to be — the old man's son-in-law! He saw enough of the old man as it was, without wanting to introduce him into his private life! God, what a nuisance old Penny was, with that loud voice and that loud manner, and those constant tiresome suggestions! He hadn't the sense to see that his sort of design and your sort of design were entirely different! The old boy was good — in his way, in his florid, elaborate way, but it was quite different from your way and you couldn't mix the two styles. But the old boy, wouldn't see it, simply wouldn't see it!

Thank goodness that contract was nearly done with — a couple of months would see it through. Shameless contract. Old Penny had paid him over and above it, lately. Generous, he wanted you to believe — an eye on the future, that was all! But nothing could alter the fact that the contract was iniquitous! If he renewed it, he could get what he wanted from Penny — in reason. But it wasn't good enough! No contract could make working for Penny worthwhile! He didn't work well — never knowing when the old man wasn't going to come blowing in all toothy smile and suggestion, all charm and hard cold eye. . . No, it wasn't good enough! He wanted to feel himself free, free to work how and where he chose. Well — another couple of months of that rotten, iniquitous contract, and he'd be his own man — free.

Free. Soon he would be free from Penny contracts, Penny influence, Penny — his mouth was wry — charm! Had he really for one mad moment thought of tangling himself up with that girl! Even if the old man were willing, even if there was not the question of exposing himself to the everlasting noise of her father, even then there was the difficulty of her money. He didn't believe in rich wives. It would take more of patience and sweetness than she possessed, to sweeten that stinking money! Not that money must necessarily stink. Money that he made for himself would be sweet enough. It was simply that he wanted neither Penny money nor Penny wife!

Then what sort of wife did he want? A man, he supposed, must marry some time! He hadn't thought, really. . . He'd like, he supposed, the sort of woman who'd make a man comfortable. But. . . she mightn't have eyes of Chinese blue, nor a little mouth that went quirking up at the corners. . .

. . .But a mouth that turns up, can so easily turn down! Especially with that girl. He'd seen it! Seen those eyes dark with temper, too! No, he'd want a different sort of girl — a girl who would put his work first, put it before herself — before both of them. And she must understand the urgency of rhythm and design. She must look at his work and understand it. Like it or not, she must *understand*... He could not do with a woman who thought in terms of merely pretty, or whether it would look well upon herself or not.

But... she mightn't have little curls flat upon her forehead like a woman on a Greek vase, little curls, round and bright like new-minted coins...

He laughed a little at himself, striding across Theatre Quadrant, and dodging for his life out of the tiresome stream of motors — they seemed to multiply day by day!

...A woman to make him comfortable? Had he jumped straight into middle-age? A woman, selfless, to share his thoughts and dreams? Was he so young, so silly a romantic, so stuck fast in adolescence? No — he was neither of these things. He was Pen Wade, and he was — he suddenly realised — an ordinary man, and he wanted his girl. And life — wise or indifferent, or merely muddling, had offered him this girl — this vital, this terribly attractive girl!

He sighed, smiling, as he turned back to Mrs Greenhalgh's.

Chapter 34

Nicholas sat alone in his "den". It was small and comfortable compared with his chilly magnificent library, and he always used it when he was disturbed.

And he *was* disturbed!... Not that there was any reason, none whatsoever! At Pennys things were going better than ever — twist-lace, burnt-lace, wool-lace — they couldn't turn it out fast enough! As for those hairnets, they alone were building him a steady fortune! That was part of the trouble. He wanted more machines for his nets. And why should he buy new ones, when his own machines at Heriots were ready and waiting!

And they *were* his machines! Ware couldn't even keep up the interest, let alone pay off the capital! Ware would have to close down — a month or two would see him finished. And that being the case, surely it was sensible to take the machines now, when he wanted them. Old Ware would have to close down a bit sooner, that was all! Well, it would stop him from throwing good money after bad!

That was sense — simply common sense. But if he called in the mortgage, Heriot would condemn him. She wouldn't say a word — but it would be clear in her voice and in her eye and in every one of her damned ladylike actions. Queer how he still minded what Heriot thought! She irritated him in a thousand ways with her ladylike manners and her bottled-up sentimentality — Ware brand! But still he craved for her approval... he couldn't get rid of it, this curious desire that she should approve...

He knew what Heriot would think. She would think it gave him pleasure to have a hand in smashing Heriots. Why should she think that? If he had wanted to smash Heriots he could have done it any time these last eight years. How could Heriot believe that he was jealous? Hadn't he something far bigger to show than Heriots, ay, bigger and finer than Heriots at its best?

The plain truth was, he wanted those machines, and he wanted them now! It was ridiculous to buy new ones when there were machines for the taking, machines that ought to have been taken long ago, that certainly ought to be taken now to prevent old Ware from ending in the workhouse!

But Heriot would never see it like that! Jealous, her eyes would say; jealous, that quiet, unspeaking mouth...

The door opened and Nicki came in. He was glad it was Nicki. A man could talk to Nicki and she would understand. She was his girl — his comfort, his protection against the treacle-and-water Wares. Nicki was firm and she was sensible. Nicki would never let you down!

Nicki crossed over and poked the fire into a cheerful blaze — for all it was late June, the night air was chilly. She came back to the table and laid her cheek on his shoulder. For a moment he rested in her youthfulness, her friendship.

"Well?" she asked presently.

"Well?"

"What's this for?" she rubbed delicately at the lines between his brows.

"Nothing. . . not really! But I'm sick of knowing that every time you open your mouth there's a good chance of Ware treacle being shoved in — ay, an' brimstone an' all!"

"Spit it out!" Nicki advised.

"I do! Right in their eye!" Nicholas chuckled." But the taste sticks. God, how it sticks! You're my girl, Nicki, thank the Lord for that! I can talk to you! You've got sense. You understand!"

He leaned back in his chair. He was feeling better already.

"It's like this, Nicki. Eight years ago I lent your grandfather some money — a lot of money — ten thousand pounds to be exact. I didn't want to. I knew it was no use. But he put it in such a way I couldn't refuse. Your mother was wild about it. That's the trouble with the Wares — do or don't, you're always wrong!

"Your grandfather bought new machines with the money and he offered them to me as security. Well, it wasn't enough! Ten used machines for ten new ones — it doesn't make sense!"

Nicki nodded.

"So Ware threw in Heriots as well! Not *such* a security! Apart from those ten, all their machines are narrow and old-fashioned. But a man has to have some sort of security somewhere! I mean you can't just go and chuck your money down a drain, now can you?

"Well, that loan didn't help — as I knew it wouldn't. Your grandfather is where he was a quarter of a century ago — he's learned nothing! He's still bleating about the wickedness of taking machines outside Nottingham. Can you credit that? But time doesn't stand still, even if he does! He doesn't realise, — actually doesn't realise, that the best part of Nottingham's trade has gone to Europe — ay, to foreigners! We, outside the city, why we've only got hold of a tiny bit of it — foreigners grabbed the rest long ago!"

Nicki sat, hands loosely clasped, giving him her whole attention. By God, it rested a man to put a matter clear to a clear intelligence!

"Nottingham lost best part of her trade not so much because of Long Eaton, or Heanor, or Beeston or Derby — there was enough for all! But because Frenchmen began making Nottingham lace — ay, making Nottingham patterns on Nottingham machines — and Nottingham twist-hands went across to help them!

"Nottingham machines! There's your stumbling-block! Nottingham let them have the machines! It began by selling 'em second-hand to Calais manufacturers. Trade wasn't so good here — so they had to go and make things better! Ay, they made things better by selling machines they weren't using, half-price! As early as '67 questions were being asked about it in Parliament. And there it ended — as you might have guessed. They didn't do a thing! Not a damn thing! When it comes to shovelling gold into your pocket, you're satisfied to be blind!"

True, Nicki thought, and truest of all of you!

She said, gently, "You couldn't blame them! An old wornout machine — turn it into bread and butter!"

"Ay — that's the way it began. But it didn't end there! Next it was machines that weren't second-hand. Ay, they sent away brand new machines, latest patterns. Your grandfather's best friend piled up a fortune that way — and the town showed its appreciation by making him mayor. Machines shipped all over the world — our machines! But your grandfather didn't see any harm in that — he couldn't see any farther than Long Eaton — or maybe, Derby! If the Japs are satisfied to work at starvation rates and bring down the price of lace, well, that doesn't matter! Japan's a hell of a long way away!

"It's men like your grandfather, blind when they should have seen; dumb when they should have spoken — were to blame. It was the men who sold Nottingham's lace machines abroad, sold the trade!"

Nicki said, "Every man for himself! That's what you'd say if you wanted to be honest! You'd have sold machines yourself — if you'd had the chance!"

"Maybe! But I didn't get the chance! Nor I didn't get the chance to stop it neither! Your grandfather did, though; he was a public man, known and respected! That's what gets me on the raw with him! Straining at the gnat and swallowing the whole damn elephant! Ware blindness and Ware bleating!"

Nicki laughed outright. "Why worry? Take what you want — if you can! That's the motto of the human race — and the Wares know it in spite of all their blindness and their bleating!"

"Nicki!" He was a little shocked. This from Nicki, Nicki who from birth had only to hold out her hands to have them filled! This went beyond common sense this did!

Nicki said, "Are you going in for Ware treacle too?" Her eyes were steady on him. "In this world, what you want, really want, you have to fight for! When I want a thing, I'll fight, too! I'll fight tooth and nail. I'll never stop fighting, till I've got what I want!"

Nicholas, oddly disturbed, said gravely, "What is it you're likely to want so badly that I'm not likely to give you?"

She sent him a long steady look, "I'll tell you some day!" she said.

Nicholas sat back in his chair. Nicki had gone, taking his comfort with her.

. . .*Take what you want — while you can!* That was a queer thing for Nicki to say! What had she meant by it? What could she have meant? Nothing. . . nothing at all. . . nothing that is, that concerned her personally. She was simply stating a fact as she saw it! *You going in for treacle, too?* That's what she'd said! And by God she was right! Getting as bad as old Ware, he was! Nicki had the sense to see clear through pretty wrappings, right down to the bone. A man must look to himself. If he doesn't no-one else will! That's the way the world goes and Nicki's got the sense to see it! She was right. . . But all the same he hadn't liked the way she'd said it. That queer personal note. . . the subject hadn't warranted it! She'd sort of twisted it round, made it personal. . . almost as if she'd been warning him. . . warning him. . .

When I want anything, I'll fight, too. I'll fight tooth and nail. I'll never stop fighting. . . But Nicki didn't have to fight him! He was her father. . . He wasn't likely to refuse her anything — not if it were possible. And she was too sensible to demand the impossible? But. . . but if she were not too sensible? Then — Nicholas shrugged — she must learn, that's all!

Nicholas was worried, more worried than he cared to admit even to himself. He was worried about Nicki — Nicki from whom he had thought no grief could come.

. . .It kept coming back to him — how odd she had been the other day. The more he thought about it, the odder it seemed. . . *When I want anything I'll fight. . . tooth and nail. I'll never stop fighting. . .* When had Nicki ever had to fight for anything? She had meant something. The more he thought about it, the surer he was that she had meant something. . . almost as if she were trying to prepare him. . . prepare him for what? What is it you are likely to want and I'm not likely to give you? He'd asked her that right away. And her answer had been queer — queer as that long look she'd given him. . . *I'll tell you some day*, she'd said.

What was it that Nicki would tell him some day? What was it she was prepared to fight for, to fight for so desperately?

Young Wade. Now why did Pen Wade leap to the mind — before everything leap to the mind? Fear — fear only. Nothing between them, he'd swear... What could be between them — Penny's employee and Penny's daughter?

Penny's son... Penny's daughter.

He turned the thought from his sick mind.

Penny's employee and Penny's daughter... it wasn't possible!

Ware's employee and Ware's daughter — that had been possible! Different. Quite, quite different. He was Nicholas Penny!

But would Nicki see the difference? Of course she would — because the difference was in Nicki herself. She was her father's girl. She understood accepted values. Heriot at Nicki's age had known no values — only the values of her adolescent dream world. But Nicki's clear eyes saw the world as it was — she was no fool — and least of all was she the world-well-lost-for-love type...

But... there was a time, and not so long ago, neither, when Nicki had seemed to be in and out of his factory, and always with a perfectly good excuse... A message from mamma. Or she had come to see papa very specially — a secret. She had wanted to ask... To ask something that could not be said over the telephone? And so secret that it might be whispered in Wade's room, where nine times out of ten he had found her!

That last time he had expressed himself pretty clearly on the subject. He had been quiet — a little whimsical in tone. But she had understood. She was no fool! The colour had blazed up in her cheeks, but she hadn't answered a word. She had taken herself off immediately and she had never set foot in Pennys since.

He had the wretched feeling that a link had been broken between himself and Nicki, broken and lost. And that he, and not Nicki, was the loser. It had come to him in the wordless obedience with which she had turned and gone — an almost contemptuous obedience. Seeming obedience — he'd swear! He knew his Nicki!

And once he had seen young Wade with a girl passing through the castle gateway. The girl's general get-up he could swear to — almost; the way she walked and the way she carried her shoulders, and that pretty tilt of the head. And he could have sworn, certainly, to the bright hat and scarf she wore. He had hurried after them — but they had gone.

Had it been Nicki? Nicki and Pen Wade? Had they, too, wandered the formal gardens, hidden in the dull galleries? But they would not talk about machines — no man would, not with Nicki! Nicki and Pen! *Pen Wade!* Out of all the world to choose Pen Wade!

He thought, because I'm afraid I think these things... my own fear driving me. Knowing what I know... I must forever be whipping at my mind...

He was a fool, a fool so to torment himself! Nicki, Nicki herself was the answer to all his fears. Nicki was proud and she was ambitious.

Nicki knew well enough her own worth in the marriage-market. He'd heard her assess the value of her looks plus her father's money. And she didn't put the value too low, neither! She wasn't the sort to throw herself away on a penniless young man, however attractive — a man worse than penniless — obscure, without background, without family. No. . . she wouldn't consider marrying such a young man!

But — suppose she found him too attractive? Not attractive enough to marry, but too attractive to leave alone? Nicki wouldn't be the first girl to lose her head! — and more than her head! Nonsense — Nicki wasn't just any girl, Nicki was Nicki! She wasn't the girl to diminish her own value! Her sense of values came before her affections — and the sense of her own value topped the list! Nicki was *his* girl, Penny through and through! None of the woolly-headed Ware about Nicki! He was a fool to go worrying himself to death! Clear the whole thing out of his mind and have done with it!

Easier said than done! And only one way to do it! Talk the whole thing out with Nicki — have a good laugh together over it.

But — suppose Nicki didn't laugh! Suppose once he'd put the idea into her head it remained there? Pen Wade was a fine-looking chap. And Nicki, if she was proud and ambitious, she was also self-willed. Through sheer obstinacy she might cherish the idea, might even come to think herself a little in love!

The thought of another's obstinacy stiffened his own will. Obstinacy he could deal with — no man better! He had given Nicki her head all her life because it suited him to do so. He liked high spirits — in his daughter! It amused him — as long as it didn't cut across his own will. But if it did, if it came to a battle of wills between himself and Nicki, then by God, Nicki would have to knuckle under!

Nicki would have to learn who was master. It would do her good! A woman had to learn to obey the guiding rein — and Nicki wasn't a child any longer. Let her learn her lesson and then he'd make it up to her. A new car — but he'd just given her one, there was damn little you could offer Nicki — a holiday abroad, another string of pearls — whatever she wanted — if what she wanted was reasonable. He wouldn't want to be hard on Nicki.

But — suppose it was not as easy as all that! Suppose Nicki honestly believed herself to be in love! After all, Stella had been no older. . . no older, but she had loved and she had suffered. . . Now why must he think of Stella, of Stella long dust? It was Nicki he must think of now, Nicki alive and able to suffer. . .

God, if Nicki were unhappy! If Nicki suffered!

Then she must suffer! She must suffer as others before her had suffered — suffered and got over it! Nicki must be made to understand that never in this world could she marry Pen Wade.

No easy job to persuade Nicki once she'd set her heart on a thing! Well, then he wouldn't try to persuade! He'd tell her straight out that it was No! He would remind her that he had never refused her anything, and if now be had to say No, the reason was good. And it *was* No. No and No and No! He'd tell her that he'd rather see her dead than living with Pen Wade!

But it wouldn't do. It wouldn't do! People didn't talk like that! It sounded pure bunk! Nicki would simply laugh. She wouldn't know that it was the truth — the absolute literal truth. She wouldn't know, either that there was nothing she could do about it, that even her iron will couldn't help her here — that there was no law in any land that would marry her to Pen Wade.

Well, if it came to it, he must *make* her understand! Tell her why she could never marry Pen Wade. Lord, what a heap of muck to rake over! And having raked it over? Having bespattered himself with muck? There was still no knowing where blind wilfulness might not lead her. Driven by anger, bewildered by grief, and ignorant — terribly ignorant — she might fly like a wild thing to Pen Wade... whether she believed it or not, it would be all one if her devil was up. Off she would fly, a bewildered fury, driven by passion for Pen Wade.

If... and if... and if... He was a fool to sicken himself with these impossible possibilities, to torture himself with the whimsies of his own fearful brain! But — how did he know it was impossible? Except for the one hidden fact, the story was common enough — his own story, his and Heriot's.

Find out. He must find out the truth. He must stop goading himself on to madness...

It was Heriot, very quiet, almost abstracted, who raised the storm.

She was sitting over the fire in her own room when Nicholas came in. He did not like Heriot's room. He disliked its pale tones. Compared with the rich reds and golds of the rest of the house it struck him as anaemic and cold — like Heriot herself! Besides — she'd been sly about this room, countermanding his orders behind his back. It was the one room in the whole house that did not shout *Nicholas*, and he avoided it whenever he could.

He came in now without knocking — it was not his way to knock. Every room in the house was his, so why knock anywhere? Standing in her doorway, it came to him that, caught unawares, Heriot lost something of her air of authority, of security. It hurt him, a little, to catch Heriot without that defence that was also his own defence. It was almost as though someone had questioned his success.

Heriot put down her knitting and smiled; it was a formal smile, cold and impersonal. He thought, she doesn't smile nowadays, not *smile* — not the way she used to. Her one beauty — and she doesn't smile! Caught off her guard, she was, he thought, a little pathetic. But even as he thought it, she stiffened into assurance.

On guard again! Even while he was pleased to see again the Heriot he admired, he asked himself why she must wear the mask with her husband. Was it because she had guessed long and long ago that he had never loved her? Well then, what was love? Love — a thing for raw boys and girls! He had not loved her, granted! But he had admired her quality, always he had admired that fineness in her, and would do so till he died.

He stood looking at her, not knowing how always he had rested upon her love for him — love unspoken, unrecognised, without value to him — but still the foundation that carried his life.

He was troubled now that there was no warmth in her greeting. He stood there tasting the faint but definite sense of loss.

. . .That smile of hers! It had gone and he had never missed it, had never even noticed that it had gone.

She put out a hand, inviting him with the small movement, nearer the warmth of the fire. He felt that she offered him courtesy — nothing more. He thought, she had never failed in courtesy all these years. Never once. But — he thought — if there had been warmth between us — not even love — kindness only — warm live kindness, we might have quarrelled and kissed and been friends. All these years and not a quarrel — not the shadow of a quarrel! I would have welcomed her rudeness; I hated her unbreakable courtesy. . . Too well-bred to quarrel. All manners and no heart!

But blaming her did not wholly satisfy him. In spite of her hateful courtesy, he felt a little sorry for her — for them both. He thought, If I went, now, and bought her something — something that cost the devil of a lot of money. An emerald ring, an emerald necklace, even. . . Women like expensive things.

(Another ring for Heriot's ringless fingers, another necklace for her unadorned neck.)

Heriot said, "Can you spare me a minute, Nicholas? I want to speak to you!"

He hesitated, wondering why his heart beat as at the warning of danger; she added gently, "I promised to speak to you, Nicholas."

He said, trying to put off the moment, "I only looked in for a second. I'm in a hurry. What is it?"

Heriot said. "It's Nicki. And young Wade. They're seeing a lot of each other!"

He felt his cold stomach rise. He said roughly, "Don't be a damned fool, putting notions into the kid's head!"

Heriot said, "When did anybody put notions into Nicki's head that she didn't want put there? And she's not a child any longer. That's where you make a mistake, Nicholas. And after all," there was that cold smile on her lips, "why not?"

Why not? Why not? Why not? Sitting there and mimming at him, and asking all quiet and ladylike, *why not?*

His temper flared.

"D'yer want ter drive me crazy wi' yer daft notions? *Why not?* Because I say so! Got that? I *say* so!"

He was beating upon her little rosewood table. A crack sprang out upon its polished surface. She thought angrily, All lovely things, all delicate things, he spoils. She thought wearily, Poor Nicholas!

She said quietly, "That won't be enough for Nicki, never mind how often or how loudly you say it! You know Nicki! You know that when her heart is set, even a good reason doesn't count!"

"This time it will! It's got to! I give no reason. I don't need to give a reason, I'm her father. I say *No*! And that's enough!"

"Not for Nicki. You're dealing with Nicki, not — with me!"

She paused, watching him... He expected obedience from her, expected it without question, without surprise. Her bitterness rose. She could feel physical bitterness in her mouth.

She thought, holding herself in to restraint, *quiet, quiet now — for Nicki's sake. If I let go now — after all these years let go...*

She said, quiet as ever, "And the objection, Nicholas?"

He was shaken with fury. He could feel the fingers thrust into his pockets, trembling in the warmth of the stuff. That she should presume to argue with him! That she should have the idiocy to argue what was not arguable!

He would like to take her by the thin shoulder and shake, shake, shake her! *And the objection, Nicholas?* By God, he'd like to wipe that smile off her face, that pleasant, aggravating, damn ladylike smile!

"Because — because —" He was choking over the words. Nothing could excuse her damn-fool meddling, nothing, nothing at all!

Suddenly speech burst forth. "Can't yer see fer yersen! Are yer daft? It wain't niver do! It wain't *do*!"

Damn her, sitting there and quiet and ladylike and dragging him back, back to the days when he was poor, unknown, Nicholas Penny. Wasn't she satisfied yet? No, there she sat and she didn't say a word, only her eyes went on demanding, demanding...

"It i'n't suitable!" He flung out each word as though it were a stone.

"Why not? I don't see it!"

God, she was goading him! She was getting under his skin with that damn fine lady air of hers!

"Suitable? What do yo' know about suitable? What do yer know abowt anythin'? Yo' wi' yer niminy, piminy, piddlin' ways — yo're just abowt as suitable as one o' them punch-an'-judy dolls! No 'eart. No guts! How suitable hev yo' bin ter me? How much enjoyment hev I had from yo'? Enjoyment — that's somethin' any woman can give, ne'er mind how silly! Enjoyment! My God! Yer've failed i' that, as yer failed in everythin'!"

It was not Heriot he was attacking, not Heriot standing there and smiling out of her cold, sick face. Even while he was spitting out the hateful words he knew that! It was the horror in his heart, in his brain, because of Nicki and Pen, because she made it seem so reasonable, so likely... Nicki and Pen... brother and sister... *brother and sister*... How could a man think of these things and not go mad? It *was* driving him mad — forcing him to shout things he hadn't meant to say ever, filthy things...

He turned from Heriot's sick face. He stood bracing himself for self control. There were things that must be said, here and now. He must make her understand that he had been driven beyond himself to say things he hadn't meant — that saying them, he had wounded himself as well as her... more than her.

His mind groped for words of apology. No use... no use. both mind and tongue were all unused to the words of humility.

His tongue moved stiffly about the words of his careful acquired speech. He said very slowly, "Maybe you think it's the same with them as it was with us. But it isn't. Believe me, it isn't. The outside circumstances — they might seem the same, that's all! But they're not the same — they're not. If things were — were what they seem — I wouldn't say a word, I swear that! But this — it's a case in a million, in ten million..."

His words dried on his tongue. Looking at her cold closed face, he thought, she thinks it just pride — pride and greed. He was angered by the injustice.

He was suddenly tired of making her understand. "After all," he said, and he was almost jaunty, "there's only one *me*, only one Nicholas Penny!"

She looked at him then, but her expression did not change. He thought, she won't ever smile again — not that smile! He thought, emeralds — ring or necklace, it's too late! And he had wanted to make her smile, the old Heriot smile, to bring back the lost beauty to her face. Now she would never smile that way again!

He felt beaten. He leaned against the mantelpiece, feeling the comfort of its support. He looked indolent, careless, warming himself against the bright fire. He thought, no good getting on the wrong side of Heriot. She's got to stand with me in this. . . Nicki's mother. In all other things she doesn't count — in this, she doubles or halves my strength!

He said, trying the humble mode, "There's a lot on my mind just now!" But the words came arrogantly, as if he wanted to make her understand that she and Nicki were of small importance because of his great affairs.

He said, "Not business —" He tried to sweeten the impression, "other things!"

She stared at him then. He could see her staring. He said slowly, "Business isn't the end of things with me — though at one time I thought it was. But it isn't now. Believe that. Do believe it, Heriot!"

He thought it was like scratching with his fingernails upon stone. Strange that this should be Heriot, who had once been warm and eager and kind! Through the long years she must have been changing, bit by bit changing, and he had not noticed — he had not cared enough to notice.

He said again, "You must believe it! And you must believe me when I say it isn't pride stands in the way. Nicki and — and that young man! I'd move heaven and earth, if I could, I swear it, to make that right! But it can't be made right. God himself couldn't make it right. Because it's wrong, utterly, horribly wrong. You couldn't know how wrong! But you could believe me, Heriot — you could trust me!"

Still she said no word, standing rigid, inimical. . . *How much enjoyment have I had from yo'. . . Yer've failed in that. . . yer failed in everythin'. . . How much enjoyment? Enjoyment?* She couldn't speak, not while she was bleeding, bleeding to death. . .

He fumbled on. "Heriot — could you take it that — when I said that — you know, before — about you, I mean — I didn't know what I was saying. . . Excited, you know, driven — a little crazy, maybe. . ."

But it's true. . . true. . . all the same true. . .

Both minds flinging the challenge, both clamouring, ruthless to hurt, to hurt each other, to hurt themselves with the hateful truth!

Heriot spoke as if she had not heard him. Quiet above her mind's clamour, her still face, her still voice. Only the voice, a little sharpened, might have betrayed her.

"I promised Nicki I'd talk to you. I promised to do my best. So you must listen, Nicholas, and then I'll say no more. Pen Wade is young and he's attractive and he's clever." She spoke as though the matter held no more interest than a much-repeated lesson. "He makes a good living — and can make a better. And they love each other. I don't know what that means to you, Nicholas — probably nothing at all — though I thought it did — once. But it means everything in the world to Nicki." She looked at him steadily. “Everything — and now,” her voice was high and clear, “I’ve kept my promise and there’s nothing more to say, Nicholas, nothing more. . .”

A hand careful about her skirts, she moved across the room. In the doorway she half turned. “Oh,” she said pitifully — but whom she pitied was not clear, “be careful, Nicholas, be *careful*!” And closed the door gently behind her.

Chapter 35

More and more machines at Heriots falling silent. . . day after day, silent. Orders so few, so negligible, it was cheaper to stop the machines altogether. American orders for the fine narrow edgings in which Heriots specialised, going straight to the continent, swelling the voice of the machines in Calais, in Plauen, in St. Gall. . . Nottingham patterns made on Nottingham machines coming back across the Channel to be finished — only to be finished.

In Long Eaton, and Bulwell and Beeston and Derby, the mills prospering, filling the air with their great voices. Miles of lace, cheap lace, common lace — lace to hang upon emancipated factory girls in China, lace to frame aspidistras in mean English streets — lace that paid!

Only Nottingham passed over, forgotten. . .

One by one the machines slackening, silent. Large factories, famous factories, silencing the machines, closing up their doors. Men and women in hundreds, in thousands — twist-hands and warpers, stretchers and bleachers, menders and folders, draughtsmen and designers, founders and moulders, porters and carters, paper-box makers, warehousemen and clerks, walking the streets helpless, hopeless.

Small wonder that John Ware who could never endure to see good workmen workless, who had that very day turned off half his hands, men and women he had known for years, known and respected, rose up in the night and quietly shot himself.

And it was not of his daughter he thought, finger on the trigger, nor of Ada his wife, nor even of Heriots, that great tradition; but of James Clark, friend as well as employee these many years, James Clark with the grey look already on his face — James Clark, and others like him, turned out upon the streets to starve.

What this might mean to Heriot, this pitiful ending, no-one ever knew. This, and the crashing of Heriots — she never spoke of them. Only where she had smiled rarely, she now smiled not at all; and her carriage lost something of its fine bearing. Nicholas ever-sensitive about himself, thought that he caught her eyes upon him sometimes, thoughtful eyes. And, he fancied, at times, unforgiving eyes.

It annoyed him whenever he thought of it. What had he done that she should, or should not, forgive? He had lent the old man ten thousand, but he had not claimed the machines till the very last minute. In spite of his talk with Nicki, he had waited — waited till the crash was imminent. . .

But all the same he felt uncomfortable when he thought of Heriot's eyes.

Still silent, she came from the pitiful reading of John Ware's will — will heavy with matters of Heriots and its affairs, with houses and property, with bonds and money in the bank — will made long ago, its grandiloquent phrases meaning exactly nothing. There was but one recipient of all — factory, houses, bonds — all to Nicholas Penny.

Nicholas was kind. He offered to allow his mother-in-law to stay on, his pensioner, in the house where Heriot had been born, the house where he had been admitted on sufferance only, where Heriot's parents, where the servants, even, had not always concealed their contempt.

But Ada Ware refused — in spite of courteous urging, refused.

Since she knew that Heriots was to be closed down, its last remaining hands dispersed, its shops dismantled of those machines that had cost her husband his life, she had turned against Nottingham. She had no anger because all the property was coming to Nicholas. He had a right to value for money — why else take securities? But that he should take away the machines that might yet give Heriots life — machines that had cost her husband his own life, that it should be her son-in-law to close the doors of Heriots, close them for ever. . .

Her sick spirit turned from the thought.

Husband and daughter, they had loved Heriots, had talked of it with easy love. But she, her own nature cautious, and a little dour, had never trusted herself to speak of what Heriots meant to her. But she was Andrew Heriot's daughter. They were apt to forget it, those two — but she, she remembered it always. Heriots was more to her than a mere miracle. It was something created, fashioned by the will and the brain and the flesh and the sweat of one man. No, she could never talk easily about the factory, for she must look back and remember her father, her mother, remember the agony of mind and the travail of body that had made Heriots.

But even if she had not this memory, Heriots had always been the centre of her life. How could it be otherwise? Every day, John going to Heriots, working for Heriots, thinking for Heriots. And now, no more Heriots.

And if one put the thing at its lowest — stream of good living pouring into her house from Heriots, comfort, luxury, beauty — all from Heriots. And now, no more good living, no more home, even; no more Heriots.

No more Heriots. To Andrew Heriot's daughter, this was the worst that could happen — the worst.

She spared herself nothing of what this must mean. Rather she tormented her flinching mind with every detail. Machines wrenched away to serve the Penny mills — those great machines that should have brought life to Heriots, life and not death. The very walls that housed them, razed to the ground — no longer would the old-fashioned building cumber the site, Nicholas knew well enough its value. One would not even be able to look upon the place and say, *this was Heriots*.

And Nicholas was to do this! Heriot's husband. Nicholas, who should have cherished Heriots as a trust. Was it nothing to him that Heriots with its proud tradition of good will between master and man, with its straight dealing and fine quality, should have crashed from its place of pride?

And he might have saved it! He might have saved it!

But Nicholas did not want to save it. Rather, she was sure, he felt satisfaction, pleasure even, in destroying Heriots. Jealousy. Because Heriots was all that Pennys never was — never could be! Pennys might coin money — and that was all! Long after Pennys had been swept away and forgotten, Heriots would be remembered. Heriots — its very name was history; the lace mill that had treated men as men, before the law compelled the masters to humanity. Heriots — why it had been mentioned in Parliament nearly fifty years ago. She had the cutting still, yellow and fragile with age. They had been pressing once again to include lace under the Factory Act; and one of the members, himself a master, had stood up and cited Heriots as a proof of good conditions in the trade.

And then — the reply. . .

But all mills are not like Heriots. Not one of these is like Heriots. Heriots is unique. . . She would never forget the pride in her heart when the words had leaped up at her from her morning paper, no, nor the look in her father's face!

And it was this, this, Nicholas was going to destroy. He was going to shut the doors of Heriots for ever, pull down the very building stone by stone.

Whenever she thought of Nicholas, nowadays, dislike rose strong as nausea. She had not, she remembered now, really disliked the young Nicholas. She had had no feelings against him — except as a husband for Heriot. She had even admired his courage, had admitted in her inmost heart, his young charm. But with growing prosperity her dislike had grown. Courage coarsened into cheap bullying — where he dared; charm treacling down into familiarity — where it paid. And now she could hardly bear to look at his handsome coarsening face. She sickened at the sound of his dominating voice. Shut away in her bedroom, she flinched at the sound of his knock upon the street door — the knocking of a man who knows that the house and all within it, are his own. If he came into the room where she sat, it was all she could do not to rise up and go away. Sometimes she felt it was more than she could endure to be in the same town as Nicholas — as if she must cry aloud what the man had done!

And her granddaughter — the girl whose ridiculous name never let you forget whose daughter she was! There was another disappointment. Yet, why should you expect otherwise? But you had expected otherwise. You had hoped once that she would grow into the rather fine sort of person Heriot should have been. . . she had had freedom, always, Nicki. But freedom, after all, didn't work miracles — it didn't work that magic the unfree dream of. . . Nicki took after her father. Handsome as paint and hard as stone. You had tried to help her, long ago, to open her eyes to hidden values of the heart. . . Useless, quite useless. Only unhappiness would teach Nicki — the sharp realisation that the world wasn't her own particular plaything — and only then, if the lesson didn't come too late! Nicki was her father's daughter! She cared nothing for Heriots — to her it was nothing but a name, a name already half forgotten. And the death of her grandfather? One supposed she was sorry — in her way — she wasn't inhuman. But the tragedy swept her by. She didn't care.

With the selfishness of the old, Ada Ware resented it. The fall of Heriots, John's death — they had broken her own life. Nicki's life should take the shadow, if only for a little while.

Heriot, too, wondered about Nicki. The child had never been one to wear her heart on her sleeve. Yet here was tragedy — violent death and ruin. But Nicki was living in a world of her own. Fighting her own difficulties, she was bound to be more or less blind to the outer world. She was in love. And her love was threatened — unless she herself had the wit to pull things straight. That was all Nicki could see. . . And no wonder, thought Heriot, remembering a little with wonder, the passion and the loneliness of her own young days. . . No, Nicki was not at all heartless she was only rather desperate. To Nicki, at this moment, Nicki's own problem came first. And Heriot remembering. . . remembering, was satisfied it should be so.

Nicki was sweet to Heriot these days, anxious to run little errands, to do little things for her It was a genuine but surface sweetness. She was trying to make up for an essential lack of sympathy. She had made a real effort to enter the difficult world of middle-age, to accept its puzzling standards, its queer values. She had tried and she had failed. She felt herself clumsy, embarrassed, lost. Reduced to this new stupidity she was angry — angry with herself, and with the odd people whose world it was. She was desperate to free herself from the stuffy sentimental tangles of the middle-aged.

She tried, once, to explain herself to Heriot. "I don't waste my sympathy on grandfather! It's you I'm sorry for, you and especially grandmother. It's you two that have got to face the music. Why all this terrible fuss about grandfather because he found it simpler to finish things himself? After all, he wasn't young! And choosing when, and how — finishing off quickly and neatly — well, old people have to face worse ways of dying!"

Difficult to know whether to laugh or cry at such terrifying simplicity! Heriot managed to smile at Nicki, Nicki secure in her knowledge that the world was hers to mould. Nicki pathetically ignorant that tarnish could ever dim her bright world. And this was the child one had thought subtle! Well, it looked as though love had stolen her wit. Or was it, that with one's mother it didn't pay to be subtle!

One's mother. People talked so easily, so stupidly, about love between parent and child. Parent and child — as if that were not the most awkward, the most difficult relationship in the world. Her own mother and herself! How had they been able to help each other? Each wrapped in isolation, wrapped securely, wrapped coldly, so that when one reached out a hand, all she could touch was the end of a cold fingertip. . . Yes, Nicki was right, right to keep her eyes clear, to refuse to be tricked. Better to accept conditions that can't be altered than to break your heart against them!

And yet — one wanted so desperately to help. And one was so powerless. There was her own mother — Ada Ware carrying her head high, denying any need, not knowing how those stricken eyes looked dumbly for sympathy!

There was no end, so it seemed, thought Heriot, to the distress that death brought. First came the loss — loss too new to be fully felt. And it brought with it its own sad dignity. But that was the only respite. And the wise woman made the most of it. For after that — at least when death brought ruin — the meannesses cropped up, the irritations, the nastiness.

Events following rapidly, inexorably. Inquest. And funeral. Selling up of the beloved home, dispersal of friendly things to the unfriendly winds of heaven.

Mamma had behaved beautifully. She was quiet and surprisingly obedient; she was courteous and self-controlled. The day of the inquest she lay in a darkened room and asked no questions. She went to the funeral on Nicholas's arm — handsome old lady leaning upon handsome son-in-law. Fortunate for her to have so strong an arm, so rich an arm, on which to lean!

Not even Heriot guessed at the withdrawal of the flesh, shrinking sickly from Nicholas, as Ada Ware stood with her son-in-law by the open grave.

She left Nottingham immediately after the funeral. All that she was called upon to endure, she would endure. But not this! To see the curious crowding in upon her house, the house to which in John's lifetime they had never been admitted, to see them swarming, appraising, criticising, pricing... No corner hidden from their prying eyes — the bed in which Heriot had been conceived and born; the hearth at which she and John had sat and talked — or did not talk, knowing each other's heart...

Feet soiling her floors and carpets, that she could endure; the soiling of those dear memories — that she was not called upon to endure — would not endure.

But Heriot endured it all, suffered it all.

She had not meant so to punish herself. But on the first day of the auction, it had struck her with a sudden bitter knowledge, that this was the last time she would ever see those things that as a child she had loved, together in one place. Even though they no longer stood in their right places, even though everything was parceled, bundled, ticketed, the old house sheltered them still, and she must see them so sheltered for the last time.

She had gone. She had seen all, sparing herself nothing. Shuffling feet upon the pale marble of the hall, careless of the mud they left — after all what did it matter? There were still the crowds warming into the dining-room where the auctioning was to take place; the crowd sitting, standing, leaning, smoking, spitting, here in the room where the young Nicholas had once sat, quiet and respectful, before John Ware. Crowds dribbling with excitement over the Ware furniture; gasps of admiration over the massive silver, the fine linen; giggles of amusement over the old-fashioned pictures, the statues, the knick-knacks.

One by one, the things that had been built into a life-time, upon whose foundations Ware lives had been securely built, laid under the tap of the hammer — going, going, gone...

In her third-rate boarding-house at Skegness, Ada Ware carried her head high.

...Now they were taking them away, the things that had been part of her life, hallowed by long years of mutual serving. Gods of the household — the old Romans had been wise! Now they were being cast forth, her household gods, carried into holes and corners all over the country. And some would be treated lovingly as was fit for old and faithful things, and some would be scratched and bruised and smeared — uncared for, degraded... She had a moment's distress as for some helpless thing betrayed.

But her thoughts pressed onwards, allowing no respite.

Tonight the house would stand empty — home to which she had come, young and exalted with love, hardly daring, even yet, to believe that such happiness could befall Ada Ware; home which had housed her vigorous middle-age, when she had accepted all dignities as her natural right; home that should have sheltered her quiet old age... home to which she would return no more.

Well, that was the way life went! Old things, known things, were left behind, scattered, lost. John was dead — and how cruelly dead! And even beloved things didn't matter any more!

But when Heriots was sold up — there was another story! Heriot had come to spend the day with her, to take her mind from what it could not be taken. All about her, sunshine and blue sea and golden sand were like the queer background to a dream. The mind dwelt where Heriots towered grim and dirty above its mean street... Tonight empty walls would brood upon empty floors. Patches white upon stone floors where once machines had stood. Silence where the voice of the machines had flung their roaring upon the air. Coldness where there had been warmth. Death where there had been life.

Emptiness... Silence... Death.

Tonight the ghosts would walk. Andrew Heriot, puzzled by that empty silence. Mary, his wife, handkerchief to lips, white handkerchief patterned with blood. Mary, whom all her husband's wealth could not keep from too early a grave. And following them, John Ware, whose hands had been too generous to hold his trust.

Let them walk — tonight. Think on them — tonight. Leave all heartbreak, till tonight. Then it will be dark. And Heriot will be gone. And in the dark and the loneliness you may break your heart with no-one to hinder you with false comfort. Now it is morning and sunshine... Heriot pale in the sunshine. You have still your duty of comfort towards Heriot. When all's gone, there's still courage...

So she took Heriot down to look at the sea; and they admired the brown children and the grey donkeys and the white kiosks and the pink peppermint rock and the ice-cream merchant in his spotless coat, and the fruit-sellers, their baskets aglow with fat William pears and dark plums and rosy apples. And she laughed and talked and joked, and pretended well enough that this day was like all other days. And Heriot laughed and joked, and pretended too. And later, they laughed again, when they looked out from the boarding-house window on to the promenade, and saw a fat woman in riding kit trying to ride a horse. Every time the fat woman tried to get on, the horse's legs spread under him — like a pantomime horse. And they went on laughing, even when their hostess told them it was a Mrs Crispin, wife of a mill-owner of Heanor, and rich as Croesus. "Life has its ups and downs!" said Ada

Ware, and then they all laughed more than ever because at that moment, Mrs Crispin decided to fall off!

But in the early hours of morning, when Ada Ware lay thinking of those three wanderers among the empty silent walls, there were tears — and to spare — in her eyes. And there was no courage at all in her heart.

Chapter 36

The new machines were in. There they stood clattering away at Pennys, working double shift, the way machines should work. More machines, more workers. Yes, in these days of distress in the trade, he had found work for twenty! In Nottingham, every day, they were turning off men, but he, Nicholas Penny, had found work for another twenty! By being sensible, by refusing to listen to Heriot's criticism — criticism unspoken, but loud enough for all that — by removing the machines, as he had hoped to do from the minute he'd signed that agreement with old Ware, he had found work for twenty unemployed.

Taking machines from where they were useless and putting them where they could work full strength, what was wrong with that? He was a benefactor. Surely he was a benefactor! Yet here was Heriot going about as though he'd done someone an injury! Not that she ever *said* anything — not in so many words — that wasn't her way! She was quiet and careful for his comfort, as ever, but — he knew Heriot!

He frowned, settling himself more deeply in the big hide chair.

. . .A good dinner. A good cigar. And all spoilt by the damn unreasonableness of Heriot! She didn't see straight — ever! She itched to "do good". But it had to be her way — her muddled Ware way. If you helped others — and managed to do yourself a spot of good the same time, that didn't count. No, it didn't count, unless, like her precious father, you managed to ruin yourself at the same time! That business of Clark, now! He was sorry about it! Damn sorry! But he'd be sorrier still, now, if he had given way to his own softness of heart!

There was a tap at the door and Heriot came in — Heriot like everyone else in the house, except Nicki, asking the master's permission to enter!

He looked up surprised. She so rarely sought his company — and never in this room. . . She looked pale, he thought.

He could not know that she was strung to meet this moment; could not guess her fear that, once again, he would show the cheap stuff of which he was made; nor how important it was, how terribly important that he should behave well this once — just this once!

She thought, It's the first time I ever asked a favour of Nicholas. First time — and last time. And I hate doing it!

She had never, after the first, asked anything, not so much as an explanation, even — never since that time, so long ago, when she had gone running to Pennys and seen his new machines, machines of which he had told her nothing. Yes — once, she had questioned his decision —

once; eight years ago it had been, when John Ware had bought his new machines — but never before or since. Nicholas must go his own way!

But now it was different. This concerned someone who was old and poor and unkindly treated. She thought, If he fails me in this, it's finished. Everything's finished!

Nervousness gave her a remote air of pride.

She said, "I want to talk to you, Nicholas!"

He went on sitting; only he shoved a chair forward with his foot. His courtesies were for Nicki; for Heriot, only when they were not alone.

Heriot went on standing. She had brought herself to this point of asking. And now she could not find the words — the right words that would give Nicholas his chance... She had to have this out with him here and now — the matter could not wait. But it was his last chance to behave decently — and he didn't know it! She could not rid herself of the feeling that in offering him this last chance, unknown to him — she was acting unfairly.

Well, fair or unfair, the thing had to be said!

"It's about Clark," she said at last. "Nicholas, couldn't you give him work?"

He thought irritably hasn't she learned yet not to meddle?

He said, "Why should I give him work?"

"Because —" she spread out her hands. "You know why, Nicholas, you know very well why! You know that Clark worked for Heriots — oh, ever since I can remember. Ever since I can remember anything at all! I've known Clark, known and respected him. And now —" *the machines are gone* — she caught back the words on her tongue. No sense in reminding him how she hated what he had done, no sense in stiffening his anger. "He's on the streets, Nicholas, a man like that! Upright. A fine worker. On the streets! Why didn't you give him work when he came to you? Why, Nicholas?"

"It isn't as easy as all that! I wish it were. Believe me I do! I was sorry — downright sorry — to refuse."

"Then why did you? You advertised for hands. I saw your advertisement in *The Guardian*. Clark saw it, too! You must have taken on fifteen or twenty... all those machines..."

She stopped abruptly... *Mustn't annoy him... mustn't.*

"Nicholas, I'm not asking for charity for Clark. He wouldn't take it! He's a good worker — one of the best. Give him a job, Nicholas — any job! He's an old man — and if you refuse, there's only the workhouse! Don't refuse me, Nicholas, *please...*"

He felt the eagerness breaking through her estrangement. He realised that she was asking him a favour, she who, all their life together, had been too proud to ask a thing for herself. He would like to have granted this apparently small thing.

His wish to please her was fretted with annoyance that she should have asked something so apparently easy — so impossible to grant. If he could make her understand! If she could trust him in this one small thing, might she not come to trust to his decency in bigger things? This question of Nicki, for instance — he needed her — *co-operation* — he baulked at the word *help* — needed it badly!

He chose his words with care. "It's hard on Clark. He's a good worker and a decent fellow. But — well, an old chap like that, used to working under union rules, used to them all his life, he's bound to be a source of trouble! Union men like him — they won't lift a hand, except to do their own bit of work. They stand about idle, the way the union orders them to! There they stand, doing nothing, because, maybe, a bolt wants tightening. I've seen that sort of thing happen scores of times wherever union men are employed. There they stand, idle, hanging about for the person whose job they think it is, to put it right!"

"Not Clark! Clark's not like that! He's desperate for a job, Nicholas!"

"Yes, Clark! He'd be just like that! He'd be all right to begin with, I grant you. But as soon as the fear of being out of work wore off, it'd be a different tale! Bound to! You can't get away from the habits of a lifetime, not at his age! Union men are a damn nuisance — you take my word for it!"

"Couldn't you try, Nicholas? Couldn't you? He's so *frightened*, Nicholas. An old man like him — a *decent* man — oughtn't to be frightened. It means everything to him, everything in the world!"

He said with careful patience, "I can't have my own men upset. They're all right, my men, all of them! They set their hand to whatever turns up and make no bones about it! It's like this. A twist-hand, if he's got time, will thread the machine for his butty on second shift. Saves time. And his butty will do it back for him. So they both stand to gain. It pays them, and it pays me! I can't run my works any other way, and —" his patience slipped, "I don't intend to try!"

She said, so low, he could hardly catch her words, "So you won't give him a chance, not even a chance to save him from the workhouse in his old age?"

"I've told you! I can't and won't have my men upset. That's all there is to it!"

"That's all there is to it!" She repeated his words almost as she accepted them. She went from the room in that quiet way of hers, as if having shown him her naked mind, she desired to efface herself altogether, to be no more seen.

Nicholas tossed his cigar into the grate. She had spoilt the taste! Confounded meddling! Couldn't a man be left in peace to settle his own business affairs? Did she think he had enjoyed turning the old chap down? Did she think he'd liked telling the old man there was no work, and seeing the trembling, knotted old hand thrust forward his own advertisement? He'd been sorry about it. He had a heart — and a damn soft one at that! But he had to consider the good of the whole — not the good of just one particular man! No one but Heriot with her damn-fool Ware notions would expect him to risk the smooth running of his factories because one old fellow was out of a job!

Still — he had been sorry! He'd offered the old fellow a sovereign. There it had lain, the bright gold on the palm of the soiled old hand... and the old chap leaning forward, his jaw out-thrust and trembling. It had looked for one moment, as though he would strike your hand upwards, your hand and the gleaming sovereign. And then, suddenly, his jaw had trembled more violently than ever, as though he were going to cry — like a baby, an old and rather frightened baby. And then, very slowly, his hand had moved out and he had taken the money. He had hated taking it. Hated you for letting him take it! "I ha'n't tekken no man's charity, iver!" he'd said. And then, as though he could hardly push the words through his obstinate lips, had added, "Thank yer, mester!"

You had been right, turning him down — though it hadn't been pleasant! A proud and difficult old man. And anyhow, why should you be responsible for Ware's pensioners?

Still you'd rather it hadn't happened!

He leaned forward, choosing a fresh cigar... Relax... a man must relax...

Another knock upon his door — sharp, imperious, not to be denied, a knock that did not ask permission, but announced a challenge. Before he could so much as answer, Nicolet, who never troubled to knock, as a rule, walked in.

He rose at once — as he never rose for Heriot. He knew, without telling, why she had come. For all her light-hearted air, her purpose was clear in the set of her chin. He could feel it through the light kiss flicked upon the top of his head. She was pretending to playfulness. But — against the chair's back, he could see her back, rigid.

He thought, I can't argue with Nicki — not now — not after that set-to with Heriot. The matter's too tremendous. Nicki's whole life. And mine!

She said lightly, "Go on smoking, papa! Nice to smoke your troubles away. I wish I could!"

"Ladies don't smoke!" God, what a remark! If this was the best he could do, it was a poor lookout!

"Yes, they do! More and more of them! You'd be surprised!"

"Reckon I should! Like to try?"

. . .Anything, anything to head her off! He was holding out the cigarette box.

Nicki ignored it. Her eyes were looking straight at him, holding him with their steel blue gaze.

. . .So, the thing was to be fought out, now — this minute. And he was not ready. Fool that he was, he was not ready! The thing had been in his mind constantly — had never been out of it, really! But he'd allowed other matters to shove it into the background. Business affairs connected with Heriots, installing those machines with the least possible waste of time. . . this matter, that matter, pushing Nicki and her problem out of the way. . . Nicki could wait! By waiting Nicki and her problem would probably settle itself! He had thought that! He had actually thought that! He — the all-wise, all-knowing, bloody fool, Nicholas Penny! Because now, Nicki wasn't going to wait any longer! And it didn't look as if the problem was going to be settled as easily as all that, neither!

Well. . . if Nicki were spoiling for a fight, he was ready! Because all the time in the world couldn't alter what he had to say!

He went on holding out the box. Nicki shook her head. "No thank you! I thought you didn't approve of women smoking! But then," — her look was a warning, a defiance "you always like me to do what I want, don't you?"

Nicholas put the box down with care. "Only if it's good for you!"

"Who's to judge?" Her tone was still light.

"I'm the judge!" Nicholas was blunt. He was no match for Nicki's tongue and he did not intend to play her game. "I and your mother. We're older than you, and —" he stumbled, hating the obvious, "a little wiser — I hope. And we only want you to be happy!"

"I know," she said prettily. "Then everything is all right. Mother says it's all right. Mother's on my side!"

"Your side?" Nicholas said. And then again, "Your side?" What was this talk of *sides*? Just a phrase of Nicki's? Or had Heriot set herself against him to punish him for some fancied wrong — Clark, for instance! That wasn't Heriot's way. . . How did he know that? What was Heriot's way? Did he know? Did anyone know? Heriot kept her own counsel. *Your side. . . my side. . .* Heriot knew his wishes on this subject, knew them clearly, definitely. Was she, because he didn't always see eye to eye with her, presuming to set herself against him, to split Nicki's loyalty! Heriot on the high horse, not knowing what she was doing, not knowing that she might bring everything down in ruin on their heads!

But — he caught at his one hope. This was just Nicki's careless way of talking! Yet Nicki when she wanted a thing was never careless. Words were her weapons — and she chose them with care.

Nicolet said, "let's not beat about the bush, papa. You know perfectly well what I mean. I'm going to marry Pen Wade."

Their eyes met, hard and bright as swords.

Nicholas said very slowly, "Nicki, I've always given you whatever you wanted — if I could — haven't I? I never refused you anything — if it wouldn't harm you and if it was in my power. But there are limits to a man's power. Even mine. No good pretending I'd pick the stars out of the sky to give you! I wouldn't even try! I couldn't reach them — and we both know it!"

"I wouldn't thank you for them if you could!" Her impatience dismissed the extravagance. "What good do you suppose they'd be to me? I don't want anything, anything at all — except Pen Wade."

"It's out of the question, Nicki!"

"There is no question, none at all! All you've got to do is to give those prehistoric notions of yours a rub up."

Nicholas said again, "It's out of the question."

"Why?" and added quickly, "But whatever you say won't make any difference!"

It sounded so much like the small defiant Nicki that his heart was shaken. He put out a hand and touched hers. "Nicki, trust me. I'm your father, Nicki!"

She said steadily, "I don't trust anyone in this but myself — myself and Pen Wade. And I won't give up my life's happiness because someone tells me to, no, not even if that someone's you! I can't and I won't — and you can't expect it! I've got to think for myself, take my own way! That's the only way a person can live. You understand that, you understand better than anyone — You do understand, don't you? Don't you?"

Quite suddenly he knew that if they sat there arguing till doomsday they would get no further. There was no winning Nicki with fair words.

He said, chin ugly, "It's no good talking any more. I say *no*. And I mean *no*! And that's my last word. I utterly and absolutely forbid it!"

"As you please!" Nicolet said. "About discussing it, I mean. As for stopping us — you can't. There's nothing you can do — unless you want a scandal. And even that won't stop us — in the end!"

His belly went cold. His face was the face of an enemy.

Looking at his face she knew that with the word *scandal* she had turned his kindness away from her — though how or why it had happened, she had no notion. It was the first time in her life this had happened, that she felt papa her enemy. She was a little frightened.

"Please," she said a little helplessly, "papa, please." It might have been a dead face for all the sign it gave — deaf and pale and cold. . .

Quite suddenly she lost her nerve. She was on her feet. She was shouting, shouting, "You can't stop us! You *can't*! You may have money enough to buy Heriots and smash it in pieces — as you smash everything that stands in your way! But you can't buy me! And you can't buy Pen! You can't smash our happiness — we won't let you! Do you hear — we won't let you!"

By the crashing of the door he knew that she was gone.

He slumped back in his chair. . . He ought to be angry with Nicki. But somehow he wasn't. He wished he could be angry — he missed his anger. Anger, it was more comfortable, more decent to bear, than this terrible pity. . . Poor Nicki. Life had played her a queer trick — the sort of trick it didn't play one in ten thousand, one in a thousand thousand! She was caught in a net she didn't know was there. And the more she fought to free herself, the more hopelessly entangled she would become.

Poor Nicki. . . and poor Nicholas. He, too, was taken in the net, he and Nicki together! He had meant no harm. He had gone quietly about his business, and suddenly he was in the net, he — and Nicki whom he loved above all things. And there was no way. . . no way.

There was a way. . . one only way. And he would have to take it! Nothing would stop Nicki, now, except the truth!

God, after all these years must he strip away the falsehood to show the long-rotten bones? Must he shame Stella long dead, disgust Nicki, antagonise Pen — and himself stand in the market-place anointing himself with dirt?

He had done no worse than many another man. . . but his punishment had been worse! And through the years it had grown heavier — more and more heavy. . . What he had done, he and Stella together, that wasn't so bad, surely not so bad — nothing a man mightn't do betrayed by youth in the blood! But. . . he had hidden it from Heriot, from Heriot his wife; he had lived with her his lying deceitful life.

. . .It was nonsense, thinking that way, sheer sentimental nonsense. Sentimentality! He had always despised it! He had spared Heriot's pride — surely any decent man would do the same! He had denied his son! Better for that son. Even Stella had seen that! And he had not refused his responsibilities — not utterly refused — he had done well enough by Pen Wade!

Then why this punishment, beyond all proportion, beyond all reason?

Because he had allowed Pen Wade within Nicki's orbit. He saw it now — now when it was over late. This was the natural result of his carelessness, his criminal carelessness. Because his pride had not foreseen the possibility that a nameless workhand could mean anything at all to Nicolet Penny; because he had recognised the rough justice of Stella's demands, he had brought Nicki into deadly peril.

He got up and paced about the room.

What was he going to do? What? There was no-one in whom he could confide, no-one whom he might ask for advice, no-one, no-one at all! Suppose he sat tight and said nothing? Who would know? Break his reputation and Nicki's heart upon a convention. After all, it *was* only tradition and convention made the thing seem horrible. Tradition and convention. What was tradition? What convention? It differed from place to place, from age to age... He'd read somewhere, or heard it, that in Ancient Egypt marriage between brother and sister had been the law — the law for the royal house of Egypt... A wise people the Egyptians, civilised beyond all others, skilled in medicine. Yet they had allowed it, insisted upon it, made it their law...

...But it is incest. *Incest!* Fantastic crime that never seems, even remotely, to touch one's own life. Incest... and Nicki!

He was suddenly wild to see Nicki again, to plead with her, to make her understand that never in this world could she marry Pen Wade... and if she refused to understand? Then he must tell Nicki the truth.

Tell Nicki the truth. Tell Nicki. Bring the knowledge of incest close to her innocence — innocence the more touching because she guarded it with her young arrogance... Yes, he must make incest a foul reality which could touch her own life.

So repulsive, so foul a crime — and Nicki!

He groaned. He went over to the fire, and bent towards it, holding his chilled hands to the bright flames.

How would she take it, Nicki? She thought herself so wise, so experienced — little young Nicki, little silly Nicki!

How would he tell her? What words would he use, trying to make her understand — yet sparing that young innocence? But for all his care, the cheek must pale, the eye darken...

He was dissolved in agonised tenderness for Nicki.

The words he would say... choosing over and over again; over and over again rejecting.

He stirred, crouched there by the fire. How did the minutes go? Swift? Slow? What time now? What time? Time to seek Nicki, to tell her that she must no longer break her heart upon Pen Wade — to break instead her world and her faith in pieces...

What words? What words?

The clock on the mantelpiece chimed. He counted the golden notes. Two? Only two? He had mistaken the number, missed them in the heaviness of his thoughts.

He went over and stared at the face of the clock. Two. The clock said two! He went back to the fire. The bright flame had gone, there was only grey, hiding a glimmer of hidden warmth. He went over to the window and pulled aside the heavy curtain. The garden lay dark and peaceful and quiet.

Two. Two in the morning. . .

He was taken with pity for himself awake in the sleeping house, awake and sick at heart in the sleeping house. They slept. All slept — Heriot, Nicki, the meanest scullery-maid, even, quiet upon their pillow. In all the house, only he kept vigil, and they had not thought, not one of them had thought, to come and ask if all was well with him, the master. . . His hand, his brain, his unresting toil, kept this great house going, kept every individual in it. All, all of them, from Heriot downwards, they looked to him, everyone looking to him, depending upon him for livelihood, for the very food they ate! And here he sat worn with grief — but what did they care as long as he could go on providing? Here be sat — and not one of them had thought of him, not one.

Who, he wondered, did he expect, might come? Heriot? It was long since she had shown any sign of tenderness towards him. Quiet and courteous, with a hard, almost glittering courtesy, as though courtesy might be a weapon to wound you with. Ever since her father's factory had closed down, he had noticed the glitter of her courtesy. Heriot — she was one of your cold women! She thought no more of her husband than she might of a dog. . . less. She had a kind way with dogs. Her husband was less in her eyes than a dog!

Tears of sheer self-pity stung his eyes.

Not Heriot, then. But Nicki. What of Nicki? Surely she might have come to say goodnight to the father who loved her so dearly! Nicki didn't think he loved her — Nicki would ask, why, if he loved her, was he trying to break her heart? She wouldn't understand that breaking her heart, he would most surely break his own. Sounded like cant. . . But it was true. Only you couldn't expect Nicki to see it! The young took a wound, but they were resilient, quick to heal. When you were older, the hurt went deep. It didn't heal. You carried it about with you, a secret hurt, until you bled to death.

Well, it was late. Thank God it was late! Tonight he need break no-one's heart but his own. . . At this moment, Nicki, in spite of her sorrow, slept. Bed. . . A warm bed. . . it was the end, for the time being, of all one's sorrow. Even the criminal, tomorrow to be hanged, slept tonight in his cell. Bed. . .

His arms went out in a yawn. He felt his very bones dissolve with weariness, as he stumbled noisily to bed.

Chapter 37

He awoke at the tick of seven — it was his habit. But he awoke unrefreshed from troubled sleep to troubled waking. In the wide bed Heriot slept, her slight figure barely rounding the bedclothes. He leaned on an elbow and looked down at her. In sleep she wore a thin and disappointed look — as though her life had been thin, disappointed. In spite of his troubles, he could afford to smile. His wife, disappointed!

His wife. Twenty-three years sleeping side-by-side. And yet she was a stranger! In sleep, light, remote, as if her body were not really there; waking, she looked at him with her stranger's eyes, smiled at him with stranger's lips... sleeping and waking a stranger!

He was taken with irritation that she should have kept herself strange from him. She had borne his child. She had grieved when she had known there could be no other. And yet she was a stranger...

But she had loved him once. He'd swear to that! And he'd been a good husband, kind, easy with money. And yet she had stopped loving him — somehow, sometime, she had stopped. Well, women were like that, thin and fickle in their affections — all except Stella — Stella who had died, loving him.

But once he would have sworn that Heriot, too, was different. He would have sworn it!

He jerked himself out of bed. The springs leaped and bounced.

Heriot lay still upon her pillow.

Asleep! Could you beat that? And she'd gone to bed early enough, he'd bet! She hadn't so much as opened an eye when he'd come to bed! Here he was, up, and facing his troubles, and still she slept!

Heriot lay still as death. The arm where her head lay, felt cramped; pins and needles of discomfort pricked it. She had been awake when Nicholas had come noisily to bed, not caring whom he disturbed. Frantic with self-pity, he'd been — she knew the signs; and while not wilfully disturbing the household, not at all displeased if a sleeper should waken for a moment and settle again to slumber.

She had lain awake the whole of the long summer night, sleepless because of the trouble Nicholas had made... unhappiness for Nicki, for Pen Wade, for Nicholas himself! And yet the thing was simple enough! If only Nicholas had behaved differently! If, in fact, Nicholas had not been Nicholas...

Only with morning pale on the window panes had she fallen to uneasy sleep.

And now here was Nicholas, bursting to begin an argument, to justify himself, to prove that all who opposed him were negligible, ridiculous. She was in no mood to argue with Nicholas — or rather to hear Nicholas lay down the law. That amazing certainty that what he said, what he did, was right! That heedless, senseless trampling on the feelings of others! She supposed she ought to be used to it. Twenty-three years was long enough! And yet, it never failed to surprise. Annoyed she might be, or humiliated or indignant, but over and above these things, surprised — surprised that any human being could be so obtuse, so consistently conceited. . .

She looked at him through half-closed eyes.

There he stood, red-faced, clumsy with eagerness to prove himself to the world. She was sorry — in a way — for Nicholas, making things so impossible for himself; but at this moment she could not endure the exhibition of hearty justification. Later perhaps, but not now. . . not now. . .

The slam of the bedroom door echoed and re-echoed in the beat of pulses about her temples. She sighed a little, stretching her cramped limbs.

No, she could not, at this moment, listen to Nicholas. His arguments — she knew them by heart. And they didn't matter. Not one of them mattered. Nothing that he had said, so far, had had the slightest effect on Nicki. Nicki knew what she wanted. Nicki meant to have what she wanted. If Nicholas went on behaving like Nicholas — then it was certain Nicki would go on behaving like Nicki!

The prospect was not pleasant. Heriot felt the strongest desire to run away — to get as far as possible from this ugly muddle Nicholas had made. She counted so little with either of them. Why should she allow herself to be buffered in between the violence of their fighting?

Because her place was here. Because Nicki, young and hard and eager as she was, might yet fail. For who, after all, had ever stood up to Nicholas and won? And Nicolet must win — for her father's sake as well as for her own. Because in this, it was right she should win!

For what. after all, did Nicki ask but the right to make her own mistakes? Make them and pay for them! Nicki knew that you couldn't hope to get through life without making mistakes; and she guessed that there might even be satisfaction in making your own mistakes and paying for it! But to listen to the advice of others — and then to pay for their mistakes — hateful!

The truth was no-one could tell Nicki whether she was right or wrong! Nicki herself, could only tell by going her own way and living it out! Being sure in one's heart was no surety. Living it out — there was the proof, the long, long proof, the sometimes bitter proof. She herself — she had been sure. Once. She had loved Nicholas so much; and she had known, deep in her heart, that Nicholas hadn't loved her in the same way. But she'd been sure, so sure, that loving him as she did, he must come to love her — some day. She'd been so sure of that day, she could afford to wait! How fine she had thought herself for standing out against mamma and papa.

It came to her now, with a shock of surprise, that she had not been fine at all. She had known so certainly that she could love no-one but Nicholas, live with no-one but Nicholas, that she had taken no risk at all. It was Nicholas, not loving, who had taken the risk! And, deny it as she would, browbeat herself as she would, withdraw herself as she would, he was still her life — stupid, blind, noisy, domineering — but still Nicholas. The day she had dreamed of, the day when Nicholas would turn to her and love her, had not come — would never come now. But, choosing again, and knowing everything, she would still choose the same, because without Nicholas there could be no life for her, no life at all. . . only she was sorry for Nicholas because he had got so little out of marrying her.

Nicholas sat in to his breakfast. Porridge, kidneys, toast, marmalade, and a cup of good strong sweet tea — he had enjoyed them all and now he felt his own man.

Marvellous what a bath and a bite could do! Daft to have lost his head last night! He and Nicki going for each other like a couple of Kilkenny cats! Nicki, he was sure, would be a sensible lass and see that it wouldn't do! And having been sensible, she'd get something nice for a present!

And that was that!

He stood up and threw his snowy, glossy napkin to the floor — an affectation that pleased him ever since he had heard the story of certain ducal comments on a napkin-ring.

Out in the hall, the man waited with his coat; at the huge car's head, the liveried chauffeur stood to attention. Different this, from those days he'd pedalled along, saving his pence, and thinking he'd gone up in the world because he'd got one of those new safety bikes!

He bent his head to the spicy smell of his yellow-streaked carnation . . .This business of Nicki and young Wade! Hard on Nicki, he wasn't the man to deny it! But even if — if certain facts about the young man were not facts at all, still it wouldn't do — it just would not do! The difference between them — difference in upbringing, in outlook, in everything, would just about dish all chance of happiness! He knew what he was talking about! And he wasn't only thinking of Nicki — it would come just as hard on the young man. Not that he cared overmuch about Wade's happiness. But Nicki did. If she could come to see that she would wreck the young man's life as well as her own, maybe she wouldn't be so damn selfish!

Yes, he would be firm. He would be wise and he would be sympathetic, but he would be absolutely firm. Lucky Nicki to have so wise a father!

He was not over-pleased with young Wade, though! That chap hadn't behaved too well. Couldn't help falling in love with Nicki, maybe! But he could have helped letting her know it! Considering the difference between their stations, he ought never to have breathed a word. If the young fellow had kept his tongue between his teeth, then all this commotion would never have come about. A young chap ought to have principles!

Young Wade deserved to lose his job. But if he sent Wade off, he'd have no hold upon the chap at all! Best keep him under one's own eye! Keep him away from the dozen firms who'll grab at him! No morals, some of these firms! It wouldn't matter to them that Wade owed everything to Penny — they'd grab! And, in any case, one ought to be fair! If Nicki cast eyes on young Wade, it wouldn't be easy to head her off. . . mustn't be too hard on the young chap. . .

Keep Wade where he would be useful to Pennys. At the same time keep him away from Nicki. . .

The problem weighed on him.

He sat back in the smooth-running car, turning the question this way and that.

It was towards the middle of the morning that the solution came — a solution so simple, so altogether admirable, that he chuckled to the tune of his own admiration. . .

Send young Wade abroad!

A couple of months — six if necessary! Let him watch Penny interests in Calais, in Saxony, in Switzerland — Italy, maybe! By the time he got back again the thing would have fizzled out! If Wade hadn't the sense himself, then Nicki's common-sense would see to it!

Cost something of course. But cheap at any price. Besides — what was money for, if not to protect a man's interests? Do the young chap a power of good an' all! Widen his outlook and his knowledge. Yes, certainly to Italy. . . those silk factors hadn't been satisfactory, maybe Wade could negotiate direct. . . He might learn something about other folk's notions of design an' all. Good as he was, it would do him a power of good to learn to respect the work of others. He'd learn then, maybe, not to think of his own designs so much as a personal expression, but rather as an expression of other folk's needs. If he could get over that one weakness, his work would gain, gain enormously. . . Yes, it would cost a mint of money, but it was worth it!

He sat there congratulating himself — congratulating Nicki and Pen

Wade. How kindly, how wisely, he had arranged everything! Lucky Nicki, lucky Wade, to have so wise, so kindly a man to deal with!

Even Nicki, hard and angry and hurt, must appreciate that!

Pen Wade showed neither surprise nor enthusiasm when Nicholas gave him his orders — it was not his way! He merely inquired when he was to start. Nicholas grunted at Wade's departing back... No sign of gratitude in the young. Open their mouths they did — and manna fell into it! What would Stella have thought of her son gallivanting like a gentleman all over Europe? What would he, himself, have given for this chance when he was Wade's age? The young were selfish — rich and poor alike, they expected to sit under a tree and let the ripe plums fall into their mouths!

Well... it showed one thing, though! It showed that young Wade didn't mind overmuch about leaving Nicki. Brisk as a bee he'd sounded to be off!

Leave things to Nicholas. He'd find the best way out for everyone.

Nicki would thank him one day!

On his way home he was not so sure about Nicki. She was not always reasonable. And she wasn't used to going without what she wanted. It would come hard on Nicki. She might even think he'd played a low-down trick, using his position to get rid of young Wade. And she wouldn't be backward in saying so! He stopped the car at Perry the jeweller's.

It wasn't a festive meal. Good food. Attractive table. Pretty daughter. Elegant wife. And a damn unpleasant meal! He'd have a belly-ache if it went on like this!

When he spoke, Heriot answered pleasantly enough — but she was aloof, as though nothing she could say to him mattered to either of them. And Nicki sat there, messing about with her food, grain by grain, like the woman in *The Arabian Nights* — damn dirty book, that!

He felt in his pocket. Something to cheer a little girl up!

But it didn't cheer her up. He called her back as she was following Heriot out of the room and thrust the little box in her hand.

Nicolet fingered the tiny platinum watch set with diamonds; the narrow bracelet twinkled with fire. She stood looking at it. He thought how much she had changed! The old Nicki would have had it on her wrist, would already be turning it this way and that, flying at him with little kisses and soft chirpings of delight.

Nicki put it back in the box and pushed it across at him. "You can't buy me like this!" she said.

He was hurt. That anyone should accuse him of trying to buy Nicki!

That Nicki herself accused him! Why, that struck at his common sense as well as at his decency! Didn't he know Nicki better than anyone else? Didn't he know the impossibility of buying her? No, he had gone into Perry's with nothing but the desire to please Nicki. All he had wanted was to see her smile again — just a little Nicki-smile. . . a smiling Nicki would be easier to deal with!

He said, "I'm not trying to buy you, Nicki. I wouldn't be such a mug! As to altering your mind — let's leave that, for the present. Meanwhile, take it — without prejudice."

She still hesitated. Then, almost unwillingly, she said, "Without prejudice!" and allowed him to snap the bracelet on her arm. She said still in that slow unwilling voice, "It's lovely. And I'm sorry I said what I did. But" she looked at him with miserable young eyes, "it *is* without prejudice, that *is* clear, isn't it?"

"Perfectly," Nicholas agreed, comfortable at the thought of his plan. But all the same he wondered when Nicki would kiss him again with the old spontaneous affection.

And she hadn't even smiled.

Nicki took the news of Pen's departure quietly. She showed neither surprise, nor emotion. If you didn't know Nicki, Nicholas thought, you might think she was completely uninterested. It worried him, bothering him when he ought to have been thinking of business — of contracts and contacts; of the sharp rise in the price of yarn; of the possibility of using that new artificial silk instead of pure silk thread — Betts said it wouldn't take the weight, it would stretch and then snap; of the way things weren't looking too bright in the direction of Germany. Let the politicians go on snoring in their beds, he would put his money on Blatchford. Read him every week in *The Sunday Dispatch* — and gospel truth every word! There'd be war with Germany all right! And before very long an' all! If there was a war — what about getting in on the Saxony trade. . . Young Wade might keep his ears and his eyes open!

The hundred thousand details of his enormous businesses! And always the worry about Nicki, stabbing and pricking and poisoning.

Young Wade! There was a dark horse for you — dark as they made 'em! Where'd he got that sly nature of his! Not from Stella — open as daylight she'd been — too open! All these years and you didn't know the first thing about Wade — except he could design like an angel. . . *like an angel*. . . Stella's words long and long ago.

Did Wade honestly care about Nicki? He couldn't. There ought to be, there must be, some instinct warning him off! Whether he cared or whether he didn't, you wouldn't know! He'd never let on what he was thinking — that young man! Why, he hadn't shown by so much as the batting of an eyelid, that he was aware that you knew about him and Nicki!

Well, let that rest — for the moment — let it rest! This very morning, this very minute indeed, young Wade was crossing the channel... and he hoped the chap would be damn seasick!

Yes, the chap was gone and you could breathe freely for a bit! Better look over that last design of his — the costing worked out a bit high. Obstinate young devil! Wouldn't alter a single thread. No, not even if it meant a substantial cut in costing, not even if the alteration didn't show! Wonderful where he got that dumb obstinacy of his!

He was deep in translating design into terms of costing, when the telephone rang sharply.

Why had that girl allowed him to be bothered! She knew he was not to be disturbed — knew it perfectly well! She'd had her orders, hadn't she? Marching orders'd be the next thing she'd get — if this was the best she could do!

Damn it all! Tearing his thoughts to ribbons with its shrill summons!

He lifted his unwilling hand; he bent his unwilling ear.

Heriot's voice.

...But she never rings me at the works, never has done.

Heriot's voice.

...Never at the works, never... not even that time Nicki fell from her horse... never...

"What's the matter?" And even as he asked, the naked fear leaped.

Heriot said, "I can't discuss it over the telephone. Please come home!"

"It's Nicki. It *is* Nicki — isn't it?"

"Yes, it's Nicki!" There came the small click of the receiver replaced.

He stood perfectly still. There was a sickness rising from his stomach. When he took a deep breath he seemed to draw the sickness up with it.

Suddenly he was at the bell, ringing, ringing... That girl standing there, eyes popping, lips drawn nervously back above her sticking-out teeth! The car! At once, the car! No, he could not sign this, could not look at that! To hell with both this and that! And with you, too, you damn-fool rabbit!

He was running down the stairs. He couldn't wait for the lift. Couldn't endure the thought of being boxed up without moving, without hastening by his own volition... Running, running downstairs, running and panting, and unable to get his breath because of the cold sickness in his belly...

He sat rigid, body bent forward, as if to force the car to greater speed.

Nicki. She's gone. Gone with Pen Wade. Nicki with Pen Wade. Never mind how swiftly one follows, or how slowly — too late... too late... Nicki spoiled... dirtied.

Dirtied. The word sickened him. He went on saying it, pressing the poison into his heart, his brain.

He knew. . . But all the same he didn't know. News untold is not yet news. He would not hear it. Would not let it become news. . .

He had the maddest impulse to order the man to turn, to drive back again, back to Pennys. . . No, not there! There the news could reach at him, get at him! Not Pennys, but away, away, where no news could reach him. . . where presage of disaster could not become news. . .

And yet — his innate optimism thrust upwards — what did he know? Nothing. Nothing at all. Heriot had said nothing. He was a fool; he was torturing himself with his own hidden fears. A thing like that couldn't happen. God wouldn't let it happen. Nicki and Pen couldn't let it happen. They'd be knowing, both of them, deep down inside them, that this was wickedness. . .

. . .No, it couldn't happen!. . . An accident? An arm. Or a leg. Her back even. . . only an accident.

Nicki chained to her bed. Nicki's feet helpless, dragging. Nicki dead, even. Anger, young rebellious anger, frozen on her mouth for ever. Even then he'd say *thank God*. . . Dragging out a dirty incestuous life — better she should lie quiet in the grave!

He thought wildly, through my own acts I must wish her dead. Nicki dead. God, let her be dead! I left her unprotected, exposed to the foulest, filthiest danger. . . Oh God, God, let her be dead. . .

He put a hand to his head. It was cold upon his tortured head. If she might be dead! If I might mourn her with decent heartbreak as fathers mourn a beloved child, an only child — know the aching, gnawing; *decent* loss, keep her beloved memory bright! But to go on, as I must go, dreading the mention of her name, dreading even the thought of her in her corrupt and dirty life, feeling the gorge rise, the heart turn in the breast. . .

Suddenly he knew that if Nicki had gone with Pen Wade, then he himself must die. He must die because he could not endure to go on living. There was nothing to it but that — he must die!

But — he thought — live or die, nothing can save Nicki, nothing!

Nearer. Nearer to what he must hear. To what he could not hear and live!

Cottages ablow with marigolds, with plumy asters and small bright chrysanthemums. Wide fields. Hayricks lying each side of the main road. More cottages.

Nearer, nearer. . .

Houses of the better sort. Red brick. White steps. Glittering brass.

Nearer, nearer.

North Road. He rapped smartly upon the glass. Now that he was near, so very near, he could not face it. A few minutes' grace, a few minutes only, that was all he asked... before the end...

The car took the longer way round by the Derby Road.

Shops. Right into town now. The corner of Chapel Bar and Derby Road. Sale's shop. And people going in and out and buying sugar and coffee and tea. Armitage's the butcher. And people coming out, their dinners under their arms. Tramcars, and motor cars, and carriages... This day like every other day. And he could have sworn that today, the order of nature must itself be reversed.

And so it was, since Nicki... Nicki... He could not allow himself to finish the thought. But the thought leaped ahead of his will, forced itself upon his will. Down Chapel Bar and across the Market Square. The Exchange holding sunlight in its quiet stone. The Exchange where he had hoped one day to sit. Councillor, Mayor — and then in his quiet old age, Alderman. That was the way it went... Perhaps — who knew — Sir Nicholas! Party funds... thirty-thousand and he'd have a handle to his name... Sir Nicholas. Sir Nicholas Penny... Finished... Quite, quite finished. His life, even, finished.

He envied the people swarming through the narrow alleys of the market stalls. Poor folk, fingering the pennies in their pockets, hovering, picking — picking here, picking there, among the bright wares of the stalls.

Pick, pick, pick... flies... picking and soiling. Well, he envied them, he Nicholas Penny, with his pockets full of gold. They soiled the cheap goods they fingered, but he — he had corrupted Nicki's immortal soul!

Up Friar Lane and the castle standing foursquare, grim behind its grey walls. So it had stood when the future was yet in his hands — unspoiled in his hands... Heriot coming to meet him, her skirts brushing the bright grass, coming in that proud way of hers because she loved him. Yes, loving him — but for all that, remote, infinitely remote because of her ways and the clothes she wore, and that voice of hers crisp with authority... remoter still now, because he had never brought her near, because he had never loved her...

There the fault. There the stumbling block. He had known, even in the moment of admiring her most, that he did not love Heriot, could never love her. There was the heart of the matter! Because he had not loved Heriot, he had not been able to confess about Stella — about Pen. He had not endured the notion of throwing himself upon her pity. She would have been generous, Heriot, with that strange unseeking generosity of hers, with that terrible uncompromising truthfulness. She had not known then, as she did not know now, how to compromise.

Down the Lenton Road, and the high grey rock on his left... patches of grass and fern nodding against the clear sky.

Heriot. . . too good, too hatefully, unspeakably good, for this bad world. No knowing where her terrible generosity might have led. Straight to the divorce court, maybe! That was Heriot. Smash herself. Smash him. Smash everything in the effort to put right that which could never be put right. . .

He was taken with anger against Heriot because she had not known how to compromise. Stella had compromised. And now Stella lay cold in the grave, had lain there these past thirteen years. . . Odd to think that Stella dying had been not so much older than Nicki was now. Stella with all the weight of her experience! Nicki so young, so untouched. What would ten years do to Nicki — now?

Chapter 38

She must have been on the lookout, for there she was at the door, she herself, mistress of the house, Mrs Nicholas Penny and mayoress-that-might-have-been. Did he have to tell Heriot that it wasn't the thing for Lady Penny to open the door, not even for Sir Nicholas, himself, no, not even for Nick, Nick, Old Nick who would never be Sir Nicholas. . .

He passed a cold hand over his face as he went up the steps.

Heriot took his hat and coat in silence. He thought she looked odd — strung tight; her face was white, but there was a flame behind it, lighting its pallor.

He thought, She looks sick. And frightened. But she looks somehow — satisfied.

He thought, wait, wait till I tell you! You won't be so satisfied then!

He followed her into his own room. In spite of the warmth of the early September day, in spite of the sunshine flooding through the windows, there was a fire. He was glad of the fire. He thought shivering, If a man has to die, a fire is a good thing to see. . . at the last!

He looked at Heriot, shining, frightened Heriot. He thought, when you know, you will want to die, too!

. . .Heriot might be a good sort of person to die with, quiet and unflinching. Dying together. . . a much more intimate thing than lying together under the trees, or sleeping side by side in one bed. At the last, Heriot and he would have achieved perfect intimacy.

On his table stood a bowl of cyclamen, pure white, the blossoms poised on pale stems. He thought, Nicki gave me those. When she bought them, she was happy, she was innocent. . . she was white and pure as those flowers. . .

Tears stung his eyelids. As ever, the sentimental moved him.

He turned to Heriot standing tall and motionless before him — Heriot still with that odd frightened exultation about her.

She said, "Sit down, Nicholas."

He said, as he had said before, "It's Nicki. It *is* Nicki!"

Heriot nodded.

"She's gone — with —" He could not bring himself to utter the name.

She nodded again. Her hand moved out towards him holding a letter. She said, "Nicki left this. For you."

He could not bring himself to take it. The written word. Irrevocable.

Heriot stood there, waiting. His hand went slowly outwards. His fumbling fingers tore at the flap with silly, ineffectual movements.

Heriot stood tall and silent, watching. He spoke, in so low a voice, that she had to guess his meaning. Easy enough to guess!

Shutting her out. Even in grief, shutting her out!

The door closed softly behind her.

Still he could not bring himself to read the letter. For when it was read, then life was finished.

He went over to the door, moving slowly, moving cautiously, over the rich carpet. The key turned in the lock. Now he would be safe, from prying eyes, for a little while safe. . .

The white page lay smooth before him. Black upon white. Nicki's beloved writing. Nicki's writing. . . he had kept every line she had ever written to him, from her first childish scrawl blotted and uncontrolled. . .

He fumbled in his drawer.

. . .Her first letter. Lay it beside her last, her very last. Next to the white paper, the pink — ruled across in slanting pencil lines, a posy of pansies in the top left-hand corner. . .

In spite of his grief, a faint smile touched the corner of his mouth. Again the easy tears stung his eyes. The tiny posy blurred and swam.

He drew the sheet of white notepaper towards him.

. . .Nicki's handwriting, no longer a childish scrawl, but firm and uncompromising as Nicki herself.

. . .*By the time you get this we shall be married*. . . No need to read further. No need. His death sentence. He would die. But she — ought she to go on living, living in corruption, passing on corruption that would cease not with her children, nor her children's children. . .? Before he died, must he not first kill Nicki?

But where would he find Nicki? And how would he kill her? And with what would he kill her? Men like him didn't kill. They didn't even know how to set about it. He could — when the moment came — kill himself. But to lift his hand to take the life of another — and that other, Nicki — the thing was impossible. The thing became sheer fantasy! Life was one too much for him — for Nicholas Penny, who had thought he could bend life, break life, to his own desire. . . He couldn't kill Nicki. She must go on living. And the knowledge of her filthy living must follow him down to the grave and beyond the grave. . .

He lifted his head from his hands. He looked about him with puzzled eyes, trying to translate the change of light. There had been bright sunshine in the room, and now there were shadows — darkness. . . Well, it was more fitting. . .

He thought quietly, as though the question were purely academic, *how does a man kill himself?*

Gas? Lingering. Uncertain. One might be missed. . . missed before the job is properly done! The door broken in. Or the window. A match, maybe, struck... dangerous. See how humane! How at the point of death, he thought for others...

Aspirin? A woman's way! A coward's way! Packing oneself with the filthy stuff... Twenty, thirty, forty... a hundred. How many of the damn things? The sour powder clogging the throat, the senses, the heart... No, if he had to die, he'd take a man's way. A bullet. A clean death...

But he hadn't a gun! Ready to shoot himself and no gun! Funny that! Damn funny! No-one could say he hadn't a sense of humour! About to die and able to see the funny side! Have to go out and buy a gun. Soon he would go. Rest a little first. He was tired. Tired to the bone. Cold. Nearer to the fire. Better. Good fire. Good company. Sleep a little. Sound idea. Face death better that way. Sleep a little... just a little...

Click went the revolver.

Click. Clicking through your head.

You put a hand to your head. A hole. A hole no bigger than a man's hand... wrong... that was wrong... than a grain of mustard seed. Yes, that was it, a mustard seed... Neat little hole. But your hand came away full of blood.

Blood. Bloody bloody hands.

But it didn't hurt. The hole in your head didn't hurt. Odd. Because all the time you went on shooting. Because, click, it went, click, click, click...

He held his two hands before him, turning them this way and that in the firelight.

Reddened... they were reddened... Of course they were reddened.

His fingers climbed his cheeks. Upwards. Smooth flesh stretching over smooth bone... no break in the smoothness...

But still the click, click...

He came slowly back.

Someone at the door. Someone rattling at the door and calling his name. A frightened voice... difficult to recognise because of its fear. But for all that he recognised it. Heriot's voice. And more than that — he could tell by the sound of it that she was frightened — frightened and trying desperately hard not to be...

Now why should Heriot be afraid? Had he ever seen her frightened before, ever, in the whole of their life together? He considered the question purely as a matter of curiosity.

No... he thought not... he was sure not.

Click... click... Stop that damn clicking while I think, while I think why Heriot is afraid Why is she afraid? Because she knows Nicki is gone. But she wanted Nicki to go, *made* her go...

But still she is frightened. . .

Not for Nicki then. . . not for Nicki. Then for whom?

Could she be afraid because of — him? Heriot the proud, the fearless, afraid because of something that might have happened to him shut up in the room alone, in the dark room alone?

He was at the door. He was turning the key. The door swung open.

Heriot and Nicholas faced each other. For the first time in their lives, faced each other.

He thought, She doesn't look satisfied any more. She is frightened — horribly frightened. . . and miserable.

He was sorry for the misery in Heriot's face, because nothing could take that away. She had driven Nicki to shame and for that he must die. And there would be no-one to comfort her ever.

He was terribly sorry for Heriot — even if she had brought it upon herself. But there was nothing now a man might say, nothing a man might do. . .

He pushed a chair forward.

Heriot sat obediently. That line of neck and shoulder, the proud line, the lovely line was gone. At long last, gone. Her head drooped between rounding shoulders.

He thought, pitying her, Must I tell her? If I die — won't that be enough?

But he knew it would not be enough. She had to know. It was her right to know.

There was silence between them, flowing between them, separating them. Nicholas thought, I have the values of the dying — the distance of the dying. I can make no contact.

Heriot sat there twisting and untwisting her fingers. Silence, destroying silence, enfolded them.

At last Heriot spoke. Her voice was toneless, lacking the authority that had made him not her lover, but her servant — a bad servant.

She said carefully, "What Nicki has done — it upset you — naturally it upset you. . . You like your own way always. But it isn't tragic, you know!"

He cried out at that. Unknowing she had played her part in this tragedy, driving it on to its obscene end. And now, she pressed upon his pain, crying out that it was no tragedy, driving the poison deeper, deeper. . .

"You don't know what you've done, Heriot. You don't know!"

She said, still with enormous care, choosing among words, holding them in her mind, uttering them with slow weight, "I know — everything — Nicholas!"

He had to laugh at that! Know! She! She whose hand had pushed the child the last step down into filthy corruption. . .

He laughed. . . laughed. The tears poured down his face. . . not the tears of laughter. But what man, he wondered sickly, would not weep?

Heriot said as gently as one speaks to a sick child, as she had, never in all their years together spoken to him, "I know more than you know yourself, Nicholas!"

He sat staring. Her words made no sense, no sense at all. She was out of her mind. Quite, quite mad! But the eyes that held his were steady. . . steady.

She said, "Don't talk. Don't try to explain — anything. . . Let me do the talking."

She said more slowly than ever, so that a man could count between her words, count one. . . two. . . three. . .

"You're frightened because of Nicki, frightened to death!"

"To death. That's right. To death."

"You think she's done something horrible — something that can't be named, don't you, Nicholas? And you think it's your fault, don't you? You think," her eyes were on the ground, the voice dead in her throat.

One, two, three, four. . . Nicholas counted.

She lifted her eyes. They were holding his eyes in their direct gaze. He wanted to turn, turn away from their unflinching truth.

She said, "You think Pen Wade is your son. You think that Nicki — Nicki —" Her voice faltered then. "Listen, Nicholas, and believe me. Because it's true. Pen Wade isn't your son. He isn't your son, Nicholas. . ."

He said wearily, "Don't lie to me, Heriot. You mean to be kind. But it only makes things worse!"

She said steadily, "I'm not a liar. And I'm not a fool. And I'm not lost to all decency, neither. If I thought — what you think — if I thought there was the hundredth thousandth chance of it being true, I would have told Nicki the truth. And she would have listened — to me." Her voice softened. "Yes — she would have listened to me — now! But," her voice rose, a little shrill, "if she hadn't listened, do you think I would have let her go, go with her brother — *her brother*, Nicholas? If she hadn't listened, I should have killed her, I think. Yes, I should have killed her — and myself, afterwards."

"And now," Nicholas said, "you have killed me!"

Heriot cried fiercely, "Stop thinking of yourself, Nicholas, just once stop thinking of yourself! Oh, Nicholas, Nicholas. Pen Wade isn't your son. He's Stella's child. But not yours. Not yours. I swear he isn't yours. I'll prove it he isn't. *Prove* it, Nicholas!"

He said, as if speaking out of a long-dead past, "So you knew — you knew about Stella and me! All the time, you knew!"

She laughed a little wildly. "Did you think I was such a fool? Did you, Nicholas? A fool I might have been for loving you — but not such a fool as to trust you! Not such a fool as that! Stella — she was the fool. She trusted you — once. And it was once too much! But," He could see the effort she put upon herself, see the throat rising to thrust back the words, "I didn't come here to quarrel. . .

"Listen, Nicholas, listen to every word, because it's true. When you've heard me, you'll *know* it's true! What happened between you and Stella was easy to understand, easy. What wasn't easy was that you could live with me and lie to me. Twenty-three years of lying! I don't *want* to be bitter, Nicholas, but bitterness creeps in, it creeps in. Twenty-three years. . . it's a long time. . .

"You loved Stella — in your way — didn't you? She must have been lovely, and you couldn't help it, could you, Nicholas? And then, she was going to have your child — or thought she was. She wasn't so lovely then — was she? So you went away and left her. And you married me.

"You married me Nicholas. I wasn't beautiful — I wasn't even pretty. And you didn't love me. But I thought you did. At first. But you never said so. . . you never said so. You were honest in that, at least!"

"I thought you must love me — at first. I couldn't see, else, why you wanted to marry me. I wasn't pretty — but plain women *do* get loved. And father wouldn't give us a farthing, and everyone was against us, so I thought you must love me. . . I was so simple, Nicholas, you can't think how simple a young girl can be when she's in love! But I didn't know about Stella then, or I shouldn't have married you. . . perhaps I should, though. I loved you so much."

His hand went out in a gesture of impatience. Even now, in this, her supreme moment, she did not count. She knew she did not count.

She said, a little sadly, "Let's come back to Stella, She was going to have a child — your child, you thought. But you went away and left her to manage as best she could. Things weren't easy with you, Nicholas, I know that. You were just beginning — and you hadn't any money, and everyone was looking on and wanting you to fail. One less out of the competition! But you could have helped Stella a little, you could have helped!

"But you let her go. And you didn't see anything of her for a long time. A year, wasn't it? Long enough for her to have got over her trouble, anyhow! Then you found her again. That wasn't difficult, was it, Nicholas? You could have put your hand on Stella whenever you wanted her. But you didn't want her — you hadn't any use for her — not while she was going to have a child! When you found her again, the child had been born. A boy. Your boy — Nicholas. That's what you believed — and she let you go on believing it! A month or so more or less on a young child's age, you wouldn't know, would you, Nicholas? Besides, you never saw it. Stella was careful — and you never saw it. Did you ever wonder why Stella was so careful, so very careful? It was because Pen Wade wasn't your son, Nicholas. He wasn't your son. . .

"That first time, when she told you she was going to have your child, she thought it was true, she honestly thought it was true. And when you left her, without doing a thing to help her, because she still thought it was true, she looked round for the help you wouldn't give.

"And she found it. She found a man. Women as attractive as she was will always find a man. Of course it was horrible. For her. You can't imagine how horrible! She was never a light woman. And she loved you always.

"And afterwards — when she found out she'd been mistaken, it was too late. . . because of Pen.

"She hated herself, then, because she'd given herself away for nothing, though the man was kind enough — wanted to marry her when he knew about Pen. He was a lace-designer and he earned good money. There's your corroborative detail. It was from his father he inherited his gift, not from you, Nicholas, not from you. . .

"But Stella wouldn't. She'd got used to the idea that her child wouldn't have a father; and she wouldn't tie herself up to any man — except you. Because she loved you, Nicholas. She went on loving you to the end. When you think about Stella, and what she did, you've got to remember that. I remember it, always.

"You see, she'd got it into her head that you were responsible for her position. And you were! Don't flatter yourself, Nicholas, that that sort of thing would have happened sooner or later to Stella, because it wouldn't. She wasn't that sort of woman. She was a one-man woman — and you were her man!

"As soon as the child was born and she was strong enough, she got work. But you know about that — because even then you wouldn't let her alone. So she lost that work, too! But still she had the child to support. So she let you go on believing it was yours. She felt she had a claim — a moral claim. And so she had! You see, Nicholas, although she went on loving you, she'd stopped trusting you. . . she'd done that once too often!

"That's what she said. That's what she thought. But the plain truth is just that she couldn't keep away from you. A burned child fears the fire! But Stella loved the fire even while it burned her. She tried to warm herself a little, just a little at the flames. Poor Stella!

"Well — she'd lost her job and she needed work. And you needed workers — cheap as you could get them! So you gave her work. But you didn't treat her better than any other of your workers. You treated her worse. You sweated them all — as long as you could. But you sweated Stella more than most because you knew she daren't try to get away. . ."

He would have spoken then, told her of those days when his fingers reached down into empty pockets; when, in spite of his growing little factory, often enough he hadn't the price of his dinner in his pocket. But she went steadily on.

"You were short of money, I know. Everything depended upon a penny saved here, and a penny saved there. But afterwards, when the money was coming in, still you sweated her; you sweated her as long as you could — which was as long as she could take it. So Stella died.

"Overwork and underpay. Long hours crouching over the lace in a steamy, smelly room — that was before you showed the world your model factories. I remember it. . . I remember it well. . . though I only saw it once. . . the gaunt badly-lit room and Stella's red head, her lovely head, bent close to the work. . . And then — a hole to sleep in, a dark unventilated hole — when she wasn't sleeping with you, Nicholas!

"Oh," she cried pitifully, "she was your mistress, but still you sweated her. Ever heard of anything meaner, Nicholas?

"Long hours. Sweated work. That's what you gave Stella whom you loved. So she went down with T.B. And that was the end of Stella!

"But not the end of Stella's son — Stella's, not yours, Nicholas. She let you go on thinking he was yours because she knew she was dying and she was desperate to get help for the child. Such a little child, Nicholas, to be left — no friends, no money, nothing! If you'd been decent, only a little bit decent, she would have told you the truth.

"She wanted to tell you the truth, wanted it terribly. She didn't want to die with such a lie on her conscience. She was terrified to die like that! But she didn't trust you. And she daren't tell you the truth.

"Yes — you did promise to keep an eye on the child — but only when she'd begged and threatened, using up the last of her poor strength to get that promise. And you kept your word. And you've been lucky there — as you've always been lucky. Your tiny bit of outlay, your grudging bit of help, it all came back a hundred-fold.

"When she had your promise, Stella went home to die. Yes, it was simple as that! You promised; and she went home to bed and she never left it again."

Nicholas said, "A good story, well told — in its way! But how are *you* so clever! How do *you* come into it?"

"I'm coming to that. . . soon. When she knew the end was near, she sent for Father Martin. You didn't know she was a Catholic, did you, Nicholas? There was so much about Stella you didn't know! She sent for the priest and she confessed everything. He told her that she dare not die with that lie on her soul. But she was brave, was Stella. She believed in hell — flames and all — but she was ready to risk hell-fire to make the child safe. She said Jesus was a baby once, and Mary would understand.

"Father Martin begged her to tell you the truth. He warned her of difficulties that might crop up if she didn't — though he never foresaw this particular difficulty, nor did I. Nor did you, Nicholas — not even you! And it was natural — the children were so young, so very young, and in every way so far apart. It wasn't likely that they would ever even meet. But Father Martin did point out that the child's life must not be built upon lies. . .

"But Stella wouldn't give in. She didn't trust you, Nicholas. She preferred hell-flames to trusting you. Then — when there seemed no other way out, he suggested telling me.

"She didn't want to. Naturally she didn't want to! The frying pan or the fire — there isn't much choice! But she daren't go on refusing. I think he might have refused her absolution. . . I don't know! She sent for me. But she hadn't made up her mind to trust me. She wanted to see me first.

"She saw me. And she trusted me. That hurt me more than anything that ever happened to me in my life. It made me proud. But it hurt too. . .

"When I stood there and I looked at her. . . I didn't know her again. I'd only seen her once before, but she was so lovely, I'd never forgotten, I *couldn't* forget. . . and now, I didn't know her. . . that glorious hair, all its colour was gone. And that red mouth of hers, it was grey, grey as the ashes in the empty hearth. . . and her eyes, *her eyes*, Nicholas. . .

"She told me everything then. And she told me, too, how she would lie crying in the night because she was going to die and there was no-one to care for the child. . . crying and sitting up in bed, and holding her lips together with her hand. . . shaking lips and shaking hand. . . not to cry out to frighten the child. . .

"And I saw Pen, too. It was the first time. He was sitting by the hearth. There wasn't a fire, did I tell you that, Nicholas? There was no-one to make it. And she was dying. It was bitterly cold. I was wearing my fur coat, but still I was cold. He was sitting there — and he was so beautiful, Nicholas. . . and his lower lip was thrust out, and his chin was trembling, though he wouldn't let himself cry. He knew what was going to happen — the way children do — not with their intelligence but in their blood.

"He was crouching down by the hearth, and what do you think he was doing? He was tracing with his finger in the dusty hearth — a pattern. I think he didn't realise he was doing it — it was, I'm sure, a sort of unconscious attempt to comfort himself.

"It was as much as I could do not to bring him home with me there and then. He was so young and so unhappy. . . and his clothes, Nicholas — his poor rags! And it would have done Nicki good, not being the only child in the house! But his mother was dying and she wanted him for the little time she had left. And I couldn't bring him home and not tell you the truth — and I'd sworn not to tell! And the impulse passed. . . and the rest of the story you know. . ."

She sat there looking at him, waiting for him to speak. Nicholas said quietly, and he was even smiling a little — he could feel the grin stretching the stiff flesh of his face, "Finished, Heriot? It was a good effort, hell-flames an' all! And Father Martin's dead — that's lucky, isn't it? You see I don't believe it. Quite simply, I don't believe it. Such luck doesn't happen — it simply doesn't happen. God isn't so good!"

Heriot's hand went out towards him. "It's here," she said, "the proof. Written down. She told me what to say. I wrote it. And here — look Nicholas — she wrote her name. She didn't write it well, poor Stella. But you know her handwriting, don't you, Nicholas? You don't believe it yet, not even yet. . . you can't make out the signature because of the way it's smeared. That's her real signature, that smear. . . her seal. She was coughing when I put the pencil in her hand, coughing and coughing. . . She put her hand up to her mouth. Her fingers came away red. The pencil slipped a little in her red fingers. . . I saw it slip, Nicholas. . . and I have the pencil, still. It was while she was writing that this smear came. . . from her fingers. She looked at it, and the expression on her face. . . it was surprised, a sort of comical surprise — almost. She laughed a little. She tried to rub the smear away. . . "It won't go," she said, and she was still surprised, "it won't *go*."

Nicholas took the paper. But, he thought stupidly, Heriot's writing, clean and firm, no mistaking it. . . But, of course, it *is* Heriot's writing!

His eye dropped to the signature he could not recognise save for a trick of the S — like a narrow curly snake she used to make it. . . The narrow S. . . and the little brown smear. . .

The smear. He could see it, touch it. It moved him more than all the sorrow and the fear and the pain Stella had known — known because of him.

His head went down on his arms, shutting out the stain he could not endure to see. . . Suddenly in the darkness of his own making he was weeping, Nicholas Penny weeping, weeping away the sense of sin, of desolation.

In the darkness, Heriot's voice was gentle. "Life's odd, Nicholas, and nothing turns out as you'd expect! I knew, ever since Nicki and Pen fell in love, how you must suffer. I could have saved you that pain, but I didn't do it — I didn't do it! I thought, *He mustn't know I know*... I was waiting for you to tell me yourself. Your pride. I was trying to save your pride. And yet..." Heriot incorrigibly honest, fatally honest, destroying her last faint hope, "I don't know. I don't know. Perhaps it wasn't that at all! Our motives, our desires — so tangled and twisted — we can't always see clear, even when we most terribly want to, least of all when we terribly want to. Perhaps I meant you to suffer a little while, because you made me suffer so long. And I hated you for bringing the knowledge of evil — such evil — close to Nicki. I did hate you for that, Nicholas!

"At least I thought I hated you. I waited for this moment — for years and years I waited. I knew the time would come when I must break my promise. But I didn't foresee such a revenge, such a perfect revenge. And I didn't foresee, either, that when it came I wouldn't be able to take it — wouldn't even want it any more.

"I thought I hated you. And now — suddenly everything's clear I don't hate you at all, Nicholas. I'm a fool, as you said. Because I love you, Nicholas, and I shall always go on loving you. It's a fool's habit I can't get rid of..."

Silence. And the soft fall of a foot. The rustle of a dress. The careful closing of the door.

Chapter 39

Nicholas lay there, head upon outstretched arm, lay biting upon bitterness.

. . .Heriot had gone. She had gone, thinking to leave comfort, her lying comfort behind. Clever Heriot. But not quite clever enough. Lying Heriot. Liar — like all women. Lying for their own advantage; or — if you could believe them so far, lying for your advantage; or for the advantage of a mythical someone else. But lying, always lying. . .

Stella. Living and swearing that the child was his. Dying and swearing that the child was not his. Lying, lying, 'till you were confused with lies and didn't know what to think!

God, if you might believe! If only you might believe! It was life to you to believe — quite literally life, life and not death. But they were not going to let you off as easily as that — the women. They drove you through the tangle of lies and lying. . . drove you so that you didn't know what was truth and what lies. You dare not believe. Dare not disbelieve. Either way they had you! Torture, the most clever, the most devilish torture. . . Heriot might posture and pose, but she had her revenge all right, her perfect revenge.

Heriot. Upon her truthfulness you would have staked your life. Truthfulness. . . and only just now lying, bolstering you up with false hopes to make your punishment more bitter, only stumbling upon the truth when she spoke of revenge. . . revenge, that at least was the truth. . .

Heriot. . . her clear eyes. Whatever her tongue said, her eyes could not lie. She was speaking the truth — as she knew it. Yes, that was evident in her eyes, and in her voice, and in the very words she used. . . *She didn't trust you. . . She preferred hell-flames to trusting you. . .* Straight words, blunt and cruel.

But still. . . she might be lying. Women were clever as the devil when they were out to punish. . . and Heriot had meant to punish. But that paper, with the signature. . . the long S, and that still more certain signature — Stella's blood.

Heriot had spoken the truth. . .

But Stella, what of Stella?

Would she, good Catholic, die with a lie on her lips? Would she risk the hell-flames she so feared, lie in her last confession, knowing there could be no real absolution? And why should she destroy the boy's chances by confessing that you were not the boy's father?

Then why had Stella told Heriot? She would be terrified that it might injure the child. But she dare not disobey her priest. It was he who had forced her to lay open her secret. Only in her last extremity had she brought herself to confess to Heriot.

Queer confession. Long delayed. . . but it bore the stamp of truth.

True. He knew it was true. Not because he needed so terribly to believe it, but because it proclaimed itself the truth. Examined in every detail, looked at from every angle, still it bore the stamp of truth. Had he not always thought the boy all Stella? In look, in manner, in character, all Stella? Only in the gift for design had he recognised the boy his own. And that gift, too, explained, so easily explained. . . Explained, too, why he had never felt an impulse of warmth towards the boy. . .

He sat there, life flowing back to his heart, his limbs.

Not to die! Life stretching steady and unbroken as far as mind could see. . .

He would go on as he had planned, on and on. . . He would extend the Long Eaton factories, he would experiment with artificial silk. He would acquire that interest in the Beeston dyeworks. He would send off that cheque. . . thirty thousand, pretty stiff. But Sir Nicholas, Sir Nicholas Penny. . . He would. . .he would. . .

Released from intolerable pressure, his brain was working freely, working eagerly. He got up and paced about the room.

Lord, he was tired! Tired as a dog! And as hungry! He hoped there'd be a specially good dinner tonight, some of his favourite dishes. . . thick steak deliciously red on the inside. . .

At the thought of dinner his juices began to flow. His mouth was full of water. He went over to the cupboard and helped himself to a generous tot of brandy.

Better. . . that was better. . .

He could not sit. Fatigue drove him on in restless pacing. He stumbled against the table. Nicki's cyclamen, top-heavy with bloom, fell sideways. The blossoms lay broken across the rim of the bowl. Nicki's flowers. . . Nicki. . .

His thoughts took a sudden, savage turn.

Fool that he had been, fool to trust any woman, to torture himself on the bare word of any woman! Stella — that pious Catholic, lying, lying; swearing he was her only love, swearing that the boy was his! Her whole life a lie, blighting his own decent life — a corrupt and dirty lie!

That man — the man who had taken Stella and begot Pen. He was taken with fury against the unknown man who had taken his fun — and left another man to pay with years of misery.

Years. . . His anger switched suddenly, switched violently to Heriot.

She had known. For years, Heriot had known. . . thirteen years.

Dumb and mum and damnably self-satisfied, she had let him carry the burden — burden which had galled his spirit and embittered his life — another man's burden. She had gone about, sly and quiet, and she had said nothing — she had said nothing.

For thirteen years, silence. Yes, even during these last weeks when she had known his agony, seen it clear in his face, even then silent. Why? Because of a promise made to a dead woman — so she said! Believe that if you liked! But what of her vows made to a living man — and that man her husband? To spare his pride — she had said that, too! Believe that, also, if you liked! It wasn't to spare his pride, it was to drag it down, to tear it to ribbons. She'd meant him to pay! Clever she might be — but she'd given herself away! Pay? Pay for what? For keeping her like a queen all the days of her life?

Because she had been Heriot Ware, they had both taken her condescension for granted! The fool, the fool he had been! The name of Heriot and the name of Ware — what did they signify both, but ruin and disaster? With his own good name he had covered the dishonour of her own name — and she babbled of revenge! Women, creatures without moral sense, without gratitude, without common kindness, even. . . all of them. . . all. . .

Nicki, even Nicki whom he had worshipped. . . He had bowed to her every whim, laden her with gifts of a princess! And how had she returned his kindness? She had gone off with the first young man that caught her fancy! Father, duty, common decency — all gone with the wind. A young man had whistled and she had followed. Nicki with her selfishness had brought the shadow of disgrace upon him. . . disgrace — and death. An hour, one hour, and he would have been lying here, a hole in his forehead, the gun dropped from his stiffening hand.

Nicki — she would never know what her selfishness had so nearly cost! But for all that she should not get off scot free! She would have to learn that the time came when you had to pay for your pleasures! And the time had come for her! He would not accept this marriage. He had spoken and Nicki had not listened. She had gone off with a toss of the head! Let her accept the consequences! Let her know what it was not to dip her fingers whenever she chose into her father's money-bags. Let her see the money melt away in her hands and know there was no more save what her husband could earn. Good enough, young Wade's money, for a woman of his own class, but not for Nicki. Not for Nicki! He would forgive her one day — he supposed. But not soon. . . by no means, soon. Let her savour to the full the pleasure of being a poor man's wife!

Women — the man was a fool who trusted in them. He, himself, had been thrice foolish — he had trusted three women.

Stella. He had given her his young love and she had answered him with lies. She had spread their poison through his life, she had mocked his success and cankered his happiness.

Heriot. He had made her his wife. She was the mistress of his house, he had set her amidst wealth and dignity. But she was empty towards him, empty as a figure of porcelain — in spite of her fine words, empty and vindictive and proud.

Nicki. He had given her all his tenderness, his unbounded father's love. He had filled her hands with gifts before she had had time to ask, before she had known, even, that she wanted them. And she, indifferent, ungrateful, had mocked him, had gone blindly to her own desire.

Women. . . the man who trusted in them was doomed and damned.

Trust no more. . . no more. . .

In the warm darkness, shadows of chairs and desk leaped against the firelit walls, shadow of Nicholas himself unstirring, sleeping, head upon outstretched arms.

Heriot sat upright on her dressing stool, her fingers playing with the trinkets of her toilet table. She stared at Heriot in the mirror, dressed and groomed for dinner — finished and self-sufficient. . . Odd, when one felt so completely insufficient, so lost. . .

She bent to the strange Heriot in the mirror.

. . .If one could see one's real self as clearly! If one might understand a little, just a little, what one wanted, where one was going! Nothing had happened, ever, as she had hoped and dreamed and planned — nothing from beginning to end, not even that last scene with Nicholas!

No, it had not been at all the scene she'd planned. All those rehearsals — what she would say to Nicholas, the contempt with which she would fling the truth at his head! Of all those carefully prepared, stinging words, she had not uttered one, not one!

Even now, from long familiarity, she heard them in her mind, heard them as clearly as though someone had spoken them.

. . .I despise you Nicholas, not so much for the things you've done, as for the things you haven't done! Not because you got Stella with child, but because you didn't stand by her, or the child! Not because you believed Pen Wade to be your son, but because you were too much of a coward to say so! Because to save your own face, you preferred the unspeakable — the risk of blighting Nicki's life, of corrupting her soul. . .

And how nearly it might have happened, how nearly!

I hate and despise you, Nicholas, because in all human relations you are rotten and shallow. Bad master — greedy, careless, heartless. Bad lover — greedy, inconstant, callous. Bad father — greedy, lazy, overbearing; lavish in things that don't matter, in things that count, mean and hard. And as a husband — as a husband, Nicholas, what shall I say, what words shall I use to make you understand? Untender, unfaithful, unkind, crushing those things of the spirit that are life — and without which, life is death. Do you remember that, Nicholas, do you? In not one relationship without reproach, in every human contact a failure... You called me a failure once, Nicholas, do you remember? But it's you, that's the failure, you — in spite of your success and your money and your power — a failure. And so Nicholas I despise you and I hate you...

That's what I meant to say. But I didn't say it... I didn't say it. Because to say it, to believe it, even, one must be blinded by anger. Seeing Nicholas then, pitying Nicholas then, I saw it was not the whole truth. Selfish he is — with the selfishness of the unimaginative. He can see, unflinching, the pain of others, because in that particular way he has never been hurt. Pain he himself has known, pain that he could see or touch or himself feel — that might not find him wanting...

Selfish, unimaginative — that's all! Enough — but not enough to bring a man's house in ruins to the dust!

If it were enough, what of me? What imagination have I shown? What unselfishness? And no excuse... none... I loved him. I knew what he was. And I was glad to take him as he was. I took him, knowing in my heart he didn't love me. But I loved him. I wanted him. That was enough for me! And then — when he didn't show the little ways that lovers do, the little tender ways, I wrapped myself in my pride, kept myself secure from hurt.

I could have helped him. But I didn't. My pride was hurt, and I didn't. In the beginning I went halfway to meet him. But it wasn't enough... it wasn't enough. Loving him, I should have gone all the way. I should have taken him by the hand and brought him over to my side. But I froze myself into my pride, empty pride, cold and bitter and useless...

Simple it seems when all's finished and one looks back. But at the time, how difficult, how unclear!

These last weeks... why didn't I say straight out, Pen Wade is not your son... weeks of anguish saved, anguish no man should be called upon to endure... whatever the fault, still he should not endure it!

Why didn't I! *Keeping my promise!*... I'd like to believe it! But wasn't it, rather, because first of all, perhaps subconsciously, and then not at all subconsciously, but quite deliberately, I meant him to suffer? And all the time blinding myself with words... *If he suffers a little... if the pain gets under his skin...* flattering myself he might learn a little kindness, pretending that pain would teach what love couldn't...

All the time untruthful, knowing well that it was to hurt and hurt again. Thinking secretly, that the pain inflicted, I might stand within the circle with him. . . no longer to be shut out, but to stand with him, with Nicholas, within the circle of pain.

Nicholas and I — together. Nicholas. . . I loved him from that first minute I saw him standing by his machine, angry and sulky, by the silent machine. Curious. . . all our life together we tried to kill that love — Nicholas with indifference, and I, with pride. . .

But it wouldn't die. Nothing could kill it. It won't ever die. Long after I'm dead myself, when the body that is I has crumbled to dust, my love for Nicholas will go on. . . because Heriot, you fool, because Nicholas, dear fool, it is imperishable, eternal. . .

She sat staring at herself in the mirror, contemplating the truth. A half smile lay upon the quiet face in the mirror.

Presently she stirred. Little thoughts, common everyday thoughts came pricking, beating upon contemplation, pushing aside contemplation.

. . .It's late. Not too late to see cook. His special sweet. . . pancakes with strawberry jam. . . Nicholas with his dear, silly, little-boy tastes. . . in spite of his fine talk about "palates", still little-boy tastes. . .

She smiled again. The old forgotten smile widened her lips. But first of all, to hell with pride for ever and ever! There's nothing but Nicholas, only Nicholas!

She trailed her silk skirts down the wide staircase. Gentle as a ghost, eager as the ghost of the young Heriot, she opened his door. In the doorway, she stood and whispered his name. "Nicholas," she said. And then, name long unused, "Nicky!"

He raised his head. Need was naked in his unguarded eyes, need most urgent for help, for kindness. Blurred by sleep, he looked unprotected, helpless.

And then, consciousness returning, the eyes set in hardness, in distrust; the whole figure stiffened into arrogance.

I don't care, she thought, that first look trusted me. . . his need for kindness, I saw it plain. Hardness, distrust. . . it's only armour. Trusting me — that was the first thing, the real thing. . .

"Dinner soon," Heriot said in her most matter-of-fact voice and went quietly away.